Where does a story truly begin? In life, there are seldom clear-cut beginnings, those moments when we can, in looking back, say that everything started. Yet there are moments when fate intersects with our daily lives, setting in motion a sequence of events whose outcome we could never have foreseen.

I'm not sure why I feel compelled to tell my story in the first place. What can be achieved by unearthing the past? After all, the events I'm about to describe happened thirteen years ago, and I suppose a case can be made that they really began two long years before that. But as I sit, I know I must try to tell it, if for no other reason than to finally put all this behind me.

This is, above all, a love story, and like so many love stories, the love story of Miles Ryan and Sarah Andrews is rooted in tragedy. At the same time, it is also a story of forgiveness. And it is my story as well. I, too, played a role in all that happened . . .

Donation

# A BEND IN
# THE ROAD

# Nicholas Sparks

TIME WARNER
BOOKS

First published in Great Britain in 2001 by Bantam Press
This paperback edition published in 2006
by Time Warner Books

Copyright © 2001 by Nicholas Sparks

The moral right of the author has been asserted.

A CIP catalogue record for this book
is available from the British Library.

ISBN-13: 978-0-7515-3893-9
ISBN-10: 0-7515-3893-0

Typeset in Goudy by Palimpsest Book Production,
Polmont, Stirlingshire
Printed and bound in Great Britain by Clays Ltd, St Ives plc

Time Warner Books
An imprint of
Little, Brown Book Group
Brettenham House
Lancaster Place
London WC2E 7EN

A member of the Hachette Livre Group of Companies

www.littlebrown.co.uk

Time Warner Books is a trademark of Time Warner Inc.
or an affiliated company. Used under licence by Little,
Brown Book Group, which is not affiliated with
Time Warner Inc.

This novel is dedicated to Theresa Park and
Jamie Raab.
They know why.

# Acknowledgments

As with all my novels, I'd be remiss if I didn't thank Cathy, my wonderful wife. Twelve years and still going strong. I love you.

I'd also like to thank my five children—Miles, Ryan, Landon, Lexie, and Savannah. They keep me grounded, and more than that, they're a lot of fun.

Larry Kirshbaum and Maureen Egen have been both wonderful and supportive throughout my career. Thank you both. (P.S. Look for your names in this novel!)

Richard Green and Howie Sanders, my Hollywood agents, are the best at what they do. Thanks, guys!

Denise Di Novi, the producer of both *Message in a Bottle* and *A Walk to Remember*, is not only superb at what she does, but has become a great friend as well.

Scott Schwimer, my attorney, deserves my thanks and gratitude, and here it is. You're the best.

Micah and Christine, my brother and his wife. I love you both.

I'd also like to thank Jennifer Romanello, Emi Battaglia, and Edna Farley in publicity; Flag, who designs the covers of my novels; Courtenay Valenti and Lorenzo Di Bonaventura of Warner Bros; Hunt Lowry of Gaylord Films; Mark Johnson; and Lynn Harris of New Line Cinema. I am where I am because of you all.

# Prologue

Where does a story truly begin? In life, there are seldom clear-cut beginnings, those moments when we can, in looking back, say that everything started. Yet there are moments when fate intersects with our daily lives, setting in motion a sequence of events whose outcome we could never have foreseen.

It's nearly two A.M., and I'm wide awake. Earlier, after crawling into bed, I tossed and turned for almost an hour before I finally gave up. Now I'm sitting at my desk, pen in hand, wondering about my own intersection with fate. This is not unusual for me. Lately, it seems it's all I can think about.

Aside from the steady ticking of a clock that sits on the bookshelf, it's quiet in the house. My wife is asleep upstairs, and as I stare at the lines on the yellow legal pad before me, I realize that I don't know where to start. Not because I'm unsure of my story, but because I'm not sure why I feel compelled to tell it in the first place. What can be achieved by unearthing the past? After all, the events I'm about to describe happened thirteen years ago, and I

1

suppose a case can be made that they really began two long years before that. But as I sit, I know I must try to tell it, if for no other reason than to finally put this all behind me.

My memories of this period are aided by a few things: a diary I've kept since I was a boy, a folder of yellowed newspaper articles, my own investigation, and, of course, public records. There's also the fact that I've relived the events of this particular story hundreds of times in my mind; they are seared in my memory. But framed simply by those things, this story would be incomplete. There were others involved, and though I was a witness to some of the events, I was not present for all of them. I realize that it's impossible to re-create every feeling or every thought in another person's life, but for better or for worse, that's what I will attempt to do.

This is, above all, a love story, and like so many love stories, the love story of Miles Ryan and Sarah Andrews is rooted in tragedy. At the same time, it is also a story of forgiveness, and when you're finished, I hope you'll understand the challenges that Miles Ryan and Sarah Andrews faced. I hope you'll understand the decisions they made, both good and bad, just as I hope you will eventually understand mine.

But let me be clear: This isn't simply the story of Sarah Andrews and Miles Ryan. If there is a beginning to this story, it lies with Missy Ryan, high-school sweetheart of a deputy sheriff in a small southern town.

Missy Ryan, like her husband, Miles, grew up in New Bern. From all accounts, she was both charming and kind, and Miles had loved her for all of his adult life. She had dark brown hair and even darker eyes, and I've been told she spoke with an accent that made men from other parts of the country go weak in the knees. She laughed easily, listened with interest, and often touched the arm of whomever she was talking to, as if issuing an invitation to be part of her world. And, like most southern women, her will was stronger than was noticeable at first. She, not Miles, ran the household; as a general rule, Miles's friends were the husbands of Missy's friends, and their life was centered around their family.

In high school, Missy was a cheerleader. As a sophomore, she was both popular and lovely, and although she knew of Miles Ryan, he was a year older than she and they hadn't had any classes together. It didn't matter. Introduced by friends, they began meeting during lunch break and talking after football games, and eventually made arrangements to meet at a party during homecoming weekend. Soon they were inseparable, and by the time he asked her to the prom a few months later, they were in love.

There are those, I know, who scoff at the idea that real love can exist at such a young age. For Miles and Missy, however, it did, and it was in some ways more powerful than love experienced by older people, since it wasn't tempered by the realities of life. They dated

3

throughout Miles's junior and senior years, and when he went off to college at North Carolina State, they remained faithful to each other while Missy moved toward her own graduation. She joined him at NCSU the following year, and when he proposed over dinner three years later, she cried and said yes and spent the next hour on the phone calling her family and telling them the good news, while Miles ate the rest of his meal alone. Miles stayed in Raleigh until Missy completed her degree, and their wedding in New Bern filled the church.

Missy took a job as a loan officer at Wachovia Bank, and Miles began his training to become a deputy sheriff. She was two months pregnant when Miles started working for Craven County, patrolling the streets that had always been their home. Like many young couples, they bought their first home, and when their son, Jonah, was born in January 1981, Missy took one look at the bundled newborn and knew motherhood was the best thing that had ever happened to her. Though Jonah didn't sleep through the night until he was six months old and there were times she wanted to scream at him the same way he was screaming at her, Missy loved him more than she'd ever imagined possible.

She was a wonderful mother. She quit her job to stay home with Jonah full-time, read him stories, played with him, and took him to play groups. She could spend hours simply watching him. By the time he was five, Missy realized she wanted another baby, and she and Miles began trying again. The seven years they were married were the happiest years of both their lives.

But in August of 1986, when she was twenty-nine years old, Missy Ryan was killed.

Her death dimmed the light in Jonah's eyes; it haunted Miles for two years. It paved the way for all that was to come next.

So, as I said, this is Missy's story, just as it is the story of Miles and Sarah. And it is my story as well.

I, too, played a role in all that happened.

# Chapter 1

On the morning of August 29, 1988, a little more than two years after his wife had passed away, Miles Ryan stood on the back porch of his house, smoking a cigarette, watching as the rising sun slowly changed the morning sky from dusky gray to orange. Spread before him was the Trent River, its brackish waters partially hidden by the cypress trees clustered at the water's edge.

The smoke from Miles's cigarette swirled upward and he could feel the humidity rising, thickening the air. In time, the birds began their morning songs, the trill whistles filling the air. A small bass boat passed by, the fisherman waved, and Miles acknowledged the gesture with a slight nod. It was all the energy he could summon.

He needed a cup of coffee. A little java and he'd feel ready enough to face the day—getting Jonah off to school, keeping rein on the locals who flouted the law, posting eviction notices throughout the county, as well as handling whatever else inevitably cropped up, like meeting with Jonah's teacher later in the afternoon. And that was just for starters. The evenings, if anything, seemed even busier. There was always so much to do, simply to keep the household running smoothly: paying the bills, shopping, cleaning, repairing things around the house. Even in those rare moments when Miles found himself with a little free time on his hands, he felt as if he had to take advantage of it right away or he'd lose the opportunity. Quick, find something to read. Hurry up, there's only a few minutes to relax. Close your eyes, in a little while there won't be any time. It was enough to wear anyone down for a while, but what could he do about it?

He really needed the coffee. The nicotine wasn't cutting it anymore, and he thought about throwing the cigarettes out, but then it didn't matter whether he did or not. In his mind, he didn't really smoke. Sure, he had a few cigarettes during the course of the day, but that wasn't real smoking. It wasn't as though he burned through a pack a day, and it wasn't as if he'd been doing it his whole life, either; he'd started after Missy had died, and he could stop anytime he wanted. But why bother? Hell, his lungs were in good shape—just last week, he'd had to run after a shoplifter and had no trouble catching the kid. A *smoker* couldn't do that.

Then again, it hadn't been as easy as it was when he'd been twenty-two. But that was ten years ago, and even if thirty-two didn't mean it was time to start looking into nursing homes, he was getting older. And he could feel it, too—there was a time during college when he and his friends would start their evenings at eleven o'clock and proceed to stay out the rest of the night. In the last few years, except for those times he was working, eleven o'clock was *late*, and if he had trouble falling asleep, he went to bed anyway. He couldn't imagine any reason strong enough to make him want to stay up. Exhaustion had become a permanent fixture in his life. Even on those nights when Jonah didn't have his night-mares—he'd been having them on and off since Missy died—Miles still awoke feeling . . . tired. Unfocused. Sluggish, as if he were moving around underwater. Most of the time, he attributed this to the hectic life he lived; but sometimes he wondered if there wasn't something more seriously wrong with him. He'd read once that one of the symptoms of clinical depression was "undue lethargy, without reason or cause." Of course, he did have cause . . .

What he really needed was some quiet time at a little beachfront cottage down in Key West, a place where he could fish for turbot or simply relax in a gently swaying hammock while drinking a cold beer, without facing any decision more major than whether or not to wear sandals as he walked on the beach with a nice woman at his side.

That was part of it, too. Loneliness. He was tired of being alone, of waking up in an empty bed, though the feeling still surprised him. He hadn't felt that way until recently. In the first year after Missy's death, Miles couldn't even begin to imagine loving another woman again. Ever. It was as if the urge for female companionship didn't exist at all, as if desire and lust and love were nothing more than theoretical possibilities that had no bearing on the real world. Even after he'd weathered shock and grief strong enough to make him cry every night, his life just felt *wrong* somehow—as if it were temporarily off track but would soon right itself again, so there wasn't any reason to get too worked up about anything.

Most things, after all, hadn't changed after the funeral. Bills kept coming, Jonah needed to eat, the grass needed to be mowed. He still had a job. Once, after too many beers, Charlie, his best friend and boss, had asked him what it was like to lose a wife, and Miles had told him that it didn't seem as if Missy were really gone. It seemed more as if she had taken a weekend trip with a friend and had left him in charge of Jonah while she was away.

Time passed and so eventually did the numbness he'd grown accustomed to. In its place, reality settled in. As much as he tried to move on, Miles still found his thoughts drawn to Missy. Everything, it seemed, reminded him of her. Especially Jonah, who looked more like her the older he got. Sometimes, when Miles stood in the doorway after tucking Jonah in, he could see his wife in the small features of his son's face, and he would have to turn away before Jonah could see the tears. But the image would stay with him for hours; he loved the way Missy had looked as she'd slept, her long brown hair spread across the pillow, one arm always resting above her head, her lips slightly parted, the subtle rise and fall of her chest as she breathed. And her smell—that was something Miles would never forget. On the first Christmas morning after her death, while sitting in church, he'd caught a trace of the perfume that Missy used to wear and he'd held on to the ache like a drowning man grasping a life preserver until long after the service was over.

He held on to other things as well. When they were first married, he and Missy used to have lunch at Fred & Clara's, a small restaurant just down the street from the bank where she worked. It was out of the way, quiet, and somehow its cozy embrace made them both feel as if nothing would ever change between them. They hadn't gone much once Jonah had been born, but Miles started going again once she was gone, as if hoping to find some remnant of those feelings still lingering on the paneled walls. At home, too, he ran his life according to what she used to do. Since Missy had gone to the grocery store on

Thursday evenings, that's when Miles went, too. Because Missy liked to grow tomatoes along the side of the house, Miles grew them, too. Missy had thought Lysol the best all-purpose kitchen cleaner, so he saw no reason to use anything else. Missy was always there, in everything he did.

But sometime last spring, that feeling began to change. It came without warning, and Miles sensed it as soon as it happened. While driving downtown, he caught himself staring at a young couple walking hand in hand as they moved down the sidewalk. And for just a moment, Miles imagined himself as the man, and that the woman was with him. Or if not her, then *someone* . . . someone who would love not only him, but Jonah as well. Someone who could make him laugh, someone to share a bottle of wine with over a leisurely dinner, someone to hold and touch and to whisper quietly with after the lights had been turned off. Someone like Missy, he thought to himself, and her image immediately conjured up feelings of guilt and betrayal over-whelming enough for him to banish the young couple from his mind forever.

Or so he assumed.

Later that night, right after crawling into bed, he found himself thinking about them again. And though the feelings of guilt and betrayal were still there, they weren't as powerful as they had been earlier that day.

11

And in that moment, Miles knew he'd taken the first step, albeit a small one, toward finally coming to terms with his loss.

He began to justify his new reality by telling himself that he was a widower now, that it was okay to have these feelings, and he knew no one would disagree with him. No one expected him to live the rest of his life alone; in the past few months, friends had even offered to set him up with a couple of dates. Besides, he knew that Missy would have wanted him to marry again. She'd said as much to him more than once—like most couples, they'd played the "what if" game, and though neither of them had ever expected anything terrible to happen, both had been in agreement that it wouldn't be right for Jonah to grow up with only a single parent. It wouldn't be right for the surviving spouse. Still, it seemed a little too soon.

As the summer wore on, the thoughts about finding someone new began to surface more frequently and with more intensity. Missy was still there, Missy would always be there . . . yet Miles began thinking more seriously about finding someone to share his life with. Late at night, while comforting Jonah in the rocking chair out back—it was the only thing that seemed to help with the nightmares—these thoughts seemed strongest and always followed the same pattern. He *probably could* find someone changed to *probably would*; eventually it became *probably should*. At this point, however—no matter how much he wanted it to be otherwise—his thoughts still reverted back to *probably won't*.

The reason was in his bedroom.

On his shelf, in a bulging manila envelope, sat the file concerning Missy's death, the one he'd made for himself in the months following her funeral. He kept it with him so he wouldn't forget what happened, he kept it to remind him of the work he still had to do.

He kept it to remind him of his failure.

A few minutes later, after stubbing out the cigarette on the railing and heading inside, Miles poured the coffee he needed and headed down the hall. Jonah was still asleep when he pushed open the door and peeked in. Good, he still had a little time. He headed to the bathroom.

After he turned the faucet, the shower groaned and hissed for a moment before the water finally came. He showered and shaved and brushed his teeth. He ran a comb through his hair, noticing again that there seemed to be less of it now than there used to be. He hurriedly donned his sheriff's uniform; next he took down his holster from the lockbox above the bedroom door and put that on as well. From the hallway, he heard Jonah rustling in his

13

room. This time, Jonah looked up with puffy eyes as soon as Miles came in to check on him. He was still sitting in bed, his hair disheveled. He hadn't been awake for more than a few minutes.

Miles smiled. "Good morning, champ."

Jonah looked up from his bed, almost as if in slow motion. "Hey, Dad."

"You ready for some breakfast?"

He stretched his arms out to the side, groaning slightly. "Can I have pancakes?"

"How about some waffles instead? We're running a little late."

Jonah bent over and grabbed his pants. Miles had laid them out the night before. "You say that every morning."

Miles shrugged. "You're late every morning."

"Then wake me up sooner."

"I have a better idea—why don't you go to sleep when I tell you to?"

"I'm not tired then. I'm only tired in the mornings."

"Join the club."

"Huh?"

"Never mind," Miles answered. He pointed to the bathroom. "Don't forget to brush your hair after you get dressed."

"I won't," Jonah said.

Most mornings followed the same routine. He popped some waffles into the toaster and poured

14

another cup of coffee for himself. By the time Jonah had dressed himself and made it to the kitchen, his waffle was waiting on his plate, a glass of milk beside it. Miles had already spread the butter, but Jonah liked to add the syrup himself. Miles started in on his own waffle, and for a minute, neither of them said anything. Jonah still looked as if he were in his own little world, and though Miles needed to talk to him, he wanted him to at least seem coherent.

After a few minutes of companionable silence, Miles finally cleared his throat.

"So, how's school going?" he asked.

Jonah shrugged. "Fine, I guess."

This question too, was part of the routine. Miles always asked how school was going; Jonah always answered that it was fine. But earlier that morning, while getting Jonah's backpack ready, Miles had found a note from Jonah's teacher, asking him if it was possible to meet today. Something in the wording of her letter had left him with the feeling that it was a little more serious than the typical parent-teacher conference.

"You doing okay in class?"

Jonah shrugged. "Uh-huh."

"Do you like your teacher?"

Jonah nodded in between bites. "Uh-huh," he answered again.

Miles waited to see if Jonah would add anything more, but he didn't. Miles leaned a little closer.

"Then why didn't you tell me about the note your teacher sent home?"

"What note?" he asked innocently.

"The note in your backpack—the one your teacher wanted me to read."

Jonah shrugged again, his shoulders popping up and down like the waffles in the toaster. "I guess I just forgot."

"How could you forget something like that?"

"I don't know."

"Do you know why she wants to see me?"

"No . . ." Jonah hesitated, and Miles knew immediately that he wasn't telling the truth.

"Son, are you in trouble at school?"

At this, Jonah blinked and looked up. His father didn't call him "son" unless he'd done something wrong. "No, Dad. I don't ever act up. I promise."

"Then what is it?"

"I don't know."

"Think about it."

Jonah squirmed in his seat, knowing he'd reached the limit of his father's patience. "Well, I guess I might be having a little trouble with some of the work."

"I thought you said school was going okay."

"School *is* going okay. Miss Andrews is really nice

16

and all, and I like it there." He paused. "It's just that sometimes I don't understand everything that's going on in class."

"That's why you go to school. So you can learn."

"I know," he answered, "but she's not like Mrs. Hayes was last year. The work she assigns is *hard*. I just can't do some of it."

Jonah looked scared and embarrassed at exactly the same time. Miles reached out and put his hand on his son's shoulder.

"Why didn't you tell me you were having trouble?"

It took a long time for Jonah to answer.

"Because," he said finally, "I didn't want you to be mad at me."

After breakfast, after making sure Jonah was ready to go, Miles helped him with his backpack and led him to the front door. Jonah hadn't said much since breakfast. Squatting down, Miles kissed him on the cheek. "Don't worry about this afternoon. It's gonna be all right, okay?"

"Okay," Jonah mumbled.

"And don't forget that I'll be picking you up, so don't get on the bus."

"Okay," he said again.

"I love you, champ."

"I love you, too, Dad."

Miles watched as his son headed toward the bus

17

stop at the end of the block. Missy, he knew, wouldn't have been surprised by what had happened this morning, as he had been. Missy would have already known that Jonah was having trouble at school. Missy had taken care of things like this.

Missy had taken care of everything.

# Chapter 2

The night before she was to meet with Miles Ryan, Sarah Andrews was walking through the historic district in New Bern, doing her best to keep a steady pace. Though she wanted to get the most from her workout—she'd been an avid walker for the past five years—since she'd moved here, she'd found it hard to do. Every time she went out, she found something new to interest her, something that would make her stop and stare.

New Bern, founded in 1710, was situated on the banks of the Neuse and Trent Rivers in eastern North Carolina. As the second oldest town in the state, it had once served as the capital and been home to the Tryon Palace, residence of the colonial governor. Destroyed by fire in 1798, the palace had been restored in 1954, complete with some of the most breathtaking and exquisite gardens in the South. Throughout the grounds, tulips and azaleas bloomed each spring, and chrysanthemums blossomed in the fall. Sarah had taken a tour when she'd first arrived.

19

Though the gardens were between seasons, she'd nonetheless left the palace wanting to live within walking distance so she could pass its gates each day.

She'd moved into a quaint apartment on Middle Street a few blocks away, in the heart of downtown. The apartment was up the stairs and three doors away from the pharmacy where in 1898 Caleb Bradham had first marketed Brad's drink, which the world came to know as Pepsi-Cola. Around the corner was the Episcopal church, a stately brick structure shaded with towering magnolias, whose doors first opened in 1718. When she left her apartment to take her walk, Sarah passed both sites as she made her way to Front Street, where many of the old mansions had stood gracefully for the past two hundred years.

What she really admired, however, was the fact that most of the homes had been painstakingly restored over the past fifty years, one house at a time. Unlike Williamsburg, Virginia, which was restored largely through a grant from the Rockefeller Foundation, New Bern had appealed to its citizens and they had responded. The sense of community had lured her parents here four years earlier; she'd known nothing about New Bern until she'd moved to town last June.

As she walked, she reflected on how different New Bern was from Baltimore, Maryland, where she'd been born and raised, where she'd lived until just a few months earlier. Though Baltimore had its own rich history, it was a city first and foremost. New Bern, on the other hand, was a small southern town, relatively isolated and largely uninterested in keeping up with the ever quickening pace of life elsewhere. Here, people would wave as she passed them on the street, and any question she asked usually solicited a long, slow-paced answer, generally peppered with references to people or events that she'd never heard of before, as if everything and everyone were somehow connected. Usually it was nice, other times it drove her batty.

Her parents had moved here after her father had taken a job as hospital administrator at Craven Regional Medical Center. Once Sarah's divorce had been finalized, they'd begun to prod her to move down as well. Knowing how her mother was, she'd put it off for a year. Not that Sarah didn't love her mother, it was just that her mother could sometimes be . . . *draining*, for lack of a better word. Still, for peace of mind she'd finally taken their advice, and so far, thankfully, she hadn't regretted it. It was exactly what she needed, but as charming as this town was, there was no way she saw herself living here forever.

New Bern, she'd learned almost right away, was not a town for singles. There weren't many places to meet people, and the ones her own age that she had met were already married, with families of their own. As in many southern towns, there was still a social order that defined town life. With most people married, it was hard for a single woman to find a place to fit in, or even to start. Especially someone who was divorced and completely new to the area.

It was, however, an ideal place to raise children, and sometimes as she walked, Sarah liked to imagine that things had turned out differently for her. As a young girl, she'd always assumed she would have the kind of life she wanted: marriage, children, a home in a neighborhood where families gathered in the yards on Friday evenings after work was finished for the week. That was the kind of life she'd had as a child, and it was the kind she wanted as an adult. But it hadn't worked out that way. Things in life seldom did, she'd come to understand.

For a while, though, she had believed anything was possible, especially when she'd met Michael. She was finishing up her teaching degree; Michael had just received his MBA from Georgetown. His family, one of the most prominent in Baltimore, had made their fortune in banking and were immensely wealthy and clannish, the type of family that sat on the boards of various corporations and instituted policies at country clubs that served to exclude those they regarded as inferior. Michael, however, seemed to reject his family's values and was regarded as the ultimate catch. Heads would turn when he entered a room, and though he knew what was happening, his most endearing quality was that he pretended other people's images of him didn't matter at all.

*Pretended*, of course, was the key word.

Sarah, like every one of her friends, knew who he was when he showed up at a party, and she'd been surprised when he'd come up to say hello a little later in the evening. They'd hit it off right away. The short conversation had led to a longer one over coffee the following day, then eventually to dinner. Soon they were dating steadily and she'd fallen in love. After a year, Michael asked her to marry him.

Her mother was thrilled at the news, but her father didn't say much at all, other than that he hoped that she would be happy. Maybe he suspected something, maybe he'd simply been around long enough to know that fairy tales seldom came true. Whatever it was, he didn't tell her at the time, and to be honest, Sarah didn't take the time to question his reservations, except when Michael asked her to sign a prenuptial agreement. Michael explained that his family had insisted on it, but even though he did his best to cast all the blame on his parents, a part of her suspected that had they not been around, he would have insisted upon it himself. She nonetheless signed the papers. That evening, Michael's parents threw a lavish engagement party to formally announce the upcoming marriage.

Seven months later, Sarah and Michael were married. They honeymooned in Greece and Turkey; when they got back to Baltimore, they moved into a home less than two blocks from where Michael's parents lived. Though she didn't have to work, Sarah began teaching second grade at an inner-city elementary school. Surprisingly, Michael had been fully supportive of her decision, but that was typical of their relationship then. In the first two years of their marriage, everything seemed perfect: She and Michael spent hours in bed on the weekends, talking and making love, and he confided in her his dreams of entering politics one day. They had a large circle of friends, mainly people Michael had known his entire life, and there was always a party to attend or weekend trips out of town. They spent their remaining free time in Washington, D.C., exploring museums, attending the theater, and walking among the monuments located at the Capitol Mall. It was there, while standing inside the Lincoln Memorial, that Michael told Sarah he was ready to start a family. She threw her arms around him as soon as he'd said the words, knowing that nothing he could have said would have made her any happier.

Who can explain what happened next? Several months after that blissful day at the Lincoln Memorial,

Sarah still wasn't pregnant. Her doctor told her not to worry, that it sometimes took a while after going off the pill, but he suggested she see him again later that year if they were still having problems.

They were, and tests were scheduled. A few days later, when the results were in, they met with the doctor. As they sat across from him, one look was enough to let her know that something was wrong.

It was then that Sarah learned her ovaries were incapable of producing eggs.

A week later, Sarah and Michael had their first major fight. Michael hadn't come home from work, and she'd paced the floor for hours while waiting for him, wondering why he hadn't called and imagining that something terrible had happened. By the time he came home, she was frantic and Michael was drunk. "You don't own me" was all he offered by way of explanation, and from there, the argument went downhill fast. They said terrible things in the heat of the moment. Sarah regretted all of them later that night; Michael was apologetic. But after that, Michael seemed more distant, more reserved. When she pressed him, he denied that he felt any differently toward her. "It'll be okay," he said, "we'll get through this."

Instead, things between them grew steadily worse. With every passing month, the arguments became more frequent, the distance more pronounced. One night, when she suggested again that they could always adopt, Michael simply waved off the suggestion: "My parents won't accept that."

Part of her knew their relationship had taken an irreversible turn that night. It wasn't his words that gave it away, nor was it the fact that he seemed to be taking his parents' side. It was the look on his face—the one that let her know he suddenly seemed to regard the problem as hers, not theirs.

Less than a week later, she found Michael sitting in the dining room, a glass of bourbon at his side. From the unfocused look in his eyes, she knew it wasn't the first one he'd had. He wanted a divorce, he began; he was sure she understood. By the time he was finished, Sarah found herself unable to say anything in response, nor did she want to.

The marriage was over. It had lasted less than three years. Sarah was twenty-seven years old.

The next twelve months were a blur. Everyone wanted to know what had gone wrong; other than her family, Sarah told no one. "It just didn't work out" was all she would say whenever someone asked.

Because she didn't know what else to do, Sarah continued to teach. She also spent two hours a week talking to a wonderful counselor, Sylvia. When Sylvia recommended a support group, Sarah went to a few of the meetings. Mostly, she listened, and she thought she was doing better. But sometimes, as she sat alone in her small apartment, the reality of the situation would bear down hard and she would begin to cry again, not stopping for hours. During one of her darkest periods, she'd even considered suicide, though no one—not the counselor, not her family—knew that. It was then that she'd realized she had to leave Baltimore; she needed a place to start over. She needed a place where the memories wouldn't be so painful, somewhere she'd never lived before.

Now, walking the streets of New Bern, Sarah was doing her best to move on. It was still a struggle at times, but not nearly as bad as it once had been. Her parents were supportive in their own way—her father said nothing whatsoever about it; her mother clipped out magazine articles that touted the latest medical developments—but her brother, Brian, before he headed off for his first year at the University of North Carolina, had been a life-saver.

Like most adolescents, he was sometimes distant and withdrawn, but he was a truly empathetic listener. Whenever she'd needed to talk, he'd been there for her, and she missed him now that he was gone. They'd always been close; as his older sister, she'd helped to change his diapers and had fed him whenever her mother let her. Later, when he was going to school, she'd helped him with his homework, and it was while working with him that she'd realized she wanted to become a teacher.

That was one decision she'd never regretted. She loved teaching; she loved working with children. Whenever she walked into a new classroom and saw thirty small faces looking up at her expectantly, she knew she had chosen the right career. In the beginning, like most young teachers, she'd been an idealist, someone who assumed that every child would respond to her if she tried hard enough. Sadly, since then, she had learned that wasn't possible. Some children, for whatever reason, closed themselves off to anything she did, no matter how hard she worked. It was the worst part of the job, the only part that sometimes kept her awake at night, but it never stopped her from trying again.

Sarah wiped the perspiration from her brow, thankful that the air was finally cooling. The sun was dropping lower in the sky, and the shadows lengthened. As she strode past the fire station, two firemen sitting out front in a couple of lawn chairs nodded to her. She smiled. As far as she could tell, there was no such thing as an early evening fire in this town. She'd seen them every day at the same time, sitting in exactly the same spots, for the past four months.

New Bern.

Her life, she realized, had taken on a strange simplicity since she'd moved here. Though she sometimes missed the energy of city life, she had to admit that slowing down had its benefits. During the summer, she'd spent long hours browsing through the antique stores downtown or simply staring at the sailboats docked behind the Sheraton. Even now that school had started again, she didn't rush anywhere. She worked and walked, and aside from visiting her parents, she spent most evenings alone, listening to classical music and reworking the lesson plans she'd brought with her from Baltimore. And that was fine with her.

Since she was new at the school, her plans still needed a little tinkering. She'd discovered that many of the students in her class weren't as far along as they should have been in most of the core subjects, and she'd had to scale down the plans a bit and incorporate more remedial work. She hadn't been surprised by this; every school progressed at a different rate. But she figured that by the end of the year, most students would finish where they needed to be. There was, however, one student who particularly concerned her.

Jonah Ryan.

He was a nice enough kid: shy and unassuming, the kind of child who was easy to overlook. On the first day of class, he'd sat in the back row and answered politely when she'd spoken to him, but working in Baltimore had taught her to pay close attention to such children. Sometimes it meant nothing; at other times, it meant they were trying to hide. After she'd asked the class to hand in their first assignment, she'd made a mental note to check his work carefully. It hadn't been necessary.

The assignment—a short paragraph about something they'd done that summer—was a way for Sarah to quickly gauge how well the children could write. Most of the pieces had the usual assortment of misspelled words, incomplete thoughts, and sloppy handwriting, but Jonah's had stood out, simply because he hadn't done what she'd asked. He'd written his name in the top corner, but instead of writing a paragraph, he'd drawn a picture of himself fishing from a small boat. When she'd questioned him about why he hadn't done what she'd asked, Jonah had explained that Mrs. Hayes had always let him draw, because "my writing isn't too good."

Alarm bells immediately went off in her head. She'd smiled and bent down, in order to be closer to him. "Can you show me?" she'd asked. After a long moment, Jonah had nodded, reluctantly.

While the other students went on to another activity, Sarah sat with Jonah as he tried his best. She quickly realized it was pointless; Jonah didn't know how to write. Later that day, she found out he could barely read as well. In arithmetic, he wasn't any better. If she'd been forced to guess his grade, having never met him, she would have thought Jonah was just beginning kindergarten.

Her first thought was that Jonah had a learning

disability, something like dyslexia. But after spending a week with him, she didn't believe that was the case. He didn't mix up letters or words, he understood everything she was telling him. Once she showed him something, he tended to do it correctly from that point on. His problem, she believed, stemmed from the fact that he'd simply never had to do his schoolwork before, because his teachers hadn't required it.

When she asked a couple of the other teachers about it, she learned about Jonah's mother, and though she was sympathetic, she knew it wasn't in anyone's best interest—especially Jonah's—to simply let him slide, as his previous teachers had done. At the same time, she couldn't give Jonah all the attention he needed because of the other students in her class. In the end, she decided to meet with Jonah's father to talk to him about what she knew, in the hope that they could find a way to work it out.

She'd heard about Miles Ryan.

Not much, but she knew that people for the most part both liked and respected him and that more than anything, he seemed to care about his son. That was good. Even in the little while she'd been teaching, she'd met parents who didn't seem to care about their children, regarding them as more of a burden than a blessing, and she'd also met parents who seemed to believe their child could do no wrong.

Both were impossible to deal with. Miles Ryan, people said, wasn't that way.

At the next corner, Sarah finally slowed down, then waited for a couple of cars to pass. Sarah crossed the street, waved to the man behind the counter at the pharmacy, and grabbed the mail before making her way up the steps to her apartment. After unlocking the door, she quickly scanned the mail and then set it on the table by the door.

In the kitchen, she poured herself a glass of ice water and carried the glass to her bedroom. She was undressing, tossing her clothes in the hamper and looking forward to a cool shower, when she saw the blinking light on the answering machine. She hit the play button and her mother's voice came on, telling Sarah that she was welcome to stop by later, if she had nothing else going on. As usual, her voice sounded slightly anxious.

On the night table, next to the answering machine, was a picture of Sarah's family: Maureen and Larry in the middle, Sarah and Brian on either end. The machine clicked and there was a second message, also from her mother: "Oh, I thought you'd be home by now . . . ," it began. "I hope everything's all right . . ."

Should she go or not? Was she in the mood?

Why not? she finally decided. I've got nothing else to do anyway.

*    *    *

Miles Ryan made his way down Madame Moore's Lane, a narrow, winding road that ran along both the Trent River and Brices Creek, from downtown New Bern to Pollocksville, a small hamlet twelve miles to the south. Originally named for the woman who once ran one of the most famous brothels in North Carolina, it rolled past the former country home and burial plot of Richard Dobbs Spaight, a southern hero who'd signed the Declaration of Independence. During the Civil War, Union soldiers exhumed the body from the grave and posted his skull on an iron gate as a warning to citizens not to resist the occupation. When he was a child, that story had kept Miles from wanting to go anywhere near the place.

Despite its beauty and relative isolation, the road he was following wasn't for children. Heavy, fully loaded logging trucks rumbled over it day and night, and drivers tended to underestimate the curves. As a homeowner in one of the communities just off the lane, Miles had been trying to lower the speed limit for years.

No one, except for Missy, had listened to him.

This road always made him think of her.

Miles tapped out another cigarette, lit it, then rolled down the window. As the warm air blew in the car, simple snapshots of the life they'd lived together surfaced in his mind; but as always, those images led inexorably to their final day together.

33

Ironically, he'd been gone most of the day, a Sunday. Miles had gone fishing with Charlie Curtis. He'd left the house early that morning, and though both he and Charlie came home with mahi-mahi that day, it wasn't enough to appease his wife. Missy, her face smudged with dirt, put her hands on her hips and glared at him the moment he got home. She didn't say anything at all, but then, she didn't need to. The way she looked at him spoke volumes.

Her brother and sister-in-law were coming in from Atlanta the following day, and she'd been working around the house, trying to get it ready for guests. Jonah was in bed with the flu, which didn't make it any easier, since she'd had to take care of him as well. But that wasn't the reason for her anger; Miles himself had been the cause.

Though she'd said that she wouldn't mind if Miles went fishing, she *had* asked him to take care of the yardwork on Saturday so she wouldn't have to worry about that as well. Work, however, had intervened, and instead of calling Charlie with his regrets, Miles had elected to go out on Sunday anyway. Charlie had teased him on and off all day—"You'll be sleeping on the couch tonight"—and Miles knew Charlie was probably right. But yardwork was yardwork and fishing was fishing, and for the life of him, Miles knew that neither Missy's brother nor his wife would care in the slightest whether there were a few too many weeds growing in the garden.

Besides, he'd told himself, he would take care of everything when he got back, and he meant it. He hadn't intended to be gone all day, but as with many of his fishing trips, one thing had led to the next and he'd lost track of time. Still, he had his speech worked out—*Don't worry, I'll take care of everything, even if it takes the rest of the night and I need a flashlight.* It might have worked, too, had he told her his plans before he'd slipped out of bed that morning. But he hadn't, and by the time he got home she'd done most of the work. The yard was mowed, the walk was edged, she'd planted some pansies around the mailbox. It must have taken hours, and to say she was angry was an understatement. Even furious wasn't sufficient. It was somewhere beyond that, the difference between a lit match and a blazing forest fire, and he knew it. He'd seen the look a few times in the years they'd been married, but only a few. He swallowed, thinking, Here we go.

"Hey, hon," he said sheepishly, "sorry that I'm so late. We just lost track of time." Just as he was getting ready to start his speech, Missy turned around and spoke over her shoulder.

"I'm going for a jog. You *can* take care of this, can't you?" She'd been getting ready to blow the grass off the walkway and drive; the blower was sitting on the lawn.

Miles knew enough not to respond.

After she'd gone inside to change, Miles got the cooler from the back of the car and brought it to the kitchen. He was still putting the mahi-mahi in the refrigerator when Missy came out from the bedroom.

"I was just putting the fish away . . . ," he started, and Missy clenched her jaw.

"What about doing what I asked you?"

"I'm going to—just let me finish here so this won't spoil."

Missy rolled her eyes. "Just forget it. I'll do it when I get back."

The martyr tone. Miles couldn't stand that.

"I'll do it," he said. "I said I would, didn't I?"

"Just like you'd finish the lawn before you went out fishing?"

He should have just bitten his lip and kept quiet. Yes, he'd spent the day fishing instead of working around the house; yes, he'd let her down. But in the whole scheme of things, it wasn't *that* big a deal, was it? It was just her brother and sister-in-law, after all. It wasn't as if the president were coming. There wasn't any reason to be irrational about the whole thing.

Yep, he should have kept quiet. Judging from the way she looked at him after he'd said it, he would have been better off. When she slammed the door on her way out, Miles heard the windows rattle.

Once she'd been gone a little while, however, he knew he'd been wrong, and he regretted what he'd done. He'd been a jerk, and she was right to have called him on it.

He wouldn't, however, get the chance to say he was sorry.

"Still smoking, huh?"

Charlie Curtis, the county sheriff, looked across the table at his friend just as Miles took his place at the table.

"I don't smoke," Miles answered quickly.

Charlie raised his hands. "I know, I know—you've already told me that. Hey, it's fine with me if you want to delude yourself. But I'll make sure to put the ashtrays out when you come by anyway."

Miles laughed. Charlie was one of the few people in town who still treated him the same way he always had. They'd been friends for years; Charlie had been the one who suggested that Miles become a deputy sheriff, and he'd taken Miles under his wing as soon as Miles had finished his training. He was older—sixty-five, next March—and his hair was streaked with gray. He'd put on twenty pounds in the past few years, almost all of it around his middle. He wasn't the type of sheriff who intimidated people on sight, but he was perceptive and diligent and had a way of getting the answers he needed. In the last three elections, no one had even bothered to run against him.

"I won't be coming by," Miles said, "unless you stop making these ridiculous accusations."

They were sitting at a booth in the corner, and the waitress, harried by the lunchtime crowd, dropped off a pitcher of sweet tea and two glasses of ice on her way to the next table. Miles poured the tea and pushed Charlie's glass toward him.

"Brenda will be disappointed," Charlie said. "You know she starts going through withdrawals if you don't bring Jonah by every now and then." He took a sip from the glass. "So, you looking forward to meeting with Sarah today?"

Miles looked up. "Who?"

"Jonah's teacher."

"Did your wife tell you that?"

Charlie smirked. Brenda worked at the school in the principal's office and seemed to know everything that went on at the school. "Of course."

"What's her name again?"

"Brenda," Charlie said seriously.

Miles looked across the table, and Charlie feigned a look of sudden comprehension. "Oh—you mean the teacher? Sarah. Sarah Andrews."

Miles took a drink. "Is she a good teacher?" he asked.

"I guess so. Brenda says she's great and that the

kids adore her, but then Brenda thinks everyone is great." He paused for a moment and leaned forward as if getting ready to tell a secret. "But she did say that Sarah was attractive. A real looker, if you know what I mean."

"What does that have to do with anything?"

"She also said that she was single."

"And?"

"And nothing." Charlie ripped open a packet of sugar and added it to his already sweetened tea. He shrugged. "I'm just letting you know what Brenda said."

"Well, good," Miles said. "I appreciate that. I don't know how I could have made it through the day without Brenda's latest evaluation."

"Oh, take it easy, Miles. You know she's always on the lookout for you."

"Tell her that I'm doing fine."

"Hell, I know that. But Brenda worries about you. She knows you smoke, too, you know."

"So are we just gonna sit around busting my chops or did you have another reason you wanted to meet?"

"Actually, I did. But I had to get you in the right frame of mind so you don't blow your stack."

"What are you talking about?"

As he asked, the waitress dropped off two plates of barbecue with coleslaw and hush puppies on the side, their usual order, and Charlie used the moment to collect his thoughts. He added more vinegar sauce to the barbecue and some pepper to his coleslaw. After deciding there was no easy way to say it, he just came out with it.

"Harvey Wellman decided to drop the charges against Otis Timson."

Harvey Wellman was the district attorney in Craven County. He'd spoken with Charlie earlier that morning and had offered to tell Miles, but Charlie had decided it would probably be better if he handled it.

Miles looked up at him. "What?"

"He didn't have a case. Beck Swanson suddenly got a case of amnesia about what happened."

"But I was there—"

"You got there after it happened. You didn't *see* it."

"But I saw the blood. I saw the broken chair and table in the middle of the bar. I saw the crowd that had gathered."

"I know, I know. But what was Harvey supposed to do? Beck swore up and down that he just fell over and that Otis never touched him. He said he'd been confused that night, but now that his mind was clear, he remembered everything."

Miles suddenly lost his appetite, and he pushed his plate off to the side. "If I went down there again, I'm sure that I could find someone who saw what happened."

Charlie shook his head. "I know it grates on you, but what good would it do? You know how many of Otis's brothers were there that night. They'd also say that nothing happened—and who knows, maybe they were the ones who actually did it. Without Beck's testimony, what choice did Harvey have? Besides, you know Otis. He'll do something else— just give him time."

"That's what I'm worried about."

Miles and Otis Timson had a long history between them. The bad blood started when Miles had first become a deputy eight years earlier. He'd arrested Clyde Timson, Otis's father, for assault when he'd thrown his wife through the screen door on their mobile home. Clyde had spent time in prison for that—though not as long as he should have—and over the years, five of his six sons had spent time in prison as well on offenses ranging from drug dealing to assault to car theft.

To Miles, Otis posed the greatest danger simply because he was the smartest.

Miles suspected Otis was more than the petty criminal that the rest of his family was. For one thing, he didn't look the part. Unlike his brothers, he shied away from tattoos and kept his hair cut short; there were times he actually held down odd jobs, doing manual labor. He didn't look like a criminal, but looks were deceiving. His name was loosely linked with various crimes, and townspeople frequently speculated that it was he who directed the flow of drugs into the county, though Miles had no way to prove that. All of their raids had come up empty, much to Miles's frustration.

Otis also held on to a grudge.

He didn't fully understand that until after Jonah was born. He'd arrested three of Otis's brothers after a riot had broken out at their family reunion. A week after that, Missy was rocking four-month-old Jonah in the living room when a brick came crashing through the window. It nearly hit them, and a shard of glass cut Jonah's cheek. Though he couldn't prove it, Miles knew that Otis had somehow been responsible, and Miles showed up at the Timson compound—a series of decrepit mobile homes arranged in a semicircle on the outskirts of town—with three other deputies, their guns drawn. The Timsons came out peacefully and, without a word, held out their hands to be cuffed and were taken in.

In the end, no charges were brought for lack of evidence. Miles was furious, and after the Timsons were released, he confronted Harvey Wellman outside his office. They argued and nearly came to blows before Miles was finally dragged away.

In the following years, there were other things: gunshots fired nearby, a mysterious fire in Miles's garage, incidents that were more akin to adolescent pranks. But again, without witnesses, there was nothing Miles could do. Since Missy's death it had been relatively quiet.

Until the latest arrest.

Charlie glanced up from his food, his expression serious. "Listen, you and I both know he's guilty as hell, but don't even think about handling this on your own. You don't want this thing to escalate like it did before. You've got Jonah to think about now, and you're not always there to watch out for him."

Miles looked out the window as Charlie went on.

"Look—he'll do something stupid again, and if there's a case, I'll be the first to come down on him. You know that. But don't go looking for trouble—he's bad news. So stay away from him."

Miles still didn't respond.

"Let it go, you got that?" Charlie was speaking now not simply as a friend, but as Miles's boss as well.

"Why are you telling me this?"

"I just told you why."

Miles looked at Charlie closely. "But there's something else, isn't there."

Charlie held Miles's gaze for a long moment. "Look . . . Otis says you got a little rough when you arrested him, and he filed a complaint—"

Miles slammed his hand against the table, the noise reverberating throughout the restaurant. People at the next table jumped and turned to stare, but Miles didn't notice.

"That's crap—"

Charlie raised his hands to stop him. "Hell, I know that, and I told Harvey that, too, and Harvey isn't gonna do anything with it. But you and him aren't exactly best friends, and he knows what you're like when you get worked up. Even though he's not gonna press it, he thinks it's possible that Otis is telling the truth and he told me to tell you to lay off."

"So what am I supposed to do if I see Otis committing a crime? Look the other way?"

"Hell, no—don't be stupid. I'd come down on you if you did that. Just keep your distance for a while, until all this blows over, unless there's no other choice. I'm telling you this for your own good, okay?"

It took a moment before Miles finally sighed. "Fine," he answered.

Even as he spoke, however, he knew that he and Otis weren't finished with one another yet.

# Chapter 3

Three hours after meeting with Charlie, Miles pulled into a parking space in front of Grayton Elementary School just as classes were being dismissed. Three school buses were idling and students began drifting toward them, clustering in groups of four or six. Miles saw Jonah at the same time his son saw him. Jonah waved happily and ran toward the car; Miles knew that in a few more years, once adolescence settled in, Jonah wouldn't do that anymore. Jonah leapt into his open arms and Miles squeezed him tight, enjoying the closeness while he could.

"Hey, champ, how was school?"

Jonah pulled back. "It was fine. How's work going?"

"It's better now that I'm done."

"Did you arrest anyone today?"

Miles shook his head. "Not today. Maybe tomorrow. Listen, do you want to get some ice cream after I finish up here?"

Jonah nodded enthusiastically and Miles put him

down. "Fair enough. We'll do that." He bent lower and met his son's eyes. "Do you think you'll be okay on the playground while I talk to your teacher? Or do you want to wait inside?"

"I'm not a little kid anymore, Dad. Besides, Mark has to stay, too. His mom's at the doctor's office."

Miles looked up and saw Jonah's best friend waiting impatiently near a basketball hoop. Miles tucked Jonah's shirt back in.

"Well, you two stay together, okay? And don't go wandering, either of you."

"We won't."

"All right, then—but be careful."

Jonah handed his father his backpack and scrambled off. Miles tossed it onto the front seat and started through the parking lot, weaving among the cars. A few kids shouted greetings, as did some mothers who drove their kids home from school. Miles stopped and visited with some of them, waiting until the commotion outside finally began to die down. Once the buses were on their way and most of the cars were gone, the teachers headed back inside. Miles took one last glance in Jonah's direction before following them into the school.

As soon as he entered the building, he was hit with a blast of hot air. The school was nearly forty years old, and though the cooling system had been replaced more than once over the years, it wasn't up to the task during the first few weeks of school, when summer was still bearing down hard. Miles could feel himself begin to sweat almost immediately, and he tugged at the front of his shirt, fanning himself as he made his way down the hallway. Jonah's classroom, he knew, was in the far corner. When he got there, the classroom was empty.

For a moment he thought he'd entered the wrong room, but the children's names on the roll sheet confirmed he was where he was supposed to be. He checked his watch and, realizing he was a couple of minutes early, wandered around the classroom. He saw some work scribbled on the chalkboard, the desks arranged in orderly rows, a rectangular table cluttered with construction paper and Elmer's Glue-All. Along the far wall were a few short compositions, and Miles was looking for Jonah's when he heard a voice behind him.

"Sorry I'm late. I was dropping off a few things at the office."

It was then that Miles saw Sarah Andrews for the first time.

In that instant, no shivers pricked the hairs on the back of his neck, no premonitions burst forth like exploding fireworks; he felt no sense of foreboding at all, and looking back—considering all that was to come—he was always amazed by that. He would, however, always remember his surprise at the fact that Charlie had been right: She *was* attractive. Not glamorous in a high-maintenance way, but definitely a woman whose passing would cause men to turn their heads. Her blonde hair was cut cleanly just above the shoulders in a style that looked both elegant and manageable. She wore a long skirt and a yellow blouse, and though her face was flushed from heat, her blue eyes seemed to radiate a freshness, as if she'd just spent the day relaxing at the beach.

"That's okay," he finally said. "I was a little early anyway." He held out his hand. "I'm Miles Ryan."

As he spoke, Sarah's eyes briefly flickered downward toward his holster. Miles had seen the look before—a look of apprehension—but before he could say anything, she met his eyes and smiled. She took his hand as if it didn't matter to her. "I'm Sarah Andrews. I'm glad you could make it in today. I remembered after I sent the note home that I hadn't offered you the chance to reschedule if today was inconvenient."

"It wasn't a problem. My boss was able to work it out."

She nodded, holding his gaze. "Charlie Curtis, right? I've met his wife, Brenda. She's been helping me get the hang of things around here."

"Be careful—she'll talk your ear off if you give her the chance."

Sarah laughed. "So I've realized. But she's been

great, she really has. It's always a little intimidating when you're new, but she's gone out of her way to make me feel as if I belong here."

"She's a sweet lady."

For a moment, neither of them said anything as they stood close together, and Miles immediately sensed that she wasn't as comfortable now that the small talk was out of the way. She moved around the desk, looking as if she were ready to get down to business. She began shuffling papers, scanning through the piles, searching for what she needed. Outside, the sun peeked out from behind a cloud and began slanting through the windows, zeroing in on them. The temperature instantly seemed to rise, and Miles tugged on his shirt again. Sarah glanced up at him.

"I know it's hot . . . I've been meaning to bring a fan in, but I haven't had the chance to pick one up yet."

"I'll be fine." Even as he said it, he could feel the sweat beginning to trickle down his chest and back.

"Well, I'll give you a couple of options. You can pull up a chair and we can talk here and maybe we both pass out, or we can do this outside where it's a little cooler. There are picnic tables in the shade."

"Would that be okay?"

"If you don't mind."

"No, I don't mind at all. Besides, Jonah's out on the playground, and that way I can keep an eye on him."

She nodded. "Good. Just let me make sure I have everything . . ."

A minute later they left the classroom, headed down the hall, and pushed open the door.

"So how long have you been in town?" Miles finally asked.

"Since June."

"How do you like it?"

She looked over at him. "It's kind of quiet, but it's nice."

"Where'd you move from?"

"Baltimore. I grew up there, but . . ." She paused. "I needed a change."

Miles nodded. "I can understand that. Sometimes I feel like getting away, too."

Her face registered a kind of recognition as soon as he said it, and Miles knew immediately that she'd heard about Missy. She didn't say anything, however.

As they seated themselves at the picnic table, Miles stole a good look at her. Up close, with the sun slanting through the shade trees, her skin looked smooth, almost luminescent. Sarah Andrews, he decided on the spot, never had pimples as a teenager.

"So . . .," he said, "should I call you Miss Andrews?"

"No, Sarah's fine."

"Okay, Sarah . . ." He stopped, and after a moment Sarah finished for him.

"You're wondering why I needed to talk to you?"

"It had crossed my mind."

Sarah glanced toward the folder in front of her, then up again. "Well, let me start by telling you how much I enjoy having Jonah in class. He's a wonderful boy—he's always the first to volunteer if I ever need anything, and he's really good to the other students as well. He's also polite and extremely well spoken for his age."

Miles looked her over carefully. "Why do I get the impression that you're leading up to some bad news?"

"Am I that obvious?"

"Well . . . sort of," Miles admitted, and Sarah gave a sheepish laugh.

"I'm sorry, but I did want you to know that it's not all bad. Tell me—has Jonah mentioned anything to you about what's going on?"

"Not until breakfast this morning. When I asked him why you wanted to meet with me, he just said that he's having trouble with some of the work."

"I see." She paused for a moment, as if trying to collect her thoughts.

"You're making me a little nervous here," Miles finally said. "You don't think there's a serious problem, do you?"

"Well . . ." She hesitated. "I hate to have to tell you this, but I think there is. Jonah isn't having trouble with some of the work. Jonah's having trouble with *all* of the work."

Miles frowned. "All of it?"

"Jonah," she said evenly, "is behind in reading, writing, spelling, and math—just about everything. To be honest, I don't think he was ready for the second grade."

Miles simply stared at her, not knowing what to say. Sarah went on. "I know this is hard for you to hear. Believe me, I wouldn't want to hear it, either, if it was my son. That's why I wanted to make sure before I talked to you about it. Here . . ."

Sarah opened the folder and handed Miles a stack of papers. Jonah's work. Miles glanced through the pages—two math tests without a single correct answer, a couple of pages where the assignment had been to write a paragraph (Jonah had managed a few, illegibly scrawled words), and three short reading tests that Jonah had failed as well. After a long moment, she slid the folder to Miles.

"You can keep all that. I'm finished with it."

"I'm not sure I want it," he said, still in shock.

Sarah leaned forward slightly. "Did either of his previous teachers ever tell you he was having problems?"

"No, never."

"Nothing?"

Miles looked away. Across the yard, he could see

Jonah going down the slide in the playground, Mark right behind him. He brought his hands together.

"Jonah's mom died right before he started kindergarten. I knew that Jonah used to put his head down on his desk and cry sometimes, and we were all concerned about that. But his teacher didn't say anything about his work. His report cards said he was doing fine. It was the same thing last year, too."

"Did you check the work he'd bring home from school?"

"He never had any. Except for projects he'd made."

Now, of course, it sounded ridiculous, even to him. Why, then, hadn't he noticed it before? *A little too busy with your own life, huh?* a voice inside him answered.

Miles sighed, angry with himself, angry with the school. Sarah seemed to read his mind.

"I know you're wondering how this could have happened, and you've got every right to be upset. Jonah's teachers had a responsibility to teach him, but they didn't. I'm sure it wasn't done out of malice—it probably started because no one wanted to push him too hard."

Miles considered that for a long moment. "This is just *great*," he muttered.

"Look," Sarah said, "I didn't bring you here just to give you bad news. If I did only that, then I'd be neglecting *my* responsibility. I wanted to talk to you about the best way to help Jonah. I don't want to hold him back this year, and with a little extra effort, I don't think I'll have to. He can still catch up."

It took a while for that to sink in, and when he looked up, Sarah nodded.

"Jonah is very intelligent. Once he learns something, he remembers it. He just needs a little more work than I can give him in class."

"So what does that mean?"

"He needs help after school."

"Like a tutor?"

Sarah smoothed her long skirt. "Getting a tutor is one idea, but it can get expensive, especially when you consider that Jonah needs help in learning the basics. We're not talking algebra here—right now we're doing single-digit addition, like three plus two. And as far as reading goes, he just needs to spend some time practicing. Same thing with writing, he just needs to do it. Unless you've got money to burn, it would probably be better if you do it."

"Me?"

"It's not all that hard. You read with him, have him read to you, help him with his assignments, things like that. I don't think you'll have any problem with anything that I've assigned."

"You didn't see my report cards as a kid."

Sarah smiled before going on. "A set schedule, too, would probably help. I've learned that kids

54

remember things best when there's a routine involved. And besides, a routine usually ensures that you're consistent, and that's what Jonah needs most of all."

Miles adjusted himself in his seat. "That's not as easy as it sounds. My schedule varies. Sometimes I'm home at four, other times I don't get home until Jonah's already in bed."

"Who watches him after school?"

"Mrs. Knowlson—our neighbor. She's great, but I don't know if she'd be up to doing schoolwork with him every day. She's in her eighties."

"What about someone else? A grandparent or someone like that?"

Miles shook his head. "Missy's parents moved to Florida after she died, so they're not around. My mother died when I was finishing up high school, and as soon as I went off to college, my father took off. Half the time, I don't even know where he is. Jonah and I have been pretty much on our own for the last couple of years. Don't get me wrong—he's a great kid, and sometimes I feel lucky to have him all to myself. But at other times, I can't help but think it would have been easier if Missy's parents had stayed in town, or if my father were a little more available."

"For something like this, you mean?"

"Exactly," he answered, and Sarah laughed again.

He liked the sound of it. There was an innocent ring to it, the kind he associated with children who had yet to realize that the world wasn't simply fun and games.

"At least you're taking this seriously," Sarah said. "I can't tell you how many times I've had this conversation with parents who either didn't want to believe it or wanted to blame me."

"Does that happen a lot?"

"More than you can imagine. Before I sent the note home, I even talked to Brenda about the best way to tell you."

"What did she say?"

"She told me not to worry, that you wouldn't overreact. That first and foremost, you'd be worried about Jonah and that you'd be open to what I was telling you. Then she told me that I shouldn't worry one little bit, even if you did have a gun with you."

Miles looked horrified. "She didn't."

"She did, but you have to have been there when she said it."

"I'm going to have to talk to her."

"No, don't—it was obvious that she likes you. She told me that, too."

"Brenda likes everyone."

At that moment, Miles heard Jonah yelling for Mark to chase him. Despite the heat, the two boys raced through the playground, whipping around some poles before spinning off in another direction.

"I can't believe how much energy they have," Sarah marveled. "They did the same thing at lunch today."

"Believe me, I know. I can't remember the last time I felt that way."

"Oh, come on, you're not that old. You're what—forty, forty-five?"

Miles looked horrified again, and Sarah winked. "Just teasing," she added.

Miles wiped his brow in mock relief, surprised to find himself enjoying the conversation. For some reason, it seemed almost as if she were flirting, and he liked that, more than he thought he should.

"Thanks—I think."

"No problem," she answered, trying and failing to hide the smirk on her face. "But now . . ." She paused. "Where were we again?"

"You were telling me that I haven't aged well."

"Before that . . . Oh yeah, we were talking about your schedule and you were telling me how impossible it was going to be to get a routine going."

"I didn't say impossible. It's just not going to be easy."

"When are you off in the afternoons?"

"Usually on Wednesdays and Fridays."

As Miles tried to work it out, Sarah seemed to come to a decision.

"Now, I don't usually do this, but I'll make a deal with you," she said slowly. "If it's okay with you, of course."

Miles raised his eyebrows. "What kind of deal?"

"I'll work with Jonah after school the other three days a week if you promise to do the same on the two days you're off."

He couldn't hide the surprise in his expression. "You'd do that?"

"Not for every student, no. But as I said, Jonah's sweet, and he's had a rough time the last couple of years. I'd be glad to help."

"Really?"

"Don't look so surprised. Most teachers are pretty dedicated to their work. Besides, I'm usually here until four o'clock anyway, so it won't be much trouble at all."

When Miles didn't answer right away, Sarah fell silent.

"I'm only going to offer this once, so take it or leave it," she finally said.

Miles looked almost embarrassed. "Thank you," he said seriously. "I can't even tell you how much I appreciate this."

"My pleasure. There's one thing that I'm going to need, though, so I can do this right. Think of it as my fee."

"What's that?"

"A fan—and make it a good one." She nodded toward the school. "It's like an oven in there."

"You got yourself a deal."

Twenty minutes later, after she and Miles had said good-bye, Sarah was back in the classroom. As she was collecting her things, she found herself thinking about Jonah and how best to help him. It was a good thing that she'd made the offer, she told herself. It would keep her more attuned to his abilities in class, and she'd be able to better guide Miles when he was working with his son. True, it was a little extra work, but it was the best thing for Jonah, even if she hadn't planned on it. And she hadn't—not until she'd said the words.

She was still trying to figure out why she'd done that.

Despite herself, she was also thinking about Miles. He wasn't what she'd expected, that's for sure. When Brenda had told her that he was a sheriff, she'd immediately pictured a caricature of southern law enforcement: overweight, pants hanging too low, small mirrored sunglasses, a mouth full of chewing tobacco. She'd imagined him swaggering into her classroom, hooking his thumbs into the waistband of his pants, and drawling, *Now, just what did you want to talk to me about, little lady?* But Miles was none of these things.

He was attractive, too. Not as Michael had been—dark and glamorous, everything always perfectly in place—but appealing in a natural, more rugged way. His face had a roughness to it, as if he'd spent many hours in the sun as a boy. But contrary to what she'd said, he didn't look forty, and that had surprised her.

It shouldn't have. After all, Jonah was only seven, and she knew Missy Ryan had died young. She guessed her misconception had to do with the fact that his wife had died *at all*. She couldn't imagine that happening to someone her age. It wasn't right; it seemed out of sync with the natural order of the world.

Sarah was still musing over this as she glanced around the room one last time, making sure she had everything she needed. She removed her purse from the bottom drawer of her desk, slipped it over her shoulder, put everything else under her other arm, and then turned off the lights on her way out.

As she walked to her car, she felt a pang of disappointment when she saw that Miles had already left. Chiding herself for her thoughts, she reminded herself that a widower like Miles would hardly be entertaining similar thoughts about his young son's schoolteacher.

Sarah Andrews had no idea how wrong she was.

# Chapter 4

*B*y the dim light on my desk, the newspaper clippings look older than they are. Though yellowed and wrinkled, they seem strangely heavy, as if burdened with the weight of my life back then.

There are some simple truths in life, and this is one of them: Whenever someone dies young and tragically, there's always interest in the story, especially in a small town, where everyone seems to know each other.

When Missy Ryan died, it was front-page news, and gasps were heard in kitchens throughout New Bern when newspapers were opened the following morning. There was a major article and three photographs: one of the accident scene and two others that showed Missy as the beautiful woman she'd been. There were two more lengthy articles in the days that followed as more information was released, and in the beginning, everyone was confident that the case would have a resolution.

A month or so after the event, another article appeared on the front page, stating that a reward had been offered by the town council for any information on the case;

and with that, confidence began to fade. And as is typical of any news event, so did the interest. People around
town stopped discussing it as frequently, Missy's name
came up less and less often. In time, another article
appeared, this one on the third page, repeating what had
been stated in the first few articles and again asking anyone
in the community with information to come forward. After
that, there wasn't anything at all.

The articles had always followed the same pattern,
outlining what was known for sure and laying out the
facts in a simple and straightforward way: On a warm
summer evening in 1986, Missy Ryan—high-school
sweetheart of a local sheriff and mother of one son—
went out for a jog, just as it was getting dark. Two people
had seen her running along Madame Moore's Lane a few
minutes after she started; each of them had been interviewed later by the highway patrol. The rest of the articles concerned the events of that night. What none of
them mentioned, however, was how Miles had spent the
last few hours before he finally learned what happened.

Those hours, I'm sure, were the ones that Miles would
always remember, since they were the last hours of nor-
malcy he would know. Miles blew off the driveway and
the walk, just as Missy had asked, then went inside. He
picked up around the kitchen, spent some time with
Jonah, and finally put him to bed. Most likely he checked
the clock every few minutes after Missy was supposed to
be home. At first, he might have suspected that Missy

had stopped to visit with someone she'd seen on her jog, something she sometimes did, and he probably chided himself for imagining the worst.

The minutes turned into an hour, then became two, and Missy still hadn't returned. By then, Miles was worried enough to place a call to Charlie. He asked him to check out the usual route Missy jogged, since Jonah was already asleep and he didn't want to leave him alone unless he had to. Charlie said he'd be glad to do it.

An hour later—during which Miles seemed to be getting the runaround from everyone he called for updates—Charlie was at the door. He'd brought his wife, Brenda, so she could watch Jonah, and she was standing behind him, her eyes red.

"You'd better come," Charlie said softly. "There's been an accident."

From the expression on his face, I'm sure that Miles knew exactly what Charlie was trying to tell him. The rest of the night was a terrible blur.

What neither Miles nor Charlie knew then, and what the investigation would later reveal, was that there were no witnesses to the hit-and-run that had taken Missy's life. Nor would anyone come forward with a confession. Over the next month, the highway patrol interviewed everyone in the area; they searched for any evidence that might provide a lead, poking through bushes, evaluating the evidence at the scene, visiting local bars and restaurants, asking if any customers had seemed intoxicated *and had left around that time. In the end, the case file was thick and heavy, chronicling everything they had learned—which in the end was essentially nothing more than what Miles knew the moment he'd pushed open the door and seen Charlie standing on the porch.*

*Miles Ryan had become a widower at the age of thirty.*

# Chapter 5

In the car, the memories of the day Missy died came back to Miles in bits and pieces, just as they had earlier when he'd driven along Madame Moore's Lane before his lunch with Charlie. Now, though, instead of running endlessly in the same loop, from his day spent fishing to the argument with Missy to all that followed, they were displaced by his thoughts of Jonah, and Sarah Andrews.

With his mind occupied, he didn't know how long they had driven in silence, but it was long enough to finally make Jonah nervous. As Jonah waited for his father to speak, his mind began focusing on the possible punishments his father might inflict, each of them worse than the last. He kept zipping and unzipping his backpack until Miles finally reached over and rested his hand on top of his son's to stop him. Still, his father said nothing, and after finally gathering his courage, Jonah looked toward Miles with wide eyes that were nearly brimming with tears.

"Am I in trouble, Dad?"

"No."

"You talked to Miss Andrews for a long time."

"We had a lot to talk about."

Jonah swallowed. "Did you talk about school?"

Miles nodded and Jonah looked toward his backpack again, feeling sick to his stomach and wishing he could keep his hands occupied again. "I'm in *big* trouble," he mumbled.

A few minutes later, sitting on a bench outside the Dairy Queen, Jonah was finishing an ice-cream cone, his father's arm around him. They'd been talking for ten minutes, and at least as far as Jonah was concerned, it wasn't half as bad as he'd thought it would be. His father hadn't yelled, he hadn't threatened him, and best of all, he hadn't been grounded. Instead, Miles had simply asked Jonah about his previous teachers and what they had—and hadn't—made him do; Jonah explained honestly that once he'd fallen behind, he was too embarrassed to ask for help. They'd talked about the things Jonah was having trouble with—as Sarah had said, it was practically everything—and Jonah promised that he'd do his best from now on. Miles, too, said that he'd help Jonah and that if everything went well, he'd be caught up in no time. All in all, Jonah considered himself lucky.

What he didn't realize was that his father wasn't finished yet.

"But because you're so far behind," Miles went on calmly, "you're going to have to stay after school a few days a week, so Miss Andrews can help you out."

It took a moment for the words to register, and then Jonah looked up at his father.

"After school?"

Miles nodded. "She said you'd catch up faster that way."

"I thought you said that you were going to help me."

"I am, but I can't do it every day. I have to work, so Miss Andrews said she'd help, too."

"But after school?" he asked again, a note of pleading in his voice.

"Three days a week."

"But . . . Dad . . ." He tossed the rest of the ice-cream cone into the garbage. "I don't want to stay after school."

"I didn't ask if you wanted to. And besides, you could have told me you were having trouble before. If you'd done that, you might have been able to avoid something like this."

Jonah furrowed his brow. "But, Dad . . ."

"Listen, I know there's a million things you'd rather do, but you're gonna do this for a while. You don't have a choice, and just think, it could be worse."

"Howww?" he asked, sort of singing the last syllable,

the way he always did when he didn't want to believe what Miles was telling him.

"Well, she could have wanted to work with you on the weekends, too. If that had happened, you wouldn't have been able to play soccer."

Jonah leaned forward, resting his chin in his hands. "All right," he finally said with a sigh, looking glum. "I'll do it."

Miles smiled, thinking, You didn't have a choice.

"I appreciate that, champ."

Later that night, Miles was leaning over Jonah's bed, pulling up the covers. Jonah's eyes were heavy, and Miles ran his hand through his son's hair before kissing his cheek.

"It's late. Get some sleep."

He looked so small in his bed, so content. Miles made sure that Jonah's night-light was on, then reached for the lamp by the bed. Jonah forced his eyes open, though one look said they wouldn't stay that way for long.

"Dad?"

"Yeah?"

"Thanks for not being too mad at me today."

Miles smiled. "You're welcome."

"And Dad?"

"Yeah?"

Jonah reached up to wipe his nose. Next to his

pillow was a teddy bear Missy had given him when he'd turned three. He still slept with it every night.

"I'm glad Miss Andrews wants to help me."

"You are?" he asked, surprised.

"She's nice."

Miles turned out the light. "I thought so, too. Now get some sleep, okay?"

"Okay. And Dad?"

"Yeah?"

"I love you."

Miles felt a tightness in his throat. "I love you, too, Jonah."

Hours later, just before four A.M., Jonah's nightmares returned.

Like the wail of someone plunging off a cliff, Jonah's screaming immediately jolted Miles awake. He staggered half-blindly from his bedroom, nearly tripping over a toy in the process, and was still trying to focus when he scooped the still-sleeping boy into his arms. He began whispering to him as he carried him to the back porch. It was, he'd learned, the only thing that would ever calm him down. Within moments the sobbing dropped to a whimper, and Miles was thankful not only for the fact that his home sat on an acre of land, but that his nearest neighbor— Mrs. Knowlson—was hard of hearing.

In the hazy humid air, Miles rocked Jonah back

and forth, continuing to whisper in his ear. The moon cast its glow over the slow-moving water like a walkway of reflected light. With low-slung oak trees and the whitewashed trunks of cypress trees lining the banks, the view was soothing, ageless in beauty. The draping veils of Spanish moss only added to the feeling that this part of the world hadn't changed in the last thousand years.

By the time Jonah's breathing had fallen into deep, regular patterns again, it was nearly five A.M. and Miles knew he wouldn't be able to get back to sleep. Instead, after putting Jonah back in bed, he went in the kitchen and started a pot of coffee. Sitting at the table, he rubbed his eyes and his face, getting the blood flowing again, then looked up. Outside the window, the sky was beginning to glow silver on the horizon and splinters of daybreak filtered through the trees.

Miles found himself thinking about Sarah Andrews once more.

He was attracted to her, that much was certain. He hadn't reacted that strongly to a woman in what seemed like forever. He'd been attracted to Missy, of course, but that was fifteen years ago. A lifetime ago. And it wasn't that he wasn't attracted to Missy during the last few years of their marriage, because he was. It's just that the attraction seemed different, somehow. The initial infatuation he'd felt when meeting Missy the first time—the desperate adolescent desire to learn everything he could about her—had been replaced with something deeper and more mature over the years. With Missy, there weren't any surprises. He knew how she looked just after getting out of bed in the mornings, he'd seen the exhaustion etched in every feature after giving birth to Jonah. He knew her—her feelings, her fears, the things she liked and didn't. But this attraction for Sarah felt . . . *new*, and it made him feel new as well, as if anything were possible. He hadn't realized how much he'd missed that feeling.

But where would it go from here? That was the part he still wasn't sure about. He couldn't predict what, if anything, would happen with Sarah. He didn't know anything about her; in the end, they might not be compatible at all. There were a thousand things that could doom a relationship, and he wasn't blind to them.

*Still, he'd been attracted to her . . .*

Miles shook his head, forcing the thought away. No reason to dwell on it, except for the reason that the attraction had once again reminded him that he wanted to start over. He wanted to find someone again; he didn't want to live the rest of his life alone. Some people could do that, he knew. There were people here in town who'd lost their spouse and never remarried, but he wasn't wired that way and never had been. He'd

71

never felt as if he'd been missing out on something when he'd been married. He didn't look at his single friends and wish that he could lead their life—dating, playing the field, falling in and out of love as the seasons changed. That just wasn't him. He loved being a husband, he loved being a father, he loved the stability that had come with all that, and he wanted to have that again.

*But I probably won't . . .*

Miles sighed and looked out the window again. More light in the lower sky, still black above. He rose from the table, went down the hall to peek in on Jonah—still asleep—then pushed open the door to his own bedroom. In the shadows, he could see the pictures he'd had framed, sitting on top of his chest of drawers and on the bedstand. Though he couldn't make out the features, he didn't need to see them clearly to know what they were: Missy sitting on the back porch, holding a bouquet of wildflowers; Missy and Jonah, their faces close to the lens, grinning broadly; Missy and Miles walking down the aisle . . .

Miles entered and sat on the bed. Next to the photo was the manila file filled with information he'd compiled himself, on his own time. Because sheriffs didn't have jurisdiction over traffic accidents—nor would he have been allowed to investigate, even if the sheriffs had—he'd followed in the footsteps of the highway patrol, interviewing the same people, asking the same questions, and sifting through the same information. Knowing what he'd been through, no one had refused to cooperate, but in the end he'd learned no more than the official investigators. As it was, the file sat on the bedstand, as if daring Miles to find out who'd been driving the car that night.

But that didn't seem likely, not anymore, no matter how much Miles wanted to punish the person who'd ruined his life. And let there be no mistake: That was exactly what he wanted to do. He wanted to make the person pay dearly for what he'd done; it was his duty both as a husband and as someone sworn to uphold the law. An eye for an eye—wasn't that what the Bible said?

Now, as with most mornings, Miles stared at the file without bothering to open it and found himself imagining the person who'd done it, running through the same scenarios he did every time, and always beginning with the same question.

If it was simply an accident, why run?

The only reason he could come up with was that the person was drunk, someone coming home from a party, or someone who made a habit of drinking too much every weekend. A man, probably, in his thirties or forties. Though there was no evidence to support that, that's whom he always pictured. In his mind's eye, Miles could see him swerving from side to side as he made his way down the road, going too fast and jerking the wheel, his mind processing everything in slow motion. Maybe he was reaching for another beer, one sandwiched between his legs, just as he caught a glimpse of Missy at the last second. Or maybe he didn't see her at all. Maybe he just heard the thud and felt the car shudder with the impact. Even then, the driver didn't panic. There weren't any skid marks on the road, even though the driver had stopped the car to see what he had done. The evidence—information that had never appeared in any of the articles—showed that much.

No matter.

No one else had seen anything. There were no other cars on the road, no porch lights flicked on, no one had been outside walking the dog or turning off the sprinklers. Even in his intoxicated state, the driver had known that Missy was dead and that he'd be facing a manslaughter charge at the least, maybe second-degree murder if he'd had prior offenses. Criminal charges. Prison time. Life behind bars. These and even more frightening thoughts must have raced through his head, urging him to get out of there before anyone saw him. And he had, without ever bothering to consider the grief he'd left in his wake.

It was either that, or someone had run Missy down on purpose.

Some sociopath who killed for the thrill of it. He'd heard of such people.

*Or killed to get back at Miles Ryan?*

He was a sheriff; he'd made enemies. He'd arrested people and testified against them. He'd helped send scores of people to prison.

One of them?

The list was endless, an exercise in paranoia.

He sighed, finally opening the file, finding himself drawn to the pages.

There was one detail about the accident that didn't seem to fit, and over the years Miles had scribbled half a dozen question marks around it. He had learned of it when he'd been taken to the scene of the accident.

Strangely, whoever had been driving the car had covered Missy's body with a blanket.

This fact had never made the papers.

For a while, there were hopes that the blanket would provide some clues to the identity of the driver. It hadn't. It was a blanket typically found in emergency kits, the kind sold in a standard package with other assorted items at nearly every auto supply or department store across the country. There'd been no way to trace it.

But . . . *why?*

This was the part that continued to nag at Miles.

Why cover up the body, then run? It made no

sense. When he'd raised the matter with Charlie, Charlie had said something that haunted Miles to this day: "It's like the driver was trying to apologize."

*Or throw us off the track?*

Miles didn't know what to believe.

But he would find the driver, no matter how unlikely it seemed, simply because he wouldn't give up. Then, and only then, could he imagine himself moving on.

# Chapter 6

On Friday evening, three days after meeting Miles Ryan, Sarah Andrews was alone in her living room, nursing her second glass of wine, feeling about as rotten as a person could feel. Even though she knew the wine wouldn't help, she knew that she'd nonetheless pour herself a third glass just as soon as this one was finished. She'd never been a big drinker, but it had been that kind of day.

Right now, she just wanted to escape.

Strangely, it hadn't started off badly. She'd felt pretty good first thing in the morning and even during breakfast, but after that, the day had nose-dived rapidly. Sometime during the night before, the hot-water heater in her apartment had stopped working and she'd had to take a cold shower before heading off to school. When she got there, three of the four students in the front of the class had colds and spent the day coughing and sneezing in her direction when they weren't acting up. The rest of the class seemed to follow their lead, and she hadn't accomplished half of what she'd wanted to. After school, she'd stayed to catch up on some of her work, but when she was finally ready to head home, one of the tires on her car was flat. She'd had to call AAA and ended up waiting nearly an hour until they showed up; and by the time she got back to her apartment, the streets had been roped off for the Flower Festival that weekend and she'd had to park three blocks away. Then, to top it all off, no more than ten minutes after she'd walked in the door, an acquaintance had called from Baltimore, to let her know that Michael was getting married again in December.

That was when she'd opened the wine.

Now, finally feeling the effects of the alcohol, Sarah found herself wishing that AAA had taken a little longer with her tire, so she wouldn't have been home to answer the phone when it rang. She wasn't a close friend of the woman's—she'd socialized with Sarah casually, since she'd originally been friends with Michael's family—and had no idea why the woman felt the urge to let Sarah know what was going on. And even though she had passed on the information with the proper mix of sympathy and disbelief, Sarah couldn't help suspecting that the woman would hang up the phone and immediately report back to Michael how Sarah had responded. Thank God she'd kept her composure.

But that was two glasses of wine ago, and now it wasn't so easy. She didn't want to hear about Michael. They were divorced, separated by law and choice, and unlike some divorced couples, they hadn't talked since their last meeting in the lawyer's office almost a year earlier. By that point, she'd considered herself lucky to be rid of him and had simply signed the papers without a word. The pain and anger had been replaced with a kind of apathy, rooted in the numbing realization that she'd never really known him at all. After that, he didn't call or write, nor did she. She lost contact with his family and friends, he showed no interest in hers. In many ways, it almost seemed as if they'd never been married at all. At least, that's what she told herself.

And now he was getting married again.

It shouldn't bother her. She shouldn't care one way or the other.

But she did, and that bothered her, too. If anything, she was more upset by the fact that his impending marriage upset her than by the upcoming marriage itself. She'd known all along that Michael would marry again; he'd told her as much.

That was the first time she'd ever really hated someone.

But real hate, the kind that made the stomach roil, wasn't possible without an emotional bond. She wouldn't have hated Michael nearly as much unless she'd loved him first. Perhaps naively, she had imagined that they would be a couple forever. They'd made their vows and promised to love each other forever, after all, and she'd descended from a long line of families that had done just that. Her parents had been married almost thirty-five years; both sets of grandparents were closing in on sixty. Even after their problems arose, Sarah believed that she and Michael would follow in their footsteps. She knew it wouldn't be easy, but when he'd chosen the views of his family over his promise to her, she'd never felt so insignificant in her entire life.

*But she wouldn't be upset now, if she was really over him . . .*

Sarah finished her glass and rose from the couch, not wanting to believe that, refusing to believe it. She was over him. If he came crawling back to her right now and begged for forgiveness, she wouldn't take him back. There was nothing he could say or do to ever make her love him again. He could marry whoever the hell he wanted, and it would make no difference to her.

In the kitchen, she poured her third glass of wine.

*Michael was getting married again.*

Despite herself, Sarah felt the tears coming. She didn't want to cry anymore, but old dreams died hard. When she put her glass down, trying to compose herself, she set the glass too close to the sink and it toppled into the basin, shattering instantly. She reached in to pick up the shards of glass, pricked her finger, and it began to bleed.

One more thing on an already terrible day.

She exhaled sharply and pressed the back of her hand against her eyes, willing herself not to cry.

"Are you sure you're okay?"

With crowds pressing in around them, the words seemed to fade in and out, as if Sarah were trying to listen to something from a distance.

"For the third time, I'm fine, Mom. Really."

Maureen reached up and brushed the hair from Sarah's face. "It's just that you look a little pale, like you might be coming down with something."

"I'm a little tired, that's all. I was up late working."

Though she didn't like lying to her mother, Sarah had no desire to tell her about the bottle of wine the night before. Her mother barely understood why people drank at all, especially women, and if Sarah explained that she'd been alone as well, her mother would only bite her lip in worry before launching into a series of questions that Sarah was in no mood to answer.

It was a glorious Saturday, and the downtown area was thronged with people. The Flower Festival was in full swing, and Maureen had wanted to spend the day browsing among the booths and in the antique

81

stores along Middle Street. Since Larry wanted to watch the football game between North Carolina and Michigan State, Sarah had offered to keep her company. She'd thought it might be fun, and it probably would have been, if it hadn't been for the raging headache that even aspirin couldn't ease. As they talked, Sarah inspected an antique picture frame that had been restored with care, though not enough care to justify the price.

"On a Friday?" her mother asked.

"I'd been putting it off for a while and last night seemed as good as any."

Her mother leaned closer, pretending to admire the picture frame. "You were in all night?"

"Uh-huh. Why?"

"Because I called you a couple of times and the phone just rang and rang."

"I unplugged the phone."

"Oh. For a while there, I thought you might be out with someone."

"Who?"

Maureen shrugged. "I don't know . . . someone."

Sarah eyed her over the top of her sunglasses. "Mom, let's not go into that again."

"I'm not going into anything," she answered defensively. Then, lowering her voice as if conversing with herself, she went on. "I just assumed you'd decided to go out. You used to do that a lot, you know . . ."

In addition to wallowing in a bottomless pit of concern, Sarah's mother could also play to perfection the part of a guilt-ridden parent. There were times when Sarah needed it—a little pity never hurt anyone—but now wasn't one of them. Sarah frowned slightly as she set the frame back down. The proprietor of the booth, an elderly woman who sat in a chair beneath a large umbrella, raised her eyebrows, clearly enjoying the little scene. Sarah's frown deepened. She backed away from the booth as her mom went on, and after a moment, Maureen trailed after her.

"What's wrong?"

Her tone made Sarah stop and face her mother. "Nothing's wrong. I'm just not in the mood to hear how worried you are about me. It gets old after a while."

Maureen's mouth opened slightly and stayed that way. At the sight of her mother's injured expression, Sarah regretted her words, but she couldn't help it. Not today, anyway.

"Look, I'm sorry, Mom. I shouldn't have snapped at you."

Maureen reached out and took her daughter by the hand. "What's going on, Sarah? And tell me the truth, this time—I know you too well. Something happened, didn't it?"

She squeezed Sarah's hand gently and Sarah

looked away. All around them, strangers were going about their business, lost in their own conversations.

"Michael's getting married again," she said quietly.

After making sure she had heard correctly, Maureen slowly enveloped her daughter in a firm embrace. "Oh, Sarah . . . I'm sorry," she whispered.

There wasn't anything else to say.

A few minutes later, they were seated on a park bench that overlooked the marina, down the street from where the crowds were still congregated. They'd moved that way unconsciously; they'd simply walked until they could go no farther, then found a place to sit.

There, they talked for a long time, or rather Sarah talked. Maureen mainly listened, unable to mask the concern she felt. Her eyes widened and occasionally filled with tears; she squeezed Sarah's hand a dozen times.

"Oh . . . that's just *terrible*," she said for what seemed like the hundredth time. "What a *terrible* day."

"I thought so."

"Well . . . would it help if I told you to try to look on the bright side?"

"There is no bright side, Mom."

"Sure there is."

Sarah raised a skeptical eyebrow. "Like what?"

"Well, you can be certain that they won't live here after they get married. Your father would have them tarred and feathered."

Despite her mood, Sarah laughed. "Thanks a lot. If I ever see him again, I'll be sure to let him know."

Maureen paused. "You're not planning on that, are you? Seeing him, I mean."

Sarah shook her head. "No, not unless I can't help it."

"Good. After what he did to you, you shouldn't."

Sarah simply nodded before leaning back against the bench.

"So, have you heard from Brian lately?" she asked, changing the subject. "He's never in when I call."

Maureen followed Sarah's lead without complaint. "I talked to him a couple of days ago, but you know how it is. Sometimes, the last thing you want to do is talk to your parents. He doesn't stay on the phone long."

"Is he making friends?"

"I'm sure he is."

Sarah stared out over the water, thinking about her brother for a moment. Then: "How's Daddy?"

"The same. He had a checkup earlier this week and he seems to be doing fine. And he's not as tired as he used to be."

"Is he still exercising?"

"Not as much as he should, but he keeps promising me that he's going to get serious about it."

"Tell him that I said he has to."

"I will. But he's stubborn, you know. It would be better if you told him. If I tell him, he thinks I'm nagging."

"Are you?"

"Of course not," she said quickly. "I just worry about him." Out in the marina, a large sailboat was heading slowly toward the Neuse River, and they both sat in silence, watching. In a minute, the bridge would swivel open to allow it passage and traffic on either side would begin to back up. Sarah had learned that if she was ever running late for an appointment, she could claim that she "got caught on the bridge." Everyone in town from doctors to judges would accept the excuse without question, simply because they had used it themselves.

"It's good to hear you laugh again," Maureen murmured after a moment.

Sarah glanced sideways at her.

"Don't look so surprised. There was a while there when you didn't. A long while." Maureen touched Sarah's knee gently. "Don't let Michael hurt you anymore, okay? You've moved on—remember that."

Sarah nodded almost imperceptibly, and Maureen pressed on with the monologue that Sarah had practically memorized by now.

"And you'll keep moving on, too. One day you'll find someone who'll love you as you are—"

"Mom . . ." Sarah interrupted, stretching out the word and shaking her head. Their conversations these days seemed always to come back to this.

For once, her mother caught herself. She reached for Sarah's hand again, and even though Sarah pulled it away at first, she persisted until Sarah relented.

"I can't help it if I want you to be happy," she said. "Can you understand that?"

Sarah forced a smile, hoping it would satisfy her mother.

"Yeah, Mom, I understand."

# Chapter 7

On Monday, Jonah began the process of settling into the routine that would come to dominate much of his life over the next few months. When the bell rang, officially ending the school day, Jonah walked out with his friends but left his backpack in the classroom. Sarah, like all the other teachers, went outside to make sure kids got in the proper cars and onto the right buses. Once everyone was on the buses and the cars were pulling out, Sarah wandered over to where Jonah was standing. He stared wistfully at his departing friends.

"I bet you wish you didn't have to stay, huh?"

Jonah nodded.

"It won't be so bad. I brought some cookies from home to make it a little easier."

He thought about that. "What kind of cookies?" he asked skeptically.

"Oreos. When I was going to school, my mom always used to let me have a couple when I got home. She said it was my reward for doing such a good job."

"Mrs. Knowlson likes to give me apple slices."

"Would you rather have those tomorrow?"

"No way," he said seriously. "Oreos are way better."

She motioned in the direction of the school. "C'mon. You ready to get started?"

"I guess so," he mumbled. Sarah reached out, offering her hand.

Jonah looked up at her. "Wait—do you have any milk?"

"I can get some from the cafeteria, if you want."

With that, Jonah took her hand and smiled up at her for a moment before they headed back inside.

While Sarah and Jonah were holding hands, heading toward the classroom, Miles Ryan was ducking behind his car and reaching for his gun, even before the echo from the last shot had died. And he intended to stay there until he figured out what was going on.

There was nothing like gunfire to get the old ticker pumping—the instinct for self-preservation always surprised Miles with both its intensity and its rapidity. The adrenaline seemed to enter his system as if he were hooked to a giant, invisible IV. He could feel his heart hammering, and his palms were slick with sweat.

If he needed to, he could put out a call saying he was in trouble, and in less than a few minutes the place would be surrounded by every law enforcement officer in the county. But for the time being, he held off. For one thing, he didn't think the gunfire was directed at him. That he'd heard it wasn't in question, but it had sounded muffled, as if it had originated from somewhere deep in the house.

Had he been standing outside someone's home, he would have made the call, figuring that some sort of domestic issue had gotten out of hand. But he was at the Gregory place, a teetering wood structure blanketed in kudzu on the outskirts of New Bern. It had decayed over the years and was completely abandoned, as it had been since Miles was a kid. Most of the time, no one bothered with the place. The floors were so old and rotten that they could give way any second, and rain poured in through the gaping holes in the roof. The structure also tilted slightly, as if a strong gust of wind would topple it someday. Though New Bern didn't have a big problem with vagrants, even the ones who were around knew enough to avoid the place for the danger it presented.

But now, in broad daylight no less, he heard the gunfire start up again—not a large-caliber gun, most likely a twenty-two—and he suspected there was a simple explanation, one that didn't pose much of a threat to him.

Still, he wasn't stupid enough to take any chances.

Opening his door, he slid forward on the seat and flicked a switch on the radio, so that his voice would be amplified, loud enough for the people inside the house to hear him.

"This is the sheriff," he said calmly, slowly. "If you boys are about finished, I'd like y'all to come out so I can talk to you. And I'd appreciate it if you set your guns off to the side."

With that, the gunfire stopped completely. After a few minutes, Miles saw a head poke out from one of the front windows. The boy was no older than twelve.

"You ain't gonna shoot us, are you?" he called out, obviously frightened.

"No, I'm not gonna shoot. Just set your guns by the door and come on down so I can talk to you."

For a minute Miles heard nothing, as if the kids inside were wondering whether or not to make a run for it. They weren't bad kids, Miles knew, just a little too rural for today's world. He was sure they'd rather run than have Miles bring them home to meet with their parents.

"Now come on out," Miles said into the microphone. "I just want to talk."

Finally, after another minute, two boys—the second a few years younger than the first—peeked out from either side of the opening where the front door used to be. Moving with exaggerated slowness, they set their guns off to the side and, hands thrust high in the air, stepped out. Miles suppressed a grin. Shaky and pale, they looked as if they believed they were going to be a source of target practice any second. Once they'd descended the broken steps, he stood from behind the car and holstered his gun. When they saw him, they stutter-stepped for a moment, then slowly continued forward. Both were dressed in faded blue jeans and torn-up sneakers, their faces and arms dirty. Country kids. As they inched forward, they kept their arms thrust above their heads, elbows locked. They'd obviously seen too many movies.

When they got close, Miles could see that both of them were practically crying.

Miles leaned against his car and crossed his arms. "You boys doin' some hunting?"

The younger one—ten, Miles guessed—looked to the older one, who met his gaze. They were clearly brothers.

"Yes, sir," they said in unison.

"What's in the house there?"

Again they looked at each other.

"Sparrows," they finally said, and Miles nodded.

"You can put your hands down."

Again they exchanged glances. Then they lowered their arms.

"You sure you weren't going after any owls?"

"No, sir," the older boy said quickly. "Just sparrows. There's a whole bunch of 'em in there."

Miles nodded again. "Sparrows, huh?"

"Yes, sir."

He pointed in the direction of the rifles. "Those twenty-twos?"

"Yes, sir."

"That's a little much for sparrows, isn't it?"

Their looks were guilty this time. Miles eyed them sternly.

"Now look . . . if you were owl hunting, I'm not gonna be too happy. I like owls. They eat the rats and the mice and even snakes, and I'd rather have an owl around than any of those creatures, especially in my yard. But I'm pretty sure from all that shooting you were doing that you didn't get him yet, now, did you?"

After a long moment, the young one shook his head.

"Then let's not try again, okay?" he said in a voice that brooked no disagreement. "It isn't safe to be shooting out here, not with the highway so close. It's also against the law. And that place isn't for kids. It's just about to fall down and you could get hurt in there. Now, you don't want me to talk to your parents, do you?"

"No, sir."

"Then you won't go after that owl again, will you? If I let you go, I mean?"

"No, sir."

Miles stared at them wordlessly, making sure he believed them, then nodded in the direction of the nearest homes. "You live out that way?"

"Yes, sir."

"Did you walk or ride your bikes?"

"We walked."

"Then I'll tell you what—I'll get your rifles and you two get in the backseat. I'll give you a ride back home and drop you off down the street. And I'll let it go this time, but if I ever catch you out here again, I'm gonna tell your parents that I caught you before and warned you and that I'm gonna have to bring you both in, okay?"

Though their eyes widened at the threat, they both nodded gratefully.

After dropping them off, Miles made his way back to the school, looking forward to seeing Jonah. No doubt the boy would want to hear all about what just happened, though Miles first wanted to find out how things had gone that day.

And despite himself, he couldn't suppress a pleasant thrill at the thought of seeing Sarah Andrews again.

"Daddy!" Jonah screamed, running toward Miles. Miles lowered himself into position to catch his son just as he jumped. Out of the corner of his eye, he saw that Sarah had followed him out in a more sedate fashion. Jonah pulled back to look at him.

"Did you arrest anyone today?"

Miles grinned and shook his head. "Not so far, but I'm not finished yet. How'd it go in school today?"

"Good. Miss Andrews gave me some cookies."

"She did?" he asked, trying to watch her approach without being too obvious.

"Oreos. The good ones—Double Stuf."

"Oh, well, you can't ask for more than that," he said. "But how'd the tutoring go?"

Jonah furrowed his brow. "The what?"

"Miss Andrews helping you with your school-work."

"It was fun—we played games."

"Games?"

"I'll explain later," Sarah said, stepping up, "but we got off to a good start."

At the sound of her voice, Miles turned to face her and again felt pleasant surprise. She was wearing a long skirt and a blouse again, nothing fancy, but when she smiled, Miles felt the same strange flut-tering he'd experienced when he'd first met her. It struck him that he hadn't fully appreciated how pretty she was the last time. Yes, he'd recognized the fact that she was attractive, and the same features immediately jumped out at him—the corn-silk hair, the delicately boned face, eyes the color of turquoise—but today she looked softer somehow, her expression warm and almost familiar.

Miles lowered Jonah to the ground.

"Jonah, would you go wait by the car while I talk to Miss Andrews for a couple minutes?"

"Okay," he said easily. Then, surprising Miles, Jonah stepped over and hugged Sarah—who returned the squeeze with a hug of her own—before he scrambled off.

Once Jonah was gone, Miles looked at her curiously. "You two seemed to have hit it off."

"We had a good time today."

"Sounds like it. If I'd known you were eating cookies and playing games, I wouldn't have been so worried about him."

"Hey . . . whatever works," she said. "But before you worry too much, I want you to know the game involved reading. Flash cards."

"I figured there was more to the story. How'd he do?"

"Good. He has a long way to go, but good." She paused. "He's a great kid—he really is. I know I've said that before, but I don't want you to forget that because of what's going on here. And it's obvious that he worships you."

"Thank you," he said simply, meaning it.

"You're welcome." When she smiled again, Miles turned away, hoping she didn't realize what he'd been thinking earlier and at the same time hoping she did.

"Hey, thanks for the fan, by the way," she went on after a pause, referring to the industrial-size fan he'd dropped off at her classroom earlier that morning.

"No problem," he murmured, torn between wanting to stay and talk to her and wanting to escape the sudden wave of nervousness that seemed to come from nowhere.

For a moment neither of them said anything. The awkward silence stretched out until Miles finally shuffled his feet and muttered, "Well . . . I guess I'd better get Jonah home."

"Okay."

"We've got some stuff to do."

"Okay," she said again.

"Is there anything else that I should know?"

"Not that I can think of."

"Okay, then." He paused, pushing his hands into his pocket. "I guess I'd better get Jonah home."

She nodded seriously. "You said that already."

"I did?"

"Yeah."

Sarah tucked a strand of loose hair behind her ear. For a reason she couldn't quite explain, she found his good-bye adorable, almost charming. He was different from the men she had known in Baltimore, the ones who shopped at Brooks Brothers and never seemed to find themselves at a loss for words. In the months following her divorce, they'd begun to seem almost interchangeable, like cardboard cutouts of the perfect man.

"Well, okay, then," Miles said, oblivious to everything except his need to depart. "Thanks again." And with that, he backed away in the direction of his car, calling for Jonah as he went.

His last image was of Sarah standing out in the school yard, waving at the retreating car with a faintly bemused smile on her face.

In the coming weeks, Miles began to look forward to seeing Sarah after school with an unchecked enthusiasm he hadn't experienced since adolescence. He thought of her frequently and sometimes in the strangest of situations—standing in a grocery store while selecting a packet of pork chops, stopped at a traffic light, mowing the lawn. Once or twice, he thought of her as he was taking a shower in the morning, and he found himself wondering about her morning routines. Ridiculous things. Did she eat cereal or toast and jelly? Did she drink coffee or was she more of a herbal tea fan? After a shower, did she wrap her head in a towel as she put her makeup on or did she style it right away?

Sometimes he would try to imagine her in the

classroom, standing in front of the students with a piece of chalk in her hand; other times he wondered how she spent her time after school. Though they exchanged small talk every time they met, it wasn't enough to satisfy his growing curiosity. He didn't know much about her past at all, and though there were moments when he wanted to ask, he held himself back from doing so for the simple reason that he had no idea how to go about it. "Mainly I had Jonah work on spelling today and he did great," she might say, and what was Miles supposed to say next? *That's good. And speaking of spelling, tell me—do you wrap your head in a towel after you shower?*

Other men knew how to do these things, but damned if he could figure it out. Once, in a moment of courage supplied by a couple of beers, he'd come close to calling her on the phone. He'd had no reason to call, and though he hadn't known what he would say, he'd hoped that something would strike him, a bolt from the sky that would imbue him with wit and charisma. He'd imagined her laughing at the things he was saying, being positively overwhelmed by his charm. He'd gone so far as to look up her name in the phone book and dial the first three numbers before his nerves got the better of him and he'd hung up.

What if she wasn't home? He couldn't dazzle her if she wasn't even there to answer the phone, and he certainly wasn't going to have his ramblings recorded on her answering machine for posterity. He supposed he could hang up if the answering machine picked up, but that was a little too adolescent, now, wasn't it? And what would happen, God forbid, if she *was* home but was on a date with someone else? It was, he realized, a distinct possibility. He'd heard a few things around the department from some of the other single men who'd finally caught on to the fact that she wasn't married, and if they knew, then others certainly knew it as well. Word was getting out, and soon, single men would start descending on her, using *their* wit and charisma, if they already hadn't.

Good Lord, he was running out of time.

The next time he picked up the phone, he actually got to the sixth number before chickening out.

That night, lying in bed, he wondered what the hell was wrong with him.

On an early Saturday morning in late September, about a month after he'd first met Sarah Andrews, Miles stood in the fields of H. J. Macdonald Junior High School, watching Jonah play soccer. With the possible exception of fishing, Jonah loved to play soccer more than anything, and he was good at it. Missy had always been athletic, even more so than Miles, and from her Jonah had inherited both agility and coordination. From Miles, as Miles would mention casually to anyone who asked, he'd inherited speed. As a result, Jonah was a terror on the field. At that age, Jonah played no more than half a game, since everyone on the team was required to play the same amount of time. Yet Jonah usually scored most, if not all, of the team's goals. In the first four games, he'd scored twenty-seven times. Granted, there were only three people to a team, goalkeepers weren't allowed, and half the kids didn't know in which direction they were supposed to kick the ball, but twenty-seven goals was exceptional. Almost every time Jonah touched the ball, he took it the length of the field and kicked it in the net.

Truly ridiculous, however, was the burst of pride Miles experienced when watching Jonah perform. He *loved* it, secretly jumped for joy when Jonah scored, even though he knew it was nothing but a temporary phenomenon and didn't mean diddly squat. Kids matured at different rates, and some kids practiced with more diligence. Jonah was physically mature and didn't like to practice; it was only a matter of time before the others caught up with him.

But in this game, by the end of the first quarter, Jonah had already scored four goals. In the second quarter, with Jonah on the sidelines, the opposing team kicked four goals to take the lead. In the third quarter, Jonah kicked two more, giving him thirty-three for the year, not that anyone was counting, and a teammate added one. By the beginning of the fourth quarter, Jonah's team was behind 8–7, and Miles crossed his arms and scanned the crowd, doing his best to appear as if he didn't even realize that without Jonah his team would be getting destroyed.

*Damn, this was fun.*

Miles was so lost in his reverie, it took a moment for the voice coming from off to the side to register.

"You got a bet riding on this game, Deputy Ryan?" Sarah asked as she walked up to him, grinning broadly. "You look a little nervous."

"No—no bet. Just enjoying the game," he answered.

"Well, be careful. Your fingernails are almost gone. I'd hate to see you accidentally nip yourself."

"I wasn't biting my nails."

"Not now," she said. "But you were."

"I think you were imagining things," he countered, wondering if she was flirting with him again. "So . . ." He pushed up the brim of his baseball hat. "I didn't expect to see you out here."

Wearing shorts and sunglasses, she looked younger than usual.

"Jonah told me he had a game this weekend and asked if I'd come."

"He did?" Miles asked curiously.

"On Thursday. He said that I would enjoy it, but

I kind of got the impression he wanted me to see him doing something he was good at."

*Bless you, Jonah.*

"It's almost over now. You've missed most of it."

"I couldn't find the right field. I didn't realize there would be so many games out here. From a distance, all these kids look the same."

"I know. Sometimes even we have trouble finding what field we're playing on."

The whistle sounded and Jonah kicked the ball to a teammate. The ball shot past him, though, and promptly rolled out of bounds. Someone on the other team chased after it, and Jonah glanced toward his father. When he saw Sarah, he waved and she returned the wave enthusiastically. Then, settling into position with a determined look on his face, Jonah waited for the throw to put the ball back in play. A moment later, he and everyone else on the field were chasing after the ball.

"So how's he doing?" Sarah asked.

"He's having a good game."

"Mark says he's the best player out here."

"Well . . . ," Miles demurred, doing his best to look modest.

Sarah laughed. "Mark wasn't talking about you. Jonah's the one out there playing."

"I know that," Miles said.

"But you think he's a chip off the old block, huh?"

"Well . . . ," Miles repeated, for lack of a clever response. Sarah lifted an eyebrow, clearly amused. *Where was that wit and charisma he was counting on?*

"Tell me—did you play soccer as a kid?" she asked.

"They didn't even *have* soccer when I was a kid. I played the traditional sports—football, basketball, baseball. But even if they'd offered soccer, I don't think I would have played it. I've got a bias against sports that require me to bounce a ball off my head."

"But it's fine for Jonah, right?"

"Sure, as long as he likes it. Did you ever play?"

"No. I wasn't much of an athlete, but once I was in college, I took up walking. My roommate got me into it."

He squinted at her. "Walking?"

"It's harder than it looks if you keep a fast pace."

"Do you still do it?"

"Every day. I have a three-mile loop that I follow. It's a good workout and it gives me a chance to unwind. You should try it."

"With all that spare time I have?"

"Sure. Why not?"

"If I went three miles, I'd probably be so sore I couldn't get out of bed the next day. That's if I could even make it."

She ran her gaze over him appraisingly. "You could make it," she said. "You might have to give up smoking, but you could make it."

"I don't smoke," he protested.

"I know. Brenda told me." She grinned, and after a moment, Miles couldn't help but smile as well. Before he could say anything else, however, a loud roar went up and both of them turned to see Jonah break away from the pack, charge down the field, and kick yet another goal, this one to tie the score. As Jonah's teammates surged around him, Miles and Sarah stood together on the sidelines, both of them clapping and cheering for the same young boy.

"Did you enjoy it?" Miles asked. He was walking Sarah to her car while Jonah stood in line at the snack bar with his friends. The game had been won by Jonah's team, and after the game, Jonah had run up to Sarah to ask her if she'd seen his goal. When she'd answered that she had, Jonah had beamed and given her a hug before scrambling off to join his friends. Miles, surprisingly, had been all but ignored, though the fact that Jonah was fond of Sarah—and vice versa—left him feeling strangely satisfied.

"It was fun," she admitted. "I wish I could have been here for the whole thing, though."

In the early afternoon sunlight, her skin glowed beneath the tan she still carried from the summer.

"It's fine. Jonah was simply glad you showed up." He glanced at her sideways. "So what's on your agenda the rest of the day?"

105

"I'm meeting my mom for lunch downtown."

"Where?"

"Fred & Clara's? It's a little place just around the corner from where I live."

"I know the place. It's great."

They reached her car, a red Nissan Sentra, and Sarah started rummaging through her handbag for her keys. As she searched for them, Miles found himself staring at her. With the sunglasses perched neatly on her nose, she looked more like the city girl she was than someone from the country. Add to that the faded jeans shorts and long legs, and she sure didn't look like any teacher Miles had ever had growing up.

Behind them, a white pickup truck began backing out. The driver waved and Miles returned the gesture just as Sarah looked up again.

"You know him?"

"It's a small town. It seems like I know everyone."

"That must be comforting."

"Sometimes it is, other times it isn't. If you've got secrets, this isn't the place for you, that's for sure."

For a moment, Sarah wondered if he was talking about himself. Before she could dwell on it, Miles went on.

"Hey, I want to thank you again for everything you're doing for Jonah."

"You don't have to thank me every time you see me."

"I know. It's just that I've noticed a big change in him these last few weeks."

"So have I. He's catching up pretty quickly, even faster than I thought he would. He actually started reading aloud in class this week."

"I'm not surprised. He's got a good teacher."

To Miles's surprise, Sarah actually blushed. "He's got a good father, too."

He liked that.

And he liked the look she'd given him when she'd said it.

As if uncertain what to do next, Sarah fiddled with her keys. She selected one and unlocked her front door. As she swung the door open, Miles stepped back slightly.

"So, how much longer do you think he'll need to keep staying after school?" he asked.

*Keep talking. Don't let her leave yet.*

"I'm not sure yet. A while, for sure. Why? Do you want to start cutting back a little?"

"No," he continued. "I was just curious."

She nodded, waiting to see if he'd add anything else, but he didn't. "Okay," she finally said. "We'll keep going like we are and see how he's doing in another month. Is that all right?"

Another month. He'd continue to see her for at least that long. Good.

"Sounds like a plan," he agreed.

For a long moment neither of them said anything, and in the silence Sarah glanced at her watch. "Listen, I'm running a little late," she said apologetically, and Miles nodded.

"I know—you've got to go," he said, not wanting her to leave just yet. He wanted to keep talking. He wanted to learn everything he could about her.

*What you really mean is that it's time to ask her out.*

And no chickening out this time. No hanging up the phone, no putzing around.

Bite the bullet!

Be a man!

Go for it!

He steeled himself, knowing he was ready . . . but . . . but . . . how should he do it? Good Lord, it had been a long time since he had been in a situation like this. Should he suggest dinner or lunch? Or maybe a movie? Or . . . ? As Sarah started to climb in her car, his mind was sorting and searching frantically, trying to come up with ways to prolong her time with him long enough to figure it out. "Wait—before you go— can I ask you something?" he blurted out.

"Sure." She looked at him quizzically.

Miles put his hands in his pockets, feeling those little butterflies, feeling seventeen again. He swallowed.

"So . . . ," he began. His mind was racing, those little wheels spinning for everything they were worth.

"Yes?"

Sarah knew instinctively what was coming.

Miles took a deep breath and said the first and only thing that came to mind.

"How's the fan working out?"

She stared at him, a perplexed expression on her face. "The fan?" she repeated.

Miles felt as if he'd just swallowed a ton of lead. *The fan? What the hell was he thinking? The fan? That was all he could come up with?*

It was as if his brain had suddenly taken a vacation, but for the life of him, he couldn't stop . . .

"Yeah. You know . . . the fan that I got you for your class."

"It's fine," she said uncertainly.

"Because I can get you a new one if you don't like it."

She reached out to touch his arm, a look of concern on her face. "Are you feeling okay?"

"Yeah, I'm fine," he said seriously. "I just wanted to make sure you're happy with it."

"You picked a good one, okay?"

"Good," he said, hoping and praying that a bolt of lightning would suddenly shoot from the heavens and kill him on the spot.


The fan?

After she pulled out of the parking lot, Miles stood

without moving, wishing that he could turn back the clock and undo everything that had just happened. He wanted to find the nearest rock to crawl under, a nice dark spot where he could hide from the world forever. Thank God no one was around to hear it!

*Except for Sarah.*

For the rest of the day, the end of their conversation kept repeating in his head, like a song he'd heard on early morning radio.

*How's the fan working out? . . . Because I can get you a new one . . . I just want to make sure you're happy with it . . .*

It was painful, physically painful, to recall it. And no matter what else he did that afternoon, the memory would lurk there under the surface, waiting to emerge and humiliate him. And on the following day, it was the same thing. He woke up with the feeling that something was wrong . . . something . . . and boom! There was the memory again, taunting him. He winced and felt the lead in his gut. And then he pulled the pillow over his head.

# Chapter 8

"So how do you like it so far?" Brenda asked.

It was Monday, and Brenda and Sarah were sitting at the picnic table outside, the same one that Miles and Sarah had visited a month earlier. Brenda had picked up lunch from the Pollock Street Deli, which in Brenda's opinion, made the best sandwiches in town. "It'll give us a chance to visit," she'd said with a wink, before running out to the deli.

Though this wasn't the first time they'd had the chance to "visit," as Brenda put it, their conversations had usually been relatively short and impersonal: where supplies were stored, whom she needed to talk to to get a couple of new desks, things like that. Of course, Brenda had also been the one whom Sarah had first asked about Jonah and Miles, and because she knew Brenda was close to them, she also understood that this lunch was Brenda's attempt to find out what, if anything, was going on.

"You mean working at the school? It's different from the classes I had in Baltimore, but I like it."

"You worked in the inner city, right?"

"I worked in downtown Baltimore for four years."

"How was that?"

Sarah unwrapped her sandwich. "Not as bad as you probably think. Kids are kids, no matter where they're from, especially when they're young. The neighborhood might have been rough, but you kind of get used to it and you learn to be careful. I never had any trouble at all. And the people I worked with were great. It's easy to look at test scores and think the teachers don't care, but that's not the way it is. There were a lot of people I really looked up to."

"How did you decide to work there? Was your ex-husband a teacher, too?"

"No," she said simply.

Brenda saw the pain in Sarah's eyes for a moment, but almost as quickly as she noticed it, it was gone.

Sarah opened her can of Diet Pepsi. "He's an investment banker. Or was . . . I don't know what he does these days. Our divorce wasn't exactly amicable, if you know what I mean."

"I'm sorry to hear that," she said, "and I'm sorrier I brought it up."

"Don't be. You didn't know." She paused before forming a lazy smile. "Or did you?" she asked.

Brenda's eyes widened. "No, I didn't know."

Sarah looked at her expectantly.

"Really," Brenda said again.

"Nothing?"

Brenda shifted slightly in her seat. "Well, maybe I did hear a couple of things," she admitted sheepishly, and Sarah laughed.

"I thought so. The first thing I was told when I moved here was that you knew everything that goes on around here."

"I don't know *everything*," Brenda said, feigning indignation. "And despite what you may have heard about me, I don't repeat everything I *do* know. If someone tells me to keep something to myself, I do." She tapped her ear with her finger and lowered her voice. "I know things about people that would make your head spin around like you're in dire need of an exorcism," she said, "but if it's said in confidence, I keep it that way."

"Are you saying this so I'll trust you?"

"Of course," she said. She glanced around, then leaned across the table. "Now dish up."

Sarah grinned and Brenda waved a hand as she went on. "I'm kidding, of course. And in the future—since we do work together—keep in mind that I won't get my feelings hurt if you tell me I've gone too far. Sometimes I blurt out questions without really thinking, but I don't do it to hurt people. I really don't."

"Fair enough," Sarah said, satisfied.

113

Brenda picked up her sandwich. "And since you're new in town and we don't know each other that well, I won't ask anything that might seem too personal."

"I appreciate that."

"Besides, it's not really my business anyway."

"Right."

Brenda paused before taking a bite. "But if you have any questions about anyone, feel free to ask."

"Okay," Sarah said easily.

"I mean, I know how it is to be new in town and feel like you're on the outside looking in."

"I'm sure you do."

For a moment, neither of them said anything.

"So . . ." Brenda drew out the syllable expectantly.

"So . . ." Sarah said in response, knowing exactly what Brenda wanted.

Again there was a period of silence.

"So . . . do you have any questions about . . . *anyone?*" Brenda prodded.

"Mmm . . . ," Sarah said, appearing to think it over. Then, shaking her head, she answered: "Not really."

"Oh," Brenda said, unable to hide her disappointment.

Sarah smiled at Brenda's attempt at subtlety.

"Well, maybe there is one person I'd like to ask you about," she offered.

114

Brenda's face lit up. "Now we're talking," she said quickly. "What would you like to know?"

"Well, I've been wondering about . . ." She paused, trailing off, and Brenda looked at her like a child unwrapping a Christmas gift.

"Yes?" she whispered, sounding almost desperate.

"Well . . ." Sarah looked around. "What can you tell me about . . . Bob Bostrom?"

Brenda's jaw dropped. "Bob . . . the janitor?"

Sarah nodded. "He's sort of cute."

"He's seventy-four years old," Brenda said, thunderstruck.

"Is he married?" Sarah asked.

"He's been married for fifty years. He's got nine kids."

"Oh, that's a shame," Sarah said. Brenda was staring wide-eyed at her, and Sarah shook her head. After a moment, she looked up and met Brenda's gaze with a twinkle in her eye. "Well, I guess that leaves Miles Ryan, then. What can you tell me about him?"

It took a moment for the words to sink in, and Brenda looked Sarah over carefully. "If I didn't know you better, I'd think you were teasing me."

Sarah winked. "You don't have to know me better: I admit it. Teasing people is one of my weaknesses."

"And you're good at it." Brenda paused for a moment before smiling. "But now, while we're on the subject of Miles Ryan . . . I hear that you two have been seeing quite a bit of each other. Not only after school, but on the weekend, too."

"You know I've been working with Jonah, and he asked me to come out to watch him play soccer."

"Nothing more than that?"

When Sarah didn't answer right away, Brenda went on, this time with a knowing look.

"All right . . . about Miles. He lost his wife a couple of years back in a car accident. Hit-and-run. It was the saddest thing I've ever seen. He really loved her, and for a long time afterwards, he just wasn't himself. She was his high-school sweetheart." Brenda paused and set her sandwich off to the side. "The driver got away."

Sarah nodded. She'd heard bits and pieces of this already.

"It really hit him hard. As a sheriff especially. He took it as his own failure. Not only wasn't there a resolution, but he blamed himself for it. He kind of shut himself off from the world after that."

Brenda brought her hands together when she saw Sarah's expression.

"I know it sounds awful, and it was. But lately, he's been a lot more like the person he used to be, like he's coming out of his shell again, and I can't tell you how happy I've been to see that. He's really a wonderful man. He's kind, he's patient, he'll go to the ends of the world for his friends. And best of all, he loves his son." She hesitated.

"But?" Sarah finally asked.

Brenda shrugged. "There are no buts, not with him. He's a good guy and I'm not saying that just because I like him. I've known him a long time. He's one of those rare men who, when he loves, he does it with all his heart."

Sarah nodded. "That's rare," she said seriously.

"It's true. And try to remember all this if you and Miles ever get close."

"Why?"

Brenda looked away. "Because," she said simply, "I'd hate to see him get hurt again."

Later that day, Sarah found herself thinking about Miles. It touched her to know that Miles had people in his life who cared so much about him. Not family, but *friends*.

She'd known that Miles had wanted to ask her out after Jonah's soccer game. The way he'd flirted and kept moving closer made his intention plain.

But in the end, he hadn't asked.

At the time, it seemed funny. She'd giggled about it, driving away—but she wasn't laughing at Miles as much as she was laughing at how hard he'd made it seem. He'd tried, God knows he'd tried, but for some reason he couldn't say the words.

And now, after talking to Brenda, she thought she understood.

Miles hadn't asked her out because he hadn't known *how*. In his entire adult life, he'd probably never had to ask a woman out—his wife had been his high-school sweetheart. Sarah didn't think she'd ever known someone like that in Baltimore, someone in his thirties who'd never once asked someone to dinner or to a movie. Oddly, she found it endearing.

And maybe, she admitted to herself, she found it a little comforting, because she wasn't all that different.

She'd started going out with Michael when she was twenty-three; they'd divorced when she was twenty-seven. Since then she'd been out only a few times, the last time with a fellow who came on a little too strongly. After that, she told herself that she just wasn't ready. And maybe she wasn't, but spending time with Miles Ryan recently had reminded her that the past couple of years had been lonely ones.

In the classroom, it was usually easy to avoid such thoughts. Standing in front of the blackboard, she was able to focus completely on the students, those small faces that stared at her with wonder. She'd come to view them as *her* kids, and she wanted to make sure they had every opportunity for success in the world.

Today, though, she found herself uncharacteristically distracted, and when the final bell rang she lingered outside, until Jonah finally came up to her. He reached for her hand.

"Are you okay, Miss Andrews?" he asked.

"I'm fine," she said absently.

"You don't look so good."

She smiled. "Have you been talking to my mother?"

"Huh?"

"Never mind. Are you ready to get started?"

"Do you have any cookies?"

"Of course."

"Then let's get going," he said.

As they walked to the classroom, Sarah noticed that Jonah wouldn't let go of her hand. When she squeezed it, he squeezed back, his small hand completely covered by hers.

It was almost enough to make her life seem worthwhile.

Almost.


When Jonah and Sarah walked out of the school after the tutoring session, Miles was leaning against his car as usual, but this time he barely looked at Sarah as Jonah came running up to give him a hug. After going through their usual routine—trading stories about work and school, and so on—Jonah climbed into the car without being asked. When Sarah approached him, Miles glanced away.

"Thinking about ways to keep the citizens safe, Officer Ryan? You look like you're trying to save the world," she said easily.

He shook his head. "No, just a little preoccupied."

"I can tell."

Actually, his day hadn't been all that bad. Until having to face Sarah. In the car, he'd been saying little prayers to himself that she'd forgotten about how ridiculous he'd sounded the other day, after the game.

"How did Jonah do today?" he asked, keeping those thoughts at bay.

"He had a great day. Tomorrow I'm going to give him a couple of workbooks that really seem to be helping. I'll mark the pages for you."

"Okay," he said simply. When she smiled at him, he shifted from one foot to the other, thinking how lovely she looked.

And what she must think of him.

He forced his hands into his pockets.

"I had a good time at the game," Sarah said.

"I'm glad."

"Jonah asked if I'd come watch him again. Would you mind?"

"No, not at all," Miles said. "I don't know what time he plays, though. The schedule is on the refrigerator at home."

She looked at him carefully, wondering why he seemed so distant all of a sudden. "If you'd rather I not go, just say the word."

"No, it's fine," he said. "If Jonah asked you to go and watch, then by all means, you should. If you want to, of course."

"Are you sure?"

"Yeah. I'll let you know tomorrow what time the game is." Then, before he could stop himself, he added, "Besides, I'd like you to go, too."

He hadn't expected to say it. No doubt he'd wanted to say it. But here he was again, blathering away uncontrollably . . .

"You would?" she asked.

Miles swallowed. "Yeah," he said, doing his best not to blow it now. "I would."

Sarah smiled. Somewhere inside, she felt a twitch of anticipation.

"Then I'll be there for sure. There's one thing, though . . ."

*Oh, no . . .*

"What's that?"

Sarah met his eyes. "Do you remember when you asked me about the fan?"

With the word *fan*, all the feelings he'd had over the weekend rushed back, almost as though he'd been punched in the stomach.

"Yeah?" he said cautiously.

"I'm also free on Friday night, if you're still interested."

It took only a moment for the words to register.

"I'm interested," he said, breaking into a grin.

# Chapter 9

On Thursday night—one night until D-Day, as Miles had begun mentally referring to it—Miles lay in bed with Jonah, trading a book back and forth so each could read a page. They were propped against the pillows, the blankets pulled back. Jonah's hair was still wet from his bath, and Miles could smell the shampoo he'd used. The odor was sweet and untainted, as if more than dirt had been washed away.

In the middle of a page that Miles was reading, Jonah suddenly looked up at him. "Do you miss Mommy?"

Miles set the book down, then slipped an arm around Jonah. It had been a few months since he'd last mentioned Missy without being asked first.

"Yeah," he said. "I do."

Jonah tugged on the material of his pajamas, making two fire trucks crash into one another. "Do you think about her?"

"All the time," he said.

"I think about her, too," Jonah said softly.

"Sometimes when I'm in bed . . ." He frowned up at Miles. "I get these pictures in my head . . ." He trailed off.

"Kind of like a movie?"

"Kinda. But not really. It's more like a picture, you know? But I can't really see it all the time."

Miles pulled his son closer. "Does that make you sad?"

"I don't know. Sometimes."

"It's okay to be sad. Everyone gets sad now and then. Even me."

"But you're a grown-up."

"Grown-ups get sad, too."

Jonah seemed to ponder this as he made the fire trucks crash again. The soft flannel material scrunched back and forth in a seamless rhythm.

"Dad?"

"Yeah?"

"Are you going to marry Miss Andrews?"

Miles's eyebrows went up. "I hadn't really thought about it," he said honestly.

"But you're going on a date, right? Doesn't that mean you're getting married?"

Miles couldn't help but smile. "Who told you that?"

"Some of the older kids at school. They say that you date first and then get married."

"Well," Miles said, "they're kind of right, but

they're kind of wrong, too. Just because I'm having dinner with Miss Andrews doesn't mean we're getting married. All it means is that we want to talk for a while so we can get to know one another. Sometimes grown-ups like to do that."

"Why?"

*Believe me, son, it'll make sense in a couple of years.*

"They just do. It's kind of like . . . well, do you know how you play with your friends? When you joke around and laugh and have a good time? That's all a date is."

"Oh," Jonah said. He looked more serious than any seven-year-old should. "Will you talk about me?"

"Probably a little. But don't worry. It'll all be good stuff."

"Like what?"

"Well, maybe we'll talk about the soccer game. Or maybe I'll tell her how good you are at fishing. And we'll talk about how smart you are . . ."

Jonah suddenly shook his head, his brows knit together. "I'm not smart."

"Of course you are. You're very smart, and Miss Andrews thinks so, too."

"But I'm the only one in my class who has to stay after school."

"Yeah, well . . . that's okay. I had to stay after school when I was a kid, too."

That seemed to get his attention. "You did?"

125

"Yeah. Only I didn't have to do it for only a couple of months, I had to do it for two years."

"Two years?"

Miles nodded for emphasis. "Every day."

"Wow," he said, "you must really have been dumb if you had to stay for two years."

*That wasn't my point, but I guess if it makes you feel better, I'll take it.*

"You're a smart young man and don't you ever forget it, okay?"

"Did Miss Andrews really say that I was smart?"

"She tells me every day."

Jonah smiled. "She's a nice teacher."

"I think so, but I'm glad you think so, too."

Jonah paused, and those fire trucks started coming together again.

"Do you think she's pretty?" he asked innocently.

*Oh my, where is all of this coming from?*

"Well . . ."

"I think she's pretty," Jonah declared. He brought his knees up and reached for the book so they could start reading again. "She kind of makes me think about Mom, sometimes."

For the life of him, Miles had no idea what to say.

Nor did Sarah, though in an entirely different context. She had to think for a moment before she finally found her voice.

126

"I have no idea, Mom. I've never asked him."

"But he's a sheriff, right?"

"Yes . . . but that's not exactly the sort of thing that's ever come up."

Her mother had wondered aloud whether Miles had ever shot someone.

"Well, I was just curious, you know? You see all those shows on TV, and with the things you read in the papers these days, I wouldn't be surprised. That's a dangerous job."

Sarah closed her eyes and held them that way. Ever since she'd casually mentioned the fact that she would be going out with Miles, her mother had been calling a couple of times a day, asking Sarah dozens of questions, hardly any of which Sarah could answer.

"I'll be sure to ask him for you, okay?"

Her mother inhaled sharply. "Now, don't do that! I'd hate to ruin things right off the bat for you."

"There's nothing to ruin, Mom. We haven't even gone out yet."

"But you said he was nice, right?"

Sarah rubbed her eyes wearily. "Yes, Mom. He's nice."

"Well, then, remember how important it is to make a good first impression."

"I know, Mom."

"And make sure you dress well. I don't care what some of those magazines say, it's important to look

127

like a lady when you go out on a date. The things some women wear these days . . ."

As her mother droned on, Sarah imagined herself hanging up the phone, but instead she simply began sorting through the mail. Bills, assorted mailers, an application for a Visa card. Caught up in that, she didn't realize that her mother had stopped talking and was apparently waiting for her to respond.

"Yes, Mom," Sarah said automatically.

"Are you listening to me?"

"Of course I'm listening."

"So you'll be coming by the house, then?"

*I thought we were talking about what I should wear . . .* Sarah scrambled to figure out what her mother had been saying.

"You mean bring him by?" she finally asked.

"I'm sure your father would like to meet him."

"Well . . . I don't know if we'll have time."

"But you just said that you weren't even sure of what you were going to do yet."

"We'll see, Mom. But don't make any special plans, because I can't guarantee it."

There was a long pause on the other end. "Oh," she said. Then, trying another tack: "I was just thinking that I'd like to at least have a chance to say hello."

Sarah began sorting through the mail again. "I can't guarantee anything. Like you said, I'd hate to ruin anything he might have planned. You can understand that, right?"

"Oh, I suppose," she said, obviously disappointed. "But even if you can't make it, you'll call me to let me know how it went, right?"

"Yes, Mom, I'll call."

"And I hope you have a good time."

"I will."

"But not *too* good a time—"

"I understand," Sarah said cutting her off.

"I mean, it is your *first* date—"

"I understand, Mom," Sarah said, more forcefully this time.

"Well . . . all right, then." She sounded almost relieved. "I guess I'll let you go, then. Unless there's something else you'd like to talk about."

"No, I think we've covered most everything."

Somehow, even after that, the conversation lasted for another ten minutes.

Later that night, after Jonah had gone to sleep, Miles popped an old videotape into the VCR and settled back, watching Missy and Jonah frolic in the surf near Fort Macon. Jonah was still a toddler then, no older than three, and he loved nothing more than to play with his trucks on the makeshift roads that Missy smoothed with her hands. Missy was twenty-six years old—in her blue bikini, she looked more like a college student than the mother she was.

In the film, she motioned for Miles to put aside the videocamera and come play with them, but on that morning, he remembered he was more interested in simply observing. He liked to watch them together; he liked the way it made him feel, knowing that Missy loved Jonah in a way that he had never experienced. His own parents hadn't been so affectionate. They weren't bad people, they just weren't comfortable expressing emotion, even to their own child; and with his mother deceased and his father off traveling, he felt almost as if he'd never known them at all. Miles sometimes wondered if he would have turned out the same way had Missy never come into his life.

Missy began digging a hole with a small plastic shovel a few feet from the water's edge, then started using her hands to speed things up. On her knees, she was the same height as Jonah, and when he saw what she was doing, he stood alongside her, motioning and pointing, like an architect in the early stages of building. Missy smiled and talked to him— the sound, however, was muffled by the endless roar of the waves—and Miles couldn't understand what they were saying to each other. The sand came out in clumps, piled around her as she dug deeper, and after a while she motioned for Jonah to get in the hole. With his knees pulled up to his chest, he fit—just barely, but enough—and Missy started filling in the sand, pushing and leveling it around Jonah's small body. Within minutes he was covered up to his neck: a sand turtle with a little boy's head poking out the top.

Missy added more sand here and there, covering his arms and fingers. Jonah wiggled his fingers, causing some sand to fall away, and Missy tried again. As she was putting the final handfuls in place, Jonah did the same thing, and Missy laughed. She put a clump of wet sand on his head and he stopped moving. She leaned in and kissed him, and Miles watched his lips form the words: "I love you, Mommy."

"I love you, too," she mouthed in return. Knowing Jonah would sit quietly for a few minutes, Missy turned her attention to Miles.

He'd said something to her, and she smiled—again, the words were lost. In the background, over her shoulder, there were only a few other people in view. It was only May, a week before the crowds arrived in full force, and a weekday, if he remembered correctly. Missy glanced from side to side and stood. She put one hand on her hip, the other behind her head, looking at him through half-open eyes, sultry and lascivious. Then she dropped the pose, laughed again as if embarrassed, and came toward him. She kissed the camera lens.

The tape ended there.

These tapes were precious to Miles. He kept them in a fire-proof box he'd bought after the funeral; he'd watched them all a dozen times. In them, Missy was alive again; he could see her moving, he could listen to the sound of her voice. He could hear her laugh again.

Jonah didn't watch the tapes and never had. Miles doubted he even knew about them, since he'd been so young when most of them were made. Miles had stopped filming after Missy had died, for the same reason he'd stopped doing other things. The effort was too much. He didn't want to remember anything from the period of his life immediately following her death.

He wasn't sure why he'd felt the urge to watch the tapes this evening. It might have been because of Jonah's comment earlier, it might have had to do with the fact that tomorrow would bring something new into his life for the first time in what seemed like forever. No matter what happened with Sarah in the future, things were changing. He was changing.

Why, though, did it seem so frightening?

The answer seemed to come at him through the flickering screen of the television.

Maybe, it seemed to be saying, it was because he'd never found out what had really happened to Missy.

132

# Chapter 10

Missy Ryan's funeral was held on a Wednesday morning at the Episcopal church in downtown New Bern. The church could seat nearly five hundred people, but it wasn't large enough. People were standing and some had crowded around the outside doors, paying their respects from the nearest spot they could.

I remember that it had begun to rain that morning. It wasn't a hard rain, but it was steady, the kind of late summer rain that cools the earth and breaks the humidity. Mist floated just above the ground, ethereal and ghostlike; small puddles formed in the street. I watched as a parade of black umbrellas, held by people dressed in black, slowly moved forward, as if the mourners were walking in the snow.

I saw Miles Ryan sitting erect in the front row of the church. He was holding Jonah's hand. Jonah was only five at the time, old enough to understand that his mother had died, but not quite old enough to understand that he would never see her again. He looked more confused than sad. His father sat tight-lipped and pale as one person after another came up to him, offering a hand or a hug. Though he seemed to have difficulty looking directly at people, he neither cried nor shook. I turned away and made my way to the back of the church. I said nothing to him.

I'll never forget the smell, the odor of old wood and burning candles, as I sat in the back row. Someone played softly on a guitar near the altar. A lady sat beside me, followed a moment later by her husband. In her hand she held a wad of tissues, which she used to dab at the corners of her eyes. Her husband rested his hand on her knee, his mouth set in a straight line. Unlike the vestibule, where people were still coming in, in the church it was silent, except for the sounds of people sniffling. No one spoke; no one seemed to know what to say.

It was then that I felt as if I were going to vomit.

I fought back my nausea, feeling the sweat bead on my forehead. My hands felt clammy and useless. I didn't want to be there. I hadn't wanted to come. More than anything, I wanted to get up and leave.

I stayed.

Once the service started, I found it difficult to concentrate. If you ask me today what the reverend said, or what Missy's brother said in his eulogy, I couldn't tell you. I remember, however, that the words didn't comfort me. All I could think about was that Missy Ryan shouldn't have died.

After the service, there was a long procession to Cedar

Grove Cemetery; it was escorted by what I assumed was every sheriff and police officer in the county. I waited until most everyone started their cars, then finally pulled into the line, following the car directly in front of me. Headlights were turned on. Like a robot, I turned mine on, too.

As we drove, the rain began to fall harder. My wipers pushed the rain from side to side.

The cemetery was only a few minutes away.

People parked, umbrellas opened, people sloshed through puddles again, converging from every direction. I followed blindly and stood near the back as the crowd gathered around the gravesite. I saw Miles and Jonah again; they stood with their heads bowed, the rain drenching them. The pallbearers brought the coffin to the grave, surrounded by hundreds of bouquets.

I thought again that I didn't want to be there. I shouldn't have come. I don't belong here.

But I did.

Driven by compulsion, I'd had no choice. I needed to see Miles, needed to see Jonah.

Even then, I knew that our lives would be forever intertwined.

I had to be there, you see.

I was, after all, the one who'd been driving the car.

# Chapter 11

Friday brought the first truly crisp air of autumn. In the morning, light frost had dusted every grassy patch; people saw their breath as they climbed in their cars to go to work. The oaks and the dogwoods and the magnolias had yet to begin their slow turn toward red and orange and now, with the day winding down, Sarah watched the sunlight filtering through the leaves, casting shadows along the pavement.

Miles would be here before long, and she'd been thinking about it on and off all day. With three messages on her answering machine, she knew her mother had been thinking about it as well—a little too much, in Sarah's opinion. Her mother had rambled on and on, leaving—it seemed to Sarah—no stone unturned. "About tonight, don't forget to bring a jacket. You don't want to catch pneumonia. With this chill, it's possible, you know," began one, and from there it went on to offer all sorts of interesting advice, from not wearing too much makeup or fancy jewelry "so he won't get the wrong impression," to making sure the nylons that Sarah was wearing didn't have any runs in them ("Nothing looks worse, you know"). The second message began by backtracking to the first and sounded a little more frantic, as if her mother knew she was running out of time to dispense the worldly wisdom she'd accumulated over the years: "When I said jacket, I meant something classy. Something light. I know you might get cold, but you want to look nice. And for God's sake, whatever you do, don't wear that big long green one you're so fond of. It may be warm, but it's ugly as sin . . ." When she heard her mother's voice on the third message, this time *really* frantic as she described the importance of reading the newspaper "so you'll have something to talk about," Sarah simply hit the delete button without bothering to listen to the rest of it.

She had a date to get ready for.

Through the window an hour later, Sarah saw Miles coming around the corner with a long box under his arm. He paused for a moment, as if he were making sure he was in the right place, then opened the downstairs door and vanished inside. As she heard him climb the stairs, she smoothed the black cocktail dress she'd agonized over while deciding what to wear, then opened the door.

"Hey there . . . am I late?"

Sarah smiled. "No, you're right on time. I saw you coming up."

Miles took a deep breath. "You look beautiful," he said.

"Thank you." She motioned toward the box. "Is that for me?"

He nodded as he handed her the box. Inside were six yellow roses.

"There's one for every week you've been working with Jonah."

"That's sweet," she said sincerely. "My mom will be impressed."

"Your mom?"

She smiled. "I'll tell you about her later. C'mon in while I find something to put these in."

Miles stepped inside and took a quick glance around her apartment. It was charming—smaller than he thought it would be, but surprisingly homey, and most of the furniture blended well with the place. There was a comfortable-looking couch framed in wood, end tables with an almost fashionable fade to the stain, a nicked-up glider rocker in the corner beneath a lamp that looked a hundred years old—even the patchwork quilt thrown over the back of the chair looked like something from the last century.

In the kitchen, Sarah opened the cupboard above the sink, pushed aside a couple of bowls, and pulled down a small crystal vase, which she filled with water.

"This is a nice place you've got," he said.

Sarah looked up. "Thanks. I like it."

"Did you decorate it yourself?"

"Pretty much. I brought some things from Baltimore, but once I saw all the antique stores, I decided to replace most of it. There are some great places around here."

Miles ran his hand along an old rolltop desk near the window, then pushed aside the curtains to peek out. "Do you like living downtown?"

From the drawer, Sarah pulled out a pair of scissors and started angling the bottoms of the stems. "Yeah, but I'll tell you, the commotion around here keeps me up all night long. All those crowds, those people screaming and fighting, partying until dawn. It's amazing that I ever get to sleep at all."

"That quiet, huh?"

She arranged the flowers in the vase, one by one. "This is the first place I've ever lived where everybody seems to be in bed by nine o'clock. It's like a ghost town down here as soon as the sun goes down, but I'll bet that makes your job pretty easy, huh?"

"To be honest, it doesn't really affect me. Except for eviction notices, my jurisdiction ends at the town limits. I generally work in the county."

"Running those speed traps that the South is famous for?" she asked playfully.

Miles shook his head. "No, that's not me, either. That's the highway patrol."

"So what you're really saying is that you don't really do much at all, then . . ."

"Exactly," he concurred. "Aside from teaching, I can't think of any job less challenging to do."

She laughed as she slid the vase toward the center of the counter. "They're lovely. Thank you." She stepped out from behind the counter and reached for her purse. "So where are we going?"

"Right around the corner. The Harvey Mansion. Oh, and it's a little cool out, so you should probably wear a jacket," he said, eyeing her sleeveless dress.

Sarah went to the closet, remembering her mother's words on her message, wishing she hadn't listened to it. She hated being cold, and she was one of those people who got cold very easily. But instead of going for the "big long green one" that would keep her warm, she picked out a light jacket that matched her dress, something that would have made her mother nod appreciatively. Classy. When she slipped it on, Miles looked at her as if he wanted to say something but didn't know how.

"Is something wrong?" she asked as she pulled it on.

"Well . . . it's cold out there. You sure you don't want something warmer?"

"You won't mind?"

"Why would I mind?"

She gladly switched jackets (the big long green one), and Miles helped her put it on, holding the sleeves open for her. A moment later, after locking the front door, they were making their way down the steps. As soon as Sarah stepped outside, the temperature nipped at her cheeks and she instinctively buried her hands in her pockets.

"Don't you think it was too chilly for your other jacket?"

"Definitely," she said, smiling thankfully. "But it doesn't match what I'm wearing."

"I'd rather you be comfortable. And besides, this one looks good on you."

She loved him for that. Take that, Mom!

They started down the street, and a few steps later—surprising herself as much as Miles—she took one hand from her pocket and looped it through his arm.

"So," she said, "let me tell you about my mother."

At their table a few minutes later, Miles couldn't stifle a laugh. "She sounds great."

"Easy for you to say. She's not your mother."

"It's just her way of showing you that she loves you."

"I know. But it would be easier if she didn't always

worry so much. Sometimes I think she does it on purpose just to drive me crazy."

Despite her obvious exasperation, Sarah looked positively luminous in the flickering candlelight, Miles decided.

The Harvey Mansion was one of the better restaurants in town. Originally a home dating from the 1790s, it was a popular romantic getaway. When it was being redesigned for its current use, the owners decided to retain most of the floor plan. Miles and Sarah were led up a curving set of stairs and were seated in what was once a library. Dimly lit, it was a medium-size room with red-oak flooring and an intricately designed tin ceiling. Along two walls were mahogany shelves, lined with hundreds of books; along the third wall, the fireplace cast an ethereal glow. Sarah and Miles were seated in the corner near the window. There were only five other tables, and though all were occupied, people talked in low murmurs.

"Mmm . . . I think you're right," Miles said. "Your mother probably lies awake at night thinking of new ways to torment you."

"I thought you said you'd never met her."

Miles chuckled. "Well, at least she's around. Like I told you when we first met, I hardly even talk to my father anymore."

"Where is he now?"

"I have no idea. I got a postcard a couple of months ago from Charleston, but there's no telling if he's still there. He doesn't usually stay in one place all that long, he doesn't call, and he very seldom makes it back to town. He hasn't seen me or Jonah for years now."

"I can't imagine that."

"It's just the way he is, but then, he wasn't exactly Ward Cleaver when I was little. Half the time, I got the impression he didn't like having us around."

"Us?"

"Me and my mom."

"Didn't he love her?"

"I have no idea."

"Oh, come on . . ."

"I'm serious. She was pregnant when they got married, and I can't honestly say they were ever meant for each other. They ran real hot and cold—one day they were madly in love, and the next day she was throwing his clothes on the front lawn and telling him never to come back. And when she died, he just took up and left as fast as he could. Quit his job, sold the house, bought himself a boat, and told me he was going to see the world. Didn't know a thing about sailing, either. Said he'd learn what he needed as he went along, and I guess he has."

Sarah frowned. "That's a little strange."

"Not for him. To be honest, I wasn't surprised

at all, but you'd have to meet him to know what I'm talking about." He shook his head slightly, as if disgusted.

"How did your mother die?" Sarah asked gently.

A strange, shuttered expression crossed his face, and Sarah immediately regretted bringing it up. She leaned forward. "I'm sorry—that was rude. I shouldn't have asked."

"It's okay," Miles said quietly. "I don't mind. It happened a long time ago, so it's not hard to talk about. It's just that I haven't talked about it in years. I can't remember the last time someone asked about my mother."

Miles drummed his fingers absently on the table before sitting up a little straighter. He spoke matter-of-factly, almost as if he were talking about someone he didn't know. Sarah recognized the tone: It was the way she spoke of Michael now.

"My mom started having these pains in her stomach. Sometimes, she couldn't even sleep at night. Deep down, I think she knew how serious it was, and by the time she finally went in to see the doctor, the cancer had spread to her pancreas and liver. There was nothing that anyone could do. She passed away less than three weeks later."

"I'm sorry," she said, not knowing what else to say.

"So am I," he said. "I think you would have liked her."

"I'm sure I would have."

They were interrupted by the waiter as he approached the table and took their drink orders. As if on cue, both Sarah and Miles reached for the menus and read them quickly.

"So what's good?" she asked.

"Everything, really."

"No special recommendations?"

"I'll probably get a steak of some sort."

"Why does that not surprise me?"

He glanced up. "You have something against steak?"

"Not at all. You just didn't strike me as the tofu and salad type." She closed her menu. "I, on the other hand, have to watch my girlish figure."

"So what are you getting?"

She smiled. "A steak."

Miles closed his menu and pushed it off to the side of the table. "So, now that we've covered my life, why don't you tell me about yours? What was it like growing up in your family?"

Sarah set her menu on top of his.

"Unlike what you had, my parents *were* Ward and June Cleaver. We lived in a suburb just outside Baltimore in the most typical of houses—four bedrooms, two bathrooms, complete with a porch, flower garden, and a white picket fence. I rode the bus to school with my neighbors, played in the front yard all weekend long, and had the biggest collection of

Barbies on the whole block. Dad worked from nine to five and wore a suit every day: Mom stayed home, and I don't think I ever saw her without an apron. And our house always smelled like a bakery. Mom made cookies for me and my brother every day, and we'd eat them in the kitchen and recite what we learned that day."

"Sounds nice."

"It was. My mom was great when we were little kids. She was the kind of mom that the other kids ran to if they hurt themselves or got in a jam of some sort. It wasn't until my brother and I got older that she started to get neurotic on me."

Miles raised both eyebrows. "Now, was it that she changed, or was she always neurotic and you were too young to notice?"

"That sounds like something Sylvia would say."

"Sylvia?"

"A friend of mine," she said evasively, "a good friend." If Miles sensed her hesitation, he gave no notice.

Their drinks arrived and the waiter took their order. As soon as he was gone, Miles leaned forward, bringing his face closer to hers.

"What's your brother like?"

"Brian? He's a nice kid. I swear, he's more grown-up than most people I work with. But he's shy and not real good at meeting people. He tends to be a little introspective, but when we're together, we just click and always have. That's one of the main reasons I came back here. I wanted to spend some time with him before he headed off to college. He just started at UNC."

Miles nodded. "So, he's a lot younger than you," he said, and Sarah looked up at him.

"Not *a lot* younger."

"Well . . . enough. You're what, forty? Forty-five?" he said, repeating what she'd said to him the first time they'd met.

She laughed. "A girl's got to stay on her toes around you."

"I'll bet you say that to all the guys you date."

"Actually, I'm out of practice," she said. "I haven't dated much since my divorce."

Miles lowered his drink. "You're kidding, right?"

"No."

"A girl like you? I'm sure you've been asked out a lot."

"That doesn't mean I say yes."

"Playing hard to get?" Miles teased.

"No," she said. "I just didn't want to hurt anyone."

"So you're a heartbreaker, huh?"

She didn't answer right away, her eyes staring down at the table.

"No, not a heartbreaker," she said quietly. "Brokenhearted."

147

Her words surprised him. Miles searched for a lighthearted response, but after seeing her expression, he decided to say nothing at all. For a few moments, Sarah seemed to be lost in a world all her own. Finally she turned toward Miles with an almost embarrassed smile.

"Sorry about that. Kind of ruined the mood, huh?"

"Not at all," Miles answered quickly. He reached over and gave her hand a gentle squeeze. "Besides, you should realize that my moods don't get ruined all that easily," he continued. "Now, if you'd thrown your drink in my face and called me a scoundrel . . ."

Despite her obvious tension, Sarah laughed.

"You'd have a problem with that?" she asked, feeling herself relax.

"Probably," he said with a wink. "But even then— considering it's a first date and all—I might let that pass, too."

It was half-past ten when they finished dinner, and as they stepped outside, Sarah was certain that she didn't want the date to end just yet. Dinner had been wonderful, their conversation liberally greased by a bottle of excellent red wine. She wanted to spend more time with Miles, but she wasn't quite ready to invite him up to her apartment. Behind them, just a few feet away, a car engine was clicking as it cooled, the sounds muffled and sporadic.

"Would you like to head over to the Tavern?" Miles suggested. "It's not that far."

Sarah agreed with a nod, pulling her jacket tighter as they started down the sidewalk at a leisurely pace, walking close together. The sidewalks were deserted, and as they passed art galleries and antique stores, a realty office, a pastry shop, a bookstore, nothing appeared to be open at all.

"Just where is this place, exactly?"

"This way," he said, motioning with his arm. "It's just up and around the corner."

"I've never heard of it."

"I'm not surprised," he said. "This is a local hangout, and the owner's attitude is that if you don't know about the place, then you probably don't belong there anyway."

"So how do they stay in business?"

"They manage," he said cryptically.

A minute later, they rounded the corner. Though a number of cars were parked along the street, there were no signs of life. It was almost eerie. Halfway down the block, Miles stopped at the mouth of a small alley carved between two buildings, one of which looked all but abandoned. Toward the rear, about forty feet back, a single light bulb dangled crookedly.

"This is it," he said. Sarah hesitated and Miles took her hand, leading her down the alley, finally

149

stopping under the light. Above the buckled doorway, the name of the establishment was written in Magic Marker. She could hear music coming from within.

"Impressive," she said.

"Nothing but the best for you."

"Do I detect a note of sarcasm?"

Miles laughed as he pushed open the door, leading Sarah inside.

Built into what appeared to have been the abandoned building, the Tavern was dingy and faintly redolent of mildewed wood, but surprisingly large. Four pool tables stood in the rear beneath glowing lamps that advertised different beers; a long bar ran along the far wall. An old-fashioned jukebox flanked the doorway, and a dozen tables were spread haphazardly throughout. The floor was concrete and the wooden chairs were mismatched, but that didn't seem to matter.

It was packed.

People thronged the bar and tables; crowds formed and dispersed around the pool tables. Two women, wearing a little too much makeup, leaned against the jukebox, their tightly clad bodies swaying in rhythm as they read through the titles, figuring out what they wanted to play next.

Miles looked at her, amused. "Surprising, isn't it?"

"I wouldn't have believed it unless I'd seen it. It's so crowded."

"It is every weekend." He scanned the room quickly, looking for someplace to sit.

"There're some seats in the back . . . ," she offered.

"Those are for the people who're playing pool."

"Well, do you want to play a game?"

"Pool?"

"Why not? There's a table open. Besides, it's probably not as loud back there."

"You're on. Let me go set it up with the bartender. Do you want a drink?"

"Coors Light, if they've got it."

"I'm sure they do. I'll meet you at the table, okay?"

With that, Miles headed toward the bar, threading his way through the crush of people. Wedging himself between a couple of stools, he raised his hand to get the bartender's attention. Based on the number of people waiting, it looked like it might take a while.

It was warm, and Sarah took off her jacket. As she folded it under her arm, she heard the door open behind her. Glancing over her shoulder, she moved aside to make room for two men. The first, with tattoos and long hair, looked downright dangerous; the second, dressed in jeans and a polo shirt, couldn't have been more different, and she wondered what they could possibly have in common.

Until she looked a little closer. It was then that she decided the second one scared her more.

Something in his expression, in the way he held himself, seemed infinitely more menacing.

She was thankful when the first one walked by without seeming to notice her. The other, though, paused as soon as he drew close, and she could feel his eyes on her.

"I haven't seen you around here before. What's your name?" he said suddenly. She could feel the cool appraisal in his gaze.

"Sylvia," she lied.

"Can I buy you a drink?"

"No, thank you," she answered with a shake of her head.

"You want to come and sit with me and my brother, then?"

"I'm with someone," she said.

"I don't see anyone."

"He's at the bar."

"C'mon, Otis!" the tattooed man shouted. Otis ignored him, his eyes locked on Sarah. "You sure you don't want that drink, Sylvia?"

"Positive," she said.

"Why not?" he asked. For some reason, even though the words came out calmly, even politely, she could feel their undercurrent of anger.

"I told you—I'm with someone," she said stepping back.

"C'mon, Otis! I need a drink!"

Otis Timson glanced toward the sound, then faced Sarah again and smiled, as if they were at a cocktail party instead of a dive. "I'll be around if you change your mind, Sylvia," he said smoothly.

As soon as he was gone, Sarah exhaled sharply and plunged into the crowd, making her way toward the pool tables, getting as far away from him as possible. When she got there, she set her coat on one of the unoccupied stools and Miles arrived with the beers a moment later. One look was enough to let him know that something had happened.

"What's wrong?" he asked, handing her the bottle of Coors.

"Just some jerk trying to pick me up. He kind of gave me the creeps. I'd forgotten what it's like in places like this."

Miles's expression darkened slightly. "Did he do anything?"

"Nothing I couldn't handle."

He seemed to study her answer. "You sure?"

Sarah hesitated. "Yeah, I'm sure," she finally said. Then, touched by his concern, she tapped her bottle against his with a wink, putting the incident out of her mind. "Now, do you want to rack or should I?"

After taking off his jacket and rolling up his sleeves, Miles retrieved two pool cues from a mount on the wall.

"Now the rules are fairly simple," Miles began. "Balls one through seven are solid, balls nine through fifteen are stripes—"

"I know," she said, waving a hand at him.

He looked up in surprise. "You've played before?"

"I think everyone's played at least once."

Miles handed her the pool cue. "Then I guess we're ready. Do you want to break? Or should I?"

"No—go ahead."

Sarah watched as Miles went around to the head of the table, chalking his pool cue as he did so. Then, leaning over, he set his hand, drew back the cue stick, and hit the ball cleanly. A loud crack sounded, the balls scattered around the table, and the four ball rolled toward the corner pocket, dropping neatly from view. He looked up.

"That makes me solid."

"I never doubted it for a minute," she said.

Miles surveyed the table, deciding on his next shot, and once again, Sarah was struck by how different he was from Michael. Michael didn't play pool, and he certainly would never have brought Sarah to a place like this. He wouldn't have been comfortable here, and he wouldn't have fit in—any more than Miles would have fit neatly into the world that Sarah used to occupy.

Yet as he stood before her without his jacket, his shirtsleeves rolled up, Sarah couldn't help but acknowledge her attraction. In contrast with a lot of people who drank too much beer with their evening pizza, Miles looked almost lean. He didn't have classic movie-star good looks, but his waist was narrow, his stomach flat, and his shoulders reassuringly broad. But it was more than that. There was something in his eyes, in the expressions he wore, that spoke of the challenges he'd faced over the last two years, something she recognized when looking in the mirror.

The jukebox fell silent for a moment, then picked up again with "Born in the USA" by Bruce Springsteen. The air was thick with cigarette smoke despite the ceiling fans that whirred above them. Sarah heard the dull roar of others laughing and joking all around them, yet as she watched Miles, it seemed almost as if they were alone. Miles sank another shot.

With a practiced eye, he looked over the table as the balls settled. He moved around to the other side and took another shot, but this time he missed the mark. Seeing that it was her turn, Sarah set her beer off to the side and picked up her cue. Miles reached for the chalk, offering it to Sarah.

"You've got a good shot at the line," he said, nodding toward the corner of the table. "It's right there on the edge of the pocket."

"I see that," she said, chalking the tip and then

setting it aside. Looking over the table, she didn't set up for her shot right away. As if sensing her hesitation, Miles leaned his cue against one of the stools.

"Do you need me to show you how to position your hand on the table?" he offered gamely.

"Sure."

"Okay, then," he said. "Make a circle with your forefinger, like this, with your other three fingers on the table." He demonstrated with his hand on the table.

"Like this?" she said, mimicking him.

"Almost . . ." He moved closer, and as soon as he reached toward her hand, gently leaning against her as he did so, she felt something jump inside, a light shock that started in her belly and radiated outward. His hands were warm as he adjusted her fingers. Despite the smoke and the stale air, she could smell his after-shave, a clean, masculine odor.

"No—hold your finger a little tighter. You don't want too much room or you lose control of your shot," he said.

"How's that?" she said, thinking how much she liked the feel of him close to her.

"Better," he said seriously, oblivious to what she was going through. He gave her a little room. "Now when you draw back, go slowly and try to keep the cue straight and steady as you hit the ball. And remember, you don't have to hit it that hard. The ball is right on the edge and you don't want to scratch."

Sarah did as she was told. The shot was straight, and as Miles predicted, the nine fell in. The cue ball rolled to a stop toward the center of the table.

"That's great," he said, motioning toward it. "You've got a good shot with the fourteen now."

"Really?" she said.

"Yeah, right there. Just line it up and do the same thing again . . ."

She did, taking her time. After the fourteen fell into the pocket, the cue ball seemed to set itself up perfectly for the next shot as well. Miles's eyes widened in surprise. Sarah looked up at him, knowing she wanted him close again. "That one didn't feel as smooth as the first one," she said. "Would you mind showing me one more time?"

"No, not at all," he said quickly. Again he leaned against her and adjusted her hand on the table; again she smelled the aftershave. Again the moment seemed charged, but this time Miles seemed to sense it as well, lingering unnecessarily as he stood against her. There was something heady and daring about the way they were touching, something . . . *wonderful*. Miles drew a deep breath.

"Okay, now try it," he said, pulling back from her as if needing a bit of space.

With a steady stroke, the eleven went in.

157

"I think you've got it now," Miles said, reaching for his beer. Sarah moved around the table for the next shot.

As she did, he watched her. He took it all in— the graceful way she walked, the gentle curves of her body as she set up again, skin so smooth it seemed almost unreal. When Sarah ran a hand through her hair, tucking it behind her ear, he took a drink, wondering why on earth her ex-husband had let her get away. He was probably blind or an idiot, maybe both. A moment later, the twelve dropped into the pocket. Nice rhythm there, he thought, trying to focus on the game again.

For the next couple of minutes, Sarah made it look easy. She sank the ten, the ball hugging the side all the way to the pocket.

Leaning against the wall, one leg crossed over the other, Miles twirled his cue stick in his hands and waited.

The thirteen ball dropped into the side pocket on an easy tap in.

With that, he frowned slightly. *Strange that she hasn't missed a shot yet . . .*

The fifteen, on what can only be described as a lucky bank shot, followed the thirteen a moment later, and he had to fight the urge to reach for the pack of cigarettes in his jacket.

Only the eight ball was left, and Sarah stood from

the table and reached for the chalk. "I go for the eight, right?" she asked.

Miles shifted slightly. "Yeah, but you've got to call the pocket."

"Okay," she said. She moved around the table until her back was toward him. She pointed with her cue stick. "I guess I'll go for the corner pocket, then."

A long shot, with a bit of an angle needed to get there. Makeable, but tough. Sarah leaned over the table.

"Be careful you don't scratch," Miles added. "If you do, I win."

"I won't," she whispered to herself.

Sarah took the shot. A moment later the eight dropped in, and Sarah stood and turned around, a big grin on her face. "Wow—can you believe that?"

Miles was still looking at the corner pocket. "Nice shot," he said almost in disbelief.

"Beginner's luck," she said dismissively. "Do you want to rack them again?"

"Yeah . . . I suppose so," he said uncertainly. "You made a few really good ones there."

"Thanks," she said.

Miles finished his beer before racking the balls again. He broke, sinking a ball, but he missed his second shot.

With a sympathetic shrug before she began, Sarah proceeded to run the table without a miss. By the time she'd finished, Miles was simply staring at her from his spot along the wall. He'd set aside the cue stick halfway through the game and had ordered two more beers from a passing waitress.

"I think that I've been hustled," he said knowingly.

"I think you're right," she said, moving toward him. "But at least we weren't betting. If we were, I wouldn't have made it look so easy."

Miles shook his head in amazement. "Where did you learn to play?"

"My dad. We always had a pool table in the house. He and I used to play all the time."

"So why didn't you stop me from showing you how to shoot before I made a fool of myself?"

"Well . . . you seemed so intent on helping me that I didn't want to hurt your feelings."

"Gee, I appreciate that." He handed her a beer, and as she took it, their fingers brushed lightly. Miles swallowed.

*Damn, she was pretty. Up close, even more so.*

Before he could think about it any further, there was a slight commotion behind him. Miles turned at the sound.

"So how are you two doing, Deputy Ryan?"

He tensed automatically at Otis Timson's question. Otis's brother was standing just behind him, holding a beer, his eyes glassy. Otis gave Sarah a mock salute, and she took a small step away from Otis, toward Miles.

"And how are *you* doing? Nice to see you again."

Miles followed Otis's eyes toward Sarah.

"He was the guy I told you about earlier," she whispered.

Otis raised his eyebrows at that but said nothing.

"What the hell do you want, Otis?" Miles said warily, remembering what Charlie had told him.

"I don't want anything," Otis answered. "I just wanted to say hello."

Miles turned away. "Do you want to go to the bar?" he asked Sarah.

"Sure," she agreed.

"Yeah, go ahead. I don't want to keep you from your date," Otis said. "You got a nice gal, there," he said. "Looks like you've found someone new."

Miles flinched, and Sarah saw how much the comment stung. Miles opened his mouth to respond, but nothing came out. His hands balled into fists, but instead he took a deep breath and turned to Sarah.

"Let's go," he said. His tone reflected a rage she'd never heard before.

"Oh, by the way," Otis added. "The whole thing with Harvey? Don't worry too much about it. I asked him to go easy on you."

A crowd, sensing trouble, was beginning to gather. Miles stared hard at Otis, who returned the gaze without moving. Otis's brother had moved off to the side, as if getting ready to jump in if he needed to.

"Let's just go," Sarah said a little more forcefully, doing her best to keep this from getting any more out of hand. She took Miles by the arm and tugged. "Come on . . . please, Miles," she pleaded.

It was enough to get his attention. Sarah grabbed both their jackets, stowing them under her arm as she pulled him through the crowd. People parted before them, and a minute later they were outside. Miles shook her hand from his arm, angry at Otis, angry at himself for almost losing control, and stalked down the alley, out toward the street. Sarah followed a few steps behind, pausing to put her jacket on.

"Miles . . . wait . . ."

It took a moment for the words to sink in, and Miles finally stopped, looking toward the ground. When she approached, holding out his jacket, Miles didn't seem to notice.

"I'm sorry about all that," he said, unable to meet her eyes.

"You didn't do anything, Miles," she said. When he didn't respond, Sarah moved closer. "Are you okay?" she asked softly.

"Yeah . . . I'm okay." His voice was so low that she barely heard it. For a moment, he looked exactly like Jonah when she assigned too much work. "You don't look okay," she finally said. "In fact, you look pretty terrible."

Despite his anger, he laughed under his breath. "Thanks a lot."

On the street, a car rolled by, looking for a parking space. A cigarette sailed out the window, landing in the gutter. It was colder now, too cold to stay in one place, and Miles reached for his jacket and slipped it on. Without a word, they set off down the street. Once they reached the corner, Sarah broke the silence.

"Can I ask what that was all about in there?"

After a long moment, Miles shrugged. "It's a long story."

"They usually are."

They took a few steps, their footsteps the only sound on the streets.

"We have a history," Miles finally offered. "Not a very good one."

"I picked up on that part," she said. "I'm not exactly dense, you know."

Miles didn't respond.

"Look, if you'd rather not talk about it . . ."

It offered Miles a way out, and he almost took her up on it. Instead, however, he pushed his hands into his pockets and closed his eyes for a long moment. Over the next few minutes, he told Sarah everything—about the arrests over the years, the vandalism in and around his home, the cut on Jonah's cheek—ending with the latest arrest and even

Charlie's warning. As he talked, they wound back through downtown, past the closed-up businesses and the Episcopal church, finally crossing Front Street and heading into the park at Union Point. Through it all, Sarah listened quietly. When he was finished, she looked up at him.

"I'm sorry I stopped you," she said quietly. "I should have let you beat him to a pulp."

"No, I'm glad you did. He's not worth it."

They passed the old women's club, once a quaint meeting place but long since abandoned, and the ruins of the building seemed to encourage silence, almost as if they were in a cemetery. Years of flooding by the Neuse had rendered the building all but uninhabitable except for birds and other assorted wildlife.

Once Miles and Sarah neared the riverbank, they stopped to stare at the tar-colored water of the Neuse drifting slowly before them. Water slapped against the marlstone along the banks in a steady rhythm.

"Tell me about Missy," she said finally, breaking the stillness that had settled over them.

"Missy?"

"I'd like to know what she was like," she said honestly. "She's a big part of who you are, but I don't know anything about her."

After a moment, Miles shook his head. "I wouldn't know where to start."

"Well . . . what do you miss the most?"

164

Across the river, a mile distant, he could see flickering porch lights, bright pinpricks in the distance that seemed to hang in the air like fireflies on hot summer nights.

"I miss having her around," he began. "Just being there when I got off work, or waking up beside her, or seeing her in the kitchen or out in the yard anywhere. Even if we didn't have much time, there was something special in knowing that she would be there if I needed her. And she would have been. We'd been married long enough to go through all those stages that married people go through—the good, the not so good, even the bad—and we'd settled into something that worked for both of us. We were both kids when we started out, and we knew people who got married around the same time we did. After seven years, a lot of friends had divorced and a few had already gotten remarried." He turned from the river to face her. "But we made it, you know? I look back on that, and it's something that I'm proud of, because I know how rare it was. I never regretted the fact that I'd married her. Never."

Miles cleared his throat.

"We used to spend hours just talking about everything, or about nothing. It didn't really matter. She loved books and she used to tell me all the stories she was reading, and she could do it in a way that made me want to read them, too. I remember she used to read in bed and sometimes I'd wake up in the middle of the night and she'd be sound asleep with the book on the end table with her reading light still on. I'd have to get out of bed to turn it off. That happened more often after Jonah was born—she was tired all the time, but even then, she had a way of acting like she wasn't. She was wonderful with him. I remember when Jonah started trying to walk. He was about seven months old, which is way too early. I mean, he couldn't even crawl yet, but he wanted to walk. She spent weeks walking through the house all bent over so he could hold her fingers, just because he liked it. She'd be so sore in the evenings that unless I gave her a massage, she wouldn't be able to move the next day. But you know . . ."

He paused, meeting Sarah's eyes.

"She never complained about it. I think it was what she was meant to do. She used to tell me that she wanted to have four kids, but after Jonah, I kept coming up with excuses why it wasn't the right time, until she finally put her foot down. She wanted Jonah to have brothers and sisters, and I realized that I did, too. I know from experience how hard it is to be an only child, and I wish I'd listened to her earlier. For Jonah, I mean."

Sarah swallowed before squeezing his arm in support. "She sounds great."

On the river, a trawler was inching its way up the channel, engines humming. When the breeze drifted in his direction, Miles caught the barest hint of the honeysuckle shampoo she'd used.

For a while they stood in companionable silence, the comfort of each other's presence cocooning them like a warm blanket in the dark.

It was getting late now. Time to call it a night. As much as he wished he could make the night last forever, he knew he couldn't. Mrs. Knowlson expected him home by midnight.

"We should go," he said.

Five minutes later, outside her building, Sarah let go of his arm so she could search for her keys.

"I had a good time tonight," she said.

"So did I."

"And I'll see you tomorrow?"

It took a second before he remembered that she was going to Jonah's game. "Don't forget—it starts at nine."

"Do you know what field?"

"I have no idea, but we'll be there. I'll watch for you."

In the brief lull that followed, Sarah thought that Miles might try to kiss her, but he surprised her by taking a small step backward.

"Listen . . . I gotta go . . ."

"I know," she said, both glad and disappointed that he hadn't tried. "Drive safe."

Sarah watched him head around the corner toward a small silver pickup truck and open the door, slipping behind the wheel. He waved one last time before starting the engine.

She stood on the sidewalk staring after his taillights until long after he was gone.

# Chapter 12

Sarah made it to the soccer game the following morning a few minutes before the game started. Dressed in jeans and boots with a thick turtleneck sweater and sunglasses, she stood out among the harried-looking parents. How she could look both casual and elegant at the same time was beyond Miles.

Jonah, who was kicking the ball with a group of friends, spotted her across the field and ran toward her to give her a hug. He took her hand and dragged her toward Miles.

"Look who I found, Dad," he said a minute later. "Miss Andrews is here."

"I see that," Miles answered, running his hand through Jonah's hair.

"She looked lost," Jonah offered. "So I went to get her."

"What would I do without you, champ?" He gazed at Sarah.

"You're beautiful and charming, and I can't stop thinking about last night."

No, he didn't say that. Not exactly, anyway. What Sarah heard was, "Hey—how are you?"

"Good," she answered. "It's a little early to start my weekend mornings, though. It sorta felt like I was heading off to work."

Over her shoulder, Miles saw the team beginning to cluster together, and he used it as an excuse to escape her gaze. "Jonah, I think your coach just got here . . ."

Jonah's head swiveled around and he started struggling with his sweatshirt before Miles helped him take it off. When his head was free, Miles tucked the sweatshirt under his arm.

"Where's my ball?"

"Weren't you just kicking it around a little while ago?"

"Yeah."

"Then where is it?"

"I don't know."

Miles dropped to one knee and began tucking Jonah's shirt in. "We'll find it later. I don't think you need it now, anyway."

"But the coach said we had to bring it for the warm-up."

"Just borrow someone else's."

"Then what will they use?" There was a tinge of worry in his tone.

"You'll be fine. Go on. The coach is waiting."

"Are you sure?"

"Trust me."

"But—"

"Go on. They're waiting for you."

A moment later, after debating whether or not his father was right, Jonah finally scrambled toward his team. Sarah watched it all with a bemused smile, enjoying their interaction.

Miles motioned to the bag. "Do you want a cup of coffee? I brought a thermos."

"No, that's okay. I had some tea before I got here."

"Herbal?"

"Earl Grey, actually."

"With toast and jelly?"

"No, with my cereal. Why?"

Miles nodded. "Just curious."

A whistle blew and the teams began to gather on the infield, setting up for the game.

"Can I ask you a question?"

"As long as it's not about my breakfast," she countered.

"It might sound strange."

"Why does that not surprise me?"

Miles cleared his throat. "Well, I was just wondering whether you wrap your head in a towel after you take a shower."

Her jaw dropped open. "Excuse me?"

"You know, after you shower. Do you wrap your head or do you style it right away?"

She looked at him closely. "You're funny."

"That's what they say."

"Who says?"

"Them."

"Oh."

The whistle blew again, and the game started.

"So . . . do you?" he persisted.

"Yes," she said finally with a mystified laugh. "I wrap my head in a towel."

He nodded, satisfied. "I thought so."

"Did you ever think about cutting back on the caffeine?"

Miles shook his head. "Never."

"You should."

He took another drink to hide his pleasure. "I've heard that."


Forty minutes later the game was over, and despite Jonah's best efforts, his team lost, not that he seemed all that upset about it. After slapping hands with the other players, Jonah ran toward his father, his friend Mark right behind him.

"You two played well out there," Miles assured both boys.

There was the murmur of distracted thanks from both of them before Jonah tugged on his dad's sweater.

"Hey, Dad?"

"Yeah?"

"Mark asked if I could spend the night."

Miles looked at Mark for confirmation. "He did?"

Mark nodded. "It's okay with my mom, but you can talk to her if you want. She's right over there. Zach is coming, too."

"C'mon, Dad. Please? I'll do my chores as soon as I get home," Jonah added. "I'll even do extra."

Miles hesitated. It was fine . . . but at the same time, it wasn't. He liked having Jonah around. The house was lonely without him. "All right, if you really want to go—"

Jonah smiled excitedly, not waiting for him to finish. "Thanks, Dad. You're the best."

"Thanks, Mr. Ryan," Mark said. "C'mon, Jonah. Let's go tell my mom it's okay."

They jogged off, pushing each other and veering through the crowd, laughing the whole way. Miles turned to Sarah, who was watching them go.

"He looks pretty broken up about the fact he won't see me tonight."

"Absolutely crushed," Sarah agreed with a nod.

"We were supposed to rent a movie together, you know."

Sarah shrugged. "It must be terrible to be forgotten so easily."

Miles laughed. He was smitten with her, no doubt about it. Really smitten. "Well, since I'm alone and all . . ."

"Yes?"

"Well . . . I mean . . ."

Her eyebrows lifted and she looked at him slyly. "You want to ask me about the fan again?"

He grinned. She'd never let him live that down. "If you're not doing anything," he said with an air of feigned confidence.

"What did you have in mind?"

"Not a game of pool, that's for sure."

Sarah laughed. "How about if I make you dinner at my place?"

"Tea and cereal?" he prompted.

She nodded. "Absolutely. And I promise to wear the towel on my head."

Miles laughed again. He didn't deserve this. He really didn't.

"Hey, Dad?"

Miles pushed his baseball hat a little higher on his head and looked up. They were in the yard, raking the year's first fallen leaves.

"Yeah?"

"I'm sorry about not renting a movie with you tonight. I forgot until just a little while ago. Are you mad at me?"

Miles smiled. "No. I'm not mad at all."

"Are you going to rent one anyway?"

Miles shook his head. "Probably not."

"Then, what are you going to do?"

He set the rake aside, took off his hat, and wiped his brow with the back of his hand. "Actually, I think I'll probably see Miss Andrews tonight."

"Again?"

Miles wondered how much he should say right now. "We had a nice time last night."

"What did you do?"

"We had dinner. Talked. Went for a walk."

"That's all?"

"Pretty much."

"That sounds boring."

"I guess you had to be there."

Jonah thought about that for a moment. "Is this a date again?"

"Kind of."

"Oh." He nodded and then looked away. "I guess that means you like her, right?"

Miles approached Jonah, lowering himself until they were eye level. "She and I are just friends right now, that's all."

Jonah seemed to consider it for a long moment. Miles took him in his arms and hugged him, squeezing him. "I love you, Jonah," he said.

"I love you too, Dad."

"You're a good kid."

"I know."

Miles laughed and stood, reaching for his rake again.

"Hey, Dad?"

"Yeah?"

"I'm getting kind of hungry."

"What do you want to eat?"

"Can we go to McDonald's?"

"Sure. We haven't gone there in a while."

"Can I have a Happy Meal?"

"Don't you think you're getting a little old for that?"

"I'm only seven, Dad."

"Oh, that's right," he said as if he'd forgotten. "C'mon, let's go inside and wash up."

They started toward the house, and Miles put his arm around Jonah. After a few steps, Jonah looked up.

"Hey, Dad?"

"Yeah?"

Jonah walked in silence for a few steps. "It's okay if you like Miss Andrews."

Miles looked down in surprise. "It is?"

"Yeah," he said seriously. "Because I think she likes you."

That feeling only grew stronger the more Miles and Sarah saw of each other.

Throughout October they went on half a dozen dates, in addition to the times he saw her after school.

They talked for hours, he took her hand whenever

they walked, and though their relationship hadn't become physical yet, there was nonetheless a sensual undercurrent to their conversations that neither could deny.

A few days before Halloween, after the final soccer game of the season, Miles asked Sarah if she would like to join him on the ghost walk that night. It was Mark's birthday, and Jonah was staying over for the night.

"What's that?" she asked.

"You get to tour some of the historic homes and listen to ghost stories."

"This is what people do in small towns?"

"We could either do that or go sit on my porch, chew some tobacco, and play banjos."

She laughed. "I think I'll take the first option."

"I thought you might. Pick you up at seven?"

"I'll be waiting with bated breath. Dinner at my place afterwards?"

"Sounds great. But you know that if you keep making me dinners, I'm going to get spoiled."

"That's okay," she said with a wink. "A little spoiling never hurt anyone."

# Chapter 13

"So tell me," Miles said to Sarah as they left Sarah's building later that night, "what do you miss most about the big city?"

"Galleries, the museums, concerts. Restaurants that are open past nine o'clock."

Miles laughed. "But what do you miss the most?"

Sarah looped her arm through his. "I miss the bistros. You know—little cafés where I could sit and sip my tea while I read the Sunday paper. It was enjoyable to be able to do that in the middle of downtown. It was like a little oasis somehow, because everyone who passed you on the street always looked like they were rushing somewhere."

They walked in silence for a few moments.

"You know, you can do that here, too," Miles finally offered.

"Really?"

"Sure. There's a place like that right over there on Broad Street."

"I've never seen it."

"Well, it's not exactly a bistro."

"What is it, then?"

He shrugged. "It's a gas station, but it's got a nice bench out front, and I'm sure if you brought in your own teabag, they'd be able to scrounge up a cup of hot water for you."

She giggled. "Sounds enticing."

As they crossed the street, they fell in behind a group of people who were obviously part of the festivities. Dressed in period clothing, they looked as if they'd just stepped out of the eighteenth century—thick, heavy skirts on the women, black pants and high boots for the men, high collars, wide-brimmed hats. At the corner they broke into two separate groups, heading in opposite directions. Miles and Sarah followed the smaller group.

"You've always lived here, right?" Sarah asked.

"Except for the years I went to college."

"Didn't you ever want to move away? To experience something new?"

"Like bistros?"

She nudged him playfully with her elbow. "No, not just that. Cities have a vibrancy, a sense of excitement that you can't find in a small town."

"I don't doubt it. But to be honest, I've never been interested in things like that. I don't need those things to make me happy. A nice quiet place to unwind at the end of the day, beautiful views, a few good friends. What else is there?"

"What was it like growing up here?"

"Did you ever see *The Andy Griffith Show*? Mayberry?"

"Who hasn't?"

"Well, it was kind of like that. New Bern wasn't quite so small, of course, but it had that small-town feel, you know? Where things seemed safe? I remember that when I was little—seven or eight—and I used to head out with my friends to go fishing or exploring or just out to play and I'd be gone until supper. And my parents wouldn't worry at all, because they didn't have to. Other times, we'd camp out down by the river all night long and the thought that something bad might happen to us never entered our minds. It's a wonderful way to grow up, and I'd like Jonah to have the chance to grow up that way, too."

"You'd let Jonah camp out by the river all night?"

"Not a chance," he said. "Things have changed, even in little New Bern."

As they reached the corner, a car rolled to a stop beside them. Just down the street, clusters of people strolled up and down the walks of various homes.

"We're friends, right?" Miles asked.

"I'd like to think so."

"Do you mind if I ask you a question?"

"I guess it depends on the question."

"What was your ex-husband like?"

She glanced toward him in surprise. "My ex-husband?"

"I've been wondering about that. You've never mentioned him in all the time we've talked."

Sarah said nothing, suddenly intent on the sidewalk in front of her.

"If you'd rather not answer, you don't have to," Miles offered. "I'm sure it wouldn't change my impression of him, anyway."

"And what impression is that?"

"I don't like him."

Sarah laughed. "Why do you say that?"

"Because you don't like him."

"You're pretty perceptive."

"That's why I'm in law enforcement." He tapped his temple and winked at her. "I can spot clues that ordinary people overlook."

She smiled, giving his arm an extra squeeze. "All right . . . my ex-husband. His name was Michael King and we met right after he finished his MBA. We were married for three years. He was rich, well educated, and good-looking . . ." She ticked those off, one right after the other, and when she paused, Miles nodded.

"Mmm . . . I can see why you don't like the guy."

"You didn't let me finish."

"There's more?"

"Do you want to hear this?"

"I'm sorry. Go on."

She hesitated before finally going on.

"Well, for the first couple of years, we were happy. At least, I was. We had a beautiful apartment, we spent all of our free time together, and I thought I knew who he was. But I didn't. Not really, anyway. In the end, we were arguing all the time, we hardly talked at all, and . . . and it just didn't work out," she finished quickly.

"Just like that?" he asked.

"Just like that," she said.

"Do you ever see him anymore?"

"No."

"Do you want to?"

"No."

"That bad, huh?"

"Worse."

"I'm sorry I brought it up," he said.

"Don't be. I'm better off without him."

"So when did you know it was over?"

"When he handed me the divorce papers."

"You had no idea they were coming?"

"No."

"I knew I didn't like him." He also knew she hadn't told him everything.

She smiled appreciatively. "Maybe that's why we get along so well. We see eye to eye on things."

"Except, of course, about the wonders of small-town living, right?"

"I never said I didn't like it here."

"But could you see yourself staying in a place like this?"

"You mean forever?"

"C'mon, you have to admit it's nice."

"It is. I've already said that."

"But it's not for you? In the long run, I mean?"

"I guess that depends."

"On what?"

She smiled at him. "On what my reason for staying would be."

Staring at her, he couldn't help but imagine that her words were either an invitation or a promise.

The moon began its slow evening arc upward, glowing yellow and then orange as it crested the weathered roofline of the Travis-Banner home, their first stop on the ghost walk. The house was an ancient two-story Victorian with wide, wraparound porches desperately in need of painting. On the porch, a small crowd had gathered as two women, dressed as witches, stood around a large pot, serving apple cider and pretending to conjure up the first owner of the house, a man who'd supposedly been beheaded in a logging accident. The front door of the home was open; from inside came faint sounds of a carnival funhouse: terrified shrieks and creaking doors, strange thumps and cackling laughter. Suddenly the two witches dropped their heads, the lights went out on the porch, and a headless ghost made a dramatic appearance in the foyer behind them—a blackened shape dressed in a cape with arms extended and bones where hands should have been. One woman yelped as she dropped her cup of cider on the porch. Sarah moved instinctively toward Miles, half turning toward him as she reached for his arm with a grip that surprised him. Up close, her hair looked soft, and though it was a different color from Missy's, he was reminded of what it had felt like to comb through Missy's hair with his fingers as they lay together in the evenings. A minute later, at the muttered incantations of the witches, the ghost vanished and the lights came back on. Amid nervous laughter, the audience dispersed.

Over the next couple of hours, Miles and Sarah visited a number of houses. They were invited inside for a quick tour of some; in others they stood in the foyer or were entertained in the garden with stories about the history of the home. Miles had taken this tour before, and as they strolled from home to home, he suggested places of particular interest and regaled her with stories about homes that weren't part of the ghost walk this year.

They drifted along the cracked cement sidewalks, murmuring to each other, savoring the evening. In time, the crowds began to thin and some of the homes began to close up for the night. When Sarah asked if he was ready for dinner, Miles shook his head.

"There's one more stop," he said.

He led her down the street, holding her hand, gently brushing his thumb against it. From one of the towering hickory trees, an owl called out as they passed, then grew silent again. Up ahead, a group of people dressed as ghosts were piling into a station wagon. At the corner, Miles pointed toward a large, two-story home, this one devoid of the crowds she'd come to expect. The windows were absolutely black, as if shuttered from the interior. Instead, the only light was provided by a dozen candles lining the porch railings and a small wooden bench near the front door. Beside the bench sat an elderly woman in a rocking chair, a blanket draped over her legs. In the eerie light, she looked almost like a mannequin; her hair was white and thinning, her body frail and brittle. Her skin looked translucent in the flickering glow of candles, and her face was lined deeply, like the cracked glaze of an old china cup. Miles and Sarah seated themselves on the porch swing as the elderly woman studied them.

"Hello, Miss Harkins," Miles said slowly, "did you have a good crowd tonight?"

"Same as usual," Miss Harkins answered. Her voice was raspy, like that of a lifetime smoker. "You know how it goes." She squinted at Miles, as if trying to make him out from a distance. "So you've come to hear the story of Harris and Kathryn Presser, have you?"

"I thought she should hear it," Miles answered solemnly.

For a moment, Miss Harkins's eyes seemed to twinkle, and she reached for the cup of tea that sat beside her.

Miles slipped his arm over Sarah's shoulder, pulling her close. Sarah felt herself relax beneath his touch.

"You'll like this," Miles whispered. His breath on her ear ran a current under her skin.

I already do, she thought to herself.

Miss Harkins set the cup of tea aside. When she spoke, her voice was a whisper.

> There are ghosts and there is love,
> And both are present here,
> To those who listen, this tale will tell
> The truth of love and if it's near.

186

Sarah stole a quick peek at Miles.

"Harris Presser," Miss Harkins announced, "had been born in 1843 to owners of a small candle-making shop in downtown New Bern. Like many young men of the period, Harris wanted to serve for the Confederacy when the War of Southern Independence began. Because he was an only son, however, both his mother and father begged him not to go. In listening to their wishes, Harris Presser irrevocably sealed his fate."

Here, Miss Harkins paused and looked at them.

"He fell in love," she said softly.

For a second, Sarah wondered if Miss Harkins was also referring to them. Miss Harkins's eyebrows rose slightly, as if she were reading Sarah's thoughts, and Sarah glanced away.

"Kathryn Purdy was only seventeen, and like Harris, she was also an only child. Her parents owned both the hotel and the logging mill, and were the wealthiest family in town. They didn't associate with the Pressers, but both families were among those that stayed in town after New Bern fell to Union forces in 1862. Despite the war and the occupation, Harris and Kathryn began meeting by the Neuse River on early summer evenings, just to talk, and eventually Kathryn's parents found out. They were angry and forbade their daughter to see Harris anymore, since the Pressers were regarded as commoners, but it had the effect of binding the young couple even closer together. But it wasn't easy for them to see each other. In time, they devised a plan, in order to escape the watchful eyes of Kathryn's parents. Harris would stand in his parents' candle shop down the street, watching for the signal. If her parents were asleep, Kathryn would put a lighted candle on the sill, and Harris would sneak over. He would climb the massive oak tree right outside her window and help her down. In this way, they met as often as they could, and as the months passed, they fell deeper and deeper in love."

Miss Harkins took another sip of her tea, then narrowed her eyes slightly. Her voice took on a more ominous tone.

"By now, the Union forces were tightening their grip on the South—the news from Virginia was grim, and there were rumors that General Lee was going to swing down with his army from northern Virginia and try to retake eastern North Carolina for the Confederacy. A curfew was instituted and anyone caught outside in the evening, especially young men, was likely to be shot. Unable now to meet with Kathryn, Harris contrived to work late in his parents' shop, lighting his own candle in the store window so that Kathryn would know he was longing to see her. This went on for weeks, until one day, he smuggled a note to Kathryn through a sympathetic preacher, asking her to elope with him. If her answer was yes, she was supposed to put two candles in the window—one that said she agreed, and the second as a signal for when it was safe for him to come and get her. That night, the two candles were lit, and despite all the odds, they were married that night under a full moon, by the same sympathetic preacher who'd delivered the note. All of them had risked their lives for love.

"But, unfortunately, Kathryn's parents discovered another secret letter that Harris had written. Enraged, they confronted Kathryn with what they knew. Kathryn defiantly told them that there was nothing they could do. Sadly, she was only partly right.

"A few days later, Kathryn's father, who had a working relationship with the Union colonel in charge of the occupation, contacted the colonel and informed him that there was a Confederate spy in their midst, someone in contact with General Lee, who was passing secret information about the town's defenses. In light of the rumors about Lee's probable invasion, Harris Presser was arrested in his parents' shop. Before he was taken out to be hanged, he asked for one favor—a candle to be lighted in the window of his shop—and it was granted. That night, from the limbs of the giant oak tree in front of Kathryn's window, Harris Presser was hanged. Kathryn was heartbroken, and she knew her father had been responsible.

"She went to see Harris's parents and asked for the candle that had been burning in the window the night that Harris died. Overcome by grief, they hardly knew what to make of the strange request, but she explained that she wanted something to remember 'the kindly young man who'd always been so courteous to her.' They gave it to her, and that night she lit both candles and set them on the windowsill. Her parents found her the next day. She'd committed suicide by hanging herself from the same giant oak tree."

On the porch, Miles pulled Sarah a little closer to him. "How do you like it so far?" he whispered.

"Shh," she answered. "We're getting to the ghost part, I think."

"Those candles burned all night and the following day, until they were nothing more than little knobs of wax. But still they burned. On into the next night, then the next. They burned for three days, as long as Kathryn and Harris had been married, and then they went out. The following year, on Harris and Kathryn's anniversary, Kathryn's unused room mysteriously caught fire, but the house was saved. More bad luck followed for the Purdy family—the hotel was lost in a flood and the logging mill was taken to pay debts. In financial ruin,

Kathryn's parents moved away, abandoning the house. But . . ."

Miss Harkins leaned forward, a look of mischief in her eyes. Her voice sank to a whisper.

"Every now and then, people would swear that they could see two candles burning in the window above. Others would swear there was only one . . . but that another was burning in another abandoned building down the street. And even now, over a hundred years later, people still claim to see candles burning in the windows of some of the abandoned houses down here. And it's strange—the only people who see them are young couples in love. Whether or not you two will see them depends on your feelings for each other."

Miss Harkins closed her eyes, as if telling the story had drained her. For a minute she didn't move, and Sarah and Miles sat frozen in place, afraid to break the spell. Then she finally opened her eyes again and reached for her tea.

After saying good-bye, Miles and Sarah descended the porch steps and returned to the gravel path. Miles took Sarah's hand again as they approached the street. As if still under the spell of Miss Harkins's story, neither Miles nor Sarah said anything for a long while.

"I'm glad we went there," Sarah finally offered.

"So you liked it?"

"All women love romantic stories."

They rounded the corner and neared Front Street; ahead, they could make out the river between the homes, gliding silently, shining black.

"Are you ready for something to eat?"

"In a minute," he said, slowing down, then finally stopping.

She looked at him. Over his shoulder, she could see moths fluttering around the glowing street lamp. Miles was staring into the distance, toward the river, and Sarah followed his eyes but didn't see anything out of the ordinary.

"What is it?" she asked.

Miles shook his head, trying to clear his thoughts. He wanted to start walking again but found he couldn't. Instead he took a step toward Sarah, pulling her gently toward him. Sarah followed his lead, her stomach tightening. As Miles leaned toward her, she closed her eyes, and when their faces drew near, it was as if nothing else mattered in the world.

The kiss went on and on, and when they finally pulled apart, Miles embraced her. He buried his face in her neck, then kissed the hollow of her shoulder. The moisture of his tongue made her shiver, and she leaned into him, savoring the safe harbor of his arms as the rest of the world went on around them.

\*       \*       \*

A few minutes later they walked back to her apartment, talking softly, his thumb moving gently over the back of her hand.

Once inside, Miles draped his jacket over the back of the chair as Sarah made her way to the kitchen. He wondered if she knew he was watching her.

"So what's for dinner?" he asked.

Sarah opened the refrigerator door and pulled out a large pan covered in tinfoil. "Lasagna, French bread, and a salad. Is that okay?"

"Sounds great. Can I give you a hand with anything?"

"It's pretty much done," Sarah answered as she put the pan in the oven. "All I have to do is heat this for a half hour or so. But if you want, you can start the fire. And open the wine—it's on the counter."

"No problem," he said.

"I'll join you in the living room in a few minutes," Sarah called out as she headed for the bedroom.

In the bedroom, Sarah picked up a hairbrush and began to pull it through her hair.

Much as she wanted to deny it, their kiss had left her feeling a bit shaky. She sensed that tonight was a turning point in their relationship, and she was scared. She knew that she had to tell Miles the real reason for the collapse of her marriage, but it wasn't easy to talk about. Especially to someone she cared about.

As much as she knew he cared about her as well, there was no telling what his response would be or if it would change his feelings about being with her. Hadn't he said that he wished that Jonah had a brother or sister? Would he be willing to give that up?

Sarah found her reflection in the mirror.

She didn't want to do this now, but she knew that if their relationship was to go any further, she would have to tell him. More than anything, she didn't want history to repeat itself, for Miles to do what Michael had done. She couldn't go through that again.

Sarah finished brushing her hair, checked her makeup through force of habit, and, resolving to face Miles with the truth, began to leave the bedroom. But instead of heading out the door, she suddenly sat on the edge of the bed. Was she really ready for this?

Right now, the answer to that question frightened her more than she could say.

By the time she finally emerged from the bedroom, the fire was blazing. Miles was returning from the kitchen, carrying the bottle of wine.

"Just thought we might need this," he said, lifting the bottle a little higher.

"I think that's probably a good idea," Sarah agreed.

The way she said it seemed off somehow to Miles, and he hesitated. Sarah made herself comfortable on the couch, and after a moment, he put the wine on the end table and sat beside her. For a long time, Sarah simply drank her wine in silence. Finally Miles reached for her hand.

"Are you okay?" he asked.

Sarah gently swirled the wine in her glass. "There's something I haven't told you yet," she said quietly.

Miles could hear the sound of cars as they rolled past her apartment. The logs in the fireplace popped, causing a shower of sparks to ascend the chimney. Shadows danced on the walls.

Sarah pulled one leg up and crossed it beneath her. Miles, knowing she was collecting her thoughts, watched her in silence before giving her hand an encouraging squeeze.

It seemed to bring her back to the present. Miles saw the flames flickering in her eyes.

"You're a good man, Miles," she said, "and these last few weeks have really meant a lot to me." She stopped again.

Miles didn't like the sound of this and wondered what had happened in the few minutes that she was in the bedroom. As he watched her, he felt his stomach begin to clench.

"Do you remember when you asked me about my ex-husband?"

Miles nodded.

"I didn't finish the story. There was more to it than just the things I told you, and . . . and I don't know exactly how to say it."

"Why?"

She glanced toward the fire. "Because I'm afraid of what you might think."

As a sheriff, a number of ideas occurred to him—that her ex had been abusive, that he'd hurt her somehow, that she'd left the relationship wounded in some way. Divorce was always painful, but the way she looked now suggested there was much more to it than simply that.

He smiled, hoping for some response, but there was nothing.

"Listen, Sarah," he finally said, "you don't have to tell me anything you don't want to. I won't ask about it again. That's your business, and I've learned enough about you in the past few weeks to know what kind of person you are, and that's all that matters to me. I don't need to know everything about you—and to be honest, I doubt that whatever you'd say would change the way I feel about you."

Sarah smiled, but her eyes refused to meet his. "Do you remember when I asked you about Missy?" she asked.

"Yes."

"Do you remember the things you said about her?"

Miles nodded.

"I remember them, too." For the first time, she met his eyes. "I want you to know that I can never be like her."

Miles frowned. "I know that," he said. "And I don't expect you to—"

She held up her hands. "No, Miles—you misunderstand me. It's not that I think you're attracted to me because I'm like Missy. I know that's not it. But I wasn't very clear."

"Then what is it?" he asked.

"Do you remember when you told me what a good mother she was? And how much you both wanted Jonah to have siblings?" She paused but didn't expect an answer. "I can't ever be like that. That's the reason Michael left me."

Her eyes finally locked on his. "I couldn't get pregnant. But it wasn't him, Miles. He was fine. It was me."

And then, as if driving the point home, in case he didn't understand, she put it as plainly as she could.

"I can't have children. Ever."

Miles said nothing, and after a long moment, Sarah went on.

"You can't imagine what it was like to find out. It just seemed so ironic, you know? I'd spent my early twenties trying not to get pregnant. I used to panic if I forgot to take my birth control pills. I never even considered that I might not be able to have children."

"How did you find out?"

"The usual way. It just didn't happen. We finally went in for tests. That was when I found out."

"I'm sorry," was all Miles could think to say.

"So am I." She exhaled sharply, as if she still had trouble believing it. "And so was Michael. But he couldn't handle it. I told him that we could still adopt, and I'd be perfectly happy with that, but he refused to even consider it because of his family."

"You're kidding . . ."

Sarah shook her head. "I wish I were. Looking back, I guess I shouldn't have been surprised. When we first started going out, he used to say that I was the most perfect woman he'd ever met. As soon as something happened that proved otherwise, he was willing to throw away everything we had." She stared into her wineglass, talking almost to herself. "He asked for a divorce, and I moved out a week later."

Miles took her hand without a word and nodded for her to continue.

"After that . . . well, it hasn't been easy. It's not the sort of thing you bring up at cocktail parties, you know. My family knows, and I talked to Sylvia about it. She was my counselor and she helped me a lot, but those four are the only ones who knew. And now you . . ."

198

She trailed off. In the firelight, Miles thought she had never looked more beautiful. Her hair caught fragments of light and cast them off like a halo.

"So why me?" Miles finally asked.

"Isn't it obvious?"

"Not really."

"I just thought you should know. I mean, before . . . Like I said, I don't want it to happen again . . ." She looked away.

Miles gently turned her face back to him. "Do you really think I'd do that?"

Sarah looked at him sadly. "Oh, Miles . . . it's easy to say that it doesn't matter right now. What I'm worried about is how you'll feel later, after you've had the chance to think about this. Let's say we keep seeing each other and things go as well as they have up to this point. Can you honestly say that it won't matter to you? That being able to have children wouldn't be important to you? That Jonah would never have a little brother or sister running around the house?"

She cleared her throat. "I know I'm jumping the gun here, and don't think that by telling you all this, I expect us to get married. But I had to tell you the truth, so you'd know what you're getting into— before this goes any further. I can't let myself go any further unless I'm certain that you're not going to turn around and do the same thing that Michael did.

If it doesn't work out for another reason, fine. I can live with that. But I can't face again what I've already gone through once."

Miles looked toward his glass, saw the light reflected there. He traced the rim with his finger.

"There's something you should know about me, too," he said. "I had a really hard time after Missy died. It wasn't just that she died—it was also that I never found out who'd been driving the car that night. That's what my job is, both as her husband and as sheriff. And for a long time, finding out who'd been driving was all I could think about. I investigated on my own, I talked to people, but whoever did it got away, and that ate at me like you can't imagine. I felt like I was going crazy for a long time, but lately . . ."

His voice was tender as he met her eyes.

"I guess what I'm trying to say is that I don't need time, Sarah . . . I don't know . . . I just know that I'm missing something in my life, and that until I met you, I didn't know what it was. If you want me to take some time to think about it, I will. But that would be for you—not for me. You haven't said anything that could change the way I feel about you. I'm not like Michael. I could never be like him."

In the kitchen, the timer went off with a ding, and both of them turned at the sound. The lasagna was ready, but neither of them moved. Sarah suddenly felt light-headed, though she didn't know if it was the wine or Miles's words. Carefully, she set her wineglass on the table and, taking a slow breath, stood from the couch.

"Let me get the lasagna before it burns."

In the kitchen, she paused to lean against the counter, the words coming once more.

*I don't need time, Sarah.*

*You haven't said anything that could change the way I feel about you.*

It didn't matter to him. And best of all, she believed him. The things he'd said, the way he'd looked at her . . . Since the divorce, she'd almost come to believe that no one she met would understand.

She left the pan of lasagna on the stovetop. When she returned to the living room, Miles was sitting on the couch, staring into the fire. She sat down and rested her head on his shoulder, letting him pull her close. As they both watched the fire, she could feel the gentle rise and fall of his chest. His hand was moving rhythmically against her, her skin tingling wherever he touched.

"Thank you for trusting me," he said.

"I didn't have a choice."

"You always have a choice."

"Not this time. Not with you."

She lifted her head then, and without another

word she kissed him, brushing her lips softly against his, once, then twice, before meeting them for good. His arms moved up her back as her mouth opened, and then she felt his tongue against hers, the wetness intoxicating. She brought one of her hands to his face, felt the rough stubble beneath her fingertips, then traced the stubble with her lips. Miles responded by moving his mouth to her neck, gently nipping and kissing, his breath hot against her skin.

They made love for a long time; the fire eventually burned itself out, painting the room with darker shadows. Throughout the night, Miles whispered to her in the darkness, his hand always in movement against her, as if trying to convince himself that she was real. Twice, he got up to add more logs to the fire. She retrieved a quilt from the bedroom to cover them up, and sometime in the early morning hours, both of them realized they were ravenous. They shared the plate of lasagna in front of the fire, and for some reason, the act of eating together—naked and beneath the quilt—seemed almost as sensual as anything else that had happened that night.

Just before dawn, Sarah finally feel asleep and Miles carried her to the bedroom, closed the drapes, and crawled in beside her. The morning was overcast and rainy, dark, and they slept until almost noon, the first time that had happened for either of them in as long as they could remember. Sarah woke first;

she felt Miles curled around her, one arm on top, and she stirred. It was enough to wake him. He lifted his head from the pillow, and she rolled over to face him. Miles reached up and traced her cheek with his finger, trying to suppress the lump that had formed in his throat.

"I love you," he said, unable to stop the words.

She took his hand in both of hers, bringing it to her breast.

"Oh, Miles," she whispered. "I love you, too."

# Chapter 14

During the next few days, Sarah and Miles spent all their free time together—not just on dates, but around the house as well. Jonah, instead of sorting through what it all meant, simply let his questions slide for the time being. In his room, he showed Sarah his collection of baseball cards, he talked about fishing and taught her how to cast a line. Occasionally he would surprise her by taking her hand as he led her off to show her something new.

Miles watched all of it from a distance, knowing that Jonah needed to figure out exactly where Sarah fit into his world and how he felt about her. It made it easier, he knew, that Sarah wasn't a stranger. But he couldn't hide his relief at seeing them get along so well.

On Halloween, they drove to the beach and spent the afternoon collecting seashells, then went trick-or-treating in the neighborhood. Jonah went around with a group of friends, Miles and Sarah trailing behind with other parents.

Brenda, of course, peppered Sarah with questions at school, once word had spread in town. Charlie, too, made mention of the news. "I love her, Charlie," Miles said simply, and though Charlie, being from the old school, wondered whether everything had moved a little too quickly, nonetheless slapped Miles on the back and invited both of them to dinner.

As for Miles and Sarah, their relationship progressed with a dreamlike intensity. When they were apart, they hungered for the sight of each other; when they were together, they longed for more time. They met for lunch, they talked on the phone, they made love whenever they had a quiet moment together.

Despite Miles's attention to Sarah, he also made sure to spend as much time alone with Jonah as he could. Sarah, too, did her best to keep things as normal as possible for Jonah. When she sat with him in the classroom after school, she made sure to treat him the same way she had before, as a student in need of help. If it seemed to Sarah that he sometimes paused in his work to watch her speculatively, she didn't press him on it.

In mid-November, three weeks after they'd first made love, Sarah cut back the number of days that Jonah had to stay after school from three to one. For the most part, he was caught up; he was doing fine in reading and spelling, and though he needed a little more help with math, she figured one day a week ought to do it. That night, Miles and Sarah took him out for pizza as a sort of celebration.

Later, however, while tucking Jonah into bed, Miles noticed that his son seemed quieter than usual.

"Why the glum face, champ?"

"I'm feeling kind of sad."

"Why?"

"Because," he said simply, "I don't have to stay after school as much anymore."

"I thought you didn't like staying after school."

"I didn't at first, but I kind of like it now."

"You do?"

He nodded. "Miss Andrews makes me feel special."

"He said that?"

Miles nodded. He and Sarah were sitting on the front steps, watching Jonah and Mark jump their bikes over a plywood ramp in the driveway. Sarah's legs were drawn up close and she had her arms wrapped around them.

"Yes, he did." Jonah went zipping by them, Mark right behind, onto the grass where they intended to circle around again. "To be honest, I've been wondering how he would handle our seeing each other, but he seems to be fine."

"That's good."

"How's he doing in school with this?"

"I really haven't noticed much of a change. For the first few days, I think some of the other kids in class were asking him about it, but it seems to have died down some."

Jonah and Mark raced by again, oblivious to their presence.

"Do you want to spend Thanksgiving with Jonah and me?" Miles asked. "I've got to work that night, but we can eat early, if you don't have plans."

"I can't. My brother's coming home from college and my mom is making a big dinner for all of us. She invited a bunch of people—aunts, uncles, cousins, and the grandparents. I don't think she'd be too understanding if I told her to count me out."

"No. I don't guess she would."

"She wants to meet you, though. She keeps bugging me to bring you over."

"Why don't you?"

"I didn't think you were ready for that, just yet." She winked. "Didn't want to scare you off."

"She can't be that bad."

"Don't be so sure. But if you're game, you can join us for Thanksgiving. That way we could spend it together."

"You sure? It sounds like you have a full house already."

"Are you kidding? A couple more won't make any

difference. And besides, that way you can meet the whole clan. Unless, of course, you're not ready for that yet, either."

"I'm ready."

"Then you'll come?"

"Plan on it."

"Good. But listen, if my mom starts asking some strange questions, just remember that I take after my father, okay?"

Later that night, with Jonah away at Mark's again, Sarah followed Miles into the bedroom. This was a first: Up until now, they'd always stayed overnight at Sarah's apartment, and the fact that they found themselves in the bed once shared by Missy and Miles wasn't lost on either of them. When they made love, there was an urgency to it, an almost frantic passion that left both of them breathless. They didn't speak much afterward; Sarah simply lay beside Miles with her head on his chest as he ran his hands gently through her hair.

Sarah had the sense that Miles wanted to be alone with his thoughts. As she gazed around the bedroom, she realized for the first time that they were surrounded by pictures of Missy, including one on the bedstand that she could reach out and touch.

Suddenly uneasy, she also spotted the manila file he'd mentioned before, the one filled with information he'd assembled after Missy died. It sat on the shelf, thick and well handled, and she found herself staring at it as her head rose and fell with every breath Miles took. Finally, when the silence between them began to feel oppressive, she slid her head onto the pillow to face him.

"Are you okay?" she asked.

"I'm fine," he said, not meeting her eyes.

"You're kind of quiet."

"Just thinking," he murmured.

"Good things, I hope."

"Only the best." He traced his finger down her arm. "I love you," he whispered.

"I love you, too."

"Will you stay with me all night?"

"Do you want me to?"

"Very much."

"Are you sure?"

"Absolutely."

Though still a little unsettled, she let him pull her close. He kissed her again, then held her until she finally fell asleep. In the morning, when she woke, it took her a moment to realize where she was. Miles ran his finger along her spine and she felt her body begin to respond.

There was something different about their lovemaking this time, something that more closely resembled their first time together, tender and unrushed.

It wasn't just the way he kissed and whispered to her, but rather the way he looked as he moved above her that spoke of how serious their relationship had become.

That, and the fact that sometime while she'd been sleeping, Miles had quietly removed the pictures and the manila file that had cast their shadow over them the night before.

# Chapter 15

"I still don't understand why I haven't had the chance to meet him yet."

Maureen and Sarah were in the grocery store, walking the aisles and filling the cart with everything they needed. To Sarah, it looked as if her mother planned to feed a few dozen people for at least a week.

"You will, Mom, in a few days. Like I said, he and Jonah will be coming by for dinner."

"But wouldn't he be more comfortable if he came over before that? So we could have a chance to get to know each other?"

"You'll have plenty of time to get to know him, Mom. You know how Thanksgiving is."

"But with everyone else around, it's just not going to be possible to visit the way I'd like."

"I'm sure he'll understand."

"And didn't you say he has to leave early?"

"He has to go to work about four o'clock."

"On a holiday?"

"He works Thanksgiving Day so he can have Christmas off. He's a sheriff, you know. It's not like they can let everyone take the day off."

"So who's going to watch Jonah?"

"I will. I'll probably bring him back to Miles's house. You know Dad—he'll be sound asleep by six o'clock, and I'll probably bring him home then."

"So early?"

"Don't worry. We'll still be there all afternoon."

"You're right," Maureen said. "It's just that I'm a little frazzled from all this."

"Don't be worried, Mom. Nothing's going to go wrong."


"Will there be other kids there?" Jonah asked.

"I don't know," Miles said. "There might be."

"Boys or girls?"

"I don't know."

"Well . . . how old are they?"

Miles shook his head. "Like I said, I don't know. I'm not even sure there will be other kids there, to tell you the truth. I forgot to ask."

Jonah furrowed his brow. "But if I'm the only kid, what will I do?"

"Watch the football game with me?"

"That's boring."

Miles reached for his son, sliding him along the front seat until he was close.

"Well, we're not going to be there all day, anyway, since I have to work. But we do have to visit at least for a little while. I mean, they were nice enough to invite us over, and it wouldn't be polite to leave right after we eat. But maybe we can go for a walk or something."

"With Miss Andrews?"

"If you'd like her to come."

"Okay." He paused, his head turned toward the window. They were rolling past a grove of loblolly pines. "Dad . . . do you think we're having turkey?"

"I'm pretty sure we are. Why?"

"Will it taste funny? Like it did last year?"

"Are you saying you didn't like my cooking?"

"It tasted funny."

"It did not."

"To me it did."

"Maybe they're better cooks than I am."

"I hope so."

"Are you picking on me?"

Jonah grinned. "Kind of. But it did taste funny, you know."

Miles and Jonah pulled up in front of a two-story brick home and parked near the mailbox. The lawn had all the markings of someone who enjoyed gardening. Pansies had been planted along the walkway, pine straw had been spread around the bases of the trees, and the only leaves in evidence were those that had fallen the night before. Sarah brushed back the curtain and waved from inside the house. A moment later, she opened the front door.

"Wow, you look impressive," she said.

Miles's hand went absently to his tie. "Thanks."

"I was talking to Jonah," she said with a wink, and Jonah glanced at his father with a victorious expression. He was wearing navy slacks and a white shirt and looked clean enough to have come straight from church. He gave Sarah a quick hug.

From behind her back, Sarah brought out a set of Matchbox cars, which she handed to Jonah.

"What's this for?" he asked.

"I just wanted you to have something to play with while you're here," she said. "Do you like them?"

He stared at the box. "This is great! Dad . . . look." He held the box in the air.

"I see that. Did you say thanks?"

"Thank you, Miss Andrews."

"You're welcome."

As soon as Miles approached, Sarah straightened and greeted him with a kiss. "I was just kidding, you know. You look nice, too. I'm not used to seeing you wearing a jacket and tie in the middle of the afternoon." She fingered his lapel slightly. "I could get used to this."

"Thank you, Miss Andrews," he said, mimicking his son. "You look pretty nice yourself."

And she did. If anything, the longer he knew her, the prettier she seemed to get, no matter what she wore.

"You ready to come inside?" she asked.

"Whenever you are," Miles answered.

"How about you, Jonah?"

"Are there any other kids here?"

"No. I'm sorry. Just a bunch of grown-ups. But they're really nice, and they're looking forward to meeting you."

He nodded and his eyes traveled to the box again. "Can I open this now?"

"If you'd like to. It's yours, so you can open it whenever you want."

"So I can play with them outside, too?"

"Sure," Sarah said. "That's why I got them—"

"But first," Miles added, cutting into the conversation, "you've got to come inside and meet everyone. And if you do head back out to play, I don't want you getting dirty before dinner."

"Okay," Jonah agreed instantly, and from the look on his face, it seemed he believed that he'd stay clean. Miles, however, was under no illusions. A seven-year-old boy, playing on the ground outside? Not a chance, but hopefully he wouldn't get too grubby.

"All right, then," Sarah said. "Let's head on in. One word of caution, though . . ."

"Is it about your mother?"

Sarah smiled. "How did you know?"

"Don't worry. I'll be on my best behavior, and Jonah will, too, right?"

Jonah nodded without looking up.

Sarah took Miles's hand and leaned close to his ear. "It's not you two that I was worried about."

"So there you are!" Maureen cried as she emerged from the kitchen.

Sarah nudged Miles. Following her eyes, Miles was surprised to see that Maureen looked nothing like her daughter. Where Sarah was blonde, Maureen's hair was graying in a way that looked as if it had been black at one time; where Sarah was tall and thin, her mother had a more matronly appearance. And while Sarah seemed to glide when she walked, Maureen seemed almost to bounce as she approached them. She was wearing a white apron over her blue dress and held her hands out as she approached, as if greeting long-lost friends. "I've heard so much about you both!"

Maureen enveloped Miles in a hug and did the same thing to Jonah, even before Sarah made the formal introductions. "I'm so glad you could come! We've got a full house, as you can see, but you two are the guests of honor." She seemed practically giddy.

216

"What's that?" Jonah asked.

"It means that everyone's been waiting for you."

"It does?"

"Yessiree."

"They don't even know me," Jonah said innocently, as he glanced around the room, feeling the eyes of strangers on him. Miles put a comforting hand on his shoulder.

"It's nice to meet you, Maureen. And thanks for having us over."

"Oh, it was my pleasure." She giggled. "We're just glad you could come. And I know that Sarah was glad, too."

"Mom . . ."

"Well, you were. No reason to deny it." She turned her attention to Miles and Jonah, talking and giggling for the next few minutes. When she'd finally finished, she began to introduce them to the grandparents, as well as the rest of Sarah's relatives, about a dozen people in all. Miles shook hands, Jonah followed his lead, and Sarah winced at the way Maureen kept introducing Miles. "This is Sarah's friend," she'd say, but it was her tone—a mixture of pride and motherly approval—that left no doubt as to what she really meant. When they'd finished, Maureen seemed almost exhausted by the performance. She turned her attention back to Miles. "Now, what can I get you to drink?"

"How about a beer?"

"One beer coming up. And how about for you, Jonah? We've got root beer or Seven-Up."

"Root beer."

"Let me go with you, Mom," Sarah said, taking hold of her mother's arm. "I think I need a drink, too."

On their way to the kitchen, her mother was beaming. "Oh, Sarah . . . I'm so happy for you."

"Thanks."

"He seems wonderful. Such a nice smile. He looks like someone you can trust."

"I know."

"And that boy of his is darling."

"Yes, Mother . . ."


"Where's Daddy?" Sarah asked a few minutes later. Her mother had finally calmed down enough to turn her attention back to her dinner preparations.

"I sent him and Brian out to the grocery store a few minutes ago," Maureen answered. "We needed some more rolls and a bottle of wine. I wasn't sure we had enough."

Sarah opened the oven and checked the turkey; the smell wafted through the kitchen.

"So Brian's finally up?"

"He was tired. He didn't get here until after midnight. He had an exam on Wednesday afternoon, so he couldn't get away earlier."

At that moment, the back door opened and Larry and Brian came in carrying a couple of bags, which they set on the counter. Brian, looking leaner and older somehow than when he'd left last August, saw Sarah and they hugged.

"So how's school going? I haven't talked to you in what seems like forever."

"It's going. You know how it is. How's the job?"

"It's good. I like it." She glanced over Brian's shoulder. "Hi, Daddy."

"Hey, sweetheart," Larry said, "it smells great in here."

As they put the groceries away, they chatted for a few minutes until Sarah finally told them there was someone she'd like them to meet.

"Yeah, Mom mentioned that you were seeing someone." Brian wiggled his eyebrows conspiratorially. "I'm glad. Is he a good guy?"

"I think so."

"Is it serious?"

Sarah couldn't help but notice that her mother stopped peeling the potatoes as she waited for the answer.

"I don't know yet," she said evasively. "Would you like to meet him?"

Brian shrugged. "Yeah, okay."

She reached out and touched his arm. "Don't worry, you'll like him." Brian nodded. "You coming, Daddy?"

"In a minute. Your mother wants me to find some of the extra serving bowls. They're in a box in the pantry somewhere."

Sarah and Brian left the kitchen and headed to the living room, though she didn't see Miles or Jonah. Her grandmother said that Miles had gone outside for a minute, but when she stepped out the front door, she still didn't see him.

"He must be around back . . ."

As they turned the corner of the house, Sarah finally spotted them. Jonah had found a small mound of dirt and was pushing the Matchbox cars along imaginary roads.

"So what's this guy do? Is he a teacher?"

"No, but that's how I met him. His son is in my class. Actually, he's a deputy sheriff. Hey, Miles!" she called out. "Jonah!" When they turned, Sarah nodded in her brother's direction. "There's someone I'd like you to meet."

When Jonah stood up from the dirt, Sarah saw that the knees of his pants were circled with brown. He and Miles met them halfway.

"This is my brother, Brian. And Brian, this is Miles and his son, Jonah."

Miles held out his hand. "How are you doing? Miles Ryan. Nice to meet you."

Brian held his hand out stiffly. "Nice to meet you, too."

220

"I hear you're in college."

Brian nodded. "Yes, sir."

Sarah laughed. "You don't have to be so formal. He's only a couple of years older than I am." Brian smiled weakly but didn't say anything, and Jonah looked up at him. Brian took a small step backward, as if uncertain how to address a young child.

"Hi," Jonah said.

"Hi," Brian answered.

"You're Miss Andrews's brother?"

Brian nodded.

"She's my teacher."

"I know. She told me."

"Oh . . ." Jonah looked suddenly bored and started fiddling with the cars in his hands. For a long moment, none of them said anything.

"I wasn't hiding from your family," Miles said a few minutes later. "Jonah asked if I'd come out here with him to see if I thought it would be okay to play here. I said it probably was—I hope that's okay."

"That's fine," Sarah said. "As long as he's having fun."

Larry had come around the corner as the four of them were talking and asked Brian if he could look in the garage for the serving dishes he'd been unable to find. Brian wandered off in that direction, then disappeared from view.

Larry, too, was quiet, though in a more speculative way than Brian. He seemed to regard Miles with a studying eye, as if watching his expressions would reveal more than the words Miles was saying as they covered the basics about each other. That feeling quickly passed as they found common interests, like the upcoming football game between the Dallas Cowboys and the Miami Dolphins. Within a few minutes, they were talking easily. Larry finally made his way back to the house, leaving Sarah alone with Miles and Jonah. Jonah went back to the mound of dirt.

"Your father's quite a character. I had the strangest feeling that when we first met, he was trying to figure out whether we'd slept together."

Sarah laughed. "He probably was. I am his baby girl, you know."

"Yeah, I know. How long's he been married to your mom?"

"Almost thirty-five years."

"That's a long time."

"Sometimes I think he should be sainted."

"Now, now . . . don't be so hard on your mom. I liked her, too."

"I think the feeling was mutual. For a while there, I thought she was going to offer to adopt you."

"Like you said, she just wants you to be happy."

"Say that to her, and I don't think she'll ever let you leave. She needs someone to take care of, now that Brian's off at college. Oh, listen—don't take Brian's shyness personally. He's really reserved when it comes to meeting people. Once he gets to know you, he'll come out of his shell."

Miles shook his head, dismissing her worries. "He was fine. Besides, he kind of reminds me of how I was at that age. Believe it or not, there are times when I don't know what to say, either."

Sarah's eyes went wide. "No . . . really? And here I thought you were the smoothest talker I'd ever met. Why, you practically swept me off my feet."

"Do you honestly believe that sarcasm is the right tone to take on a day like today? A day to be with family and offer thanks for all our blessings?"

"Of course."

He put his arms around her. "Well, in my defense, then, whatever I did seemed to work, didn't it?"

She sighed. "I suppose."

"You suppose?"

"What do you want? A medal?"

"For starters. A trophy would be nice, too."

She smiled. "What do you think you're holding right now?"

The rest of the afternoon passed uneventfully. After the meal was cleared away, some of the family went to watch the game, others went to the kitchen to help store the mountains of leftovers. The afternoon was unhurried, and after stuffing himself with two pieces of pie, even Jonah seemed to find the atmosphere soothing. Larry and Miles chatted about New Bern, Larry quizzing Miles about local history. Sarah wandered from the kitchen, where her mother repeated (and repeated) the fact that Miles seemed like a wonderful young man, back to the living room to make sure that Miles and Jonah didn't feel as if she'd abandoned them. Brian, dutifully, spent most of his time in the kitchen, washing and drying the china that his mother had used for dinner.

A half hour before Miles had to head home to get dressed for work, Miles, Sarah, and Jonah went for a walk, just as Miles had promised. They headed toward the end of the block and into the wooded area that fronted the development. Jonah grabbed Sarah's hand and led her through the woods, laughing as he did so, and it was while watching them weave their way among the trees that it gradually dawned on Miles where all this might lead. While he knew he loved Sarah, he'd been touched that she had chosen to share her family with him. He liked the feeling of closeness, the holiday atmosphere, the casual way her relatives had seemed to respond to him, and he was certain that he didn't want this to be an isolated invitation.

It was then that he first thought of asking Sarah to marry him, and once the idea came to him, he found it nearly impossible to dismiss.

Up ahead, Sarah and Jonah were tossing stones in a small creek, one after the next. Jonah then hopped over it, and Sarah followed.

"C'mon!" she shouted. "We're exploring!"

"Yeah, Dad, hurry up!"

"I'm coming—you don't have to wait! I'll catch up."

He didn't rush to do so. Instead, he was lost in his thoughts as they continued to move farther and farther away, eventually vanishing behind a thick grove. Miles pushed his hands into his pockets.

*Marriage.*

It was still early in their relationship, of course, and he had no intention of dropping to his knees here and now to pop the question. At the same time, he suddenly knew that there would come a moment when he would. She was right for him; of that he was certain. And she was wonderful with Jonah. Jonah seemed to love her, and that, too, was important, because if Jonah hadn't liked her, he wouldn't even be considering what a future with Sarah might bring.

And with that, something inside clicked, a key

fitting neatly into a lock. Though he wasn't even consciously aware of it, the question of "if" had become a question of "when."

With this decision, he unconsciously felt himself relax. He couldn't see Sarah or Jonah as he crossed over the creek, but he followed the direction he'd last seen them going. A minute later he spotted them, and as he closed the distance between them, he realized he hadn't been this happy in years.


From Thanksgiving Day through mid-December, Miles and Sarah grew even closer, both as lovers and as friends, their relationship blossoming into something deeper and more permanent.

Miles also started dropping hints about their possible future together. Sarah wasn't blind to what he really meant by his words; in fact, she found herself adding to his comments. Little things—when they were lying in bed, he might mention that he thought the walls should be repainted; Sarah would respond that a pale yellow might look cheery and they picked out the color together. Or Miles would mention that the garden needed some color and she'd say that she'd always loved camellias, and that's what she'd plant if she lived here. That weekend, Miles planted five of the bushes along the front of the house.

The file stayed in the closet, and for the first time

in a long time, the present seemed more alive to Miles than the past. But what neither Sarah nor Miles could know was that although they were ready to put the past behind them, events would soon conspire to make that impossible.

# Chapter 16

*I* had another sleepless night, and as much as I want to go back to bed, I realize I can't. Not until I tell you how it happened.

The accident didn't happen the way you probably imagine, or the way that Miles imagined. I hadn't, as he suspected, been drinking that night. Nor was I under the influence of any drugs. I was completely sober.

What happened with Missy that night was, quite simply, an accident.

I've gone over it a thousand times in my mind. In the fifteen years since it happened, I've felt a sense of déjà vu at odd times—when carrying boxes to a moving van a couple of years ago, for instance—and the feeling still makes me stop whatever it is I'm doing, if only for a moment, and I find myself drawn back in time, to the day that Missy Ryan died.

I'd been working since early that morning, unloading boxes onto pallets for storage in a local warehouse, and I was supposed to be off at six. But a late shipment of plastic pipes came in right before closing time—my employer that day was the supplier for most of the shops in the Carolinas—and the owner asked if I wouldn't mind staying for an extra hour or so. I didn't mind; it meant overtime, time and a half, a great way to pick up some much needed extra cash. What I hadn't counted on was how full the trailer was, or that I'd pretty much end up doing most of the job alone.

There were supposed to be four guys working, but one had called in sick that day, another couldn't stay since his son was playing a baseball game and he didn't want to miss it. That left two of us to do the job, which still would have been okay. But a few minutes after the trailer pulled in, the other guy turned his ankle, and the next thing I knew, I was all by myself.

It was hot, too. The temperature outside was in the nineties, and inside the warehouse it was even hotter, over a hundred degrees and humid. I'd already put in eight hours, with another three hours to go. Trucks had been pulling up all day, and because I didn't work there regularly, most of my work was the backbreaking type. The other three guys rotated turns using the forklift, so they might get a break now and then. Not me. My job was to sort the boxes and then haul them from the back of the trailer to where the door slid up, loading everything on pallets so the forklift could move them into the warehouse. But by the end of the day, since I was the only one there, I had to do it all. By the time I finished up, I was bone-tired. I could barely move my arms, I had spasms in my back, and since I'd missed dinner, I was starving, too.

That's why I decided to go to Rhett's Barbecue instead of heading straight home. After a long, hard day, there's nothing better in the world than barbecue, and when I finally crawled into my car, I was thinking to myself that in just a few minutes, I'd finally be able to relax.

My car back then was a real beater, dented and banged up all over, a Pontiac Bonneville that had a dozen years on the road already. I'd got it used the summer before and paid only three hundred dollars for it. But even though it looked like hell, it ran good and I'd never had a problem with it. The engine started up whenever I turned the key, and I'd fixed the brakes myself when I first bought it, which was all it really needed at the time.

So I got in my car just as the sun was finally going down. At that time of night, the sun does funny things as it arcs downward in the west. The sky is changing color almost by the minute, shadows are spreading across the roads like long, ghostly fingers, and since there wasn't so much as a cloud in the sky, there were moments when the glare would slant sharply through the window and I'd have to squint so I could see where I was going.

Just ahead of me, another driver seemed to be having even more problems seeing than I was. Whoever it was was speeding up and slowing down, hitting the brakes every time the sunlight shifted, and more than once veering across the white line onto the other side of the road. I kept reacting, hitting my own brakes, but finally I got fed up and decided to put some distance between me and him. The road was too narrow for passing, so instead I slowed my car, hoping the person would pull farther away.

But whoever it was did just the opposite. He slowed down, too, and when the distance had closed between us again, I saw the brake lights blinking on and off like Christmas lights, then suddenly staying red. I hit my own brakes hard, my tires squealing as my car jerked to a stop. I doubt if I missed the car in front of me by more than a foot.

That's the moment, I think, when fate intervened. Sometimes, I wish I'd hit the car, since I would have had to stop and Missy Ryan would have made it home. But because I missed—and because I'd had enough of the driver in front of me—I took the next right, onto Camellia Road, even though it added a little extra time, time I now wish I could have back. The road swung through an older part of town, where oaks were full and lush, and the sun was dipping low enough that the glare was finally gone. A few minutes later, the sky started darkening more quickly and I turned on my headlights.

The road veered left and right, and soon the houses began to spread out. The yards were bigger, and fewer people seemed to be about. After a couple of minutes, I made another turn, this time onto Madame Moore's Lane. I knew this road well and comforted myself with the knowledge that in a couple of miles, I'd find myself at Rhett's.

I remember turning the radio on and fiddling with the dial, but I didn't really take my eyes off the road. Then I turned it off. My mind, I promise you, was on the drive.

The road was narrow and winding, but like I said, I knew this road like the back of my hand. I automatically applied the car's brakes as I entered a bend in the road. That was when I saw her, and I'm pretty sure I slowed even more. I don't know for sure, though, since everything that happened next went so fast that I couldn't swear to anything.

I was coming up behind her, the gap between us closing. She was off to the side, on the grass shoulder. I remember she was wearing a white shirt and blue shorts and not going real fast, kind of gliding along in a relaxed sort of way.

In this neighborhood, the houses sat on half an acre, and no one was outside. She knew I was coming up behind her—I saw her glance quickly to the side, maybe enough to catch sight of me from the corner of her eye, and she moved another half step farther from the road. Both my hands were on the wheel. I was paying attention to everything I should have and thought I was being careful. And so was she.

Neither of us, however, saw the dog.

Almost as if lying in wait for her, it charged out from

a gap in a hedge when she was no more than twenty feet from my car. A big black dog, and even though I was in my car, I could hear its vicious snarl as it charged right at her. It must have caught her off-guard because she suddenly reared back, away from the dog, and took one step too many into the road.

My car, all three thousand pounds of it, smashed into her in that instant.

# Chapter 17

Sims Addison, at forty, looked something like a rat: a sharp nose, a forehead that sloped backward, and a chin that seemed to have stopped growing before the rest of his body did. He kept his hair slicked back over his head, with the help of a wide-toothed comb he always carried with him.

Sims was also an alcoholic.

He wasn't, however, the kind of alcoholic who drank every night. Sims was the kind of alcoholic whose hands shook in the morning prior to taking his first drink of the day, which he usually finished long before most people headed for work. Although he was partial to bourbon, he seldom had enough money for anything other than the cheapest wines, which he drank by the gallon. Where he got his money he didn't like to say, but then, aside from booze and the rent, he didn't need much.

If Sims had any redeeming feature, it was that he had the knack of making himself invisible and, as a result, had a way of learning things about people.

When he drank, he was neither loud nor obnoxious, but his normal expression—eyes half-closed, mouth slack—gave him the appearance of someone who was far drunker than he usually was. Because of that, people said things in his presence.

Things they should have kept to themselves.

Sims earned the little money he did by calling in tips to the police.

Not all of them, though. Only the ones where he could stay anonymous and still get the money. Only the ones where the police would keep his secret, where he wouldn't have to testify.

Criminals, he knew, had a way of keeping grudges, and he wasn't stupid enough to believe that if they knew who'd turned them in, they'd just roll over and forget it.

Sims had spent time in prison: once in his early twenties for petty theft and twice in his thirties for possession of marijuana. The third time behind bars, however, changed him. By then, his alcoholism was full-blown, and he spent the first week suffering from the most severe case of withdrawal imaginable. He shook, he vomited, and when he closed his eyes, he saw monsters. He nearly died, too, though not from withdrawal. After a few days of listening to Sims scream and moan, the other man in the cell beat him until he was unconscious, so he could get some sleep. Sims spent three weeks in the infirmary and was released by a parole board sympathetic to what he'd been through. Instead of finishing the year he still had to serve, he was placed on probation and told to report to a parole officer. He was warned, however, that if he drank or used drugs, his sentence would be reinstated.

The possibility of going through withdrawal, coupled with the beating, left Sims with a deathly fear of going back to jail.

But for Sims it wasn't possible to face life sober. In the beginning, he was careful to drink only in the privacy of his home. In time, however, he began to resent the impingement on his freedom. He began meeting a few buddies for drinks again while maintaining a low profile. In time, he began taking his luck for granted. He began drinking on his way to see them, his bottle covered with the traditional brown paper bag. Soon enough, he was drunk wherever he went, and though there might have been a little warning signal in his brain, telling him to be careful, he was too blasted out of his mind to listen to it.

Still, everything might have been okay, had he not borrowed his mother's car for a night out. He didn't have a license, but he nonetheless drove to meet some friends at a dingy bar, located on a gravel road outside the town limits. There, he drank more than he should have and sometime after two A.M.

staggered out to his car. He barely made it out of the parking area without hitting any other cars, but somehow he managed to head in the direction of home. A few miles later, he spotted the flashing red lights behind him.

It was Miles Ryan who stepped out of the car.

"Is that you, Sims?" Miles called out, approaching slowly. Like most of the deputies, he knew Sims on a first-name basis. Nonetheless, he had the flashlight out and was shining it inside the car, scanning quickly for any sign of danger.

"Oh, hey, Deputy." The words came out slurred.

"Have you been drinking?" Miles asked.

"No . . . no. Not at all." Sims eyed him unsteadily. "Just visiting with some friends."

"You sure about that? Not even a beer?"

"No, sir."

"Maybe a glass of wine with dinner or something?"

"No, sir. Not me."

"You were swerving all over the road."

"Just tired." As if to make his point, he brought one hand to his mouth and yawned. Miles could smell the booze on his breath as he exhaled.

"Aw, come on . . . not even one little drink? All night long?"

"No, sir."

"I need to see your license and registration."

"Well . . . um . . . I don't exactly have my license with me. Must have left it at home."

Miles stepped back from the car, keeping his flashlight pointed at Sims. "I need you to step out of the car."

Sims looked surprised that Miles didn't believe him. "For what?"

"Just step out, please."

"You're not going to arrest me, are you?"

"C'mon, don't make this any harder than you have to."

Sims seemed to debate what to do, though even for Sims, he was more drunk than usual. Instead of moving, he stared through the front windshield until Miles finally opened the door.

"C'mon."

Though Miles held a hand out, Sims simply shook his head, as if trying to tell Miles that he was fine, that he could do this on his own.

Getting out, though, proved more difficult than Sims anticipated. Instead of finding himself eye to eye with Miles Ryan, where he could plead for mercy, Sims found himself on the ground and passed out almost immediately.

Sims woke shivering the following morning, completely lost in his surroundings. All he knew was that he was behind bars, and the realization sent his mind spinning with a paralyzing fear. In bits and pieces, parts of the evening came back to him slowly. He remembered heading to the bar and drinking with friends . . . after that, everything was fairly foggy until he saw images of flashing lights. From the deep recesses of his mind, he also dragged out the fact that Miles Ryan had brought him in.

Sims, though, had more important things on his mind than what had happened the night before, and his thoughts centered primarily on the best way to avoid going back to jail. The very thought brought beads of perspiration to his forehead and upper lip.

He couldn't go back. No way. He'd die there. He knew it with an absolute certainty.

But he was going back. Fear cleared his mind further, and for the next few minutes, all he could think about were the things he simply couldn't face again.

Jail.

Beatings.

Nightmares.

Shaking and vomiting.

*Death*.

He stood shakily from the bed and used the wall for balance. He staggered over to the bars, looking down the corridor. Three of the other cells were occupied, but no one seemed to know if Deputy Ryan was around. When he asked, he was told to shut up twice; the third person didn't answer at all.

*This is your life for the next two years.*

He wasn't naive enough to believe that they'd let him off, nor was he under any illusions that the public defender would do any good at all. His probation had been quite clear on the fact that any violation would result in mandatory reincarceration, and because of his previous record and the fact that he was driving, there wasn't any way this would slide. Not a chance. Pleading for mercy wouldn't work, pleading for forgiveness would be like spitting in the wind. He'd rot away in prison until his case came up, and then, when he lost, they'd throw away the key.

He brought his hand up to wipe his forehead and knew then he had to do something. Anything to avoid the fate that certainly awaited him.

His mind began to click faster, hobbled and broken, but faster nonetheless. His only hope, the only thing that could help him, was to turn back the clock somehow and undo the arrest from the night before.

How the hell, though, was he going to do that?

*You have information*, a little voice answered.

Miles had just stepped out of the shower when he heard the phone ringing. Earlier, he'd made Jonah breakfast and seen him off to school, but instead of picking up around the house, he'd crawled back into bed, hoping to get another couple of hours of sleep. Though he hadn't gotten much, he'd been able to doze for a little while. He would work from noon to eight, and he was looking forward to a relaxing evening after that. Jonah would be gone—he was going to the movies with Mark—and Sarah had offered to come by so they could spend some time together.

The phone call would change all that.

Miles grabbed a towel and fastened it around his waist, answering the phone just before the recorder picked up. Charlie was on the other end. After exchanging pleasantries, Charlie got right to the point.

"You better head on in now," he said.

"Why? What's up?"

"You brought Sims Addison in last night, didn't you?"

"Yea, I did."

"I can't find the report."

"Oh . . . about that. Another call came in and I had to rush back out again. I was coming in early anyway to finish it up. Is there a problem?"

"I'm not sure yet. How soon can you be here?"

Miles wasn't sure what to make of that, nor did he really understand the tone Charlie was using.

"I just got out of the shower. Half an hour, maybe?"

"When you get in, make sure you come and talk to me. I'll be waiting."

"Can't you at least tell me what the rush is all about?"

There was a long pause on the other end.

"Just get here as quick as you can. We'll talk then."

"So what's all this about?" Miles asked. As soon as he'd arrived, Charlie had pulled him into the office and closed the door behind him.

"Tell me about last night."

"With Sims Addison, you mean?"

"Start from the beginning."

"Um . . . it was a little after midnight, and I was parked down the road from Beckers—you know, the bar out near Vanceboro?"

Charlie nodded, crossing his arms.

"Just waiting around. It had been quiet, and I knew that the place was closing. A little after two in the morning, I saw someone leave the bar and I followed the car on a hunch, and it was a good thing I did. The car was weaving all over the road, so I pulled him over to give him a sobriety test. That's when I found out it was Sims Addison. I could smell the booze on his breath as soon as I got close to the window. When I asked him to get out of the car, he fell. He passed out, so I put him in the back of the car and brought him here. By then, he'd revived enough so that I didn't have to carry him to the cell, but I had to support him. I was going to do the paperwork, but I got another call and had to go out immediately. I didn't

242

get back until after my shift was over, and since I'm filling in for Tommie today, I figured I'd do the paperwork before my shift started."

Charlie said nothing, but his eyes never left Miles. "Anything else?"

"No. Is this about him being hurt or something? Like I said, I didn't touch him—he fell. He was blasted, Charlie. Absolutely hammered—"

"No, it's not about that."

"Then what is it?"

"Let me make certain first—he didn't say anything to you at all last night."

Miles thought for a moment. "Not really. He knew who I was, so he called me by name . . ." He trailed off, trying to recall if there was anything else.

"Was he acting strange?"

"It didn't seem like it . . . just sort of out of it, you know?"

"Huh . . . ," Charlie mumbled, and he seemed lost in thought again.

"C'mon, Charlie, tell me what's going on."

Charlie sighed. "He says he wants to talk to you."

Miles waited, knowing there was more coming.

"Only to you. He says he has information."

Miles knew Sims's history as well. "And?"

"He won't talk to me. But he says that it's a matter of life and death."

\*    \*    \*

Miles stared at Sims through the bars, thinking the man looked almost on the verge of death. Like other chronic alcoholics, his skin was a sickly yellow. His hands were shaking, and sweat poured from his forehead. Sitting on the cot, he'd been absently scratching at his arms for hours, and Miles could see the red trails, tinged with blood, like streaks of lipstick applied by a child.

Miles pulled up a chair and sat forward, his elbows propped on his knees.

"You wanted to talk to me?"

Sims turned at the sound of his voice. He hadn't noticed that Miles had arrived, and it seemed to take a moment for him to focus. He wiped his upper lip and nodded.

"Deputy."

Miles leaned forward. "What do you have to say, Sims? You've got my boss pretty nervous upstairs. He said you told him that you have information for me."

"Why'd you bring me in last night?" Sims asked. "I didn't hurt nobody."

"You were drunk, Sims. And you were driving. That's a crime."

"Then why haven't you charged me yet?"

Miles debated his answer, trying to figure out where Sims was going with all this.

"I didn't have the time," he said honestly. "But according to the laws of this state, it doesn't matter if I did it last night or not. And if that's what you wanted to talk to me about, then I've things to do."

Miles made a show of standing from his chair and took a step down the corridor.

"Wait," Sims said.

Miles stopped and turned. "Yes?"

"I've got something important to tell you."

"You told Charlie it was a matter of life and death."

Sims wiped his lips again. "I can't go back to jail. If you charge me, that's where I'll go. I'm on probation."

"That's the way it goes. You break the law, you go to jail. Didn't you ever learn that?"

"I can't go back," he repeated.

"You should have thought of that last night."

Miles turned again and Sims rose from the cot, a panicked look on his face. "Don't do this."

Miles hesitated. "I'm sorry, Sims. I can't help you."

"You could let me go. I didn't hurt nobody. And if I go back to jail, I'll die for sure. I know that as sure as I know the sky is blue."

"I can't do that."

"Sure you can. You can say you was mistaken, say I fell asleep at the wheel and that's why I was swerving . . ."

Miles couldn't help but feel a little pity for the man, but his duty was clear. "I'm sorry," he said again, and he started down the corridor. Sims moved to the bars, grasping them.

"I got information . . ."

"Tell me later, once I get you upstairs to do the paperwork."

"Wait!"

There was something in his tone that made Miles stop once more.

"Yes?"

Sims cleared his throat. The other three men who'd been in the adjoining cells had been brought upstairs, but he looked around to make absolutely certain he hadn't overlooked anyone else. He motioned with his finger for Miles to come closer, but Miles stayed where he was and crossed his arms.

"If I got important information, would you drop the charges?"

Miles suppressed a smile. *Now we're talking.*

"That's not up to just me, you know that. I'd have to talk to the district attorney."

"No. Not that kind. You know how I work. I don't testify, and I remain anonymous."

Miles said nothing.

Sims looked around, making sure he was still alone.

"There ain't no proof of what I'm saying, but it's true and you'll want to know it." He lowered his voice, as if confiding a secret. "I know who did it that night. I *know.*"

The tone he used and the obvious implications made the hairs on the back of Miles's neck suddenly stand on end.

"What are you talking about?"

Sims wiped his lip again, knowing he had Miles's full attention now.

"I can't tell you no more unless you let me go."

Miles moved toward the cell, feeling off-balance. He stared at Sims until Sims stepped back from the bars.

"Tell me what?"

"I need a deal first. You gotta promise me you'll get me out of here. Just say that because I didn't take the Breathalyzer, you don't have any proof I was drinking."

"I told you—I can't make deals."

"No deal, no information. Like I said, I can't go back to prison."

They stood facing each other, neither of them looking away.

"You know exactly what I'm talking about, don't you?" Sims said finally. "Don't you want to know who did it?"

Miles's heart began to race, and his hands clenched involuntarily at his side. His mind was spinning.

"I'll tell you if you let me go," Sims added.

Miles's mouth opened, then closed as everything—all the memories—rushed back, spilling over him like the water from an overflowing sink. It seemed unbelievable, preposterous. Yet . . . what if Sims was telling the truth?

*What if he knew who killed Missy?*

"You'll have to testify," was all he could think to say.

Sims raised his hands. "No way. I didn't see nothing, but I overheard people talking. And if they find out that I'm the one who told, I'm as good as dead. So I can't testify. I won't. I'll swear that I don't remember telling you nothing. And you can't tell 'em where you learned it from, either. This is just between us—you and me. But . . ."

Sims shrugged, his eyes narrowing, playing Miles perfectly.

"You don't really care about that now, do you? You just want to know who did it, and I can do that. And may God strike me dead if I ain't telling the truth."

Miles grabbed the bars, his knuckles turning white. "Tell me!" he shouted.

"Get me out of here," Sims responded, somehow keeping his cool in spite of Miles's outburst, "and I will."

For a long time, Miles simply stared at him.

"I was at the Rebel," Sims finally began, after Miles had agreed to his demands. "You know the place, right?"

Sims didn't wait for an answer. He swiped his greasy hair with the back of his hand. "This was a couple of years back or so—I can't really recall when it was, exactly—and I was having a few drinks, you know? Behind me, in one of the booths, I saw Earl Getlin. You know him?"

Miles nodded. Another in a long line of people well-known in the department. Tall and thin, pock-marked face, tattoos up both arms—one that showed a lynching, the other a skull with a knife driven through it. Had been arrested for assault, breaking and entering, dealing in stolen goods. Suspected drug dealer. A year and a half ago, after being caught stealing a car, he'd been sent up to Hailey State Prison. Not due for release for another four years.

"He was kind of antsy, fidgeting with his drink, like he was waiting for someone. That's when I saw them come in. The Timsons. They stood in the door for just a second, looking around until they found him. They ain't the kind of people I like being around, so I didn't draw no attention to myself. Next thing I know, they were sitting across from Earl. And they were talking real low, almost whispering, but from where I was, I could hear every word they were saying."

Miles's back had gone rigid with Sims's story. His mouth was dry, as though he'd been outside in the heat for hours.

"They were threatening Earl, but he kept saying that he didn't have it yet. That's when I heard Otis speak up—until then, he'd let his brothers do the talking. He told Earl that if he didn't have the money by the weekend, he'd better watch out, because nobody screwed with him."

He blinked. Blood had drained from his face.

"He said the same thing would happen to Earl that had happened to Missy Ryan. Only this time, they'd back up and run him over again."

# Chapter 18

*I* remember that I was screaming even before I brought the car to a halt.

I recall the impact, of course—the slight shudder of the wheel and the nauseating thud. But what I remember most are my own screams from inside the car. They were ear-shattering, echoing off the closed windows, and they went on until I turned the ignition off and was finally able to push open the door. My screams then turned into panicked prayer. "No, no, no . . ." is all I remember saying.

Barely able to breathe, I ran to the front of the car. I didn't see any damage: The car was, as I said, an older model, one structured to withstand more impact than the cars of today. But I didn't see the body. I had a sudden premonition that I'd run over her, that I'd find her body wedged beneath the car, and as the horrible vision passed in front of my eyes, I felt my stomach muscles constrict. Now, I'll tell you that I'm not the kind of person who is easily rattled—people often comment on my self-control—but I confess that at that moment I put my hands on my knees and nearly vomited. As the feeling finally subsided, I forced myself to look beneath the car. I didn't see anything.

I ran from side to side, looking for her. I didn't see her, not right rightaway, and I had a strange sense that maybe I'd been mistaken, that it must have been my imagination.

I started to jog then, checking one side of the road and then the other, hoping against hope that somehow I'd simply grazed her, that maybe she'd merely been knocked unconscious. I looked behind the car and still didn't find her, and I knew then where she had to be.

As my stomach started doing flip-flops again, my eyes scanned the area in front of the car. My headlights were still on. I took a few hesitant steps forward, and it was then that I spotted her in the ditch, about twenty yards away.

I debated whether I should run to the nearest house and call an ambulance or whether I should go to her. At the time, the latter seemed like the right thing to do, and as I approached, I found myself moving more and more slowly, as if slowing down would make the outcome less certain.

Her body, I noticed right off, was lying at an unnatural angle. One leg looked bent somehow, sort of crossed over the other at the thigh, the knee twisted at an impossible angle and the foot facing the wrong way. One arm was sandwiched beneath her torso, the other above her head. She was on her back.

Her eyes were open.

I remember that it didn't strike me that she was dead, at least in that first instant. But it didn't take more than a couple of seconds to realize that there was something about the glaze in her eyes that wasn't right. They didn't seem real—they were almost a caricature of the way eyes look, like the eyes of a mannequin in a department store window. But as I stared, I think it was their utter stillness that really drove the point home. In all the time I stood above her, she didn't blink at all.

It was then that I noticed the blood pooling beneath her head, and everything sort of hit at once—her eyes, the position of her body, the blood . . .

And for the first time, I knew with certainty that she was dead.

I think I collapsed then. I can't remember making the conscious decision to get close to her, but that's exactly where I found myself a moment later. I put my ear to her chest, I put my ear to her mouth, I checked for a pulse. I checked for any movement at all, any flicker of life, anything to prod me to further action.

There was nothing.

Later, the autopsy would show—and the newspapers would report—that she died instantly. I say this so that you'll know I'm telling the truth. Missy Ryan had no chance at all, no matter what I might have done later.

I don't know how long I stayed beside her, but it couldn't have been long. I do remember staggering back to my car and opening my trunk; I do remember finding the blanket and covering her body. At the time, it seemed like the right thing to do. Charlie suspected that I'd been trying to say that I was sorry, and looking back, I think that was part of it. But the other part was that I simply didn't want anyone to see her the way that I had. So I covered her up, as if covering my own sin.

My memories after that are hazy. The next thing I remember was that I was in my car, heading for home. I really can't explain it, other than that I wasn't thinking clearly. Had the same thing happened now, had I known the things I do now, I wouldn't have done that. I would have run to the nearest house and called the police. For some reason, that night, I didn't.

I don't think, however, that I was trying to hide what I had done. Not then, anyway. In looking back and trying to understand it now, I think I started driving home because that was where I needed to be. Like a moth drawn to a porch light, I didn't seem to have a choice. I simply reacted to a situation.

Nor did I do the right thing when I got home. All I can remember about that is that I'd never felt more exhausted in my life, and instead of making the call, I simply crawled into bed and went to sleep.

The next thing I knew, it was morning.

There is something terrible in the moments after waking up, when the subconscious knows that something terrible has happened but before all the memories flash back in *their entirety.* That's what I experienced as soon as my eyes fluttered open. It was as if I couldn't breathe, as if all the air had been forced out of me somehow, but as soon as I inhaled, it all came surging back.

The drive.

The impact.

The way Missy had looked when I found her.

I brought my hands to my face, not wanting to believe it. I remember that my heart started beating hard in my chest, and I prayed fervently that it had simply been a dream. I'd had dreams like that before, ones that seemed so real that it took a few moments of serious reflection before I realized my error. This time, the reality never went away. Instead, it grew steadily worse, and I felt myself sink inward, as if drowning in my own private ocean.

A few minutes later, I was reading the article in the newspaper.

And this was when my real crime occurred.

I saw the photos, I read what had happened. I saw the quotes from the police, vowing to find whoever had done this, no matter how long it took. And with that came the horrible realization that what had happened— this terrible, terrible accident—wasn't regarded as an accident. Somehow, it was regarded as a crime.

Hit-and-run, the article said. A felony.

I saw the phone sitting on the counter, as if beckoning to me.

I had run.

In their minds, I was guilty, no matter what the circumstances were.

I'll say again that despite what I had done the night before, what happened then wasn't a crime, no matter what the article said. I wasn't making a conscious decision to flee that night. I wasn't thinking clearly enough for that.

No, my crime hadn't occurred the night before.

My crime occurred in the kitchen, when I looked at the phone and didn't make the call.

Though the article had rattled me, I was thinking clearly then. I'm not making excuses for that, since there are none. I weighed my fears against what I knew was right, and my fears won out in the end.

I was terrified of going to jail for what I knew in my heart was an accident, and I began to make excuses. I think I told myself that I would call later; I didn't. I told myself that I would wait a couple of days until things settled down, then call; I didn't. Then I decided to wait until after the funeral.

And by then, I knew it was too late.

# Chapter 19

In the car a few minutes later, the sirens blaring and lights flashing, Miles fishtailed around a corner, almost losing control of the car, and pressed the accelerator to the floor again.

He'd dragged Sims out of the cell and up the stairs, leading him quickly through the office without stopping to acknowledge the stares. Charlie was in his office on the phone, and the sight of Miles—his face white—made him hang up, but not soon enough to stop Miles from reaching the door with Sims. They went out at the same time, and by the time Charlie reached the sidewalk, Miles and Sims were heading in opposite directions. Charlie made an instant decision to go after Miles, and he called after him to stop. Miles ignored him and reached the squad car.

Charlie picked up his pace, reaching Miles's car just as it was pulling out on the street. He tapped the window even as the car was still moving.

"What's going on?" Charlie demanded.

Miles waved him out of the way, and Charlie froze

with a look of confusion and disbelief. Instead of rolling down the window, Miles flicked on the siren, hit the gas, and tore out of the parking lot, his tires squealing as he turned onto the street.

A minute later, when Charlie called on the radio, demanding that Miles let him know what had happened, Miles didn't bother to respond.

From the sheriff's department, it normally took less than fifteen minutes to reach the Timson compound. With the siren blaring and the squad car speeding, it took less than eight minutes—he was already halfway there by the time Charlie had reached him by radio. On the highway, he hit ninety miles an hour, and by the time he reached the turnoff to the mobile home where Otis lived, his adrenaline was pumping. He was holding the wheel hard enough to make parts of his hands go numb, though in his state he didn't realize it. Rage was surging through him, blocking out everything else.

Otis Timson had hurt his son with a brick.

Otis Timson had killed his wife.

Otis Timson had nearly gotten away with it.

On the dirt drive, Miles's car slid from side to side as he accelerated again. The trees he flew past were a blur; he saw nothing but the road directly in front of him, and as it veered to the right, Miles finally removed his foot from the accelerator and began to slow the car. He was almost there.

For two years, Miles had waited for this moment.

For two years, he'd tortured himself, lived through the failure.

*Otis.*

A moment later, Miles brought the car to a skidding halt in the center of the compound and pushed his way out of the car. Standing by the open door, he surveyed the area, watching for movement, watching for anything at all. His jaw was clenched as he tried to keep control.

He unsnapped his holster and began moving for his gun.

*Otis Timson had killed his wife.*

*He'd run her down in cold blood.*

It was ominously quiet. Aside from the ticking of the engine as it cooled, there were no other sounds at all. Trees were motionless, their branches absolutely still. No birds sat chirping on fenceposts. The only sounds that Miles could hear were his own: the rustle of the gun sliding out of his holster, the harsh rhythm of his breathing.

It was cold, the air crisp and cloudless, a spring sky on a winter day.

Miles waited. In time, a screened door cracked open, squeaking like a rusty squeezebox.

"What do you want?" a voice rang out. The sound was raspy, as if ravaged by years of smoking unfiltered cigarettes. Clyde Timson.

Miles lowered himself, using the car door as a shield in case shots broke out.

"I'm here for Otis. Bring him out."

The hand vanished and the door slapped shut.

Miles slipped the safety off and found his hand on the trigger, his heart thumping hard. After the longest minute of his life, he saw the door creak open again, pushed by the same anonymous hand.

"What's the charge?" the voice demanded.

"Get him out here, *now*!"

"What for?"

"He's under arrest! Now get him out here! Hands above his head!"

The door slammed shut again, and with that, Miles suddenly realized the precarious nature of his position. In his haste, he'd put himself in danger. There were four mobile homes—two in front, one off to each side—and though he'd seen no one in the others, he knew there were people inside. There were also countless junked cars, a few on blocks, between the homes, and he couldn't help but wonder whether the Timsons were stalling for time, closing in around him.

Part of him knew he should have brought help with him; he should call for help now. He didn't.

No way. Not now.

In time, the door pushed open again and Clyde appeared on the doorstep. His hands were by his side; in one hand he held a cup of coffee, as if things like this happened every day. When he saw Miles's gun pointed at him, however, he took a small step backward.

"What the hell do you want, Ryan? Otis ain't done nothin'."

"I've got to bring him in, Clyde."

"You still ain't said what for yet."

"He'll be charged when he gets to the station."

"Where's your warrant?"

"I don't need a warrant for this! He's under arrest."

"A man's got rights! You can't come barging in here and making demands. I got rights! And if you ain't got no warrant, you get the hell out of here! We've had enough of you and your charges!"

"I'm not kidding around, Clyde. Get him out here or I'll have every sheriff in the county here in a couple of minutes and you'll all be under arrest for harboring a criminal."

It was a bluff, but somehow it worked. A moment later, Otis appeared from behind the door and nudged his father. Miles shifted the gun, taking aim at Otis. Like his father, he didn't seem particularly worried.

"Step aside, Daddy," Otis said calmly. The sight of Otis's face made Miles want to pull the trigger. Biting back the wave of choking rage, he raised himself, keeping the gun pointed at Otis. He began moving around the car, into open view.

"Out here! I want you on the ground!"

Otis moved in front of his father but stayed on the porch. He crossed his arms. "What's the charge, Deputy Ryan?"

"You know damn well what the charge is! Now put your hands in the air."

"I'm afraid I don't."

Despite the possible danger, which suddenly didn't matter at all, Miles continued to approach the house, his gun still pointing at Otis. His finger was on the trigger and he could feel it tightening.

*Make a move . . . Just make a move . . .*

"Get down off the porch!"

Otis glanced at his father, who looked ready to erupt, but when he turned back to Miles, he saw an uncontrollable fury in Miles's eyes that made him step down quickly from the porch.

"All right, all right—I'm coming."

"Hands up! Let me see your hands in the air."

By now, a few others had poked their heads out of their mobile homes and were watching what was going on. Though rarely on the right side of the law, none of them considered running for his gun. They too saw the look in Miles's face, the one that made it clear that he was looking for any excuse to shoot.

"Get on your knees! *Now!*"

Otis did as he was told, but Miles didn't holster his gun. Instead he kept it pointed at Otis. He glanced from side to side, making sure that no one would stop him from what he was about to do, and closed the gap between them.

*Otis had killed his wife.*

As he approached, the rest of the world seemed to vanish. It was just the two of them now. There was fear and something else—weariness?—in Otis's eyes, but he said nothing. Miles paused as they stared at each other, then he began moving slowly around him, to the back.

He inched the gun closer to Otis's head.

Like an executioner.

He could feel the trigger under his finger. One tug, one quick pull, and this would be over.

God, he wanted to shoot him, he wanted to end this now. He owed it to Missy, he owed it to Jonah.

*Jonah . . .*

The sudden image of his son brought a burst of reality to what was happening.

No . . .

Still, he debated for a couple of breaths before finally exhaling hard. He reached for his handcuffs and slipped them from his belt. With a practiced move, he slipped one of the cuffs around the nearest of Otis's upraised wrists, then moved his hand behind Otis's back. After holstering his gun, he slipped on the other cuff, locked them both down until Otis winced, then pulled him up.

"You have the right to remain silent . . . ," he began, and Clyde, who'd been frozen in place, suddenly exploded into activity, like an anthill that had been stepped on.

"This ain't right. I'm calling my lawyer! You've got no right coming in here like this and pointing your gun that way!"

He continued to scream long after Miles had finished with the Miranda warning, loaded Otis into the back of his car, and started toward the highway.

In the car, neither Miles nor Otis spoke until they'd reached the highway. Miles's eyes remained locked on the road. Despite the fact that he had Otis in custody, he didn't want to so much as glance in the rearview mirror at Otis for fear of what he would do to him.

He'd wanted to shoot him.

With God as his witness, he'd wanted to do it.

And one wrong move, from anyone who'd been out there, and he would have.

*But that would have been wrong.*

*And you were wrong in the way you handled it out there.*

How many regulations had he broken? Half a dozen? Letting Sims go, failing to obtain a warrant, ignoring Charlie, not requesting help, pulling his gun straight off, putting it to Otis's head . . . He was going to catch hell for this, and not only from Charlie. Harvey Wellman, too. The yellow broken lines came at him, passing rhythmically from sight.

*I don't care. Otis is going to jail, no matter what happens to me. Otis will rot away in prison like he made me rot for two years.*

"So what are you bringing me in for this time?" Otis asked flatly.

"Shut the hell up," Miles responded.

"I have a right to know what the charge is."

Miles turned around, stifling the anger that bubbled up in him at the sound of Otis's voice. When Miles made no response, Otis continued, oddly calm.

"I'll let you in on a little secret. I knew you weren't going to shoot. You just couldn't do it."

Miles bit his lip, his face turning red. Keep control, he told himself. Keep control . . .

Otis, however, went on.

"Tell me, are you still seeing that girl you were with at the Tavern? I was just wondering, because—"

Miles slammed on the brakes, the wheels screeching, black scars left on the highway. Because he was unbuckled, Otis shot forward into the safety cage. Miles pressed the accelerator to the floor again, and like a yo-yo, Otis was flung back into his seat.

For the rest of the ride, Otis didn't say another word.

# Chapter 20

"So what the hell is going on?" Charlie demanded.

A few minutes earlier, Miles had shown up with Otis and had walked him through the station down to one of the holding cells. After locking him in, Otis asked to see his lawyer, but Miles simply headed back up the stairs to Charlie's office. Charlie closed the door behind them; other sheriffs stole quick glances through the window, trying their best to hide their curiosity.

"I think that seems pretty obvious, doesn't it?" Miles answered.

"This isn't the time or place for jokes, Miles. I need some answers and I need them now, starting with Sims. I want to know where the paperwork is, why you let him go, and what the hell he meant by this matter of life and death. And then, I want answers as to why you went charging out of here and why Otis is locked up downstairs."

Charlie crossed his arms and leaned against the desk.

Over the next fifteen minutes, Miles told him what had happened. Charlie's jaw dropped open, and by the end, he was pacing around the office.

"When did all this happen?"

"A couple of years ago. Sims didn't remember exactly."

"But you believed the rest of it?"

Miles nodded. "Yeah," he said. "I believed him. Either he was telling the truth, or he's the best actor I've ever seen." In the wake of the adrenaline rush that was slowly dissipating, Miles felt tired.

"So you let him go." A statement, not a question.

"I had to."

Charlie shook his head, closing his eyes for a moment. "That wasn't your call to make. You should have come to me first."

"You had to have been there, Charlie. He wouldn't have said anything at all if I started running around here, trying to cut deals with you and Harvey. I made a judgment call. You might think I was wrong, but in the end I got the answer I needed."

Charlie looked out the window, thinking. He didn't like it. Not at all. And not just the fact that Miles had overstepped his bounds and there was a whole lot of explaining to do.

"You got an answer all right," he said finally.

Miles looked up. "What's that supposed to mean?"

"It just doesn't sound right, that's all. He knows

267

he's going back to jail unless he can cut a deal, and he suddenly has information about Missy?" He turned to face Miles. "Where was he the last couple of years? There's been a reward, and you know how Sims earns his money. Why hasn't he come forward before now?"

He hadn't thought of that. "I don't know. Maybe he was afraid."

Charlie's eyes darted toward the ground. *Or maybe he's lying now.*

Miles seemed to read Charlie's mind.

"Look, we'll go talk to Earl Getlin. If he corroborates the story, we could cut a deal so he testifies."

Charlie said nothing. Christ, this was a mess.

"He ran down my wife, Charlie."

"*Sims says* that *Otis said* he ran down your wife. There's a big difference between the two, Miles."

"You know my history with Otis."

Charlie turned, holding up his hands. "Of course I do. I know every part of it. And that's why Otis's alibi was among the first we checked out, or don't you remember that? There were witnesses that put him at his house the night of the accident."

"They were his brothers . . ."

Charlie shook his head in frustration. "Even though you weren't in on the investigation, you know how hard we looked for an answer. We aren't a bunch of buffoons running around here, and neither are the men at the highway patrol. We all know how to investigate a crime, and we did it right, because we wanted the answer as badly as you did. We talked to the right people, we sent the right information into the state labs. But nothing tied Otis to this thing—nothing."

"You don't know that."

"I'm a lot more sure of it than I am of what you're telling me," he answered. He drew a deep breath. "I know this thing has eaten you up since it happened, and you know what? It's eaten me up, too. And if it had happened to me, I would have acted the same way you are. I would have gone crazy had someone run down Brenda and gotten away with it. I probably would have looked for answers on my own, too. But you know what?"

He stopped, making sure that Miles was listening to him.

"I wouldn't have believed the first story that came my way that promised an answer, especially if it was from a guy like Sims Addison. Think about who you're talking about here. *Sims Addison*. That guy would turn on his own mother if he could get money for it. When his own freedom is at stake, how far do you think he'd be willing to go?"

"This isn't about Sims—"

"Of course it is. He didn't want to go back to prison, and he was willing to say anything to ensure that. Doesn't that make more sense than what you're telling me?"

"He wouldn't lie to me about this."

Charlie met Miles's gaze. "And why not? Because it's too personal? Because it means too much? Because it's too important? Did you ever stop to think that he knew what it would take to get you to let him out of here? He's not stupid, despite his boozing habit. He'd say anything to get himself out of trouble, and from the looks of it, that's exactly what happened."

"You weren't there when he told me. You didn't see his face."

"No? To tell you the truth, I don't think I had to be there. I can imagine exactly how it went. But let's just say you're right, okay? Say Sims was telling you the truth—and let's totally disregard the fact that you were wrong in letting him go without talking to me or to Harvey, okay? Then what? You said that he overheard people talking. That he wasn't even a witness."

"He doesn't have to be."

"Oh, come on, Miles. You know the rules. In court, that's nothing more than hearsay. You don't have a case."

"Earl Getlin can testify."

"Earl Getlin? Who's gonna believe him? One look at his tattoos and his rap sheet and there goes half the jury. Throw in the deal I'm sure he'll want, and there goes the other half." He paused. "But you're forgetting something important, Miles."

"What's that?"

"What if Earl doesn't back it up?"

"He will."

"But what if he doesn't?"

"Then we'll have to get Otis to confess."

"And you think he'll do that?"

"He'll confess."

"You mean if you lean on him hard enough . . ."

Miles stood up, not wanting to listen anymore. "Look, Charlie—Otis killed Missy, it's as simple as that. You might not want to believe it, but maybe you guys did overlook something back then, and I'll be damned if I'm going to let it go now." He reached for the door. "I've got a prisoner to interrogate—"

With a swing, Charlie caught the door, closing it.

"I don't think so, Miles. Right now, I think it would be best if you stay out of this for a little while."

"Stay out of it?"

"Yeah. *Stay. Out. Of. It.* That's an order. I'll take it from here."

"We're talking about Missy, Charlie."

"No. We're talking about a deputy who over-stepped his bounds and shouldn't have gotten involved in the first place."

They stood eye to eye for a long moment before

Charlie finally shook his head. "Look, Miles, I understand what you're going through, but you're out of it now. I'll talk to Otis, I'll find Sims and talk to him, too. And I'll make a trip up to see Earl. And as for you, I think you should probably head on home. Take the rest of the day off."

"I just started my shift—"

"And now you're finished." Charlie reached for the doorknob. "Now go on, go home. Let me handle this, okay?"

He still didn't like it.

Twenty minutes later, sitting in his office, Charlie wasn't convinced.

He'd been a sheriff for almost thirty years, and he'd learned to trust his instincts. And his instincts now were flashing like strobe lights, cautioning him to be careful.

Right now, he wasn't even sure quite where to start. Otis Timson, probably, since he was downstairs, but he really wanted to talk to Sims first. Miles said he was certain that Sims was telling the truth, but for Charlie, that wasn't quite enough.

Not now. Not in these circumstances.

Not when it was about Missy.

Charlie had witnessed firsthand the struggle that Miles went through after Missy died. God, they'd been in love. Like two young kids, they couldn't keep their eyes and hands off each other. Hugging and kissing, holding hands, flirty looks—it was like no one ever bothered to tell them that marriage was supposed to be hard. It hadn't even changed when Jonah came along, for God's sake. Brenda used to joke that Miles and Missy would probably be making out in a nursing home, fifty years from now.

And when she died? If it wasn't for Jonah, Miles probably would have joined her. As it was, he practically killed himself anyway. Drinking too much, smoking, losing sleep, losing weight. For a long time, all he could think about was the crime.

The crime. Not an accident. Not in Miles's mind. Always the *crime*.

Charlie tapped a pencil on the desk.

*Here we go again.*

He knew all about Miles's investigation, and despite his better judgment, he'd looked the other way. Harvey Wellman had cursed up and down when he'd learned about it, but so what? They both knew Miles wouldn't have stopped his search, no matter what Charlie had said; if it had come right down to it, Miles would have turned in his badge and kept investigating on his own.

He had, though, been able to keep him away from Otis Timson. Thank God for that. There was something between those two, something more than the normal tension between good guys and bad guys. All those stunts the Timsons had pulled—Charlie didn't need proof to know who'd done it—were a big part of it. But combine it with Miles's tendency to arrest the Timsons first and figure the rest out later, and it became a combustible mix.

Could Otis have run down Missy Ryan?

Charlie pondered that. Possible . . . but though Otis had something of a chip on his shoulder and got into a few fights, he had never crossed the line. So far. At least that they could prove. Besides, they'd quietly checked him out. Miles had insisted on it, but Charlie was already a step ahead of him. Was it possible they'd missed something?

He grabbed a pad and, as was his habit, started jotting down his thoughts, trying to keep them straight.

*Sims Addison. Was he lying?*

He'd given good information in the past. In fact, it had always been good. But this was different. He wasn't doing this for money now, and the stakes were a lot higher. He was doing it to save himself. Did that make him more likely to tell the truth? Or less?

Charlie had to have a talk with him. Today, if possible. Tomorrow at the latest.

Back to the pad. He jotted the next name.

*Earl Getlin. What was he going to say?*

If he didn't corroborate, end of subject. Let Otis out of jail and spend the next year convincing Miles that Otis was innocent—at least of this particular crime. But if he did corroborate, then what? With his record, he wasn't exactly the most believable witness in the world. And he'd no doubt want something in return, which never played well to the jury.

Either way, Charlie had to talk to him right away.

Charlie moved Earl to the top of the list and jotted another name.

*Otis Timson. Guilty or not?*

If he'd killed Missy, Sims's story made sense, but then what? Hold him while they investigated openly this time, looking for additional evidence? Let him go and do the same thing? No matter what, Harvey wouldn't look too kindly on a case that relied solely on Sims Addison and Earl Getlin. But after two years, what could they hope to find?

He had to look into it, no doubt about it. As much as he didn't think they'd find anything, he'd have to start the investigation again. For Miles. For himself.

Charlie shook his head.

Okay, assuming Sims was telling the truth and Earl backed him up—a big assumption, but possible— why would Otis have said it? The obvious answer was that he'd said it because he'd done it. If so, it was back to the problems of building a case again. But . . .

It took a moment for the thought to coalesce into the form of a question.

But what if Sims was telling the truth? And what if Otis was lying that night?

Is that possible?

Charlie closed his eyes, thinking.

If so, why?

For his reputation? *Look what I did and got away with . . .*

To scare Earl into getting the money? *This will happen to you, unless . . .*

Or had he meant to say that he'd simply arranged it but hadn't done the dirty work himself?

His thoughts circled and zigzagged from one extreme to the next as he considered them.

But how the hell would he have known she'd be out jogging that night?

This whole thing was a mess.

Getting nowhere, he set aside the pencil and rubbed his temples, knowing there was more to consider than the situation with just those three.

What was he going to do about Miles?

His friend. His deputy.

Cutting a deal with Sims and losing the paper-work? Letting him go? Then charging out like this was the Wild West to bring Otis to justice without even bothering to talk to Earl Getlin?

Harvey wasn't a bad guy, but he was going to have problems with this. Serious problems.

*They all were.*

Charlie sighed. "Hey, Madge?" he called out.

The secretary popped her head into the office. Plump and graying, she'd been around almost as long as he had and knew everything that went on in the department. He wondered if she'd been listening.

"Is Joe Hendricks still the warden up at Hailey?"

"I think it's Tom Vernon, now."

"That's right," Charlie said, nodding, remembering he'd read about it somewhere. "Can you look up the number for me?"

"Sure. Let me get it. It's in the Rolodex on my desk."

She was back in less than a minute, and when Charlie took the slip, she stood for a moment, not liking the look in his eyes. She waited to see if he wanted to talk about it.

He didn't.

It took almost ten minutes to get Tom Vernon on the phone.

"Earl Getlin? Yeah, he's still here," Vernon answered.

Charlie was doodling on the paper in front of him. "I need to talk to him."

"Official business?"

"You could say that."

"No problem from this end. When are you planning to come up?"

"Would it be possible this afternoon?"

"That fast, huh? Must be serious."

"It is."

"All right. I'll send word down that you're coming. What time do you think you'll make it?"

Charlie checked his watch. A little after eleven. If he skipped lunch, he could be there by midafternoon.

"How about two o'clock?"

"You got it. I assume you'll need someplace to talk to him alone."

"If that's possible."

"It's no problem. See you then."

Charlie hung up the phone, and as he was reaching for his jacket, Madge peeked in.

"Are you heading up there?"

"Have to," Charlie said.

"Listen, while you were on the phone, Thurman Jones called. He needs to talk to you."

Otis Timson's attorney.

Charlie shook his head. "If he calls again, tell him that I'll be back around six or so. He can reach me then."

Madge shuffled her feet. "He said it was important. That it couldn't wait."

278

Lawyers. If they wanted to talk, it was important. If he needed to reach them, it was another story.

"Did he say what it was about?"

"Not to me. But he sounded angry."

Of course he did. His client was behind bars and hadn't been charged yet. No matter—Charlie had the right to hold him for now, anyway. The clock was ticking, though.

"I don't have time to deal with him now. Tell him to call later."

Madge nodded, her lips together. There was more she seemed to want to say.

"Anything else?"

"A few minutes later, Harvey called, too. He needs to talk to you as well. He says it's urgent."

Charlie slipped into his jacket, thinking, Of course he did. On a day like today, what else could I have expected?

"If he calls back, give him the same message."

"But—"

"Just do it, Madge. I don't have time to argue." Then, after a moment: "Have Harris come in here for a second. I've got something for him to take care of."

Madge's expression made it clear she didn't like his decision, but she did as she was told. Harris Young, a deputy, came into the office.

"I need you to find Sims Addison for me. And I need you to watch him."

Harris looked a little uncertain of what he was being asked to do. "Do you want me to bring him in?"

"No," Charlie said. "Just find him for me. And baby-sit him. But don't let him know you're there."

"For how long?"

"I'll be back around six, so at least until then."

"That's almost my whole shift."

"I know."

"What do I do if I get a call and have to leave?"

"Don't. Your job today is Sims. I'll call and get another deputy in here today to cover for you."

"All day?"

Charlie winked, knowing that Harris would be bored out of his mind. "You got it, Deputy. Ain't working law enforcement grand?"

Miles didn't go home after leaving Charlie's office. Instead he drove around town, drifting from one turn to the next, making a haphazard circuit through New Bern. He didn't concentrate on his route, but propelled by instinct, he soon found himself approaching the marlstone archway of Cedar Grove Cemetery.

He parked the car and got out, then wove his way among the headstones, toward Missy's grave. Set against the small marble marker there was a batch of flowers, dried and withered, as if they'd been placed there a few weeks back. But there were always flowers here, no matter when he seemed to visit. They were never left with a card, but Miles understood that no card was necessary.

Missy, even in death, was still loved.

# Chapter 21

*T*wo weeks after Missy Ryan's funeral, I was lying in bed one morning when I heard a bird begin to chirp outside the window. I'd left it open the night before, hoping for a break in the heat and humidity. My sleep had been fitful since the accident; more than once, I awoke to find my body covered in sweat, the sheets damp and oily, the pillow soaked through. That morning was no different, and as I listened to the bird, the odor of perspiration, sweet ammonia, surrounded me.

I tried to ignore the bird, the fact that it was in the tree, the fact that I was still alive and Missy Ryan wasn't. But I wasn't able to. It was right outside my window, on a branch that overlooked my room, its call shrill and piercing. I know who you are, it seemed to say, and I know what you did.

I wondered when the police would come for me.

It didn't matter if it was an accident or not; the bird knew they would come, and it was telling me that they would be here soon. They would find out what kind of car had been driven that night; they would find out who owned it. There would be a knock at the door and they would come in; they would hear the bird and know I was guilty. It was ludicrous, I know, but in my half-crazed state, I believed it.

I knew they would come.

In my room, wedged between the pages of a book I kept in the drawer, I kept the obituary from the paper. I'd also saved the clippings about the accident, and they were folded neatly beside it. It was dangerous to have kept them. Anyone who happened to open the book would find them and would know what I had done, but I kept them because I needed to. I was drawn to the words, not for comfort, but to better understand what I had taken away. There was life in the words that were written, there was life in the photographs. In this room, on that morning with the bird outside my window, there was only death.

I'd had nightmares since the funeral. Once I dreamed that I'd been singled out by the preacher, who knew what I had done. In the middle of the service, I'd dreamed that he suddenly stopped talking and looked over the pews, then slowly raised his finger in my direction. "There," he said, "is the man who did this." I saw faces turn toward me, one after the other, like a wave in a crowded stadium, each focusing on me with looks of astonishment and anger. But neither Miles nor Jonah turned to look at me. The church was silent and eyes were wide; I sat without moving, waiting to see if Miles and Jonah would finally turn to see who had killed her. But they did not.

In the other nightmare, I dreamed that Missy was still alive in the ditch when I'd found her, that she was breathing raggedly and moaning, but that I turned and walked away, leaving her to die. I awoke nearly hyperventilating. I bounded from the bed and paced around the room as I talked to myself, until I was finally convinced it had been only a dream.

Missy had died of head trauma. I learned that in the article as well. A cerebral hemorrhage. As I said, I hadn't been driving fast, but the reports said she had somehow landed in a way that slammed her head against a protruding rock in the ditch. They called it a fluke, a one in a million occurrence.

I wasn't sure I believed it.

I wondered if Miles would suspect me on sight, whether, in some flash of divine inspiration, he would guess it was me. I wondered what I would say to him, if he confronted me. Would he care that I like to watch baseball games, or that my favorite color is blue, or that when I was seven, I used to sneak outside and study the stars, even though nobody would have guessed that about me? Would he like to know that until the moment I hit Missy with my car, I felt sure that I would eventually make something of myself?

No, he wouldn't care about those things. What he'd want to know was the obvious: He would want to know that the killer's hair is brown, that his eyes are green, that he's six feet tall. He would want to know where he could find me. And he would want to know how it happened.

Would he, though, like to hear that it was an accident? That if anything, it was more her fault than my own? That had she not been running at night on a dangerous road, more than likely she would have made it home? That she jumped right in front of my car?

Outside, I noticed that the bird stopped chirping. The trees were still, and I could hear the faint hum of a passing car. Already, it was getting hot again. Somewhere, I knew that Miles Ryan was awake, and I imagined him sitting in his kitchen. I imagined Jonah beside him, eating a bowl of cereal. I tried to imagine what they were saying to each other. But the only thing I could imagine was steady breathing, punctuated by the sounds of spoons clanking against the bowl.

I brought my hands to my temples, trying to rub the pain away. It seemed to throb from somewhere deep inside, stabbing me with fury, matching every heartbeat. In my mind's eye, I saw Missy in the road, her eyes open, staring up at me.

Staring at nothing at all.

# Chapter 22

Charlie made it to Hailey State Prison a little before two, his stomach growling, his eyes tired, and his legs feeling as if the blood had stopped flowing sometime about an hour ago. He was getting too old to sit for three hours without moving.

He should have retired last year, when Brenda told him to, so he could spend his time doing something productive. Like fishing.

Tom Vernon met him at the gates.

Dressed in a suit, he looked more like a banker than the warden of one of the toughest prisons in the state. His hair was parted neatly on the side and streaked with gray. He stood ramrod straight, and when he extended his hand, Charlie couldn't help but notice that his fingernails looked manicured.

Vernon led the way inside.

Like all prisons, it was drab, cold . . . concrete and steel everywhere, all bathed in fluorescent light. They made their way down a long hallway, past a small reception area, and finally into Vernon's office.

At first glance, it was as cold and drab as the rest of the place. Everything was government issue, from the desk to the lamps to the file cabinets in the corner. A small, barred window overlooked the yard. Outside, Charlie could see the prisoners milling about; some were lifting weights, others were sitting around or clustered in groups. Every other person, it seemed, was smoking.

Why on earth would Vernon wear a suit to a place like this?

"I just need you to fill out some forms," Vernon said. "You know how it is."

"Sure enough." Charlie tapped his chest, feeling for a pen. Vernon handed him one before he found it.

"Did you tell Earl Getlin that I was coming?"

"I assumed you didn't want me to."

"Is he ready for me yet?"

"Once we have you set up in the room, we'll bring him in."

"Thanks."

"I did want to talk to you for a second about the prisoner. Just so you're not surprised."

"Oh?"

"There's something you should know."

"And what's that?"

"Earl was in a scuffle last spring. Couldn't really get to the bottom of it—you know how things work in here. No one sees anything, no one knows anything. Anyway . . ."

Charlie looked up when Vernon sighed.

"Earl Getlin lost an eye. Had it gouged out in a brawl down in the yard. He's filed half a dozen lawsuits alleging that we were at fault somehow." Vernon paused.

Why is he telling me this? Charlie wondered.

"The point is, he's been saying all along that he didn't belong here in the first place. That he was set up." Vernon raised his hands. "I know, I know—everyone in here says they're innocent. That's an old song, and we've all heard it a million times. But the point is, if you're here to get information from him, I wouldn't get your hopes up, unless he thinks you can get him out of here. And even then, he might be lying."

Charlie looked at Vernon in a new light. For such a natty dresser, he sure as hell seemed to know a lot about what went on in his prison. Vernon handed him the forms, and Charlie scanned them for a moment. Same ones as always.

"Any idea who he says set him up?" he asked.

"Hold on," Vernon said, raising a finger. "I'll get that for you." He went to the phone on his desk, dialed a number, and waited until someone came on. He asked the question, listened, then thanked the person.

"From what we've heard, he says it was some guy named Otis Timson."

Charlie didn't know whether to laugh or cry.

Of course Earl blamed Otis.

That made one part of his job a whole lot easier.

But the other part suddenly became that much harder.

Even if he hadn't lost an eye, prison had been less kind to Earl Getlin than most people. His hair looked hacked off in places, longer in others, as if he did it himself with a pair of rusty scissors, and his skin had taken on a sallow color. Always on the thin side, he'd lost weight and Charlie could see the bones under the skin of his hands.

But most of all, he noticed the patch. Black, like a pirate, like a bad guy in the old war movies.

Earl was manacled in the typical way, his wrists chained together and connected further to his ankles. He shuffled into the room, stopped for a moment as soon as he saw Charlie, then proceeded to take his seat. He sat across from him, a wooden table separating them.

After checking with Charlie, the guard backed quietly out of the room.

Earl stared with his one good eye. It seemed as if he had been practicing the stare, knowing that most people would be forced to look away. Charlie pretended not to notice the patch.

"Why are you here?" Earl growled. If his body looked weaker, his voice had lost none of its edge. He was wounded but wasn't about to give up. Charlie would have to keep an eye on him after he was released.

"I came to talk to you," Charlie said.

"About what?"

"About Otis Timson."

Earl stiffened at the name. "What about Otis?" he asked warily.

"I need to know about a conversation you had with him a couple of years back. You were waiting for him at the Rebel, and Otis and his brothers sat at your booth. Remember that?"

It wasn't what Earl seemed to have been expecting. He took a few seconds to process Charlie's words, then blinked.

"Refresh me," he said. "That was a long time ago."

"It concerned Missy Ryan. Does that help?"

Earl raised his chin slightly, looking down his nose. He glanced from one side to the other.

"That depends."

"On what?" Charlie asked innocently.

"On what's in it for me."

"What do you want?"

"Come on, Sheriff—don't play stupid. You know what I want."

He didn't have to say it. It was obvious to both of them.

"I can't make any promises unless I've listened to what you have to say."

Earl leaned back in his chair, playing it cool. "Then I guess we're in a bit of a bind, aren't we?"

Charlie looked at him. "Maybe," he said. "But I figure you'll tell me in the end."

"Why do you think that?"

"Because Otis set you up, right? You tell me what was said back then, and I'll listen to your side of events later. And when I get back to town, I promise to look into your story. If Otis set you up, we'll find out. And in the end, you two just might find yourselves trading places."

It was all Earl needed to talk.

"I owed him money," Earl said. "But I was a little short, you know?"

"How short?" Charlie asked.

Earl sniffed. "A few thousand."

Charlie knew the situation was illegal, most probably drug money. But he simply nodded, as if he knew this already and weren't concerned about it.

"And the Timsons come in. All of 'em. And they start telling me that I gotta pay up, that it's making 'em look bad, that they can't keep carrying me. I kept telling them that I'd give them the money as soon as I got it. Meanwhile, while all this is going on, Otis is real quiet, you know, like he's really listening to what I have to say. He had this sort of cool expression, but he was the only one who seemed to care about anything I was saying. So I start kind of explaining the situation to him and he starts nodding and the others pipe down. Right after I finished, I waited for him to say something, but he didn't say anything for a long while. Then he leans forward and he says that if I don't pay up, the same thing is gonna happen to me that happened to Missy Ryan. Except that this time, they'd run me over again."

Bingo.

So Sims was telling the truth. Interesting.

Charlie's face, though, showed nothing.

Either way, he knew that was the easy part. Getting him to talk about it wasn't what he was worried about anyway. He knew the hard part was still coming.

"When was this?"

Earl thought about it. "January, I guess. It was cold out."

"So you're there, sitting across from him, and he says this to you. How did you react when he said it?"

"I didn't know what to think. I know I didn't say anything."

"Did you believe him?"

"Of course." Big nod, as if emphasizing his point. *Too big?*

Charlie glanced toward his hand, examining his nails. "Why?"

Earl leaned forward, the chain clinking against the table. "Why else would he say something like that? Besides, you know what kind of guy he is. He'd do something like that in a heartbeat."

*Maybe. Maybe not.*

"Again, why do you think that?"

"You're the sheriff—you tell me."

"What I think isn't important. It's what you think that matters."

"I told you what I thought."

"You believed him."

"Yes," he said.

"And you thought he'd do the same to you?"

"He said it, didn't he?"

"So you were frightened, right?"

"Yes," he snapped.

*Getting impatient?*

"When did you get arrested? For stealing the car, I mean."

The change of subject threw Earl for a moment. "End of June."

Charlie nodded as if this made sense, as if he'd checked it out beforehand. "What do you like to drink? When you're not in prison, I mean."

293

"What does that matter?"

"Beer, wine, liquor. I'm just curious."

"Beer mainly."

"Were you drinking that night?"

"Just a couple. Not enough to be drunk."

"Before you got there? Maybe you were a little buzzed . . ."

Earl shook his head. "No, I had them while I was there."

"How long did you stay at the table with the Timsons?"

"What do you mean?"

"It's an easy question. Were you there for five minutes? Ten? Half an hour?"

"I can't remember."

"But long enough for a couple beers."

"Yeah."

"Even though you were afraid."

He finally saw what Charlie was getting at. Charlie waited patiently, his expression bland.

"Yeah," Earl said. "They're not the type of people you just walk away from."

"Oh," Charlie said. He seemed to accept that, and he brought his fingers to his chin. "Okay . . . so let me make sure I understand. Otis told you—no, suggested—that they killed Missy, and you thought they'd do the same to you because you owed them a bunch of money. So far, so good?"

Earl nodded warily. Charlie reminded him of that damn prosecutor who'd put him away.

"And you knew what they were talking about, right? With Missy, I mean. You knew she'd died, right?"

"Everyone knew."

"Did you read about it in the papers?"

"Yeah."

Charlie opened his palms. "So, why didn't you tell the police about it?"

"Yeah, right," he sneered. "Like you guys would have believed me."

"But we should believe you now."

"He said it. I was there. He said he killed Missy."

"Will you testify to that?"

"Depends on the deal I get."

Charlie cleared his throat. "Okay, let's change gears for a second. You got caught stealing a car, right?"

Earl nodded again.

"And Otis was responsible—you say—for you getting caught."

"Yeah. They were supposed to meet me out by the old Falls Mill, but they never showed. I ended up taking the fall."

Charlie nodded. He remembered that from the trial.

"Did you still owe him money?"

"Yeah."

"How much?"

Earl shifted in his seat. "A couple thousand."

"Isn't that what you owed before?"

"About the same."

"Were you still afraid they'd kill you? Even after six months?"

"It was all I could think about."

"And you wouldn't be here if it wasn't for them, right?"

"I told you that already."

Charlie leaned forward. "Then why," he asked, "didn't you try to use this information to lighten your sentence? Or put Otis away? And why, in all this time here when you were complaining that Otis set you up, did you never mention that he'd killed Missy Ryan?"

Earl sniffed again and glanced toward the wall.

"No one would have believed me," he finally answered.

*I wonder why.*

In the car, Charlie ran through the information again.

Sims was telling the truth about hearing what he'd heard. But Sims was a known alcoholic and was boozing that night.

He'd heard the words, but had he heard the tone?

Was Otis joking? Or serious?

Or lying?

And what had the Timsons talked about with Earl for the next thirty minutes?

Earl hadn't really cleared any of that up. It was obvious he didn't even remember the conversation until Charlie brought it up, and his account pretty much fell apart after that. He'd believed they would kill him, but he'd stayed for a few beers afterward. He'd been terrified for months, but not enough to scrounge up the money he owed, even though he stole cars and could have gotten the money. He'd said nothing when he'd been arrested. He blamed Otis for setting him up and blabbed to people in the prison about it, but he didn't mention the fact that Otis had confessed to killing someone. He'd lost an eye and still had said nothing. The reward had meant nothing to him.

A boozing alcoholic, providing information to get off free. A convict with a grudge, suddenly remembering critical information, but with serious holes and flaws in the story.

Any defense lawyer worth his salt would have a field day with both Sims Addison and Earl Getlin. And Thurman Jones was good. Real good.

Charlie hadn't stopped frowning since he'd been in the car.

He didn't like it.

Not at all.

But the fact was that Otis had indeed said "the same thing is gonna happen to you that happened to Missy Ryan." Two people had heard him, and that counted for something. Enough to hold him, maybe. At least for the time being.

But was it enough for a case?

And, most important, did any of it actually prove that Otis did it?

# Chapter 23

*I* couldn't escape that image of Missy Ryan, her eyes focused on nothing, and because of that, I became someone I'd never known before.

Six weeks after her death, I parked the car about half a mile away from my final destination, in the parking lot of a gas station. I made the rest of the way on foot.

It was late, a little past nine, and it was a Thursday. The September sun had set only half an hour earlier, and I knew enough to keep out of sight. I was wearing black and kept to the side of the road, going so far as to cower behind some bushes when I saw headlights closing in on me.

Despite my belt, I had to keep grabbing for my trousers, which kept slipping over my hips. I had begun doing that so frequently, I had stopped noticing, but on that evening, with branches and twigs pulling at them, I realized how much weight I had lost. Since the accident, I'd lost my appetite; even the idea of eating seemed to repulse me.

My hair, too, had begun to fall out. Not in clumps,

but in strands, as if decaying slowly but steadily, like termites ravaging a home. There would be strands on my pillow when I woke, and when I brushed my hair, I would have to use my fingers to clear the bristles before I finished or the brush would slide without catching. I would flush the hair down the toilet, watching it swirl downward, and once it was gone, I would flush again for no other reason than to postpone the reality of my life.

That night, as I was climbing through a hole in the fence, I cut my palm on a jagged nail. It hurt and it bled, but instead of turning around, I simply squeezed my hand into a fist and felt the blood seeping between my fingers, thick and sticky. I did not care about the pain that night, just as I do not care about the scar today.

I had to go. In the last week, I had gone to the site of Missy's accident and had also visited Missy's grave. At the grave, I remember, the headstone had been placed and there were still remnants of fresh earth, where the grass had yet to grow, almost like a small hole. It bothered me for a reason I couldn't quite explain, and that was where I set the flowers. Then, not knowing what else to do, I sat down and simply stared at the granite. The cemetery was mostly empty; in the distance, I could see a few people here and there, tending to their own business. I turned away, not caring if they saw me.

In the moonlight, I opened my hand. The blood was black and shone like oil. I closed my eyes, remembering

Missy, then moved forward again. It took half an hour to get there. Mosquitoes buzzed around my face. Toward the end of my trek, I had to cut across yards to stay off the road. The yards here are wide, the houses set far from the road, and it was easier going. My eyes were locked on my destination, and as I approached, I slowed down, careful not to make any sound. I could see light streaming from the windows. I saw a car parked in the driveway.

I knew where they'd lived; everyone did. This was a small town, after all. I had seen their house in the daytime, too; like the scene of the accident and Missy's grave, I'd been there before, though I'd never been this close. My breathing slowed as I reached the side of the house. I could smell the scent of freshly mowed grass.

I stopped, my hand pressed against the brick. I listened for squeaky floorboards, a movement toward the door, shadows flickering over the porch. No one seemed to realize I was there.

I inched my way to the living room window, then crept onto the porch, where I wedged myself into a corner, my body hidden from those who might pass on the road by an ivy-covered trellis. In the distance, I heard a dog begin to bark, then pause, then finally bark again to see if anything would stir. Curiously, I peeked in.

I saw nothing.

But I was unable to turn away. This is how they lived, I thought. Missy and Miles sat on that couch, they set their cups on that end table. Those are their pictures on

301

the wall. Those are their books. As I looked around, I noticed that the television was on, the sounds of conversation running together. The room was tidy, uncluttered, and for some reason, that made me feel better.

It was then that I saw Jonah enter the living room. I held my breath as he approached the television, since he was nearing me as well, but he never looked my way. Instead he sat, crossing his legs, and stared at the program without moving, as if hypnotized.

I pressed a little closer against the glass to see him better. He had grown in the past two months, not much, but noticeable. Though it was late, he was still in jeans and his shirt, not in his pajamas. I heard him laugh, and my heart nearly burst in my chest.

That was when Miles came into the room. I pulled back into the shadows, but still I watched him. He stood there for a long moment, watching his son, saying nothing. His expression was void, unreadable . . . hypnotized. He held a manila file in his hands, and a moment later, I saw him glance at his watch. His hair on one side was puffed out, as if he'd been running his hands through it.

I knew what would happen next, and I waited. He'd start talking to his son. He'd ask what Jonah was watching. Or, because it was a school night, he'd say something about Jonah having to go to bed or putting his pajamas on. He'd ask if he wanted a cup of milk or a snack.

But he didn't.

*Instead, Miles simply passed through the living room and vanished into a darkened hallway, almost as if he'd never been there at all.*

*A minute later I crept away.*

*I didn't sleep the rest of the night.*

# Chapter 24

Miles made it home at the same time Charlie was pulling up at Hailey State Prison, and the first thing he did was head to his bedroom.

Not to sleep. Instead, from the closet where he'd hidden it, he retrieved the manila file.

There, he spent the next few hours flipping and turning the pages, studying the information. There was nothing new, nothing he'd overlooked in the past, but still, he found it impossible to put down.

Now, he knew what to look for.

Sometime later, he heard the phone ring; he didn't answer it. It rang again twenty minutes later, with the same result. At his usual time, Jonah got off the bus, and seeing his father's car, he went home instead of to Mrs. Knowlson's. He scrambled into the bedroom excitedly because he hadn't expected to see his father until later and thought they could do something together before he went out with Mark. But he saw the file and knew immediately what that meant. Though they talked for a few moments, Jonah sensed his father's need to be alone and didn't bother asking for anything. He wandered back to the living room and turned on the television.

The afternoon sun began to sink; at dusk, Christmas lights throughout the neighborhood began twinkling. Jonah checked on his father, even spoke from the doorway, but Miles never looked up.

Jonah had a bowl of cereal for dinner.

Still, Miles scoured the file. He jotted questions and notes in the margins, beginning with Sims and Earl and the need to get them to testify. Then he turned to the pages that dealt with the investigation of Otis Timson, wishing he'd been there in the first place. More questions, more notes. *Did they check every car on the property for damage—even the junked ones? Could he have borrowed one, and from where? Would someone at an auto parts shop remember if Otis ever bought an emergency kit? Where would they have disposed of the car if it had been damaged? Call other departments— see if any illegal chop shops had been closed down within the last couple of years. Interview, if possible. Cut a deal if they can recall something.*

A little before eight o'clock, Jonah came back into the bedroom, dressed and ready to go to the movies with Mark. Miles had forgotten about the outing completely. Jonah kissed him good-bye and headed out; Miles went straight back to the file without asking when he'd be back.

He didn't hear Sarah come in until she called his name from the living room.

"Hello? . . . Miles? Are you here?"

A moment later she appeared in the doorway, and Miles suddenly remembered that they were supposed to have a date.

"Didn't you hear me knock?" she asked. "I was freezing out there, waiting for you to answer, and I finally just gave up. Did you forget that I was coming over?"

When he looked up, she saw the distracted, distant look in his eyes. His hair looked as if he'd been running his hand through it for hours.

"Are you okay?" she asked.

Miles started shuffling the papers back together. "Yeah . . . I'm fine. I've just been working . . . I'm sorry . . . I lost track of time."

She recognized the file and her brow arched up. "What's going on?" she asked.

Seeing Sarah made him realize how exhausted he felt. His neck and back were stiff, and he felt as if he were coated in a thin layer of dust. He closed the file and set it aside, his mind still on the contents. He rubbed his face with both hands, then looked at her over his fingers.

"Otis Timson was arrested today," he said.

"Otis? What for?"

Before she'd finished her question, she suddenly

306

realized the answer, and she inhaled sharply.

"Oh . . . Miles," she said, moving toward him instinctively. Miles, aching everywhere, stood up and she slipped her arms around him. "Are you sure you're okay?" she whispered, holding him tight.

As he embraced her, everything he'd felt during the day came rushing back. The mixture of disbelief, anger, frustration, rage, fear, and exhaustion magnified the renewed feelings of loss, and for the first time that day, Miles gave in to them all. Standing in the room with Sarah's arms around him, Miles broke down, the tears coming as though he'd never cried before.

Madge was waiting for Charlie when he got back to the station. Normally off at five, she stayed for an extra hour and a half waiting for him. She was standing in the parking lot, her arms crossed, hugging her long wool jacket against her.

Charlie stepped out of the car and brushed the crumbs from his pants. He'd grabbed a burger and fries on the way home, washing it all down with a cup of coffee.

"Madge? What are you still doing here?"

"Waiting for you," she answered. "I saw you pull up and I wanted to talk to you out of earshot."

Charlie reached into the car and grabbed his hat. In the chill, he needed one. He didn't have enough hair anymore to keep his head warm.

"So what's up?"

Before she answered, a deputy pushed through the door and Madge looked over her shoulder. Buying time, she said simply, "Brenda called."

"Is she okay?" Charlie asked, playing along.

"Fine, as far as I can tell. She wants you to give her a call, though."

The deputy nodded at Charlie as he strode past. Once he was near his car, Madge moved a little closer.

"I think there's a problem," Madge said quietly.

"With what?"

She motioned over her shoulder. "Thurman Jones is waiting for you inside. So is Harvey Wellman."

Charlie looked at her, knowing there was more.

"They both want to talk to you," she said.

"And?"

Again she looked around, making sure they were alone. "They're here together, Charlie. They want to talk to you together."

Charlie simply stared at her, trying to anticipate what she was going to say, knowing he wouldn't like it. Prosecutors and defense attorneys got together only under the most dire circumstances.

"It's about Miles," she said. "I think he might have done something out there. Something that he shouldn't have."

\*    \*    \*

Thurman Jones was fifty-three, of average height and weight, with wavy brown hair that always looked windblown. He wore navy suits, dark knit ties, and black running shoes while in court, which gave him a sort of country bumpkin appearance. When in court, he spoke slowly and clearly and never lost his cool, and that combination, along with his appearance, played extremely well to a jury. Why he represented the likes of Otis Timson and his family was beyond Charlie, but he did and he had for years.

Harvey Wellman, on the other hand, dressed in tailored suits and Cole-Haan shoes and always looked as if he were heading off to a wedding. At thirty, he had begun to go gray at the temples; now, at forty, his hair was nearly silver, giving him a distinguished appearance. In another life, he could have been a news anchor. Or maybe a funeral director.

Neither one of them looked happy as they waited outside Charlie's office.

"You two wanted to see me?" Charlie asked.

They both stood.

"It's important, Charlie," Harvey answered.

Charlie led them into the office and closed the door. He motioned to a couple of seats, but neither of them accepted. Charlie moved behind his desk, putting a little space between him and the visitors.

"So what can I do for you?"

"We've got a problem, Charlie," Harvey said

simply. "It concerns the arrest this morning. I tried to talk to you earlier, but you were already out."

"Sorry about that. I had to take care of some business out of town. What's this problem you're referring to?"

Harvey Wellman met Charlie's gaze directly. "It seems that Miles Ryan went a little too far."

"Oh?"

"We've got witnesses. A lot of witnesses. And they're all saying the same thing."

Charlie said nothing, and Harvey cleared his throat before going on. Thurman Jones stood off to the side, his expression blank. Charlie knew he was taking in every word.

"He put his gun to Otis Timson's head."

Later, in the living room, Miles was nursing a beer and absently peeling the label as he told Sarah everything that had happened. Like his own feelings, the story came out jumbled at times. He jumped from one point in the story to another, then backtracked, repeating himself more than once. Sarah never interrupted, never looked away, and though there were moments in which he was unclear, she didn't press him to clarify for the simple reason that she wasn't sure he could.

Unlike with Charlie, however, Miles went further. "You know, for the past two years, I've wondered

310

what would happen when I came face-to-face with the guy who did it. And when I found out it was Otis . . . I don't know . . ." He paused. "I wanted to pull the trigger. I wanted to kill him."

Sarah shifted, not knowing what to say. It was understandable, at least on some level, but . . . a little frightening, too.

"But you didn't," she finally said.

Miles didn't notice the tentativeness of her answer. His mind was back there, with Otis.

"So now what happens?" she asked.

His hand went to the back of his neck and he squeezed. Despite how emotionally caught up he was in this, the logical side of him knew they'd need more than they had now. "There's got to be an investigation—witnesses to interview, places to check out. It's a lot of work, and it's harder now that time has passed. I'm gonna be busy for I don't know how long. Lot of late nights, lot of weekends. It's back to where it was a couple of years ago."

"Didn't Charlie say he was going to handle this?"

"Yeah, but not like I would."

"Are you allowed to do that?"

"I don't have a choice."

It wasn't the time or place to discuss his role, and she let it go.

"Are you hungry?" she asked instead. "I can throw

311

something together in the kitchen for us. Or we can order a pizza?"

"No. I'm fine."

"You want to go for a walk?"

He shook his head. "Not really."

"You up for a movie? I grabbed a video on my way over."

"Yeah . . . sure."

"Don't you want to know what it is?"

"It doesn't really matter. Whatever you picked up is fine."

She rose from the couch and found the movie. A comedy, it succeeded in making Sarah laugh a couple of times, and she glanced over at Miles to see his reaction. There wasn't one. After an hour, Miles excused himself to go to the bathroom. When he didn't come back in a few minutes, Sarah went to make sure he was okay.

She found him in the bedroom, the manila folder open beside him.

"I just have to check something," he said. "It'll only take a minute."

"Okay," she answered.

He didn't come back.

Long before it was over, Sarah stopped the movie and ejected it, then found her jacket. She peeked in on him once more—not knowing that Jonah had done the same thing—then slipped quietly from the house. Miles didn't realize she'd left until Jonah got back from the movies.

Charlie was in the office until almost midnight. Like Miles, he was looking over the case file and wondering what he was going to do.

It had taken quite a bit of cajoling to cool Harvey down, especially after he threw in the incident in Miles's car as well. Not surprisingly, Thurman Jones remained fairly quiet throughout it all. Charlie guessed that he thought it would be better if Harvey did the talking for him. He did, however, flash the tiniest of smiles when Harvey said that he was seriously considering bringing Miles up on charges.

That was when Charlie told them why Otis had been arrested in the first place.

Seemed that Miles hadn't bothered to tell Otis what the charge was. They were going to have a serious heart-to-heart the following day—if Charlie didn't wring his neck first.

But in the presence of Harvey and Thurman, Charlie acted as if he'd known all along.

"No reason to start flinging accusations when I wasn't sure they were even warranted."

As expected, both Harvey and Thurman had problems with that. They had further problems with Sims's story, until Charlie told them he'd met with Earl Getlin.

"And he confirmed the whole thing" was how he phrased it.

He wasn't about to tell Thurman about his doubts, nor was he willing to share them with Harvey just yet. As soon as he'd finished, Harvey gave him a look that meant they should meet later to talk in private. Charlie, knowing he needed more time to digest things, pretended not to notice.

They did spend a great deal of time talking about Miles after Charlie finished. Charlie had no doubts that Miles had done exactly what was described, and though he was . . . *upset*, to put it mildly, he'd known Miles long enough to know that it wasn't out of character in a situation like this. But Charlie hid his anger, even as he kept his defense of Miles to a minimum.

In the end, Harvey recommended that Miles be placed on suspension for the time being, while they sorted everything out.

Thurman Jones asked that Otis either be released or charged right away, without further delays.

Charlie told them that Miles was already gone for the day, but that he would make a decision on both counts first thing in the morning.

Somehow, he hoped things would be clearer by then.

But they wouldn't be, as he discovered when he finally headed home.

314

Before he left the office, he got in touch with Harris at his house, asking how it went.

Turned out he hadn't been able to find Sims all day.

"How hard did you look?" Charlie snapped.

"I looked everywhere," Harris answered groggily. "His house, his mom's place, his hangouts. I went to every bar and liquor store in the county. He's gone."

Brenda, wearing a bathrobe over her pajamas, was waiting up for him when he got home. He recounted most of what had happened, and she asked what would happen if Otis was actually brought to trial.

"It'll be the typical defense," Charlie responded wearily. "Jones will argue that Otis wasn't even there that night and find others who will verify it. Then he'll argue that even if Otis was there, he didn't say what's attributed to him. And even if he did say it, he'll say it was taken out of context."

"Will that work?"

Charlie sipped his coffee, knowing he still had more work to do. "No one can ever predict what a jury will do. You know that."

Brenda put her hand on Charlie's arm. "But what do you think?" she asked. "Honestly."

"Honestly?"

She nodded, thinking he looked a dozen years older than when he'd left for work that morning.

"Unless we find something else, Otis is gonna walk."

"Even if he did it?"

"Yeah," he said, no energy in his voice, "even if he did it."

"Would Miles accept that?"

Charlie closed his eyes. "No. Not a chance."

"What would he do?"

He finished the cup of coffee and reached for the file. "I have no idea."

# Chapter 25

*I* began stalking them regularly, carefully, so that no one would know what I was up to.

I would wait for Jonah at school, I would visit Missy's grave, I went to their house at night. My lies were convincing; no one suspected a thing.

I knew it was wrong, but it didn't seem as if I could control my actions anymore. As with any compulsion, I couldn't stop. When I did these things, I wondered about my state of mind. Was I a masochist, who wanted to relive the agony I'd inflicted? Or was I a sadist, someone who secretly enjoyed their torment and wanted to witness it firsthand? Was I both? I didn't know. All I knew was that I didn't seem to have a choice.

I could not escape the image I'd seen the first night, when Miles walked past his son without speaking to him, as if oblivious to his presence. After all that had happened, it wasn't supposed to be that way. Yes, I knew that Missy had been taken from their lives . . . but didn't people grow closer after a traumatic event? Didn't they look to each other for support? Especially family?

This was what I had wanted to believe. This was how I had made it through the first six weeks. It became my mantra. They would survive. They would heal. They would turn to each other and become even closer. It was the singsong chant of a tortured fool, but it had become real in my mind.

But that night, they had not been doing okay. Not that night.

I am not naive enough now, nor was I naive enough then, to believe that a single snapshot of a family at home reveals the truth. I told myself after that night that I was mistaken in what I saw, or even if I was correct, that it didn't mean anything. Nothing can be read into isolated instances. By the time I got to my car, I almost believed it.

But I had to make certain.

There is a path one takes when moving toward destruction. Like someone who has one drink on a Friday night, and two the next, only to gradually and completely lose control, I found myself proceeding more boldly. Two days after my nighttime visit, I needed to know about Jonah. I can still remember the train of thought I used to justify my action. It went like this: I'll watch for Jonah today, and if he's smiling, then I'll know I was wrong. So I went to the school. I sat in the parking lot, a stranger sitting behind the wheel in a place I had no right to be, staring out the windshield. The first time I went, I barely caught a glimpse of him, so I returned the following day.

A few days later, I went again.

And again.

It got to the point where I recognized his teacher, his class, and I was soon able to pick him out immediately, just as he left the building. And I watched. Sometimes he would smile, sometimes he wouldn't, and for the rest of the afternoon, I would wonder what it meant. Either way, I was never satisfied.

And night would come. Like an itch I couldn't reach, the compulsion to spy nagged at me, growing stronger as the hours rolled on. I would lie down, eyes wide open, then get out of bed. I'd pace back and forth. I'd sit, then lie down again. And even though I knew it was wrong, I'd make the decision to go. I'd talk to myself, whispering the reasons I should ignore the feeling inside me, even as I reached for the car keys. I would drive the darkened stretch, urging myself to turn around and head back home, even as I parked the car. And I would make my way through the bushes surrounding their house, one step after the next, not understanding what had driven me there.

I watched them through the windows.

For a year, I saw their life unfold in little bits and pieces, filling in what I didn't know already. I learned that Miles continued to work at night sometimes, and I wondered who was taking care of Jonah. So I charted Miles's schedule, knowing when he'd be gone, and one day I followed Jonah's bus home from school. I learned that he stayed with a neighbor. A peek at the mailbox told me who she was.

Other times, I watched them eating dinner. I learned what Jonah liked to eat, and I learned what shows he liked to watch afterward. I learned that he liked to play soccer but didn't like reading. I watched him grow.

I saw good things and bad things, and always, I looked for a smile. Something, anything, that might lead me to stop this insanity.

I watched Miles, too.

I saw him pick up around the house, sliding items into drawers. I saw him cook dinner. I watched him drink beer and smoke cigarettes on the back porch, when he thought no one was around. But most of all, I watched him as he sat in the kitchen.

There, concentrating, one hand moving through his hair, he stared at the file. At first I assumed he brought his work home with him, but gradually I came to the conclusion that I was wrong. It wasn't different cases that he was studying, it was a single case, since the file never seemed to change. It was then, with a sudden jolt of comprehension, that I knew what the file was about. I knew that he was looking for me, this person who watched him through the windows.

Again, after that, I justified what I was doing. I started coming to see him, to study his features as he peered at the file, to look for an "aha," followed by a frantic phone call that would portend a visit to my home. To know when the end would come.

When I would finally leave the window to return to

my car, I would feel weak, completely spent. I would swear that it was over, that I'd never do it again. That I would let them lead their lives without intrusion. The urge to watch them would be satiated and guilt would set in, and on those evenings, I would despise what I had done. I would pray for forgiveness, and there were times I wanted to kill myself.

From someone who once had dreams of proving myself to the world, I now hated who I had become.

But then, no matter how much I wanted to stop, no matter how much I wanted to die, the urge would come again. I'd fight it until I could fight no longer, then I'd say to myself that this would be the last time. The very last.

And then, like a vampire, I would creep out into the night.

# Chapter 26

That night, while Miles studied the file in the kitchen, Jonah had his first nightmare in weeks.

It took Miles a moment to register the sound. He'd studied the file until nearly two in the morning; that, coupled with the all-night shift the evening before and everything that had happened during the day, had drained him completely, and his body seemed to rebel when he heard Jonah's cries. Like being forced to move through a room filled with wet cotton, consciousness returned slowly, and even as he moved toward Jonah's room, it was more of a Pavlovian response than a desire to comfort his son.

It was early in the morning, a few minutes before dawn. Miles carried Jonah to the porch; by the time his cries finally stopped, the sun was already up. Because it was Saturday and he didn't have to go to school, Miles carried Jonah back to the bedroom and started a pot of coffee. His head was pounding, so he took two aspirin and washed them down with orange juice.

He felt as if he had a hangover.

While the coffee was brewing, Miles retrieved the file and the notes he'd made the night before; he wanted to go over them one more time before heading into work. Jonah surprised him, however, by returning to the kitchen before he had a chance to do so. He padded in, his eyes puffy as he rubbed them, then sat at the table.

"Why are you up?" Miles asked. "It's still early."

"I'm not tired," Jonah answered.

"You look tired."

"I had a bad dream."

Jonah's words caught Miles off-guard. Jonah never remembered having the dreams before.

"You did?"

Jonah nodded. "I dreamed you were in an accident. Like Mommy was."

Miles went to Jonah's side. "It was just a dream," he said. "Nothing happened, okay?"

Jonah wiped his nose with the back of his hand. In his race car pajamas, he looked younger than he was.

"Hey, Dad?"

"Yeah?"

"Are you mad at me?"

"No, not at all. Why would you think I'm mad?"

"You didn't talk to me at all yesterday."

"I'm sorry. I wasn't mad at you. I was just trying to figure out some stuff."

"About Mommy?"

Miles was caught off-guard again. "Why do you think it's about Mommy?" he asked.

"Because you were looking at those papers again." Jonah pointed to the file on the table. "They're about Mommy, aren't they?"

After a moment, Miles nodded. "Kind of."

"I don't like those papers."

"Why not?"

"Because," he said, "they make you sad."

"They don't make me sad."

"Yeah, they do," Jonah said. "And they make me sad, too."

"Because you miss Mommy?"

"No," he said, shaking his head, "because they make you forget about me."

The words made Miles's throat constrict. "That's not true."

"Then why didn't you talk to me yesterday?"

He sounded almost on the verge of tears, and Miles pulled Jonah closer. "I'm sorry, Jonah. It won't happen again."

Jonah looked up at him. "Do you promise?"

Miles made an X over his chest and smiled. "Cross my heart."

"And hope to die?"

With Jonah's wide eyes piercing him, that was exactly what Miles felt like doing.

After having breakfast with Jonah, Miles called Sarah to apologize to her as well. Sarah interrupted before he had a chance to finish.

"Miles, you don't have to say you're sorry. After all that happened, it was pretty obvious that you needed to be alone. How are you feeling this morning?"

"I'm not sure. About the same, I guess."

"Are you going in to work?"

"I have to. Charlie called. He wants me to meet him in a little while."

"Will you call me later?"

"If I get the chance. I'll probably be pretty tied up today."

"With the investigation, you mean?"

When Miles didn't answer, Sarah twirled a few strands of hair. "Well, if you need to talk and can't reach me, I'll be at my mom's house."

"Okay."

Even after hanging up the phone, Sarah couldn't escape the feeling that something terrible was about to happen.

By nine in the morning, Charlie was working on his fourth cup of coffee and told Madge to keep them coming. He'd slept only a couple of hours and had made it back to the station before the sun had risen.

He'd been busy ever since. He'd met with Harvey, interviewed Otis in his cell, and spent some time with Thurman Jones. He'd also called in extra deputies to look for Sims Addison. So far, nothing.

He had, though, come to some decisions.

Miles arrived twenty minutes later and found Charlie waiting for him outside his office.

"You doing okay?" Charlie asked, thinking Miles looked no better than he did.

"Tough night."

"Tough day, too. Need some coffee?"

"Had plenty at the house."

He motioned over his shoulder. "C'mon in, then— we have to talk."

After Miles entered, Charlie closed the door behind him and Miles sat in the chair. Charlie leaned against the desk.

"Listen, before we begin," Miles started, "I guess you should know that I've been working on this since yesterday, and I think I might have some ideas—"

Charlie shook his head, not letting him finish. "Look, Miles, that's not why I wanted to see you. Right now, I need you to listen, okay?"

There was something in his expression that told

Miles he wasn't going to like what he was about to hear, and he stiffened.

Charlie glanced at the tile floor, then back at Miles again.

"I'm not going to beat around the bush here. We've known each other too long for that." He paused.

"What is it?"

"I'm going to release Otis Timson today."

Miles's mouth opened, but before he said anything, Charlie raised his hands.

"Now before you think I'm jumping to conclusions, hear me out. I didn't have a choice, not based on the information that I have so far. Yesterday, after you left, I went up to visit with Earl Getlin."

He told Miles what Getlin had said.

"Then you have the proof you need," Miles shot back.

"Now hold on. Let me also say I think there are some serious questions about his possible testimony. From what I heard, Thurman Jones would eat him alive, and there's not a jury that would believe a word he said."

"So leave that up to the jury," Miles protested. "You can't just let him go."

"My hands are tied. Believe me, I stayed up all night, looking over the case. As it stands, we don't have enough to hold him. Especially now that Sims has flown the coop."

"What are you talking about?"

"Sims. I had deputies looking for him yesterday, last night, and this morning. After he left here, he just vanished. No one's been able to find him, and Harvey isn't willing to let any of this go on unless he can talk to Sims."

"For God's sake, Otis admitted it."

"I don't have a choice," Charlie said.

"He killed my wife." Miles spoke through clenched teeth.

Charlie hated the fact that he had to do this.

"This isn't just my decision. Right now, without Sims, we don't have a case and you know it. Harvey Wellman said there was no way that the DA's office would file charges as things stand now."

"Harvey's making you do this?"

"I spent the morning with him," Charlie answered, "and I also talked to him yesterday. Believe it when I say he's been more than fair. It's nothing personal—he's just doing his job."

"That's crap."

"Put yourself in his position, Miles."

"I don't want to put myself in his position. I want Otis charged with murder."

"I know you're upset—"

"I'm not upset, Charlie. I'm pissed off like you wouldn't believe."

"I know you are, but this isn't the end. You've got

328

to understand that even if we let Otis go, that doesn't mean he won't be charged in the future. It just means that we don't have enough to hold him now. And you should also know the highway patrol is reopening the investigation. This isn't over yet."

Miles glared. "But until then, Otis is free to go."

"He'd be free on bail, anyway. Even if we did charge him with hit-and-run, he'd walk out of here. You know that."

"Then charge him with murder."

"Without Sims? Without other evidence? There's no way that would fly."

There were times when Miles despised the criminal justice system. His eyes darted around the room before settling on Charlie again.

"Did you talk to Otis?" he finally asked.

"Tried to this morning. His lawyer was there and advised him not to answer most of my questions. Didn't get any information that would help."

"Would it help if I tried to talk to him?"

Charlie shook his head. "There's no chance of that, Miles."

"Why not?"

"I can't allow that."

"Because it's about Missy?"

"No, because of the stunt you pulled yesterday."

"What are you talking about?"

"You know exactly what I'm talking about."

Charlie stared at Miles, watching for his reaction. Miles seemed to have none, and Charlie got up from behind the desk.

"Let me be frank, okay? Even though Otis wouldn't answer any questions about Missy, he did volunteer information about your behavior yesterday. So now I'm going to ask you about it." He paused. "What happened in the car?"

Miles shifted in his chair. "I saw a raccoon in the road and had to hit the brakes."

"Do you think I'm stupid enough to believe that?"

Miles shrugged. "It's what happened."

"And if Otis tells me that you did it simply to hurt him?"

"Then he's lying."

Charlie leaned forward. "Is he also lying when he tells me that you pointed your gun at his head, even though he was on his knees with his hands up? And that you held it there?"

Miles squirmed uncomfortably. "I had to keep the situation under control," he said evasively.

"And you think that was the way to go?"

"Look, Charlie, no one was hurt."

"So in your mind, it was completely justified?"

"Yes."

"Well, Otis's lawyer didn't think so. And neither did Clyde. They're threatening to file a civil lawsuit against you."

330

"A lawsuit?"

"Sure—excessive force, intimidation, police brutality, the whole works. Thurman has some friends at the ACLU and they're thinking of joining the lawsuit as well."

"But nothing happened!"

"It doesn't matter, Miles. They have a right to file whatever they want. But you should know that they've also asked Harvey to file criminal charges."

"Criminal charges?"

"That's what they say."

"And let me guess—Harvey's going to go along with that, right?"

Charlie shook his head. "I know you and Harvey don't get along, but I've worked with Harvey for years and I think he's fair most of the time. He was pretty hot about the whole thing last night, but when we met this morning, he said he didn't think he was going to go forward with it—"

"So there's no problem, then," Miles interrupted.

"You didn't let me finish," Charlie said. He met Miles's gaze. "Even though he may not go forward, that's not set in stone. He knows how caught up you are in this, and even though he doesn't think you had the right to let Sims go or take it on yourself to arrest Otis, he knows you're human. He understands the way you felt, but that doesn't change the fact that you acted inappropriately, to say the least. And because of that, he told me that he thinks it would be best if you're placed on suspension—with pay, of course—until all this works itself out."

Miles's face registered disbelief. "Suspend me?"

"It's for your own good. Once tempers cool down, Harvey thinks he can get Clyde and the lawyer to back off. But if we act as if we—or I—feel you did nothing whatsoever that was wrong, he isn't so sure he'll be able to talk Clyde out of it."

"All I did was arrest the man who killed my wife."

"You did a lot more than that, and you know it."

"So you're gonna do what he says?"

After a long moment, Charlie nodded. "I think he's giving me good advice, Miles. Like I said, it's for your own good."

"Let me get this straight. Otis goes free, even though he killed my wife. And I get booted from the force for bringing him in."

"If that's the way you want to look at it."

"That's how it is!"

Charlie shook his head, keeping his voice steady. "No, it's not. And in a little while, when you're not so wound up, you'll see that. For now, though, you're officially on suspension."

"C'mon, Charlie—don't do this."

"It's for the best. And whatever you do, don't escalate the situation. If I find out you're hassling Otis or snooping around where you shouldn't, I'll be forced to take further action and I won't have the option of being so lenient."

"This is ridiculous!"

"It's the way it is, my friend. I'm sorry." Charlie began making his way to the chair on the other side. "But like I said, it's not over. Once we find Sims and talk to him, we'll look into his story. Maybe someone else heard something, and we might find someone to corroborate it—"

Miles tossed his badge onto the desk before Charlie finished talking. His holster and gun were draped over the chair.

He slammed the door behind him.

Twenty minutes later, Otis Timson was released.

After storming out of Charlie's office, Miles got into his car, his head spinning from the events of the past twenty-four hours. He turned the key, grinding the engine, and pulled away from the curb, accelerating hard and swinging into the other lane before righting the car.

Otis was going free while he was on suspension.

It made no sense at all. Somehow, the world had gone completely crazy.

He thought briefly about going home but decided against it, because Jonah—who was at Mrs. Knowlson's—would come home if he did, and Miles knew he couldn't face him right now. Not after what

Jonah had said this morning. He needed time to calm down, to figure out what he was going to say first.

He needed to talk to someone, someone who would be able to help him make sense of all this.

The traffic clear, Miles made a U-turn and was on his way to find Sarah.

# Chapter 27

S arah was in the living room with her mother when she saw Miles pull up in front of the house. Since she hadn't told Maureen anything about recent events, Maureen jumped up from the couch and opened the door, her arms spread wide.

"What a nice surprise!" she cried. "I didn't expect you to come by!"

Miles muttered a greeting as she hugged him but turned down her offer of a cup of coffee. Sarah quickly suggested a walk and reached for her jacket. They were out the door a couple of minutes later. Maureen, misreading the whole thing as "young people in love who wanted to be alone," practically blushed as she watched them walk away.

They went to the woods where they'd gone with Jonah on Thanksgiving Day. As they walked, Miles didn't say anything. Instead he formed a fist with his hands tight enough for his fingers to turn white before opening them again.

They sat on a toppled pine tree, overgrown with

moss and ivy. Miles was still opening and closing his hands, and Sarah reached for one of them. After a moment, he seemed to relax and their fingers intertwined.

"Bad day, huh?"

"You could say that."

"Otis?"

Miles snorted. "Otis. Charlie. Harvey. Sims. Everyone."

"What happened?"

"Charlie let Otis go. Said the case wasn't strong enough to hold him."

"Why? I thought there were witnesses?" she said.

"So did I. But I guess the facts aren't worth a damn in this case." He picked at the bark on the tree and threw a piece off to the side, disgusted. "Charlie suspended me from duty."

She squinted, as if she weren't sure she had heard him correctly. "Excuse me?"

"This morning. That's why he wanted to talk to me."

"You're kidding."

He shook his head. "No."

"I don't understand . . ." She trailed off.

But she did. Deep down, she understood even as she said the words.

He threw another piece of bark. "He said that my behavior was inappropriate during the arrest and that I'm suspended while they look into it. But that's not all." He paused, looking straight ahead. "He also said that Otis's lawyer and Clyde want to file a lawsuit. And to top it off, they might bring charges against me."

She wasn't sure how to respond. Nothing seemed appropriate. Miles exhaled sharply and let go of her hand, as if needing space.

"Can you believe that? I bring in the guy who killed my wife, and I get suspended. He goes free, and I'm the one brought up on charges." He finally turned to face her. "Does that make any sense to you?"

"No, it doesn't," she answered honestly.

Miles shook his head and turned away again.

"And Charlie—good old Charlie—he's going along with it all. I used to think he was my friend."

"He is your friend, Miles. You know that."

"No, I don't. Not anymore."

"So they're bringing you up on charges?"

Miles shrugged. "They might. Charlie said there's a chance that he can get Otis and his lawyer to back off. That's the other reason he suspended me."

Now she was confused.

"Why don't you start from the beginning, okay? What did Charlie actually say to you?"

Miles repeated the conversation. When he was finished, Sarah reached for his hand again.

"It doesn't seem like Charlie's got it in for you. It sounds like he thinks he's doing what's best to help you."

"If he wanted to help, he'd keep Otis in jail."

"But without Sims, what can he do?"

"He should have filed murder charges anyway. Earl Getlin verified the story—that's really all he needs, and no judge around here would have let Otis out on bail. I mean, he knows that Sims will turn up eventually. The guy's not exactly a world traveler; he's around here someplace. I can probably find him in a couple of hours, and when I do, I'll get him to sign an affidavit as to what happened. And believe me, he will, after I talk to him."

"But aren't you on suspension?"

"Don't start taking Charlie's side now. I'm not in the mood for that."

"I'm not taking his side, Miles. I just don't want you to get in more trouble than you're already in. And Charlie did say that the investigation would probably be reopened."

He looked over at her. "So you think I should just let the whole thing go?"

"I'm not saying that—"

Miles cut her off. "What are you saying, then? Because it sounds to me like you want me to just step back and hope for the best." He didn't wait for a response. "Well, I can't do that, Sarah. I'll be damned if Otis gets away without paying for what he did."

She couldn't help but remember the night before

as he spoke. She wondered when he'd finally realized that she'd left.

"But what happens if Sims doesn't turn up?" she finally asked. "or if they don't think they have enough for a case? Then what will you do?"

His eyes narrowed. "Why are you doing this?"

Sarah blanched. "I'm not doing anything . . ."

"Yeah, you are—you're questioning everything."

"I just don't want you to do anything that you'll regret later."

"What's that supposed to mean?"

She squeezed his hand. "I mean that sometimes, things don't work out the way we want them to."

He stared at her for a long moment, his expression hard, his hand lifeless. *Cold.* "You don't think he did it, do you?"

"I'm not talking about Otis now. I'm talking about you."

"And *I'm* talking about Otis." He let go of her hand and stood. "Two people said that Otis practically bragged about killing my wife, and right now he's probably on his way home. They let him go and you want me to sit back and do nothing. You've met him. You've seen what kind of guy he is, so I want to know what *you* think about it. Do you think he killed Missy or not?"

Put on the spot, she answered quickly. "I don't know what to think about any of this."

Though she spoke the truth, it wasn't what he wanted to hear. Nor had it come across the right way. He turned away, unwilling to look at her.

"Well, I do," he said. "I know he did it, and I'm going to find the proof of it, one way or the other. And I don't care what you think about it. It's my wife we're talking about here."

*My wife.*

Before she could respond, he turned to leave. Sarah rose and started after him.

"Wait—Miles. Don't leave."

Without stopping, he spoke over his shoulder. "Why? So you can get on my case some more?"

"I'm not on your case, Miles. I'm just trying to help."

He stopped and faced her. "Well, don't. I don't need your help. This isn't your business either."

She blinked back her surprise, stung by his words. "Of course it's my business. I care about you."

"Then the next time I come because I need you to listen, don't preach to me. Just listen, okay?"

With that, he left Sarah in the woods, completely at a loss.

Harvey stepped into Charlie's office, looking more worn than usual.

"Any luck yet with Sims?"

Charlie shook his head. "Not yet. He's gone and hidden himself good."

"You think he'll turn up?"

"Has to. He can't go anywhere else. He's just keeping a low profile for now, but he can't do that for long."

Harvey casually closed the door behind him. "I just talked to Thurman Jones," he said.

"And?"

"He's still pressing charges, but I don't think his heart's in it. I think he's following Clyde's lead with this."

"So what does that mean?"

"I'm not sure yet, but I get the feeling that he'll eventually back off. The last thing he wants is to give everyone in the department a reason to do some serious digging when it comes to his client, and he knows that's exactly what'll happen if he presses this thing. And besides, he knows it'll come down to a jury, and they're far more likely to side with a sheriff than someone with a reputation like Otis's. Especially when you consider that Miles didn't fire a shot the whole time he was out there."

Charlie nodded. "Thanks, Harvey."

"No problem."

"I don't mean for the update."

"I know what you mean. But you have to make sure Miles is on a leash for a few days until this blows over. If he does something stupid, all bets are off and I'd be forced to file charges."

"Okay."

"You'll talk to him?"

"Yeah. I'll let him know."

*I just hope he'll listen.*

When Brian arrived home around noontime for Christmas break, Sarah breathed a sigh of relief. Finally, someone she could talk to. She'd been avoiding her mother's curious scrutiny all morning. Over sandwiches, Brian talked about school ("It's okay"), how he thought his grades went ("Okay, I guess"), and how he'd been feeling ("Okay").

He didn't look nearly as good as he had the last time she'd seen him. He was pale, with the pallor of someone who seldom ventured outside the library. Though he claimed exhaustion from finals, Sarah wondered how it was really going at school.

Inspecting him closely, she thought he looked almost like someone who'd gotten involved with drugs.

The sad part was, as much as she loved him, it wouldn't really surprise her if he had. He'd always been sensitive, and now that he was on his own with new stresses, it would be easy to fall prey to something like that. It had happened to someone in her dorm her freshman year, and the girl had reminded her of Brian in a lot of ways. She'd dropped out before the second semester started, and Sarah hadn't thought about her in years. But now, staring at Brian, she couldn't escape the fact that he looked exactly the same way the girl had looked.

What a day this was turning out to be.

Maureen, of course, fretted about his appearance and kept adding food to his plate.

"I'm not hungry, Mom," he protested as he pushed away his half-eaten plate, and Maureen finally gave in and brought the plate to the sink, biting her lip.

After lunch, Sarah walked out to the car with Brian to help him bring in his things.

"Mom's right, you know—you look terrible."

He pulled the keys from his pocket. "Thanks, sis. I appreciate that."

"Tough semester?"

Brian shrugged. "I'll survive." He opened the trunk and started unloading a bag.

Sarah forced him to put the bag down and reached for his arm. "If you need to talk to me about anything, you know I'm here, right?"

"Yeah, I know."

"I'm serious. Even if it's something you don't think you want to tell me."

"Do I really look that bad?" Brian raised an inquiring eyebrow.

"Mom thinks you're on drugs."

It was a lie, but it wasn't as though he'd head inside and ask his mother.

"Well, tell her I'm not. I'm just having a tough

time adjusting to school. But I'll manage." He cracked a crooked smile. "That's the answer for you, too, by the way."

"Me?"

Brian reached for another bag. "Mom wouldn't think I was using drugs if she caught me smoking pot in the living room. Now, if you'd said that she was worried that my roommates were making things hard for me because I was so much smarter than them, I might have believed you."

Sarah laughed. "You're probably right."

"I'll be fine, really. How are you doing?"

"Pretty well. School will finish up this Friday for me, and I'm looking forward to a few weeks off."

Brian handed Sarah a duffel bag full of dirty clothes. "Teachers need a break, too?"

"We need it more than the kids, if you want to know the truth."

After Brian shut the trunk, he reached for his bags. Sarah glanced over his shoulder to make sure her mom hadn't come out.

"Listen, I know you just got in a little while ago, but can we talk?"

"Sure. This can wait." He set down the bags and leaned against the car. "What's up?"

"It's about Miles. We kind of had an argument today, and it's not something I can talk to Mom about. You know how she is."

344

"What about?"

"I think I told you the last time he was here that his wife had died a couple of years ago in a hit-and-run. They never caught the guy who did it, and he really had a hard time with that. And then yesterday, new information surfaced and he arrested someone. But it didn't stop at just that. Miles went a little too far. He told me last night that he came close to killing the guy."

Brian looked taken aback, and Sarah quickly shook her head.

"Nothing bad happened in the end—well, not really. No one was actually hurt, but . . ." She crossed her arms, forcing the thought away. "Anyway, he got suspended from the department today for what he did. But that's not what I'm really worried about. To make a long story short, they had to release the guy, and now I don't know what to do. Miles isn't thinking all that clearly, and I'm afraid he might do something that he'll end up regretting."

She paused for a moment, then continued. "I mean, this whole thing is complicated by the fact that there's already a lot of bad blood between Miles and the guy he arrested. Even though Miles was suspended, he's not going to give up. And this guy . . . well, he isn't the kind of guy he should be messing with."

"But didn't you just say they had to let the guy go?"

"Yeah, but Miles won't accept that. You should have heard him today. He wouldn't even listen to anything I was saying. Part of me thinks I should call his boss and let him know what Miles said, but he's already on suspension and I don't want him to get in any more trouble than he's already in. But if I say nothing . . ." She trailed off before meeting her brother's eyes. "What do you think I should do? Wait and see what happens? Or should I call his boss? Or should I stay out of it?"

Brian took a long time before answering. "I guess that comes down to how you feel about him and how far you think he'll go."

Sarah ran a hand through her hair. "That's just it. I love him. I know you didn't get much of a chance to talk to him, but he's made me really happy these last couple of months. And now . . . this whole thing scares me. I don't want to be the one who gets him fired, but at the same time, I'm really worried about what he'll do."

Brian stood without moving for a long moment, thinking.

"You can't let someone innocent go to prison, Sarah," he said finally, looking down at her.

"That's not what I'm afraid of."

"What—you think he'll go after the guy?"

"If it comes to that?" She remembered how Miles had looked at her, his eyes flashing with frustrated rage. "I think he just might."

"You can't let him do that."

"So you think I should call?"

Brian looked grim.

"I don't think you have a choice."

After leaving Sarah's house, Miles spent the next few hours trying to track down Sims. But like Charlie, he had no luck.

He then thought about visiting the Timson compound again, but he held off. Not because he ran out of time, but because he remembered what had happened earlier that morning in Charlie's office.

He didn't have a gun with him anymore.

There was, though, another one at his house.

Later that afternoon, Charlie received two telephone calls. One was from Sims's mother, who asked Charlie why everyone was suddenly interested in her son. When asked what she meant, Sims's mother answered, "Miles Ryan came by today asking the same questions you did."

Charlie frowned as he hung up the phone, angry that Miles had ignored everything they'd talked about this morning.

The second call was from Sarah Andrews.

After she said good-bye, Charlie swiveled his chair toward the window and stared over the parking lot, twirling a pencil.

A minute later, with the pencil broken in half, he turned toward the door and tossed the remains in the garbage.

"Madge?" he bellowed.

She appeared in the doorway.

"Get me Harris. Now."

She didn't have to be asked twice. A minute later, Harris was standing in front of the desk.

"I need you to go out to the Timson place. Stay out of sight, but keep an eye on whoever goes in and out of there. If anything looks out of the ordinary—and I mean *anything*—I want you to call. Not just me—I want you to put it out on the radio. I don't want any trouble out there tonight. None at all, you got me?"

Harris swallowed and nodded. He didn't need to ask whom he was watching for.

After he left, Charlie reached for the phone to call Brenda. He knew then that he, too, was going to be out late.

Nor could he escape the feeling that the whole thing was on the verge of spinning out of control.

# Chapter 28

After a year, my nocturnal visits to their home ceased as suddenly as they'd started. So did my visits to the school to see Jonah, and the site of the accident. The only place I continued to visit with regularity after that was Missy's grave, and it became part of my weekly schedule, mentally penciled into its Thursday slot. I never missed a day. Rain or shine, I went to the cemetery and traced the path to her grave. I never looked to see if anyone was watching anymore. And always, I brought flowers.

The end of the other visits came as a surprise. Though you might think that the year would have diminished the intensity of my obsession, that wasn't the case at all. But just as I'd been compelled to watch them for a year, the compulsion suddenly reversed itself and I knew I had to let them live in peace, without me spying on them.

The day it happened was a day I'll never forget.

It was the first anniversary of Missy's death. By then, after a year of creeping through the darkness, I was almost invisible as I moved. I knew every twist and turn I had to make, and the time it took to reach their home had dropped by half. I'd become a professional voyeur: In addition to peering through their windows, I had been bringing binoculars with me for months. There were times, you see, when others were around, either on the roads or in their yards, and I hadn't been able to get close to the windows. Other times, Miles closed the living room drapes, but because the itch was not satisfied by failure, I had to do something. The binoculars solved my problem. Off to the side of their property, close to the river, there is an ancient, giant oak. The branches are low and thick, some run parallel to the ground, and that was where I sometimes made my camp. I found that if I perched high enough, I could see right through the kitchen window, my view unobstructed. I watched for hours, until Jonah went to bed, and afterward, I watched Miles as he sat in the kitchen.

Over the year, he, like me, had changed.

Though he still studied the file, he did not do it as regularly as he once had. As the months from the accident had increased, his compulsion to find me decreased. It wasn't that he cared any less, it had more to do with the reality of what he faced. By then, I knew the case was at a standstill; Miles, I suspected, realized this as well. On the anniversary, after Jonah had gone to bed, he did bring out the file. He didn't, however, brood over it as he had before. Instead he flipped through the pages, this time without a pencil or pen, and he made no marks at all, almost as if he were turning the pages of a photo album, reliving memories. In time, he pushed it aside, then vanished into the living room.

When I realized he wasn't coming back, I left the tree and crept around to the porch.

There, even though he'd drawn the shades, I saw that the window had been left open to catch the evening breeze. From my vantage point, I could glimpse slivers of the room inside, enough to see Miles sitting on the couch. A cardboard box sat beside him, and from the angle he faced, I knew he was watching television. Pressing my ear close to the window's opening, I listened, but nothing I heard seemed to make much sense. There were long periods where nothing seemed to be said; other sounds seemed distorted, the voices jumbled. When I looked toward Miles again, trying to see what he was watching, I saw his face and I knew. It was there, in his eyes, in the curve of his mouth, in the way he was sitting.

He was watching home videos.

With that, recognition settled in, and when I closed my eyes, I began to recognize who was speaking on the tape. I heard Miles, his voice rising and falling, I heard the high-pitched squeal of a child. In the background, faint but noticeable, I heard another voice. Her voice.

Missy's.

It was startling, foreign, and for a moment I felt as if I couldn't breathe. In all this time, after a year of watching Miles and Jonah, I thought I had come to know them, but the sound I heard that night changed all that. I didn't know Miles, I didn't know Jonah. There is observation and study, and there is knowledge, and though I had one, I didn't have the other and never would.

I listened, transfixed.

Her voice trailed away. A moment later, I heard her laugh.

The sound made me jump inside, and my eyes were immediately drawn to Miles. I wanted to see his reaction, though I knew what it would be. He would be staring, lost in his memories, angry tears in his eyes.

But I was wrong.

He wasn't crying. Instead, with a tender look, he was smiling at the screen.

And with that, I suddenly knew it was time to stop.

After that visit, I honestly believed that I'd never return to their house to spy on them. In the following year, I tried to get on with my life, and on the surface, I succeeded. People around me remarked that I looked better, that I seemed like my old self.

Part of me believed that was so. With the compulsion gone, I thought I had put the nightmare behind me. Not what I had done, not the fact that I had killed Missy, but the obsessive guilt I had lived with for a year.

What I didn't realize then was that the guilt and anguish never really left me. Instead they had simply gone dormant, like a bear hibernating in the winter, feeding on its own tissue, waiting for the season yet to come.

# Chapter 29

On Sunday morning, a little after eight, Sarah heard someone knocking at her front door. After hesitating, she finally got up to answer it. As she walked toward the door, part of her hoped it was Miles.

Another part hoped that it wasn't.

Even as she reached for the handle, she wasn't sure what she was going to say. A lot depended on Miles. Did he know that she'd called Charlie? And if so, was he angry? Hurt? Would she understand she'd done it because she'd felt she didn't have a choice?

When she opened the door, however, she smiled in relief.

"Hey, Brian," she said. "What are you doing here?"

"I need to talk to you."

"Sure . . . come in."

He followed her inside and sat on the couch. Sarah sat next to him.

"So what's up?" she asked.

"You ended up calling Miles's boss, didn't you?"

Sarah ran a hand through her hair. "Yeah. Like you said, I didn't have a choice."

"Because you think he'll go after the guy he arrested," Brian stated.

"I don't know what he'll do, but I'm scared enough to try to head it off."

He nodded slightly. "Does he know that you called?"

"Miles? I don't know."

"Have you talked to him?"

"No. Not since he left yesterday. I tried calling him a couple of times, but he wasn't home. I kept getting the answering machine."

He brought his fingers to the bridge of his nose and squeezed.

"I have to know something," he said. In the quiet of the room, his voice seemed strangely amplified.

"What?" she asked, puzzled.

"I need to know if you really think that Miles would go too far."

Sarah leaned forward. She tried to get him to meet her eyes, but he looked away.

"I'm not a mind reader. But yeah, I'm worried, I guess."

"I think you should tell Miles to just let it go."

"Let what go?"

"The guy he arrested . . . he should just let him go."

354

Sarah stared at him in bafflement. He finally turned to her, his eyes pleading.

"You've got to get him to understand that, okay? Talk to him, okay?"

"I've tried to do that. I told you."

"You've got to try harder."

Sarah sat back and frowned. "What's going on?"

"I'm just asking what you think Miles will do."

"But why? Why's this so important to you?"

"What would happen to Jonah?"

She blinked. "Jonah?"

"Miles would think about him, wouldn't he? Before he did anything?"

Sarah shook her head slowly.

"I mean, you don't think he would risk going to jail, do you?"

She reached for his hands and took them forcefully. "Now wait, okay? Stop with the questions for a minute. What's going on?"

*This was, I remember, my moment of truth, the reason I had come to her house. It was finally time to confess what I had done.*

*Why, then, did I not just come out and say it? Why had I asked so many questions? Was I looking for a way out, another reason to keep it buried? The part of me that had lied for two years may have wanted that, but I honestly think the better part of me wanted to protect my sister.*

I had to make sure I didn't have a choice.

I knew my words would hurt her. My sister was in love with Miles. I had seen them at Thanksgiving, I had seen the way they looked at each other, the comfortable way they related when they were close, the tender kiss she'd given him before he left. She loved Miles, and Miles loved her—she'd told me as much. And Jonah loved them both.

The night before, I finally realized that I could keep the secret no longer. If Sarah really thought Miles might take matters into his own hands, I knew that by keeping silent, I was running the risk that more lives would be ruined. Missy had died because of me; I couldn't live with another needless tragedy.

But to save myself, to save an innocent man, to save Miles Ryan from himself, I also knew I would have to sacrifice my sister.

She, who had been through so much already, would have to look Miles in the eye, knowing that her own brother had killed his wife—and face the risk of losing him as a result. For how could he ever look at her the same way?

Was it fair to sacrifice her? She was an innocent bystander; with my words, she would be irrevocably trapped between her love for Miles Ryan and her love for me. But as much as I didn't want to, I knew I had no choice.

"I know," I finally said hoarsely, "who was driving the car that night."

*She stared back, almost as if she didn't understand my words.*

*"You do?" she asked.*

*I nodded.*

*It was then, in the long silence that preceded her question, that she began to understand the reason I had come. She knew what I was trying to tell her. She slumped forward, like a balloon being slowly deflated. I, for my part, never looked away.*

*"It was me, Sarah," I whispered. "I was the one."*

# Chapter 30

A t his words, Sarah reared back, as if seeing her brother for the first time.

"I didn't mean for it to happen. I'm so, so sorry . . ."

After trailing off, unable to continue, Brian started to cry.

Not the quiet, repressed sounds of sadness, but the anguished cries of a child. His shoulders shook violently, as if in spasm. Until that moment, Brian had never cried for what he had done, and now that he had started, he wasn't sure that he would ever stop.

In the midst of his grief, Sarah put her arms around him, and her touch made his crime seem even worse than the terrible thing it was, for he knew then that his sister still loved him in spite of it. She said nothing at all as he cried, but her hand began gently moving up and down his back. Brian leaned into her, holding her tightly, somehow believing that if he let go, everything would change between them.

But even then, he knew it had.

He wasn't sure how long he cried, but when he

finally stopped, he began to tell his sister how it happened.

He did not lie.

He did not, however, tell her about the visits.

During his entire confession, Brian never met her eyes. He didn't want to see her pity or her horror; he didn't want to see the way she really saw him.

But at the end of his story, he finally steeled himself to meet her gaze.

He saw neither love nor forgiveness on her face.

What he saw was fear.

Brian stayed with Sarah most of the morning. She had many questions; in the process of answering them, Brian told her everything once more. Some questions, though—like why he hadn't gone to the police—had no meaningful answer, except for the obvious: that he was in shock, he was frightened, that too much time eventually passed.

Like Brian, Sarah justified his decision, and like Brian, she questioned it. They went back and forth, time and time again, but in the end, when she finally grew silent, Brian knew it was time for him to leave.

On his way out the door, he glanced back over his shoulder.

On the couch, hunched over like someone twice her age, his sister was quietly crying, her face buried in her hands.

# Chapter 31

That same morning, while Sarah sat crying on the couch, Charlie Curtis strode up Miles Ryan's walkway. He was dressed in his uniform; it was the first Sunday in years that he and Brenda wouldn't make it to church, but as he'd explained to her earlier, he didn't feel he had a choice. Not after the two phone calls he'd received the day before.

Not after staying up for most of the night and watching Miles's house because of them.

He knocked; Miles came to the door wearing jeans, a sweatshirt, and a baseball hat. If he was surprised to see Charlie standing on his porch, he gave no indication.

"We need to talk," Charlie said without preamble.

Miles put his hands on his hips, not hiding the anger he still felt at what Charlie had done.

"So talk."

Charlie pushed the brim of his hat up. "Do you want to do this on the porch where Jonah can hear, or do you want to talk in the yard? Your choice. It doesn't matter to me."

A minute later, Charlie was leaning against the car, his arms crossed. Miles stood facing him. The sun was still low in the sky, and Miles had to squint to see him.

"I need to know if you went looking for Sims Addison," Charlie said, getting right to the point.

"Are you asking or do you already know?"

"I'm asking because I want to know if you're willing to lie directly to my face."

After a moment, Miles glanced away. "Yeah. I went looking for him."

"Why?"

"Because you said you couldn't find him."

"You're on suspension, Miles. Do you know what that means?"

"It wasn't anything official, Charlie."

"It doesn't matter. I gave you a direct order and you disregarded it. You're just lucky that Harvey Wellman didn't find out. But I can't keep covering for you, and I'm too old and too tired to put up with crap like that." He shifted his weight from one leg to the other, trying to keep warm. "I need the file, Miles."

"My file?"

"I want it admitted as evidence."

"Evidence? For what?"

"It concerns the death of Missy Ryan, doesn't it? I want to see those notes you've been scribbling."

"Charlie . . ."

"I'm serious. Either you hand it over or I'll take it. It's one or the other, but in the end, I'm going to have it."

"Why are you doing this?"

"I'm hoping it'll knock some sense into you. You obviously didn't listen to a thing I said yesterday, so let me say it again. Stay out of this. Let us handle it."

"Fine."

"I need your word that you're going to stop looking for Sims and that you'll stay away from Otis Timson."

"It's a small town, Charlie. I can't help it if we happen to bump into each other."

Charlie's eyes narrowed. "I'm tired of playing games, Miles, so let me make something clear. If you so much as get within a hundred yards of Otis, or his house or even the places he spends his time, I'll throw you in jail."

Miles looked at Charlie incredulously. "For what?"

"For battery."

"Battery?"

"That little stunt you pulled in the car." He shook his head. "You don't seem to realize you're in a heap of trouble here. Either you keep your distance, or you'll end up behind bars."

"This is crazy . . ."

"You brought it on yourself. Right now, you're so worked up that I don't know what else to do. Do you know where I was last night?" He didn't wait for an answer. "I was parked right down the street, making sure you didn't leave. Do you know how it makes me feel to think I can't trust you after all we've been through? It's a crappy feeling, and I don't want to have to do that again. So if you don't mind—and I can't make you do this—along with the file, I'd appreciate it if you'd just let me hold on to your other guns for a while, the ones you keep in the house. You can have 'em back when all this is over. If you say no, I'm gonna have to put you under surveillance, and believe me, I will. You won't be able to buy a cup of coffee without someone watching every move you make. And you should also know that I've got deputies out at the Timson place and they're watching for you, too."

Miles stubbornly refused to meet his eyes. "He was driving the car, Charlie."

"Do you really think that? Or do you just want an answer—any answer?"

Miles's head snapped up. "That's not fair."

"Isn't it? I'm the one who talked to Earl, not you. I'm the one who reviewed every step of the highway patrol's investigation. I'm telling you, there's no physical evidence linking Otis to the crime."

"I'll find the evidence—"

"No, you won't!" Charlie shot back. "That's just the thing! You won't find anything because you're out of this!"

Miles said nothing, and after a long moment, Charlie put his hand on Miles's shoulder.

"Look, we're still looking into this—you've got my word on that." He let out a long sigh. "I don't know . . . maybe we'll find something. And if we do, I'll be the first one to come and tell you that I was wrong and that Otis will get what's coming to him. Okay?"

Miles's jaw clenched involuntarily as Charlie waited for a response. Finally, sensing that none was coming, Charlie went on.

"I know how hard this is—"

With that, Miles shrugged off Charlie's hand and stared at him. His eyes flashed.

"No, you don't," Miles snapped, "and you never will, Charlie. Brenda's still around, remember? You still wake up in the same bed, you can call her anytime you want. No one ran her down in cold blood, no one got away with it for years. And mark my words, Charlie, no one's gonna get away with it now."

Despite Miles's words, Charlie left ten minutes later with the file and the guns. Neither man said another word.

There was no need for that. Charlie was doing his job.

And Miles was going to do his.

Once she was alone, Sarah sat in the living room, numb to everything around her. She hadn't moved from the couch even after she'd stopped crying, feeling somehow that the slightest movement would shatter her tenuous composure.

Nothing made sense.

She didn't have the energy to separate her emotions; instead they were jumbled together, indistinguishable. Like an overloaded outlet, she felt as if a breaker had tripped inside her, leaving her incapable of any action.

How on earth had this happened? Not Brian's accident—she could understand that, at least on the surface. It was terrible, and what he had done afterward was wrong, no matter how she looked at it. But it was an accident. She knew that. Brian couldn't have avoided it, any more than she would have been able to avoid it.

And in the blink of an eye, Missy Ryan had died.

Missy Ryan.

Jonah's mother.

Miles's wife.

That's what didn't make any sense.

Why had Brian hit *her*?

And why, of all the people in the world, had it been Miles who later came into her life? It was almost impossible to believe, and as she sat on the couch, she couldn't reconcile everything she'd just learned— her horror at Brian's confession and the obvious guilt he was suffering . . . her anger and revulsion at the fact that he'd hidden the truth, set against the implacable knowledge that she would always love her brother . . .

And Miles . . .

Oh God . . . *Miles* . . .

What was she supposed to do now? Call him with what she knew? Or wait a little until she composed herself and figured out exactly what to say?

*The way Brian had waited?*

Oh, God . . .

What would happen to Brian?

*He would go to jail . . .*

She felt ill.

Yes, that's what he deserved, even if he was her brother. He broke the law and should pay for his crime.

Or should he? He was her little brother, just a kid when it happened, and it hadn't been his fault.

She shook her head, suddenly wishing Brian hadn't told her.

Yet in her heart, she knew why he had told her. For two years, Miles had paid the price of his silence.

*And now, Otis was going to pay.*

She inhaled deeply, bringing her fingers to her temples.

No, Miles wouldn't go that far. Would he?

*Maybe not now, but it would eat away at him as long as he believed Otis was guilty, and one day he might—*

She shook her head, not wanting to think about that.

Still, she didn't know what to do.

Nor had any answers come to her a few minutes later, when Miles showed up at her door.

"Hi," Miles said simply.

Sarah stared at him as if in shock, unable to move her hand from the doorknob. She felt herself tense, her thoughts veering in opposite directions.

*Tell him now, just get it over with . . .*

*Wait until you've figured out what to say first . . .*

"Are you okay?" he asked.

"Oh . . . yeah . . . um . . . ," she stammered. "Come in."

She stepped back, and Miles closed the door behind him. He hesitated for a moment before heading toward the window, where he pulled the curtains and scanned the road; then he made a circuit of the living room, obviously distracted. Stopping at the mantel, he absently adjusted a picture of Sarah and her family, angling it so it faced the living room. Sarah stood in the center of the room without moving. The whole thing felt surreal. All she could think as she watched him was that she knew who'd killed his wife.

"Charlie came by this morning," he said suddenly, and the sound of his voice brought her back. "He took the file I had on Missy."

"I'm sorry."

It sounded ridiculous, but it was the first and only thing that came to mind.

Miles didn't seem to notice.

"He also told me that he'd have me arrested if I so much as look at Otis Timson."

This time, Sarah didn't respond. He'd come to vent; the defensive posture he held made that clear. Miles turned toward her.

"Can you believe that? All I did was arrest the guy who killed my wife and this is what happens."

It took all the control she could summon to keep her composure.

"I'm sorry," she said for the second time.

"So am I." He shook his head. "I can't look for Sims, I can't look for evidence, I can't do anything. I'm supposed to sit at home and wait for Charlie to handle everything."

She cleared her throat, struggling for a way out. "Well . . . don't you think that might be a good idea? For a little while, I mean?" she offered.

"No, not really. Christ, I'm the only one who kept

looking after the initial investigation dried up. I know more about this case than anyone."

*No, Miles, you don't.*

"So what are you going to do?"

"I don't know."

"You'll listen to Charlie, though, won't you?"

Miles looked away, refusing to answer, and Sarah felt something drop in her stomach.

"Listen, Miles," she said, "I know you don't want to hear this, but I think Charlie's right. Let other people handle Otis."

"Why? So they can screw it up a second time?"

"They didn't screw it up."

His eyes flashed. "No? Then why is Otis still walking around? Why was it up to me to find the people who fingered him? Why didn't they look harder for any evidence back then?"

"Maybe there wasn't any," she answered quietly.

"Why do you keep playing devil's advocate about this?" he demanded. "You did the same damn thing yesterday."

"No, I didn't."

"Yeah, you did. You didn't listen to anything I said."

"I didn't want you to do anything—"

He held up his hands. "Yeah—I know. You and Charlie both. Neither one of you seems to realize what the hell is going on here."

"Of course I do," she said, trying to hide the tension in her voice. "You think Otis did it and you want revenge. But what happens if you find out later that Sims and Earl were wrong somehow?"

"Wrong?"

"With what they heard, I mean . . ."

"You think they're lying about this? Both of them?"

"No. I'm just saying that maybe they heard it wrong. Maybe Otis said it, but he didn't mean it. Maybe he didn't do it."

For a moment, Miles was too thunderstruck to speak. Sarah pressed on, talking over the lump in her throat.

"I mean, what if you find out that Otis is innocent? I know you two don't get along—"

"Don't get along?" he said, cutting her off. He stared hard at her before taking a step toward her. "What the hell are you talking about? He killed my wife, Sarah."

"You don't know that."

"Yes, I do," he said. He moved even closer to her. "What I don't know is why you're so convinced that he's innocent."

She swallowed. "I'm not saying that he is. I'm just saying that you should let Charlie handle this so that you don't do anything . . ."

"Like what? Kill him?"

Sarah didn't answer and Miles stood before her.

His voice was strangely calm. "Like he killed my wife, you mean?"

She paled. "Don't start talking like that. You've got Jonah to think about."

"Don't bring him into this."

"It's true, though. You're all he's got."

"Don't you think I know that? What do you think kept me from pulling the trigger in the first place? I had the chance but I didn't do it, remember?" Miles exhaled sharply as he turned from her, almost as if he were disappointed that he hadn't. "Yeah, I wanted to kill him. I think he deserves it for what he did—an eye for an eye, right?" He shook his head and looked up at her. "I just want him to pay. And he will. One way or another."

With that, Miles abruptly walked to the door, slamming it as he left.

# Chapter 32

Sarah couldn't sleep that night.

She was going to lose her brother.

And she was going to lose Miles Ryan.

As she lay in bed, she was reminded of the evening she and Miles had first made love in this room. She remembered it all—the way he'd listened when she told him she couldn't have children, his expression when he'd told her that he loved her, how they'd whispered together for hours afterward, and the peace she'd felt in his arms.

It had seemed so right, so perfect.

The hours after Miles had left produced no answers. If anything, she was more confused than she had been earlier; now that the shock had passed and she was able to think more clearly, she knew that no matter what decision she made, nothing would ever be the same again.

It was over.

If she didn't tell Miles, how could she face him in the future? She couldn't imagine Miles and Jonah in her home, sitting around the Christmas tree and opening gifts, she and Brian smiling, pretending that nothing had ever happened. She couldn't imagine looking at Missy's pictures in his house, or sitting with Jonah, knowing that Brian had killed his mother. Nor, of course, would it be the right thing to do. Not with Miles hell-bent on making sure that Otis paid for the crime. She had to tell him the truth, if for no other reason than to make sure that Otis Timson wasn't punished for something he didn't do.

More than that, Miles had the right to know what really happened to his wife. He deserved that.

But if she did tell him, then what? Would Miles simply believe Brian's story and let it go? No, not likely. Brian had broken the law, and once she told him, Brian would be arrested, her parents would be devastated, Miles would never speak to her again, and she would lose the man she loved.

Sarah closed her eyes. She could live with never having met Miles.

But to fall in love with him and then lose him?

And what was going to happen to Brian?

She felt sick to her stomach.

She got out of bed, slid into a pair of slippers, and went to the living room, wanting desperately to find something, anything, to think about instead. But even there, she was reminded of all that had happened, and she knew with sudden certainty what she had to do. As painful as it was going to be, there was no other way around it.

When the phone rang the following morning, Brian knew it was Sarah on the other end. He'd been expecting the call, and he reached for the phone before his mother would have the chance to answer it.

Sarah got right to the point; Brian listened quietly. In the end, he said that he would. A few minutes later, his feet leaving foot-prints in the light snow, Brian made his way to the car.

His mind wasn't on the drive; instead it was on the things he'd said the day before. He had known when he'd told her that Sarah would be unable to keep his secret. Despite her worries about him, about her future with Miles, she would want him to turn himself in. That was her nature; above all, his sister knew what it was like to be betrayed, and keeping silent would be a betrayal of the worst kind.

It was the reason, he thought, that he'd told her.

Brian spotted her just before he parked the car, outside the Episcopal church, where he'd once attended Missy's funeral. Sarah was sitting on a bench, one that overlooked a small cemetery, so old that most of the writing on the headstones had worn away over the centuries. Even before he stepped out the door, Brian could see her plainly. She looked forlorn, truly lost in a way that he'd seen only once before.

Sarah heard him pull up and turned, though she did not wave. A moment later, Brian sat next to her.

Sarah, he knew, must have called in sick. The school where she taught, unlike his, had another week to go before vacation. As he sat there, he couldn't help but wonder what would have happened had he not come home for Thanksgiving and seen Miles at the house or if Otis hadn't been arrested.

"I don't know what to do," she finally whispered.

"I'm sorry," he said quietly.

"You should be."

Brian could hear the bitterness in her tone.

"I don't want to go over all of it again, but I need to know that you were telling me the truth." She turned to face him. Her cheeks were flushed in the chill, as if someone had pinched them.

"I was."

"I mean about all of it, Brian. Was it really an accident?"

"Yes," he said.

She nodded, though his answer didn't seem to comfort her. "I didn't sleep last night," she said. "Unlike you, I can't ignore this."

Brian didn't respond. There was nothing he could say.

"Why didn't you tell me?" she asked at last. "When it happened, I mean?"

"I couldn't," Brian answered. The day before, she

had asked the same question, and he had answered in the same way.

She sat in silence for a long moment. "You have to tell him," she said, staring out over the headstones. Her voice sounded like a shadow of itself.

"I know," he whispered.

She lowered her head, and he thought he saw tears beginning to form. She was worried about him, but it wasn't her worry that caused the tears. Sitting beside her, Brian knew that she was crying for herself.

Sarah went with Brian to Miles's house. As she drove, Brian stared out the window. The movement of the car seemed to drain Brian of energy, but he was strangely unafraid of what was coming. His fear, he knew, had been passed to his sister.

They crossed the bridge, then turned on Madame Moore's Lane, following the winding curves until they reached Miles's driveway. Sarah pulled alongside his pickup and turned the key, extinguishing sound.

Sarah didn't get out right away. Instead, she sat, holding the keys in her lap. She took a deep breath, then finally faced him. Her mouth was set in a tight, forced smile of support, then vanished. She slid her keys into her purse, and Brian pushed open the door. Together they started toward the house.

Sarah hesitated at the step, and for a moment, Brian's eyes darted to the corner of the porch, where he'd stood so many times. As soon as it happened, he knew that he would tell Miles about the crime, but just as he had with his sister, he would keep silent about the other things he had done.

Steeling herself, Sarah walked to the door and knocked. A moment later, Miles opened the door.

"Sarah . . . Brian . . . ," he said.

"Hi, Miles," Sarah answered. Her voice, Brian thought, was surprisingly steady.

At first, no one moved. Still upset from the day before, Miles and Sarah simply stared at each other, until Miles took a small step backward.

"Come in," he said, leading them inside. He closed the door behind them. "Can I get you something to drink?"

"No, thank you."

"How about you, Brian?"

"No. I'm fine."

"So what's up?"

Sarah absently adjusted her purse strap. "There's something I . . . I mean we, have to talk to you about," she said awkwardly. "Can we sit down?"

"Sure," Miles answered. He motioned toward the couch.

Brian took a seat next to Sarah, across from Miles. Brian took a deep breath, almost starting then, but Sarah cut him off.

"Miles . . . before we start, I want you to know that

I wish I didn't have to be here. I wish that more than anything. Try to keep that in mind, okay? This isn't easy for any of us."

"What's going on?" he asked.

Sarah glanced toward Brian. She nodded, and with that, Brian felt his throat suddenly go dry. He swallowed.

"It was an accident," he said.

At that, the words poured forth, the way he'd rehearsed them a hundred times in his head. Brian told him everything about that night two years ago, leaving nothing out. His mind, however, wasn't on the words.

Instead it was on Miles's reaction. At first there was none. As soon as Brian began, Miles slipped into a different posture, that of someone who wanted to listen objectively, without interruption, the way he'd been trained as a sheriff. Brian, he knew, was making a confession, and Miles had learned that silence was the best way to get an uncensored version of events. It wasn't until later, when Brian mentioned Rhett's Barbecue, that Miles finally began to realize what Brian was telling him.

Then the shock set in. As Brian went on, Miles froze, his face draining of color. His hands tightened reflexively on the armrest. Nonetheless, Brian pressed forward. In the background, as if from somewhere far away, Brian heard his sister inhale sharply as he described the accident. He ignored the sound, continuing with his story, stopping only when he described the next morning in the kitchen, and his decision to keep silent.

Miles sat like a statue through it all, and when Brian lapsed into silence. Miles seemed to take a moment to register everything that Brian had told him. Then, finally, his eyes focused on Brian, as if seeing him for the first time.

In a way, Brian knew he was.

"A dog?" he rasped out. His voice was low and gravelly, as if he'd been holding his breath through the confession. "You're saying she jumped in front of your car because of a dog?"

"Yes." Brian nodded. "A black dog. A big one. There was nothing I could do."

Miles's eyes narrowed slightly as he tried to keep control. "Then why did you run?"

"I don't know," he said. "I can't explain why I ran that night. The next thing I knew, I was in the car."

"Because you don't remember." The anger in Miles's tone was unmistakable, barely suppressed. Ominous.

"I don't remember that part of it, no."

"But the rest of it you do. You remember everything else about that night."

"Yes."

"Then tell me the real reason you ran that night."

Sarah reached out to touch Miles's arm. "He's telling the truth, Miles. Believe me—he wouldn't lie about this."

Miles shook off her hand.

"It's okay, Sarah," Brian said. "He can ask whatever he wants."

"You're damn right I can," Miles added, his voice lowering even more.

"I don't remember why I ran," Brian answered. "Like I said, I don't remember even leaving the scene. I remember being in the car, but that's it."

Miles stood from the chair, glaring. "And you expect me to believe that?" he said. "That it was Missy's fault?"

"Wait a minute!" Sarah said, coming to her brother's defense. "He told you how it happened! He's telling the truth!"

Miles swiveled to face her. "Why the hell should I believe him?"

"Because he's here! Because he wanted you to know the truth!"

"Two years later he wants me to know the truth? How do you know it's the truth?"

He waited for an answer, but before she could respond, he suddenly took a small step backward. He turned from Sarah to Brian and back to Sarah again, as he considered what the answers to his questions meant.

Sarah had *known* exactly what her brother was going to say . . .

Which meant . . . that she'd known Otis was innocent. She'd tried to get him to back off. Let Charlie handle it, she'd said. What if Sims and Earl were wrong somehow?

She'd said those things because she'd *known* Brian was guilty.

But that made sense, didn't it?

Hadn't she said that she was close to her brother? Hadn't she said he was the one person she could really talk to, and vice versa?

Miles's thoughts, fed by adrenaline and anger, raced from one conclusion to the next.

She'd *known* but she hadn't told him. She'd known and . . . and . . .

Miles stared at Sarah wordlessly.

Hadn't she volunteered to help Jonah, even though it was out of the ordinary?

And hadn't she befriended him as well? Gone out with him? Listened to him, tried to help him move on with his life?

Miles's face began to twitch with barely suppressed rage.

*She'd known all along.*

She'd used him to assuage her own guilt. Everything they'd had was built on lies.

*She betrayed me.*

Miles stood without moving, without speaking, frozen in place. In the silence, Brian heard the heater come on.

"You knew," he finally rasped out. "You knew he'd killed Missy, didn't you?"

It was then, at that moment, that Brian understood not only that it was over between Sarah and Miles, but that, in Miles's mind, they had never had anything at all. Sarah, though, seemed baffled, and she answered Miles as if the answer to his question were obvious.

"Of course. That's why I brought him here."

Miles raised his hand to stop her, jabbing his finger in her direction with every point he made.

"No, no . . . you knew he'd killed her and didn't tell me . . . That's why you knew that Otis was innocent . . . That's why you kept trying to tell me to listen to Charlie . . ."

Sarah finally seemed to register the implication, and she suddenly, frantically, began shaking her head.

"No—wait—you don't understand—"

Miles cut her off, unwilling to listen, each statement more furious than the last.

"You knew all along . . ."

"No—"

"You've known since the moment we met."

"No—"

"That's why you offered to help Jonah."

"No!"

For a moment, it seemed as if Miles would strike her, but he didn't. Instead he lashed out in another direction. He kicked the end table over, sending the lamp crashing. Sarah flinched and Brian rose from the couch to reach for her; Miles grabbed him before he could and spun him around. Miles was both stronger and heavier, and Brian could do nothing to stop him from wrenching his wrist up his back toward his shoulder blades. Sarah instinctively moved away from the commotion before she even realized what was happening. Brian didn't resist, even as pain shot through his shoulder. He winced, his eyes closing, his face contorting.

"Stop! You're hurting him!" Sarah screamed.

Miles held up a warning hand in her direction. "Stay out of this!"

"Why are you doing this! You don't have to hurt him!"

"He's under arrest!"

"It was an accident!"

But Miles was beyond reason, and he twisted Brian's arm hard again, forcing him away from the couch, away from Sarah, toward the front door. Brian almost stumbled, and Miles grabbed at him, his fingers digging into Brian's flesh. Miles pushed Brian into the wall as he reached for the handcuffs that were hanging on a peg near the door. Miles slapped them around one wrist and then the next, pinching them tightly.

"Miles! Wait!" Sarah shouted.

Miles opened the door and pushed Brian out, forcing him onto the porch.

"You don't understand!"

Miles ignored her. He grabbed Brian's arm and began dragging him toward the car. It was difficult for Brian to keep his balance, and he stumbled. Sarah rushed up behind them.

"Miles!"

Miles spun around. "I want you out of my life," he hissed.

The hatred in his voice shocked Sarah into stopping.

"You betrayed me," Miles said. "You used me." He didn't wait for Sarah to respond. "You wanted to try to make things better—not for me and Jonah, but for you and Brian. You thought if you did that, you'd feel better about yourself."

She paled, incapable of saying anything.

"You knew from the beginning," he went on. "And you were willing to let me go on without ever knowing the truth until someone else got arrested for it."

"No, that's not the way it happened—"

"Stop lying to me!" he boomed. "How the hell can you live with yourself?"

The comment lashed at her, and she responded

defensively. "You've got it all wrong, and you don't even care."

"I don't care? I'm not the one who did anything wrong here."

"Neither did I."

"And you expect me to believe that?"

"It's the truth!" Then, despite her anger, Brian saw her eyes begin to well up with tears.

Miles paused momentarily but showed no sympathy at all. "You don't even know what the truth *is*."

With that, he turned and opened the door to the car. He shoved Brian in, then slammed the door and reached in his pocket for his keys. He pulled them out as he got in behind the wheel.

Sarah was too shocked to say anything more. She watched as Miles started the car, pressed the accelerator, then jammed the car into gear. The tires squealed as the car moved into reverse, backing toward the road.

Miles never glanced her way, and a moment later, he vanished from sight.

# Chapter 33

Miles drove erratically, smashing the accelerator and slamming on the brakes, as if testing how hard he could push the car before one or the other ceased to work. More than once, his arms locked behind him, Brian nearly toppled over as the car careened through a turn. From his vantage point, Brian could see the muscle in Miles's jaw tensing and relaxing, as if someone were flicking a switch. Miles held the wheel with both hands, and though he seemed to be concentrating on the road, his eyes continually darted to the rearview mirror, where they sometimes caught Brian's.

Brian could see the anger in his eyes. It was reflected plainly in the mirror, yet at the same time, he saw something else there, something he hadn't expected. He saw the anguish in Miles's eyes, and Brian was reminded of the way Miles had looked at Missy's funeral, trying and failing to make sense of all that had happened. Brian wasn't sure if the anguish Miles was feeling came from Missy or Sarah, or even both. All he knew was that it didn't have anything to do with him.

From the corner of his eye, Brian watched the trees whizzing past his window. The road curved, and again Miles took the turn without slowing down. Brian planted his feet; despite that, his body shifted and he slid toward the window. In a few minutes, he knew, they would pass the spot of Missy's accident.

The Good Shepherd Community Church was located in Pollocksville, and the driver of the church van, Bennie Wiggins, had never had so much as a speeding ticket in his fifty-four years of driving. Though it was a source of pride for Bennie, the reverend would have asked him to drive even if his record hadn't been so good. Volunteers were hard to find, especially when the weather wasn't so good, but Bennie was one he could always count on.

On that morning, the reverend had asked Bennie to drive the van to New Bern to pick up the donations of food and clothing that had been collected over the weekend, and Bennie had shown up promptly. He'd driven in, had a cup of coffee and two doughnuts while he waited for others to load the van, then had thanked everyone for their help before getting behind the wheel to head back to the church.

It was a little before ten when he turned onto Madame Moore's Lane.

He reached for the radio, hoping to find some gospel music to liven up the ride back. Even though the road was slick, he began fiddling with the knob.

Up ahead and out of sight, he had no way of knowing that another car was heading his way.

"I'm sorry," Brian finally said, "I didn't mean for any of it to happen."

At the sound of his voice, Miles glanced in the mirror again. Instead of responding, however, he cracked the window.

Cold air rushed in. After a moment, Brian huddled down, his unzipped jacket flapping in the wind.

In the reflection, Miles stared at Brian with unbridled hatred.

Sarah sped around the corner much as Miles had done, hoping to catch up with his car. He had a head start—not much, maybe a couple of minutes, but how far was that? A mile? More? She wasn't exactly sure, and as the car hit a straight stretch, she pressed the accelerator even harder.

She had to catch them. She couldn't leave Brian in his care, not after the uncontrolled fury she had seen in his face, not after what he'd nearly done to Otis.

She wanted to be there when Miles brought Brian in, but the problem was that she didn't know where the sheriff's department was. She knew where the police station was, the courthouse, even the City Hall, since they were all located downtown. But she'd never been to the sheriff's department. For all she knew, it was located in the outer reaches of the county somewhere.

She could stop and call, or check a phonebook somewhere, but that would only put her farther behind, she thought frantically. She would stop if she had to. If she didn't see him in the next couple of minutes . . .

Commercials.

Bennie Wiggins shook his head. Commercials and more commercials. That's all there was on the radio these days. Water softeners, car dealerships, alarm systems . . . after every other song, he heard the same litany of businesses hawking their wares.

The sun was beginning to peek over the treetops, and the glare from the snow caught Bennie off-guard. He squinted and pulled down the visor just as the radio faded into silence for a moment.

Another commercial. This one promised to teach your child to read. He reached for the knob.

He didn't notice that as he eyes locked on the dial, he began drifting over the center line . . .

"Sarah didn't know," Brian finally offered into the silence. "Sarah didn't know about any of it."

Over the wind, Brian wasn't sure if Miles could hear him, but he had to try. He knew this was the last chance he would get to speak to Miles without other people around. Whatever lawyer his father would arrange for him would advise him to say nothing more than he had already said. And Miles, he suspected, would be ordered to stay away from him.

But Miles had to know the truth about Sarah. Not so much for the future—as Brian saw it, they had no chance at all—but because he couldn't bear the thought of Miles believing that Sarah had known all along. He didn't want Miles to hate her. Sarah, above everyone, didn't deserve that. Unlike Miles or him, Sarah hadn't had any part in this at all.

"She never told me who she was seeing. I was away at school and I didn't find out until Thanksgiving that it was you. But I didn't tell her about the accident until yesterday. She didn't know anything until then. I know you don't want to believe me . . ."

"You think I should believe you?" Miles shot back.

"She didn't know anything," Brian repeated. "I wouldn't lie to you about that."

"What would you lie about, then?"

Brian regretted the words as soon as he'd said them and felt the chill cut through him as he imagined his answer. *Going to the funeral. His dreams. Watching Jonah at school. Stalking Miles at his home . . .*

Brian shook his head slightly, forcing the thought away. "Sarah didn't do anything wrong," he said instead, avoiding the question.

But Miles persisted. "Answer me," he said. "What would you lie about? The dog, maybe?"

"No."

"Missy didn't jump in front of your car."

"She didn't mean to. She couldn't help it. It wasn't anyone's fault. It just happened. It was an accident."

"*No, it wasn't!*" Miles boomed, wheeling around. Despite the roar of the wind from the open windows, the sound seemed to ricochet in the car. "You weren't paying attention and you ran her down!"

"No," Brian insisted. He was less afraid of Miles than he knew he should be. He felt calm, like an actor reciting his lines by rote. No fear. Just a sense of profound exhaustion. "It happened just like I told you."

Miles pointed his finger at Brian, halfway turned in his seat now. "You killed her and you ran!"

"No—I stopped and I looked for her. And when I found her . . ." Brian trailed off.

In his mind he saw Missy, lying in the ditch, her body angled wrong. Staring up at him.

Staring at nothing.

"I felt sick, like I was going to die, too." Brian paused, turning away from Miles. "I covered her up with a blanket," he whispered. "I didn't want anyone else to see her that way."

Bennie Wiggins finally found a song he wanted. The glare was intense and he sat straight in his seat just as he realized where he was on the road. He righted the van, guiding it back in his lane.

The approaching car was close now.

He still didn't see it.

Miles flinched when Brian mentioned the blanket, and for the first time Brian knew that he was really listening, despite his shouts to the contrary. Brian kept talking, oblivious to Miles, oblivious to the cold.

Oblivious to the fact that Miles's attention was focused entirely on him and not on the road.

"I should have called then, that night, after I got home. It was wrong. There's no excuse for it, and I'm sorry. I'm sorry for what I did to you and I'm sorry for what I did to Jonah."

To Brian, his voice sounded as if it belonged to someone else.

"I didn't know that keeping it inside was worse. It ate away at me. I know you don't want to believe that, but it did. I couldn't sleep. I couldn't eat—"

"I don't care!"

"I couldn't stop thinking about it. And I've never stopped thinking about it. I even bring flowers to Missy's grave . . ."

Bennie Wiggins finally saw the car as he rounded a bend in the road.

It was happening so fast, it almost didn't seem real. The car was headed right at him, jumping from slow motion to full speed with terrifying inevitability. Bennie's mind clicked into overdrive, trying frantically to process the information.

*No, that couldn't be . . . Why would he be driving in my lane? That doesn't make sense . . . But he is driving in my lane. Doesn't he see me? He's got to see me . . . He'll jerk the wheel and right himself.*

All this happened in less than a few seconds, but in their span, Bennie knew with utter certainty that whoever was driving was going too fast to get out of the way in time.

They were heading straight for each other.

Brian caught the reflection of the sun against the windshield of the approaching van just as it rounded the corner. He stopped talking in midsentence and his first instinct was to use his hands to brace himself for the impact. He jerked hard enough for the handcuffs to cut into his wrists as he arched his back, screaming, *"Watch out!"*

Miles whipped around, then immediately, instinctively, jerked the wheel hard as the cars closed in on each other. Brian tumbled to the side, and as his head slammed into the side window, he was struck by the utter absurdity of what was happening.

This had all started with him in a car on Madame Moore's Lane.

And this was how it would end.

He braced himself for the thunderous impact that was coming.

Only it never came.

He did feel a hard thump, but it was toward the rear of the car, on his side. The car began to slide and left the road just as Miles slammed on the brakes. The car shot over the snow, just off the road, closing in on a speed limit sign. Miles struggled to keep control, then felt the wheels catch at the last moment. The car swerved again and jerked suddenly, coming to a halt in a ditch.

Brian landed on the floor, dazed and confused, crumpled between the seats; it took a moment for him to orient himself. He gasped for air, as if surfacing from the bottom of a pool. He didn't feel the cuts on his wrist.

Nor did he see the blood that had been smeared against the window.

# Chapter 34

"Are you okay?"

Sounds were fading in and out, and Brian groaned. He was struggling to get off the floor of the car, his arms still manacled behind his back.

Miles pushed open the door, then opened Brian's. Cautiously he pulled Brian out and helped him to his feet. The side of Brian's head was matted with blood that was also dripping down his cheek. Brian tried to stand on his own but staggered, and Miles took his arm again.

"Hold on—your head's bleeding. You sure you're okay?"

Brian swayed a little as the world around them moved in circles. It took a moment for him to understand the question. In the distance, Miles could see the driver of the van climbing out of his vehicle.

"Yeah . . . I think so. My head hurts . . ."

Miles kept his hand on Brian's arm as he glanced up the road again. The driver of the van—an elderly man—was crossing the road now, coming toward them. Miles bent Brian forward and gently checked the wound, then stood Brian up again, looking relieved. Despite Brian's dizziness, the expression on Miles's face struck him as preposterous, considering the last half hour.

"It doesn't look deep. Just a surface cut," Miles said. Then, holding up a couple of fingers, he asked, "How many?"

Brian squinted, concentrating as they came into focus. "Two."

Miles tried again. "Now how many?"

Same routine. "Four."

"How's the rest of your vision? Any spots? Black around the edges?"

Brian shook his head gingerly, his eyes halfway closed.

"Broken bones? Your arms okay? Your legs?"

Brian took a moment, testing out his limbs, still having trouble keeping his balance. As he rolled his shoulders, he winced. "My wrist hurts."

"Hold on a second." Miles pulled the keys from his pocket and removed the handcuffs. One of Brian's hands went immediately to his head. One wrist felt bruised and achy, the other seemed stiff to the point of immobility. With his hand on the wound, blood seeped between his fingers.

"Can you stand on your own?" Miles asked.

Brian knew he was still swaying slightly, but he nodded and Miles went to his door again. On the floor was a T-shirt that Jonah had left in the car, and Miles grabbed it. He brought it back and pressed it against the gash in Brian's head.

"Can you hold this?"

Brian nodded and took it just as the driver, looking pale and scared, came huffing up.

"Are you guys okay?" he asked.

"Yeah, we're fine," Miles answered automatically.

The driver, still shaken up, turned from Miles to Brian. He saw the blood trickling down Brian's cheek, and his mouth contorted.

"He's bleeding pretty bad."

"It's not as bad as it looks," Miles offered.

"Don't you think he needs an ambulance? Maybe I should call—"

"It's all right," Miles said, cutting him off. "I'm with the sheriff's department. I've checked it out and he'll be fine."

Brian felt like a bystander, despite the pain in his wrists and head.

"You're a sheriff?" The other driver took a step back and glanced toward Brian for support. "He was over the line. It wasn't my fault . . ."

Miles held up his hands. "Listen . . ."

The driver's eyes locked on the handcuffs Miles still held and his eyes widened. "I tried to get out of the way, but you were in my lane," he said, suddenly defensive.

"Hold on—what's your name?" Miles asked, trying to control the situation.

"Bennie Wiggins," he answered. "I wasn't speeding. You were in my lane."

"Hold on . . . ," Miles said again.

"You were over the line," the driver repeated. "You can't arrest me for this. I was being careful."

"I'm not going to arrest you."

"Then who are those for?" he said, pointing at the handcuffs.

Before Miles could answer, Brian cut in. "They were on me," he said. "He was bringing me in."

The driver looked at them as if he didn't understand, but before he could say anything, Sarah's car came to a sliding halt near them. They all turned as she scrambled out, looking frightened, confused, and angry all at once.

"What happened?" she shouted. She looked them all over before her eyes finally locked on Brian. When she saw the blood she went toward him. "Are you okay?" she asked, pulling him away from Miles.

Though still woozy, Brian nodded. "Yeah, I'm okay . . ."

She turned toward Miles furiously. "What the hell did you do to him? Did you hit him?"

"No," Miles answered with a quick shake of the head. "There was an accident."

"He was over the line," the driver suddenly offered, pointing toward Miles.

"An accident?" Sarah demanded, turning toward him.

"I was just driving along," he continued, "and when I rounded the curve, this guy was coming right at me. I swerved, but I couldn't get out of the way. It was his fault. I hit him, but I couldn't help it—"

"Barely," Miles interrupted. "He grazed the rear end of my car and I swerved off the road. We barely bumped each other."

Sarah turned her attention to Brian again, suddenly not knowing what to believe. "Are you sure you're okay?"

Brian nodded.

"What really happened?" she asked.

After a long moment, Brian pulled his hand away from his head. The shirt was wet and spongy, soaked in red. "It was an accident," he said. "It wasn't anyone's fault. It just happened."

It was, of course, the truth. Miles hadn't seen the van because he was turned around in his seat. Brian knew he hadn't meant for it to happen.

What Brian didn't realize was that these were the same words he'd used when describing the accident with Missy, the same words he'd said to Miles in the car, the same words he'd repeated to himself ad nauseam for the last two years.

Miles, though, didn't miss it.

Sarah closed in on Brian again, slipping her arm around him. Brian closed his eyes, feeling suddenly weak again.

"I'm taking him to the hospital," Sarah announced. "He needs to see a doctor."

With a gentle nudge, she began to lead him away from the car.

Miles took a step toward them. "You can't do that—"

"Try and stop me," she cut him off. "You're not getting anywhere near him again."

"Hold on," Miles said, and Sarah turned, looking at him contemptuously.

"You don't have to worry. We're not going to make a run for it."

"What's going on?" the driver asked, panic in his voice. "Why are they leaving?"

"None of your business," Miles answered.

All he could do was stare.

He couldn't bring Brian in looking the way he did, nor could he leave the scene until the situation there was settled. He supposed that he could have stopped them, but Brian needed to see a doctor, and if he held on to him, he'd have to explain what was going on to whoever came to investigate—something he didn't feel up to right then. So instead, feeling almost helpless, he did nothing. When Brian glanced back, however, he heard the words once more.

*It was an accident. It wasn't anyone's fault.*

Brian, Miles knew, was wrong about that. He hadn't been watching the road—hell, he hadn't even been facing the right direction—because of the things Brian had been saying.

About Sarah. About the blanket. About the flowers.

He hadn't wanted to believe him then, nor did he want to believe him now. Yet . . . he knew Brian wasn't lying about those things. He'd seen the blanket, he'd seen flowers at the grave every time he'd gone . . .

Miles closed his eyes, trying to shake the thought. *None of that matters and you know it. Of course Brian was sorry. He'd killed someone. Who wouldn't be sorry?*

That was what he'd been screaming at Brian when it happened. When he should have been watching the road. But instead—ignoring everything but his own anger—he'd almost driven head-on into another driver.

He'd almost killed them all.

But afterward, even though Brian had been hurt,

Brian had covered for him. And as he watched Brian and Sarah shuffling off, he knew instinctively that Brian would always cover for him.

Why?

Because he felt guilty and it was another way to ask for forgiveness? To hold something over Miles? Or had he really believed what he'd said?

In his mind, that might be how he saw it. Miles hadn't meant for it to happen, after all, so that made it an accident.

*As it had been with Missy?*

Miles shook his head. *No . . .*

That was different, he told himself. And it wasn't Missy's fault, either.

The breeze kicked up, swirling with light snow flurries.

*Or was it?*

It doesn't matter, he told himself again. Not now. It's too late for that.

Up on the road, Sarah was opening the car door for Brian. She helped him in and glanced toward Miles, not hiding her anger.

Not hiding how much she'd been hurt by his words.

Sarah hadn't known until yesterday, Brian had said. *She never even told me who you were.*

At the house only minutes ago, it seemed so obvious that Sarah had known all along. But now, with the way she was looking at him, it suddenly wasn't so clear. The Sarah he'd fallen in love with wasn't capable of deceit.

He felt his shoulders give just a little.

No, he knew that Brian hadn't lied about that. Nor had he lied about the blanket or the flowers or how sorry he'd been. And if he'd told the truth about those things . . .

*Could he be telling the truth about the accident as well?*

That question kept coming back to him, no matter how much he resisted it.

Sarah turned away and went around to the driver's side. Miles knew he could still stop them. If he really wanted to, he could stop them.

But he didn't.

He needed time to think—about everything he'd heard today, about Brian's confession . . .

And more than that, he decided as he watched Sarah slide behind the wheel, he needed time to think about Sarah.

Within a few minutes, a highway patrolman arrived—a resident of one of the nearby houses had called the incident in—and began making the report. Bennie was busy explaining his version just as Charlie pulled up. The officer took a moment to talk to him up on the road. Charlie nodded before approaching Miles.

He was leaning against the car, his arms crossed,

apparently lost in thought. Charlie ran a slow hand along the dent and scrape.

"For such a little dent, you look like hell."

Miles glanced up in surprise. "Charlie? What are you doing here?"

"Heard you were in an accident."

"Word travels fast."

Charlie shrugged. "You know how it goes." He dusted the snowflakes from his jacket. "You okay?"

Miles nodded. "Yeah. A little rattled, that's all."

"What happened?"

Miles shrugged. "Just lost control. The roads were a little slick."

Charlie waited to see if Miles would add anything else.

"That's it?"

"Like you said, it's just a little dent."

Charlie studied him. "Well, at least you're not hurt. The other driver seems fine, too."

Miles nodded, and Charlie joined him against the car.

"Anything else you want to tell me?"

When Miles didn't answer, Charlie cleared his throat. "The officer tells me that there was someone else in the car with you, someone who was wearing handcuffs, but that a lady came and took him away. Said she was taking him to the hospital. Now . . ." He paused, pulling his jacket a little tighter. "An accident is one thing, Miles. But there's a lot more than that going on here. Who was in the car with you?"

"He wasn't hurt that bad, if that's what you're worried about. I checked him out and he'll be okay."

"Just answer the question. You're in enough trouble already. Now, who were you bringing in?"

Miles shifted from one foot to the other. "Brian Andrews," he answered. "Sarah's brother."

"So she's the one who took him to the hospital?"

Miles nodded.

"And he was wearing handcuffs?"

No use trying to lie about it. He nodded shortly.

"Did you somehow forget that you're on suspension?" Charlie asked. "That officially, you're not allowed to arrest anyone?"

"I know."

"Then what the hell were you doing? What was so damn critical that you couldn't call it in?" He paused, meeting Miles's eyes. "I need the truth now— I'll get it eventually, but I want to hear it from you first. What was he doing, dealing drugs?"

"No."

"You catch him stealing a car?"

"No."

"A fight of some sort?"

"No."

"Then what was it?"

Though a part of Miles was tempted to tell Charlie

the whole crazy truth, to tell him that Brian had killed Missy, he couldn't seem to find the words. Not yet, anyway. Not until he'd figured everything out.

"It's complicated," Miles finally answered.

Charlie pushed his hands into his pockets. "Try me."

Miles glanced away. "I need a little time to figure things out."

"Figure what out? It's a simple question, Miles."

*Nothing is simple about this.*

"Do you trust me?" Miles asked suddenly.

"Yeah, I trust you. But that's not the point."

"Before we go into everything that happened, I have to think this through."

"Oh, c'mon—"

"Please, Charlie. Can you give me just a little time? I know I've had you jumping through hoops these last couple of days and I've been acting crazy, but I really need this from you. And it has nothing to do with Otis or Sims or anything like that—I swear I won't go anywhere near them."

Something in the earnestness of Miles's plea, the weary confusion he saw in his eyes, told Charlie how much Miles needed this from him.

He didn't like it, not at all. Something was going on here, something big, and he didn't like not knowing what it was.

*But . . .*

Despite his better judgment, he sighed and pushed

away from the car. He said nothing at all, nor did he look back as he left, knowing that if he did, he would change his mind.

A minute later, almost as if he'd never been there at all, Charlie was gone.

In time, the highway patrolman finished the report and left. Bennie, too, drove off.

Miles, though, stayed at the scene for almost an hour, his mind a tangled mess of contradictory thoughts. Oblivious to the cold, he sat in the car with the window open, absently running his hands over the steering wheel, over and over.

When he realized what he had to do, he closed the window and turned the key, heading onto the road again. The car barely had time to get warm before he pulled off to the side again and got back out. The temperature had warmed slightly and the snow was beginning to melt. Drops fell from the branches of trees with steady *plinks*, like the ticking of a clock.

He couldn't help but notice the overgrown bushes along the side of the road. Though he'd passed them a thousand times, until this morning, they'd meant nothing to him.

Now, as he stared at them, they were all he could think about. They blocked his view of the lawn, and one look was enough to tell him they were thick enough to have kept Missy from seeing the dog.

407

Too thick to charge through?

He paced the row of bushes, slowing when he reached the area where they assumed that Missy had been hit. Bending down for a closer look, he froze when he saw it. A gap between the bushes, like a hole. No prints were evident, but black leaves were matted on the ground and branches had been torn away on either side.

Obviously a passageway for something.

A black dog?

In the distance, he listened for the sound of barking. He scanned the yards, looking there as well.

There was nothing.

Too cold to be out today?

He'd never checked for a dog. No one had.

He looked up the road, wondering. He pushed his hands into his pockets. They were stiff from the cold, difficult to bend, and as they warmed, they began to sting. He didn't care.

Not knowing what else to do, he drove to the cemetery, hoping to clear his mind. He saw them even before he'd reached the grave. Fresh flowers, propped against the headstone.

His mind flashed to Charlie and something he once had said.

*Like someone was trying to apologize.*

Miles turned and walked away.

\*　　\*　　\*

Hours passed. Dark now. Outside the window, the winter sky was black and ominous.

Sarah turned from the window and paced her apartment again. Brian was home from the hospital. The cut wasn't serious, three stitches only, and there were no broken bones. It had taken less than an hour.

Despite the fact that she'd practically begged him, Brian hadn't wanted to stay with her. He'd needed to be alone. He was back at home, wearing a hat and sweatshirt, hiding the injuries from his parents.

"Don't tell them what happened, Sarah. I'm not ready for that yet. I want to be the one who tells them. I'll do it when Miles comes by."

Miles would come to arrest Brian. She was sure of that.

She wondered what was taking so long.

For the past eight hours, she'd veered from anger to worry, from frustration to bitterness and back again, one right after the other. There were too many different emotions for her to begin to sort through.

In her mind, she rehearsed the words she should have responded with when Miles lashed out at her so unfairly. *So you think you're the only one who got hurt here?* she would have said. *That no one else in the world can understand it? Did you stop to think how hard it was for me to bring Brian by this morning? To turn my own brother in? And your response—oh, that was the kicker, wasn't it? I betrayed you? I used you?*

In frustration, she picked up the remote and turned on the television, scanned the channels. Turned it off.

Take it easy, she told herself, trying to calm down. He'd just found out who'd killed his wife. Nothing harder than that, especially coming out of the blue the way it had. Especially coming from me.

And Brian.

Can't forget to thank him for ruining everyone's life.

She shook her head. That wasn't fair, either. He was just a kid back then. It was an accident. She knew he'd do anything to change what happened back then.

Back and forth it went. She circled the living room again, ending up at the window. Still no sign of him. She went to the phone and picked up the receiver, checking to make sure it had a dial tone. It did. Brian had promised to call her as soon as Miles came over.

So where was Miles, and what was he doing? Calling for reinforcements?

She didn't know what to do. Couldn't leave the house, couldn't use the phone. Not while she was waiting for the call.

Brian spent the rest of the day hiding in his room.

In his bed, he stared at the ceiling, his arms at his sides, legs straight, as though he were lying in a coffin. He knew he'd fallen asleep at times, because the shifting light made things look different in his room. Over the hours, the walls turned from white to faded gray, then to shadows as the sun traveled slowly across the sky and finally went down. He hadn't eaten lunch or dinner.

Sometime during the afternoon, his mother had knocked at his door and come in; Brian had closed his eyes, pretending to be asleep. He knew she thought he was sick, and he could hear her as she crossed the room. She'd put a hand to his forehead, feeling for a fever. After a minute, she'd crept out, closing the door behind her. In hushed tones, Brian had heard her speaking to his father.

"He must not be feeling well," she'd said. "He's really out."

When he wasn't sleeping, he thought about Miles. He wondered where Miles was, he wondered when Miles would come. He thought about Jonah, too, and what he would say when his father told him who had killed his mother. He wondered about Sarah and wished she hadn't been any part of this.

He wondered what prison was like.

In the movies, prisons were worlds of their own, with their own laws, their own kings and pawns, and gangs. He imagined the dim fluorescent lights and the cold permanence of the steel bars, doors clanging shut. In his mind, he heard toilets flushing, people talking and whispering and yelling and moaning; he imagined a place that was never silent, even in the middle of the night. He saw himself staring toward the tops of concrete walls covered with barbed wire and seeing guards in the towers, holding guns pointed toward the sky. He saw other prisoners, watching him with interest, taking bets on how long he would survive. He had no doubt about this: If he ended up there, he would be a pawn.

He would not survive in a place like that.

Later, as the sounds from the house began to settle down, Brian heard his parents go to bed. Light spilled under his door, then finally turned black. He fell asleep again, and later, when he woke suddenly, he saw Miles in the room. Miles was standing in the corner by the closet, holding a gun. Brian blinked, squinted, felt the fear constrict his chest, making it difficult to breathe. He sat up and held his hands in a defensive posture before he realized he'd been mistaken.

What he'd thought was Miles was nothing but his jacket on the coat rack, mingling with the shadows, playing tricks with his mind.

Miles.

He'd let him go. After the accident, Miles had let him go, and he hadn't come back.

Brian rolled over, curling into a ball.

But he would.

\* \* \*

Sarah heard the knock a little before midnight and glanced through the window on the way to the door, knowing who had come. When she opened it, Miles neither smiled nor frowned, nor did he move. His eyes were red, swollen with fatigue. He stood in the doorway, looking as if he didn't want to be here.

"When did you know about Brian?" he asked abruptly.

Sarah's eyes never left his. "Yesterday," she answered. "He told me yesterday. And I was as horrified as you were."

His lips, dry and cracked, came together. "Okay," he said.

With that, he turned to leave, and Sarah reached out to stop him, taking hold of his arm. "Wait . . . please."

He turned.

"It was an accident, Miles," she said. "A terrible, terrible accident. It shouldn't have happened, and it wasn't fair that it happened to Missy. I know that and I feel so sorry for you . . ."

She trailed off, wondering if she was reaching him. His expression was glazed, unreadable.

"But?" he said. There was no emotion in the question.

"No buts. I just want you to keep that in mind. There's no excuse for him running, but it was an accident."

She waited for his response. When there was none, she let go of his arm. He made no move to leave.

"What are you going to do?" she finally asked.

Miles glanced away. "He killed my wife, Sarah. He broke the law."

She nodded. "I know."

He shook his head without responding, then started down the hall. A minute later, outside the window, she watched as he got into his car and drove off.

She went to the couch again. The phone was on the end table and she waited, knowing it would ring soon.

# Chapter 35

Where, Miles wondered, was he supposed to go? What should he do, now that he knew the truth? With Otis, the answer had been simple. There was nothing to consider, nothing to debate. It didn't matter whether all the facts had fit or that everything had an easy explanation. He'd learned enough to know that Otis hated Miles enough to kill Missy; that was enough for Miles. Otis deserved whatever punishment the law could fashion, except for one thing.

That's not the way it happened.

The investigation had unearthed nothing. The file he'd painstakingly assembled over two years had meant nothing. Sims and Earl and Otis meant nothing. Nothing had provided the answer, but suddenly and without warning, it had arrived at his doorstep, dressed in a windbreaker and ready to cry.

This was what he wanted to know:

Did it matter?

He'd spent two years of his life thinking that it

did. He'd cried at night, he'd stayed up late, he'd taken up smoking, and he'd struggled, certain that the answer would change all of that. It had become the mirage on the horizon that was always just out of reach. And now, at this moment, he held it in his hand. With a single call, he could be avenged.

He could do that. But what if, on closer inspection, the answer wasn't what he had imagined it would be? What if the killer wasn't a drunk, wasn't an enemy; what if it wasn't an act of reckless behavior? What if it was a boy with pimples and baggy pants and dark brown hair, and he was afraid and sorry for what happened and swore it was an accident that couldn't have been avoided?

Did it matter then?

How should a person answer that? Was he supposed to take the memory of his wife and the misery of the last two years, then simply add his responsibility as a husband and a father and his duty to the law to come up with a quantifiable answer? Or did he take that total and subtract a boy's age and fear and obvious sorrow along with his love for Sarah, thus bringing the number back to zero?

He didn't know. What he did know was that whispering Brian's name aloud left a bitter taste in his mouth. Yes, he thought, it mattered. He knew with certainty that it would always matter, and he had to do something about it.

In his mind, he didn't have a choice.

Mrs. Knowlson had left the lights on and they cast a yellow glow over the walk as Miles approached the door. He could smell the faint odor of chimney smoke in the air as he knocked before inserting his key and gently pushing the door open.

Dozing beneath a quilt in her rocking chair, all white hair and wrinkles, she looked like a gnome. The television was on, but the volume was low, and Miles crept inside. Her head tilted to the side and she opened her eyes, merry eyes that never seemed to dim.

"Sorry I'm so late," he said, and Mrs. Knowlson nodded.

"He's sleeping in the back room," she said. "He tried to wait up for you."

"I'm glad he didn't," Miles said. "Before I get him, can I help you to your room?"

"No," she said. "Don't be silly. I'm old, but I can still move good."

"I know. Thanks for watching him today."

"Did you get everything worked out?" she asked.

Though Miles hadn't told her what was going on, she'd seen how troubled he'd been when he'd asked if she would watch Jonah after school.

"Not really."

She smiled. "There's always tomorrow."

417

"Yeah," he said, "I know. How was he today?"

"Tired. A little quiet, too. He didn't want to go outside, so we baked cookies."

She didn't say he was upset, but then, she didn't have to. Miles knew what she meant.

After thanking her again, he retreated to the bedroom and scooped Jonah into his arms, adjusting him so that the boy's head was on his shoulder. He didn't stir, and Miles knew he was exhausted.

Like his father.

Miles wondered if he would have nightmares again.

He carried him back to the house, then to bed. He pulled the covers up, turned on a night-light, and sat on the bed beside him. In the pale glow, he looked so vulnerable. Miles turned toward the window.

He could see the moon through the blinds, and he reached up to close them. He could feel the cold radiating through the glass. He pulled the covers higher and ran his hand through Jonah's hair.

"I know who did it," he whispered, "but I don't know if I should tell you."

Jonah was breathing steadily, his eyelids still.

"Do you want to know?"

In the darkness of the room, Jonah didn't answer.

After a while, Miles left the room and retrieved a beer from the refrigerator. He hung his jacket in the closet. On the floor was the box where he kept the home videos, and after a moment, he reached for it. He brought the box to the living room, set it on the coffee table, and opened it.

He selected one at random and popped it into the VCR, then settled back into the couch.

The screen was black at first, then out of focus, then everything came clear. Kids were seated around the table in the kitchen, wiggling furiously, little arms and legs waving like flags on a windy day. Other parents either stood close by or wandered in and out of the picture. He recognized the voice on the tape as his own.

It was Jonah's birthday party, and the camera zoomed in on him. He was two years old. Sitting in a booster seat, he was holding a spoon and thumping the table, grinning with every bang.

Missy came into the picture then, carrying a tray of cupcakes. One of them had two lit candles, and she set it in front of Jonah. She was singing "Happy Birthday," and the parents joined in. Within moments, hands and faces were smeared with chocolate.

The camera zoomed in on Missy, and Miles heard himself call her name on the tape. She turned and smiled; her eyes were playful, full of life. She was a wife and mother, in love with the life she lived. The camera faded to black and a new scene emerged in its place, one where Jonah was opening his gifts.

After that, the tape jumped a month forward, to Valentine's Day. A romantic table had been set, and Miles remembered it well. He'd set out the fine china, and the flickering glow of candlelight made the wineglasses sparkle. He'd cooked dinner for her: sole stuffed with crab and shrimp and topped with a lemon cream sauce, wild rice on the side, spinach salad. Missy was in the back room getting dressed; he'd asked her to stay there until everything was ready.

He'd caught her on tape as she entered the dining room and saw the table. That night, unlike at the birthday party, she looked nothing like a mother and wife; that evening, she looked as if she were in Paris or New York and were ready for opening night at the theater. She was wearing a black cocktail dress and small hooped earrings; she wore her hair in a bun, and a few curled strands framed her face.

"It's beautiful," she'd breathed. "Thank you, honey."

"So are you," Miles had answered.

Miles remembered that she'd asked him to turn off the camera so they could sit at the table; he also remembered that after dinner, they had gone to the bedroom and made love, lost in the blankets for hours. Thinking back to that night, he barely heard the small voice behind him.

"Is that Mommy?"

Miles used the remote to stop the tape just as he

turned and saw Jonah at the end of the hallway. He felt guilty and knew he looked it, but he tried to hide it with a smile.

"What's up, champ?" he asked. "Having trouble sleeping?"

Jonah nodded. "I heard some noises. They woke me up."

"I'm sorry. That was probably just me."

"Was that Mommy?" he asked again. He was gazing at Miles, his eyes fixed and steady. "On the television?"

Miles heard the sadness in his voice, as though he'd accidentally broken a favorite toy. Miles tapped the couch, not knowing exactly what to say. "C'mere," he said. "Sit with me."

After hesitating briefly, Jonah shuffled to the couch. Miles slipped his arm around him. Jonah looked up at him, waiting, and scratched the side of his face.

"Yeah, that was your mom," Miles finally said.

"Why's she on television?"

"It's a tape. You know the kind we used to make with the videocamera sometimes? When you were little?"

"Oh," he said. He pointed to the box. "Are all of those tapes?"

Miles nodded.

"Is Mommy on those, too?"

"Some of them."

"Can I watch 'em with you?"

Miles pulled Jonah a little closer. "It's late, Jonah—I was almost done, anyway. Maybe some other time."

"Tomorrow?"

"Maybe."

Jonah seemed satisfied with that, at least for the moment, and Miles reached behind him to turn the lamp off. He leaned back on the couch, and Jonah curled against him. With the lights off, Jonah's eyelids began to droop. Miles could feel his breathing begin to slow. He yawned. "Dad?"

"Yeah."

"Did you watch those tapes because you're sad again?"

"No."

Miles ran his hand through Jonah's hair methodically, slowly.

"Why did Mom have to die?"

Miles closed his eyes. "I don't know."

Jonah's chest went up and down. Up and down. Deep breaths. "I wish she was still here."

"So do I."

"She's never coming back." A statement, not a question.

"No."

Jonah said no more before he fell asleep. Miles

held him in his arms. Jonah felt small, like a baby, and Miles could smell the faint odor of shampoo in his hair. He kissed the top of his head, then rested his cheek against him.

"I love you, Jonah."

No answer.

It was a struggle to get up from the couch without waking Jonah, but for the second time that night, he carried his son to his room and put him in bed. On his way out, he closed the door partway behind him.

*Why did Mom have to die?*

*I don't know.*

Miles went back to the living room and put the tape back into the box, wishing Jonah hadn't seen it, wishing he hadn't talked about Missy.

*She's never coming back.*

*No.*

He carried the box back to the bedroom closet, wishing with a terrible ache that he could change that, too.

On the back porch, in the darkened chill of night, Miles took a long drag on the cigarette, his third of the night, and stared at the blackened water.

He'd been standing outside since he'd put the videos away, trying to put the conversation with Jonah behind him. He was exhausted and angry, and he didn't want to think about Jonah or what he should tell him. He didn't want to think about Sarah or Brian or Charlie or Otis or a black dog darting between the bushes. He didn't want to think about blankets or flowers or a bend in the road that had started it all.

He wanted to be numb. To forget everything. To go back in time before all this began.

He wanted his life back.

Off to the side, fed by the lights from inside the house, he saw his own shadow following him, like the thoughts he couldn't leave behind.

Brian, he assumed, would go free, even if Miles brought him in.

He'd get probation, maybe have his license revoked, but he wouldn't end up behind bars. He'd been a minor when it happened; there were mitigating circumstances, the judge would acknowledge his sorrow and take pity.

And Missy·was never coming back.

Time passed. He lit another cigarette and smoked it down. Dark clouds spanned the sky above; he could hear the rain as it soaked the earth. Over the water, the moon made an appearance, peeking through the clouds. Soft light spilled into the yard. He stepped off the porch and onto the flat slate he'd sunk into the ground as a pathway. The path led to the tin-roofed shed where he kept his tools, his lawn mower, weed killer, a can of gasoline. During the marriage, it had been his place, and Missy seldom ventured there.

*She had, though, on the last day he saw her . . .*

Small puddles had collected on the slate, and he felt the water splash around his feet. The pathway curved along the house, past a willow tree he'd planted for Missy. She'd always wanted one in her yard, thinking they looked both sad and romantic. He passed a tire swing, then a wagon that Jonah had left outside. A few steps later, he reached the shed.

It was padlocked, and Miles reached above the door and found the key. The lock opened with a click. He opened the door and was greeted with a musty smell. There was a flashlight on the shelf, and he reached for it. He turned it on and looked around. A spiderweb that started in the corner stretched toward a small window.

Years ago, when his father had left, he'd given Miles a few things to keep. He'd packed them away in a large metal box; Miles hadn't been given the key. The lock, though, was small, and now Miles reached for the hammer that hung on the wall. He swung the hammer and the lock popped open. He lifted the lid.

A couple of albums, a leather-covered journal, a shoebox full of arrowheads that his father had found near Tuscarora. Miles looked past them to the bottom and found what he was looking for. His father had kept the box, and the gun was neatly tucked inside. It was the only gun that Charlie hadn't known about.

Miles knew he was going to need it, and that night he oiled the gun, making sure it was ready to go.

# Chapter 36

M iles didn't come for me that night.

Bone tired, I remember forcing myself from my bed at dawn the following morning to shower. I was stiff from the accident, and as I turned the faucet on, I felt a shooting pain from my chest to my back. My head was tender when I washed my hair. My wrists ached when I ate breakfast, but I finished before my parents made it to the table, knowing that if they saw me wince, they would ask questions I wasn't prepared to answer. My father was heading into work; because it was nearly Christmas, I knew my mother would head out for errands as well.

I would tell them later, after Miles came for me.

Sarah called that morning to check on me. I asked the same questions of her. She told me that Miles had come by the night before, that they talked for a minute, but that she didn't know what to make of it.

I told her that I didn't, either.

But I waited. Sarah waited. My parents went on with their lives.

In the afternoon, Sarah called again.

"No, he still hasn't come," I told her. He hadn't called her, either.

The day passed, the evening came. Still no Miles.

On Wednesday, Sarah went back to school. I told her to go, that I'd reach her at the school if Miles came. It was the last week of school before Christmas break, and she had work to do. I stayed home, waiting for Miles.

I waited in vain.

Then it was Thursday and I knew what I had to do.

In the car, Miles waited as he sipped a cup of coffee he'd picked up at a convenience store. The gun was on the seat beside him, beneath a fold of newspapers, fully loaded and ready to go. The side window was beginning to steam with his breath, and he wiped it with his hand. He needed to see clearly.

He was in the right place; he knew that. Now all he had to do was watch carefully, and when the time was right, he would act.

That afternoon, just before dusk, the sky was glowing red and orange over the horizon as I got in the car. Though it was still chilly, the bitter cold had passed and temperatures had returned to normal. The rain over the previous couple of days had melted all the snow; where I once saw lawns blanketed in white, I now saw the familiar brown of centipede grass, gone dormant over the winter. Wreaths and red bows decorated windows and doors in my neighborhood, but in the car I felt disconnected from the season, as if I'd slept through it all and had another year to wait.

I made a single stop on my way, my usual. I think the man there had come to know me, since I made the same purchase every time. When he saw me come in, he waited by the counter, nodded when I told him what I wanted, then returned a few minutes later. We had never shared small talk in all the time I'd been coming to his shop. He didn't ask me what they were for; he never did.

He did, however, say the same thing every time he handed them to me:

"They're the freshest I've got."

He took my money and rang up the purchase. On my way back to the car, I could smell them, their sweet, honeyed fragrance, and I knew he was right. The flowers, once again, were beautiful.

I set them on the car seat beside me. I followed roads familiar to me, roads I wish I'd never traveled, and I parked outside the gates. I steeled myself as I stepped out of the car.

I saw no one in the cemetery. Gripping my jacket near the collar to pull it tighter, I walked with my head down; I didn't have to watch where I was going. The ground was wet, clinging to my feet. In a minute, I was at the grave.

As always, I was struck by how small it was.

429

*It was ridiculous to think this, but as I stared, I couldn't help it. The grave, I noticed, was well tended. The grass was neatly trimmed, and there was a silk carnation in a small holder in front of the headstone. It was red, as was every other carnation near every other headstone I could see, and I knew that the groundskeeper had placed them all.*

*I bent over and propped the flowers against the granite, making sure not to touch the stone. I never had. It wasn't, nor had it ever been, mine.*

*Afterwards, my mind drifted. Usually, I thought about Missy and the wrong decisions I had made; on that day, I found my thoughts drawn to Miles.*

*I think that was the reason why I didn't hear the approaching footsteps until they were already upon me.*

"Flowers," Miles said.

Brian turned at the sound of his voice, half-surprised, half-terrified.

Miles was standing near an oak tree whose limbs fanned out over the ground. He was wearing a long black coat and jeans; his hands were buried in his pockets.

Brian felt the blood drain from his face.

"She doesn't need flowers anymore," Miles said. "You can stop bringing them."

Brian didn't respond. What was there really to say?

Miles stared at him. With the sun sinking below the horizon, his face was shadowed and dark, his features hidden. Brian had no idea what he was thinking. Miles pushed the coat outward with both hands, as if he were holding something beneath its folds.

Hiding something.

Miles made no move toward Brian, and for a fleeting second, Brian had the urge to run. To escape. He was younger by fifteen years, after all—a quick burst might be enough to allow him to reach the road. Cars would be there, people would be all around.

But just as quickly as the thought came, it left him, draining whatever energy he had. He didn't have any reserves left. He hadn't eaten for days. He'd never make it, not if Miles really wanted to catch him.

And more than that, Brian knew he didn't have any place to go.

So Brian faced him. Miles was twenty feet away, and Brian saw his chin rise slightly. Miles met his gaze. Brian waited for him to do something, make a gesture; perhaps, he thought, Miles was waiting for the same thing. It struck Brian that they must have looked like a couple of gunfighters in the Old West, preparing to draw.

When the silence became too much to bear, Brian looked away, toward the street. He noticed that Miles's car was parked behind his, the only two he could see. They were alone here, among the gravestones.

"How did you know I was here?" Brian finally asked.

Miles took his time in answering. "I followed you," he said. "I figured you'd be leaving the house sometime and I wanted to be alone with you."

Brian swallowed, wondering how long Miles had been watching him.

"You bring flowers, but you don't even know who she was, do you?" Miles said quietly. "If you knew her, you would have been bringing tulips. Those were the ones she would have wanted here. Those were her favorite—yellows, reds, pinks—she loved them all. She used to plant a garden every spring with tulips. Did you know that?"

No, Brian thought, I didn't. In the distance, he heard the whistle of a train.

"Did you know that Missy used to worry about the wrinkles in the corners of her eyes? Or that her favorite breakfast was French toast? Or that she always wanted to own a classic Mustang convertible? Or that when she laughed, it was all I could do to keep my hands off her? Did you know she was the first woman I'd ever loved?"

Miles paused, willing Brian to look at him.

"That's all I have left now. Memories. And there will never be any more. You took that from me. And you took that from Jonah, too. Did you know that Jonah has had nightmares since she died? That he still cries out for his mother in his sleep? I have to take him in my arms and hold him for hours until it finally stops. Do you know how that makes me feel?"

His eyes pierced Brian's, pinning him to the patch of ground where he stood.

"I spent two years looking for the man who ruined my life. Jonah's life. I lost those two years because it was all I could think about."

Miles glanced toward the ground and shook his head.

"I wanted to find the person who killed her. I wanted that person to know how much he'd taken away from me that night. And I wanted the man who killed Missy to pay for what he did. You have no idea how much those thoughts consumed me. Part of me still wants to kill him. To do the same thing to his family that he did to mine. And now, I'm looking at the man who did it. And this man is putting the wrong flowers on my wife's grave."

Brian felt his throat constrict.

"You killed my wife," he said. "I'll never forgive you, and I'll never forget. When you look in the mirror, I want you to remember that. And I don't want you to ever forget all that you took from me. You took away the person that I loved most in the world, you took my son's mother, and you took two years from my life. Do you understand?"

After a long moment, Brian nodded.

"Then understand something else. Sarah can know what happened here, but only her. You take this conversation—and everything else—to your grave. Tell no one else about any part of it. Ever. Not your parents, not your wife, not your kids, not your minister, not your buddies. And make sure you do something with your life, something that doesn't make me regret what I'm doing. Promise me those things."

Miles stared, making sure Brian had heard him, until Brian nodded again. Then, Miles turned to leave. A minute later, he was gone.

Only then did Brian realize that Miles was letting him go.

Later that night, when Miles opened the door, Sarah simply stood on the doorstep looking at him wordlessly, until Miles finally stepped out, closing the door behind him.

"Jonah's home," he said. "We'll talk outside."

Sarah crossed her arms and looked out over the yard. Miles followed her eyes.

"I'm not sure why I'm here," she said. "Thanking you doesn't seem very appropriate, but I can't ignore what you did, either."

Miles nodded almost imperceptibly.

"I'm so sorry for everything. I can't even begin to imagine what you've been going through."

"No," he said. "You can't."

"I didn't know about Brian. I really didn't."

"I know." He glanced toward her. "I shouldn't have believed it otherwise. And I'm sorry for the accusations."

Sarah shook her head. "Don't be."

He looked away, seeming to struggle for words. "I guess I should thank you for letting me know what really happened."

"I had to. I didn't have a choice." Then, after he grew quiet again, Sarah brought her hands together. "How's Jonah doing with all this?"

"Okay. Not great. He doesn't know anything, but I think he sensed that something was going on by the way I was acting. He's had a couple of nightmares in the last few days. How's he doing in school?"

"So far, he's fine. In the last couple of days, I haven't noticed anything unusual."

"That's good."

Sarah ran a hand through her hair. "Can I ask you a question? You don't have to answer if you don't want to."

Miles turned. "Why did I let Brian go?"

She nodded.

It took a long time to answer. "I saw the dog."

She turned toward him in surprise.

"A big black dog, just like Brian said. He was running around in a yard a couple of houses up from where the accident happened."

"You just drove by and happened to see him?"

"No, not exactly. I went looking for him."

"To find out if Brian was telling the truth?"

He shook his head. "No, not really. I pretty much knew that he was telling the truth by then. But I had this crazy notion in my head that I just couldn't get rid of."

"What notion?"

"Like I said, it was crazy."

She looked at him curiously, waiting.

"When I got home that day—when Brian told me, I mean—I just got to thinking that I had to do something. Someone had to pay for what happened, but I just didn't know who until it hit me. So I got my father's gun, and the next night, I went out to look for the damn dog."

"You were going to shoot the dog?"

He shrugged. "I wasn't sure I'd even get the chance, but as soon as I pulled up, there he was. He was chasing a squirrel through the yard."

"So you did it?"

"No. I got close enough to do it, but when I got him in my sights, I got to thinking how insane it was. I mean, I was out hunting somebody's pet. Only someone seriously deranged would do that. So I turned around and got in my car. I let him go."

She smiled. "Like Brian."

"Yeah," he said. "Like Brian."

She reached for his hand, and after a moment, he let her take it. "I'm glad," she said.

"I'm not. Part of me wishes that I would have. At least then I'd know that I'd done something."

"You did do something."

Miles squeezed her hand before letting go. "I did it for me, too. And for Jonah. It was time to let it go. I'd already lost two years of my life, and I couldn't see the point in prolonging it anymore. Once I realized that . . . I don't know . . . it just seemed like it was the only thing I could do. No matter what happened to Brian, Missy wasn't coming back."

He brought his hands to his face and rubbed his eyes, and neither one of them said anything for a while. The stars were out in full glory above them, and Miles found his eyes traveling to Polaris, the North Star.

"I'm going to need some time," he said softly.

She nodded, knowing he was talking about them, now. "I know."

"I can't tell you how long it'll be, either."

Sarah glanced toward him. "Do you want me to wait?"

It took a long moment for him to answer.

437

"I can't make any promises, Sarah. About us, I mean. It's not that I don't love you anymore, because I do. I've spent the last couple of days agonizing over that fact. You're the best thing that's happened to me since Missy died. Hell, you're the only good thing that happened. For Jonah, too. He asked why you haven't been over lately, and I know he misses you. But no matter how much I want that to go on, part of me just can't imagine it. It's not as if I can forget what happened. And you're his sister."

Sarah's lips tightened. She said nothing.

"I don't know if I can live with that, even though you had nothing to do with it, because being with you means that in a way, I have to be with him, too. He's your family and . . . I'm not ready for that. I wouldn't be able to handle that. And I don't know whether I'll ever be ready."

"We could move away," she suggested. "We could try to start over."

He shook his head. "No matter how far I go, this will follow. You know that . . ."

He trailed off, then looked at her. "I don't know what to do."

She smiled sadly. "Neither do I," she admitted.

"I'm sorry."

"So am I."

After a moment, Miles moved closer and put his

arms around her. He kissed her gently, then held her for a long time, burying his face in her hair.

"I do love you, Sarah," he whispered.

She forced aside the lump in her throat and leaned into him, feeling his body close to hers and wondering whether this would be the last time he held her like this.

"I love you, too, Miles."

After he let her go, Sarah stepped back, trying to stop the tears. Miles stood without moving, and Sarah reached for her keys in the pocket of her jacket. She heard the jingle as she pulled them out. She couldn't form the words to say good-bye, knowing that this time, it might be forever.

"I'll let you get back to Jonah," she said.

In the soft glow of the porch light, she thought she saw tears in his eyes as well.

Sarah swiped at her tears. "I bought a Christmas gift for Jonah. Would it be all right to bring it by?"

Miles glanced away. "We might not be here. I was thinking of heading up to Nags Head next week. Charlie's got a place up there and he said I could use it. I just need to get away for a while, you know?"

She nodded. "I'll be around if you want to reach me by phone."

"Okay," he murmured.

No promises, she thought.

She took a step backward, feeling empty, wishing

for something to say that would change everything. With a tight smile, she turned and went to the car, doing her best to keep control. Her hands trembled slightly as she opened the door, and she looked back at him. He hadn't moved; his mouth was set in a straight line.

She slid behind the wheel.

As Miles watched her, he wanted to call out her name, to ask her to stay, to tell her that he would find some way to make this work between them. That he loved her now and always would.

But he didn't.

Sarah turned the key and the engine hummed to life. Miles moved toward the stairs and her heart surged, but she realized he was moving toward the door. He wasn't going to stop her. She put the car in reverse and started to back out.

His face was shadowed now, growing smaller as the car rolled backward. She could feel her cheeks getting wet.

As he opened the door, Sarah had the sinking realization that this would be her last image of him. She couldn't stay in New Bern the way things were. Seeing Miles around town would be too hard; she'd have to find another job. Somewhere she could start over.

Again.

On the road, she accelerated slowly into the darkness, willing herself not to look back.

I'll be fine, she told herself. No matter what happens, I'll make it, just as I made it before. With or without Miles, I can do that.

*No, you can't*, a voice inside her cried suddenly.

She broke down then, the tears coming hard, and she pulled to the side of the road. As the car idled and steam began to cloud the windows, Sarah cried as she'd never cried before.

# Chapter 37

"Where were you?" Jonah asked. "I looked around, but I couldn't find you."

Sarah had left half an hour earlier, but Miles had stayed on the porch. He'd just stepped inside when Jonah spotted him and came to a halt. Miles motioned over his shoulder.

"I was on the porch."

"What were you doing out there?"

"Sarah came by."

Jonah's face brightened. "She did? Where is she?"

"No, she isn't here. She couldn't stay."

"Oh . . ." Jonah looked up at his father. "Okay," he said, not hiding his disappointment. "I just wanted to show her the Lego tower that I built."

Miles went to his side and squatted until he was eye level with Jonah. "You can show me."

"You've already seen it."

"I know. But you can show me again."

"You don't have to. I wanted Miss Andrews to see it."

"Well, I'm sorry about that. Maybe you can bring it to school tomorrow and show her then."

Jonah shrugged. "That's okay."

Miles looked at him closely. "What's wrong, champ?"

"Nothing."

"Are you sure?"

Jonah didn't answer right away. "I guess I just miss her, that's all."

"Who? Miss Andrews?"

"Yeah."

"But you see her in school every day."

"I know. But it's not the same."

"As when she's here, you mean?"

He nodded, looking lost. "Did you guys have a fight?"

"No."

"But you're not friends anymore."

"Of course we are. We're still friends."

"Then why doesn't she come over anymore?"

Miles cleared his throat. "Well, things are kind of complicated right now. When you're a grown-up, you'll understand."

"Oh," he said. He seemed to think about that. "I don't want to be a grown-up," he finally declared.

"Why not?"

"Because," he said, "grown-ups always say that things are complicated."

"Sometimes they are."

"Do you still like Miss Andrews?"

"Yeah," he said, "I do."

"Does she like you?"

"I think so."

"Then what's so complicated?" His eyes were pleading, and Miles knew then with certainty that Jonah not only missed Sarah, he loved her as well.

"Come here," he said, drawing Jonah close, not knowing what else to do.

Two days later, Charlie pulled up in front of Miles's house as he was loading a few things into the car.

"Taking off already?"

Miles turned. "Oh . . . hey, Charlie. I figured it'd be better if we got going a little early. I don't want to be stuck in traffic."

He closed the trunk and stood. "Thanks again for letting us use your place out there."

"No problem. You need a hand?"

"No. I'm just about done."

"How long you gonna stay?"

"I don't know. Maybe a couple of weeks, until just after the New Year. You sure it's okay?"

"Don't worry about it—you've got enough vacation time to spend a month up there."

Miles shrugged. "Who knows? Maybe I will."

Charlie cocked an eyebrow. "Oh, by the way, I

came by to let you know that Harvey isn't going to press charges. Seems that Otis told him to drop it. So, officially, your suspension is over and you'll be able to work again when you get back."

"Good."

Jonah came bursting out the door, and both of them turned at the sound. Jonah called hello to Charlie, then turned around and ran back inside as if he'd forgotten something.

"So is Sarah going to join you up there for a few days? She's more than welcome to."

Miles was still looking toward the door, and he turned back to Charlie. "I don't think so. Her family is here, and with the holidays, I don't think she's going to make it."

"That's too bad. You'll see her when you get back, though, right?"

Miles dropped his gaze, and Charlie knew what that meant. "Not going so well?"

"You know how it goes."

"Not really. I haven't dated in forty years. But that's a shame."

"You don't even know her, Charlie."

"Didn't have to. I meant that it's a shame for you."

Charlie pushed his hands into his pockets. "Listen, I didn't come here to pry. That's your own business. Actually, there's another reason. Something I'm still not exactly sure about."

"Oh?"

"I got to wondering about that phone call—you know, when you let me know that Otis was innocent and suggested we stop the investigation."

Miles said nothing, and Charlie squinted at him from beneath his hat. "I take it you're still convinced of that."

After a moment, Miles nodded. "He's innocent."

"Despite what Sims and Earl said?"

"Yeah."

"You're not just saying that so you can handle this on your own, are you?"

"You've got my word on that, Charlie."

Charlie searched his face, sensing that he was telling the truth. "All right," he said. He brushed his hands against his shirt, as if wiping them off, then tipped his hat. "Well, listen—have a good time up there at Nags Head. Try to do some fishing for me, okay?"

Miles smiled. "You got it."

Charlie took a few steps, then suddenly stopped and turned. "Oh—wait, there's one more thing."

"What's that?"

"Brian Andrews. I'm still a little foggy on why you were bringing him in that day. Is there anything you want me to take care of while you're gone? Anything I should know about?"

"No," he answered.

"It was . . . what? You never were real clear about it."

"A mistake of sorts, Charlie." Miles studied the trunk of his car. "Just a mistake."

Charlie gave a startled laugh. "You know, that's funny."

"What is?"

"Your choice of words. Brian said exactly the same thing."

"You talked to Brian?"

"I had to check in on him, you know. He had an accident while in the custody of one of my deputies. I had to make sure he was doing okay."

Miles paled.

"Don't worry, I made sure that no one else was home." He let that sink in, then, bringing his hand to his chin, he gave the appearance of someone groping for the right words. "You see," he finally went on, "I got to thinking about those two things, and the investigator in me had the feeling that they just might be connected somehow."

"They weren't," Miles said quickly.

Charlie nodded, his face serious. "I thought you might say that, but like I said, I had to make sure. I just want to be clear—there's nothing I should know about Brian Andrews?"

Miles should have known that Charlie would figure it out. "No," he said simply.

"Okay," Charlie said. "Then let me give you some advice."

Miles waited.

"If you're telling me it's over, then follow your own advice, okay?"

Charlie made sure that Miles heard the seriousness in his tone.

"What's that supposed to mean?" Miles asked.

"If it's over—if it's really over—then don't let it screw up the rest of your life."

"I don't follow you."

Charlie shook his head and sighed.

"Yes, you do," he said.

# Epilogue

*I*t's nearly dawn now, and my story is almost over. It's time, I think, to let you know the rest.

I'm thirty-one years old now. I've been married three years to a woman named Janice, whom I met in a bakery. She, like Sarah, is a teacher, though she teaches high school English. We live in California, where I attended medical school and did my residency. I'm an emergency room physician, out of school for a year now, and in the past three weeks, with the help of many others, I've saved the lives of six people. I'm not saying this to brag, I'm telling you this because I want you to know that I've done my best to honor Miles's words to me in the cemetery.

I've also kept my word about telling no one.

It wasn't for me that Miles made me promise silence, you see. My silence, I was convinced at the time, was for his own protection.

Believe it or not, letting me go that day was a crime. A sheriff who has absolute knowledge that someone has committed a crime must turn that person in. Though our

449

*crimes were far from equal, the law is clear on this point, and Miles broke the law.*

*At least that's what I believed back then. After years of reflection, however, I came to realize that I'd been wrong.*

*I know now that he'd asked me because of Jonah.*

*If it had become widely known that I was the one driving the car, people in town would have forever gossiped about Miles's past. It would have become part of his general description—"The most awful thing happened to him," people would say—and Jonah would have had to grow up with those words all around him. How would something like that affect a child? Who knows. I don't, and Miles didn't. But he wasn't willing to take that chance.*

*Nor will I risk it even now. When I am finished, I plan to burn these pages in the fireplace. I just needed to get it out.*

*It's still hard, though, for all of us. I talk to my sister infrequently on the phone, usually at odd hours, and I seldom visit. I use distance as an excuse—she lives across the country from my wife and me—but we both know the real reason I stay away. She does, though, sometimes come to see me. She is always alone when she does so.*

*As for what happened with Miles and Sarah, I'm sure you've figured it out . . .*

It happened on Christmas Eve, six days after Miles and Sarah said good-bye on the porch. By then Sarah had finally, reluctantly, come to grips with the fact that it was over. She hadn't heard from Miles, nor did she expect to.

But that night, after getting home from visiting her parents, Sarah got out of her car, glanced up toward her apartment—and froze. She couldn't believe what she saw. She closed her eyes, then opened them slowly, hoping and praying it was true.

It was.

Sarah couldn't help but smile.

Like tiny stars, two candles were flickering in her windows.

And Miles and Jonah were waiting for her inside.

# *THE NOTEBOOK*

## Nicholas Sparks

Set amid the austere beauty of the North Carolina coast, *The Notebook* begins with the story of Noah Calhoun, a rural Southerner recently returned from the Second World War. Noah is restoring a plantation home to its former glory, and he is haunted by images of the beautiful girl he met fourteen years earlier, a girl he loved like no other. Unable to find her, yet unwilling to forget the summer they spent together, Noah is content to live with only memories . . . until she unexpectedly returns to his town to see him once again.

Like a puzzle within a puzzle, the story of Noah and Allie is just the beginning. As it unfolds, their tale miraculously becomes something different, with much higher stakes. The result is a deeply moving portrait of love itself, the tender moments and the fundamental changes that affect us all. It is a story of miracles and emotions that will stay with you for ever.

# THE WEDDING

## Nicholas Sparks

The long-awaited follow up to his classic *The Notebook* – a romantic surprise that is sure to delight fans, old and new alike.

Despite the shining example of Allie and Noah's marriage, son-in-law Wilson Lewis is a man who has always found it difficult to express his emotions. A hardworking estate tax attorney, he has provided well for his family, but now, with his daughter's upcoming wedding coinciding with his thirtieth wedding anniversary, he confronts the fact that he and his wife Jane have grown apart and he wonders if she even loves him any more.

Wilson is sure of one thing: his love for his wife has only deepened and intensified over the years. With the memories of his in-laws' magnificent fifty-year love affair as his guide – and some patient advice from Noah – Wilson struggles to find his own way back into the heart of the woman he adores . . .

# MESSAGE IN A BOTTLE

## Nicholas Sparks

Divorcée Theresa Osborne, newspaper columnist and mother of a twelve-year-old son, picks up a bottle on the beach during a seaside vacation. Inside is a letter from a man called Garrett.

*My dearest Catherine, I miss you my darling, as I always do, but today is particularly hard because the ocean has been singing to me, and the song is that of our life together . . .*

For Garrett, his message is the only way he knows to express his undying love for a woman he has lost. For Theresa, wary of romance since her husband shattered her trust, the message raises questions that intrigue her. Who are Garrett and Catherine? What is their story? Challenged by the mystery and unaccountably drawn to find him, Theresa embarks on a search that takes her to a sunlit coast town and an unexpected confrontation . . .

# A WALK TO REMEMBER

## Nicholas Sparks

The last person Landon thought he would fall for was Jamie Sullivan, daughter of the town's Baptist minister. A quiet girl, Jamie seemed content living in a world apart from the other teens. She took care of her widowed father, rescued hurt animals and volunteered at the local orphanage.

Landon would never have dreamed of asking her out, but a twist of fate threw them together when he found himself, without a partner for the school dance. In the months that followed, Landon discovered truths that most people take a lifetime to learn – about the joy of giving, the pain of loss and, most of all, the transforming nature of love. Being with Jamie would show him the depths of the human heart and lead him to a decision so stunning it would send him irrevocably on the road to manhood . . .

Other bestselling Time Warner Books
titles available by post:

| | | | |
|---|---|---|---|
| ☐ | The Guardian | Nicholas Sparks | £6.99 |
| ☐ | The Wedding | Nicholas Sparks | £5.99 |
| ☐ | The Notebook | Nicholas Sparks | £6.99 |
| ☐ | A Walk to Remember | Nicholas Sparks | £6.99 |
| ☐ | The Rescue | Nicholas Sparks | £6.99 |
| ☐ | Message in a Bottle | Nicholas Sparks | £6.99 |
| ☐ | Nights in Rodanthe | Nicholas Sparks | £6.99 |
| ☐ | True Believer | Nicholas Sparks | £5.99 |

TIME WARNER
BOOKS

**TIME WARNER BOOKS**
**PO Box 121, Kettering, Northants NN14 4ZQ**
**Tel: 01832 737525, Fax: 01832 733076**
**Email: aspenhouse@FSBDial.co.uk**

**POST AND PACKING:**
Payments can be made as follows: cheque, postal order (payable to Time Warner Books), credit card or Switch Card. Do not send cash or currency.
All UK Orders        **FREE OF CHARGE**
EC & Overseas       25% of order value

Name (BLOCK LETTERS) . . . . . . . . . . . . . . . . . . . . . . . . . . . . . . . . . . . .

Address . . . . . . . . . . . . . . . . . . . . . . . . . . . . . . . . . . . . . . . . . . . . . . . . . .

. . . . . . . . . . . . . . . . . . . . . . . . . . . . . . . . . . . . . . . . . . . . . . . . . . . . . . . .

Post/zip code: . . . . . . . . . . . . . . . . . . . . . . . . . . . . . . . . . . . . . . . . . . . .

☐ Please keep me in touch with future Time Warner publications

☐ I enclose my remittance £ . . . . . . . . .

☐ I wish to pay by Visa/Access/Mastercard/Eurocard/Switch Card

| | | | | | | | | | | | | | | | |
|---|---|---|---|---|---|---|---|---|---|---|---|---|---|---|---|

Card Expiry Date [ ][ ][ ][ ]        Switch Issue No. [ ][ ]